MW00605962

EIGHTH
WONDER
The Thomas
Bethune Story

To: Mr. Zhrich
Enjoy! 2016
♡ A.M. Cal

A Novel
By
A.M. Cal

ACKNOWLEDGMENTS

Thanks to my mother Frances Ophelia Cal and my grandmother Bernice Johnson for encouraging me to write this book and supporting me all the years of my life. Madea, as we called grandma, told me once when I was down, "Don't get discouraged 'nita, your ship'll come in." Mom, your words of encouragement were a precious spring in a vast desert, and how can a child who's had a mother's love ever repay it? There are no words adequate enough to express the depth of thankfulness. The rest of my family, daddy Clarence Cal Sr., sister Daria, brother Barry, and nephew Landon and niece Jillian, thank you for believing in me, and big brother Clarence, big sister Sherry, thanks for your support, and Theron. It takes a village to climb to the top of a mountain and I'm forever grateful for the support and words of encouragement from my aunties Margie, Arlene, and Melvar. To my good friend and fellow author, Christopher J. Moore, thank you for picking up the baton and urging me to start writing this novel, as well as coaching me through the post-writing process. Thanks to my favorite 3rd and 5th grade teacher Ms. Stephanie Cuelho for encouraging me to write, and my public school teachers and administrators in LAUSD who've supported my work and hired me week after week to guest teach: especially Ms. Vanessa Culp, Ms. Cheng, Ms. Hardacre, Ms. Goldstein, Mr. Escamilla, Cornelia Romey, and Ms. Debra Bryant. I also appreciate the support of Dean Helen Williams and my Pepperdine family, Zeta Phi Beta sorority (Bibliana Bovery, Stacye Montez, Denise Irving, Tamara Scott, Lula), as well as my Rainier Beach High and Sealth High School friends, in addition to my University of Washington family. Special thanks to my closest friends: Germaine Tarpinian, Satise Roddy, Anne Zohner, Ambrit Millhouse, Cheryl J., Mary S., Lisa Washington, Diedre Andrus, Eugene S., Casey Lee, Lee Garrett, Vanessa and Gary Springer, Ed Conley, Rachel Oden, Kevin and Elizabeth, April and Andrea, Denise and Michael, Mo, Sheena, Vernita Lynn Adkins, Monica Mallet, Lisa Jefferson, Angela Witherspoon, and my little sister Crystal Garrett, your support gave me strength to believe in myself, to endure. To my goddaughter Nakiesha Alexander, never forgotten. Over six years, there were hundreds of drafts of this book and I'm thankful to my good friend Vivian Louie for her notes, and to my creative editor, Susan M. Wyler for falling in love with Thomas and putting heart and soul into helping read drafts, providing guidance to help me tell the story I wanted to tell, in addition to notes provided by associate editor Cara Underwood early on. A special thanks to Jacqui Corn-Uys for copy editing the book at such short notice. Assistant Professor in Composition, Huck Hodge, DMA, FAAR, at the University of Washington enriched the musical experience with his artistic comments on Thomas's compositions. I also thank the Oak Alley Foundation for granting the use of their iconic plantation home for the cover. It was my graduate work at Cal State University, Northridge that introduced me to Thomas Bethune while researching prodigies for my master's thesis. I saw a picture of this slave boy next to his master, in the same pages as renowned prodigies Beethoven and Mozart. He captured my imagination. I've spent almost two decades thinking about Thomas. It was my heart's desire to do him justice, to somehow right the wrongs that made him famous, while at the same time impacting his legacy as a true American virtuoso. I strived to tell a riveting story that would entertain, as well as restore Thomas to greatness. I hope I have done his story justice and I thank you, all of you, who have supported me in this journey and I pray that I made you proud. To God be the glory.

Atina Books Edition 2015

Copyright © 2015 by Anita M. Cal

All rights reserved under International and Pan-American copyright conventions. Published in the United States under Atina Books, 13547 Ventura Blvd., Box 168, Sherman Oaks, CA 91423. No part of this publication may be reproduced, distributed, or transmitted in any form or by any means, including photocopying, recording, or other electronic or mechanical methods, without the prior written permission of the publisher, except in the case of brief quotations embodied in critical reviews and certain other noncommercial uses permitted by copyright law. For permission requests, write to the publisher, addressed "Attention: Permissions Coordinator," at the address below:

Atina Books c/o R. Oden
13547 Ventura Blvd. Box #168
Sherman Oaks, CA 91423
www.anitamcal.com

Images provided via licensing from Oak Alley Plantation. Use of said images does not constitute any official endorsement or approval by Oak Alley Foundation or Oak Alley Plantation. Opinions and statements made herein are solely those of the author and do not necessarily represent the opinion of Oak Alley Plantation. Furthermore, Oak Alley Plantation neither controls nor guarantees the accuracy, timelines, appropriateness, or completeness of the information contained in this book. Oak Alley Plantation is in no way responsible for the content of this book.

Special discounts are available on quantity purchases by corporations, associations, and others. For details, contact the publisher at the address above.

Orders by U.S. trade bookstores and wholesalers. Please contact Atina Distribution

Tel: Fax: (270) 596-3797 or visit www.anitamcal.com

Printed in the United States of America

Publisher's Cataloging-in-Publication data

Cal, A.M.

Eighth Wonder : The Thomas Bethune Story/ A.M. Cal.

p. cm.

ISBN 978-0-9968425-1-8

1. The main category of the book —Historical Fiction —Other category. 2. Biography —From one perspective. 3. Classical music. I. Cal, A.M. II. Eighth Wonder.

HF0000.A0 A00 2010

299.000 00–dc22 2010999999

First Edition 14 13 12 11 10 / 10 9 8 7 6 5 4 3 2 1

BENEFACTORS

Clarence A. Cal Sr. and Frances O. Cal

PART ONE

I.

1905

Elway Plantation, Warrenton, VA

On that blustery afternoon before his life of tea and servants descended into madness, his freedom was taken away, and he was rightly and falsely accused; the ebb and flow of the most rapturous music drifted into Colonel Bethune's drawing room. The old Colonel limped into his study humming along with a sonata that trickled through the vents. He shuffled across the worn Oriental rug with his cane. The piano sonata was as beautiful as it was in the royal courts of Switzerland decades earlier, and the old boy played it with a virtuosity afforded only the rarest form of genius.

The Colonel lowered his craggy body into his custom Birds-eye rocker. He slipped off his slippers and with his bare feet, set the chair in motion. It was good to hear exquisite music on the plantation grounds again. For months it had been disturbingly silent, but for the crowing of cocks and the pounding of wooden mortar to mill rice. The Colonel took pleasure in the piano, thinking of how he yearned to master the instrument during his youthful studies in Vienna. But he did not have the gift. No, that honor went to his son downstairs.

Ready for a relaxing read, the Colonel leaned over to the antique bookcase, settling on Alcott's Little Women. He marveled at the piano's wondrous capabilities and was savoring the moment, until a loud scream from the grand parlor pierced the walls.

The Colonel stopped his rocker. More horrible screams came and the bone-chilling clang of piano pitches clashing off key. He clutched the head of his golden walking stick and with great effort lifted his ancient eighty-three-year old body from the chair. His heart raced and his hand trembled atop his cane.

Down two winding flights of creaking stairs, he moved as fast as his frail legs would allow. "Don't be dreadful, old boy!" he called out to his son from the vast hallway.

At the far end of the long corridor, he could see his son seated at the black grand piano.

A heavy-set man, his son wore a tight worn frock and ill-fitting frayed pants. His short gray hair was thick like cotton, his skin the color of coal. Mozart's Sonata #2 Third Movement in D-major flowed beneath the chunky digits of his one hand, until he slammed the keys again. Of course this man was a Negro and the Negro was not the Colonel's son, but he was always treated like one. "Hold on, old boy, you mustn't ruin Mozart," he said, chastising as if speaking to a young boy. His breaths short and heavy, the Colonel made his way toward the double doors.

The Negro ignored his father, released another agonizing wail and collapsed to the floor.

The Colonel made his way into the *grand parlor* with fear in his blue eyes. He limped close to his son and nudged the Negro with his cane.

"The angels have stopped singing," the Negro whispered. "Isn't that terrible? Tom is done." His voice was a soft murmur and his body went stiff.

"Come now, quit with your tomfoolery," the Colonel said. His son had a long-held penchant for pranks and was not beyond the most-extreme trickery.

The French nurse had emerged from the *petit parlor* and was on her knees, feeling the Negro's forehead. "We need to call a *docteur*, Colonel," she said in French. The Colonel hesitated. "Colonel?"

He ignored the nurse and bent over as far as his ancient body would allow and whispered in the old boy's ear. "I'll take care of you, son, I always do," he said.

"Colonel, you need to take him into town, now," the nurse said with more urgency. "If you don't take him *maintenant*. He's going to die."

The Colonel turned ashen and brought his hand to his mouth. How could he call a doctor? It wasn't safe. Was there no other option?

"Colonel, *maintenant!*" The nurse tugged on his feeble arm. The Colonel heaved a deep sigh and nodded.

Heavy rains fell. Servants carried the ailing Negro on a makeshift stretcher and lifted him into a gold-trimmed Barouche. A steam trumpet from the train blared in the distance. From the back seat, the Colonel was nauseous. He listened to the squeaking of the plantation gate, his mind racing. The soft tone of the Colored cook came lightly through the carriage walls, "Make sure you bring 'im back home, Colonel. Bring 'im back on home." The Colonel clutched the ivory handle of his gilded cane, hoping his face didn't betray his most horrible fears. They were two hours away from town. He hoped he would bring him back alive. As the vehicle pulled away, he maintained his composure, hoping to instill confidence in his servants—even the brown ones with the blue eyes, the ones who'd brought his now dead wife so much pain.

The carriage creaked toward town past motor buggies and maneuvered around a black convertible Model K stranded in a ditch. Inside, the Colonel leaned forward in his seat to look at the Negro, who was barely holding on to life. He touched his bloated cheek with the back of his hand. *Will he ever open his eyes again?*

Pulling the curtains back, the Colonel peeked out of the window at the busy street, and saw heads turning to watch his gilded carriage pass by. He tried to assess the danger. It was important for him not to be seen. Indeed, maintaining his anonymity was an obsession of his ever since the War of Northern Aggression had ended.

The Colonel was so uncompromisingly solitary that for the past forty years he hadn't attended church on Sundays, never used his box at the opera in

Washington City and didn't bother with shopping on Main Street. He never received visitors at *Elway* and never conducted business by day, always sending one of his Colored servants to carry out his bidding. So peculiar were his ways, people who lived in town thought him mad. Indeed the Colonel, once a very sociable gentleman, stayed out of sight and remained firmly secluded behind the white pillars of his big mansion. He was unmoved by speculations or rumors, as he knew he was not as the rumors suggested. Indeed, it was all a matter of the sick Negro that was dying on the opposite seat from him.

It was dark and cloudy. The old carriage turned onto a floral-lined pathway, past a long white picket fence that stretched a half-mile to the front door of Dr. Lawrence Paige's three-storied house. A small clinic set in a private cottage stood adjacent to the main home, discretely tucked behind a cluster of oak trees.

Dr. Paige was in the living room delighting his wife and two young daughters with a harpsichord when the urgent knocking came at the front door. He walked through the living room with his candle. The flame threw a faint light on the stranger when he opened the door. Standing before him was a bent, proud, near white domestic in black livery with gold trim and blue buttons. He stood on the front terrace, wet from the rain.

"Good evening Doctor Paige," the blue-eyed domestic said. He informed Dr. Paige that the gentleman, Colonel James Bethune, was in the gilded carriage perched in front of his home with cash and a request for him to see about a sick Negro.

Eyebrows lifted, Dr. Paige nodded. "Certainly, of course."

Colonel James Bethune? Dr. Paige stretched his neck to get a glimpse of the famous tycoon who lived as an eccentric recluse. But the Colonel was hidden from view in the back seat behind velvet curtains. The domestic jaunted back to the gilded coach, boots plopping up mud. The old man emerged only once he had gained assurance from the domestic that the doctor would treat the ill Colored inside.

Dr. Paige heaved excitedly when the elderly tycoon stepped down the carriage stairs with his imported Italian leather boots and wool frock, his cravat tightly wrapped about his neck. A black umbrella kept him from getting wet. He was French in manner and dress, Dr. Paige thought. He had all the embellishments of a gentleman, down to his fancy expensive cane. The Colonel met his gaze with piercing, fierce blue eyes. Eyes, Dr. Paige noted by the candlelight that were very troubled.

"A pleasure to meet you, Colonel Bethune. Come in, come in." Dr. Paige was too fascinated to contemplate why the Colonel's eyes and his Colored domestic's eyes looked like one and the same.

The Colonel tilted his head, but did not speak.

"Come. Follow me, follow me. My clinic is around the back," Dr. Paige said. He led them around the terrace along the side of the house.

The nurse-in-residence was summoned from her quarters and water was boiled in the hearth. The Colonel was led to a waiting room and the domestics carried the sick Negro into Dr. Paige's office. After removing the Negro's clothes, leeches were drawn from clay urns and placed strategically on his body. The nurse pressed one parasite onto his chest, four more on his neck and arms.

Dr. Paige continued the bloodletting long into the night. Across the room, the nurse squeezed blood out of a rag into the washbasin by the sink. She grabbed a fresh towel, dipped it in boiling water and placed it on the Negro's forehead.

Hours had passed by the time Dr. Paige carefully peeled away the final leech, fattened with blood. Based on his examinations, he estimated the Negro looked to be about sixty, a few years younger than his own age. He tilted his head for a closer look. The left side of the patient's face hung down to his swollen neck and his oversized body was paralyzed on one side: clear signs of a stroke. Peering closer, Dr. Paige lifted the skin covering his eyes. His lids were folded up, revealing pink rims. And where the pupils were supposed to be there was only pure white. He was blind.

Dr. Paige couldn't help but wonder the identity of the ill, blind Negro he was treating. When he'd asked, the Colonel had not bothered to provide him a name. He merely tipped his top hat and settled on the chaise in the waiting room, as if he deemed him unworthy of enlightenment. But it was a needling question, sticking in his thoughts. Had he seen the Negro before?

In the wee hours of the next morning, Dr. Paige took rest on a cot in the clinic thinking about the mysterious black man in his office. Why had he been dressed as if ready for the opera, in a smart frock, and full cape at a time when opera season didn't start for another month? And why was no information offered, not even a first name? He went on to ponder other answerless questions until at last he leaned over, blew out the yellowish flame, and slipped deeper beneath the covers.

But Dr. Paige couldn't sleep. A distant memory began to stir in the darkness of his mind like the first rays of sunlight emerging at dawn. It lingered over his thoughts like a thick haze. A remembrance needled his sleep that he could not shake in those early hours when only the piercing symphony of whirring cicadas could be heard in the woods.

Suddenly, Dr. Paige opened his eyes, swung his legs out the cot, and padded barefoot toward his office. The night nurse was sleeping in a vacant patient room and woke up upon hearing footsteps. She grabbed a robe and emerged from the room, and watched Dr. Paige with curious sleepy eyes. The doctor was in his office gliding alongside a row of bookshelves. He ran his finger across medical books, and novels, before pulling out a leather portfolio of discolored newspaper clippings. He sifted through the pile of old articles and announcements before picking up a yellowed music program. On the cover was a photo. He lifted the paper closer to his eyes.

"Oh, my land. This can't be." Dr. Paige went ashen and had to steady himself, his hands groping for a nearby chair to sit. "He died long ago."

"Dr. Paige," came the night nurse's alarmed murmur. Gazing curiously at him, the nurse asked, "are you all right, doctor?"

The nurse's voice pierced his musings. Dr. Paige motioned for her to come closer. He spoke quickly, his voice lowered with urgency. He whispered the unthinkable into her ear. In shock, she covered her mouth. The doctor knew her mind had to process what had just been said, for the titles of "slave" and "master" to sink in, for the old Negro patient was one of Colonel Bethune's former slaves, a famous musician. The color drained from the nurse's face. The old Negro was still under the control of his former master?

"His master, doctor? Even though he'd been freed...?"

"Even though he's been freed," Dr. Paige said. There was heaviness when he said those words. An ominous reality trickled into the room like the first mist of a heavy storm.

"Perhaps there's an explanation," the nurse offered. "He's blind. Maybe...maybe he took pity on him and took him in?"

Dr. Paige was shaking his head. "No. I know the Colonel's kind," he said. Shock had turned to anger. Dr. Paige had deep anti-slavery ties. Long before the war, his childhood home had been used as a station for escaped slaves. He remembered back to those tense nights seeing men, women, and children hidden in the cellar, frightened, packed together like wet fish in a net. He dropped onto his desk near the hearth. "Unconscionable," he muttered, his voice resolute with old resurrected convictions.

An involuntary look of fear emerged in the nurse's eyes. She lifted up both hands in a gesture to remove herself from the weight of it. "Oh no, Dr. Paige. I have a family to care for," she said. She didn't want anything to do with it. But Dr. Paige shook his head. He was already at the wall, jaws pressed tight, the black phone's spitcup mouthpiece at his lips.

The smell of wet cattle drifted in the waiting room. The Colonel slept upright on a chaise longue underneath a blanket. He snored, Aristotle's *Poetics* open on his lap. Suddenly, a popping sound woke him. A great commotion took place outside. Car doors slammed and horses whinnied. Suddenly, the waiting room door burst open with a thud and a small band of voluntary police swarmed in with the sheriff. A rustle of voices rose, charges of enslavement were hurled about, and there was a jostling for position, as the floor shook, and furniture tipped over. He was being lifted out of his seat.

The Colonel trembled. The men shouted, and pointed, and escorted him out. He closed his eyes and the crowd of bodies surrounding him began to fade away. He was twenty-seven-years-old, looking at slaves to purchase for *Solitude*, the four-thousand-acre plantation he'd recently purchased in Columbus, Georgia. It was the day he'd acquired his son, a sweltering November afternoon. He could hear the soft high-pitched sobs of slaves, long low moans, and the frantic bark of hounds.

II.

1851

Harris County, Columbus, Georgia

Beyond a thick tangle of fruit trees the slash of Wiley Jones' whip cracked over loud cries and raging voices. "Pull off dem pants an' take dem skirts off!" a Colored driver shouted against a clang of iron. "Y'all heard 'em. Clothes off!" the overseer barked. The smell of warm feces hung in the air. Colonel Bethune hobbled out from beneath the cool shade of the peach tree holding an embroidered handkerchief to his nose. It was unusually hot that afternoon, even for Columbus, Georgia. The sun's rays reached down and spilled across the fields where the lilies swayed and the cherry blossoms danced in the warm breeze.

As soon as he cleared the last branch, the Colonel took out his gold pocket watch and glanced at the time. He'd been inspecting slaves four long hours in a private sale and was ready to buy more. Though a young man of twenty-seven, there was a slight tilt when he walked; from a squaw's knife to his knee during the war with the Indians. And although maimed, the Colonel still carried himself tall, with a commanding air. He strode, stab-by-stab, deliberate and erect with his Faberge cane, over a large patch of brittle sunburned grass toward the auction block.

As he walked, he took in the dismal disrepair Wiley had let happen around the once stunning property. The garden pathways were overgrown with weeds, the windows on the main house were boarded up, and his father's once luxurious Landau was broken down. "Damn, shame," the Colonel muttered, as he came to a stop before a long cement platform.

The Colored slave driver shouted at two shivering Colored children. He shoved the chained teary-eyed boys toward the auction block and snarled. His red eyes bulged and sweat poured from his wide face. The concrete block was actually the extension of a side porch. The sun-torched ground in front of it was covered with patches of tall brown dandelions. Off to the side of the stairs, a knotted pile of the slaves' clothes lay crumpled in the dirt. Frightened and suffering, Wiley's naked slaves dragged up the stone steps like exhausted sheep.

"This is the lot of them," Wiley Jones barked to the Colonel. He was an ugly, rough-featured man, his pocked face flush from heat and whiskey. About forty years old, the Colonel thought he had the refinement of a pirate: knotted greasy hair, dark tough skin that was scarred from chickenpox, brown teeth, wrinkled frock, and dirt beneath his fingernails.

"They's all kin, jus' like ya wanted," he spat, pointing toward his slaves.

In the center of the chattel was a naked coal-Colored woman surrounded by fifteen of her children, aged three to sixteen. The family was smashed together on the block, bodies wet with urine, eyes wide with fear. Wiley aimed his whip.

"Come on up here," he sneered at the mother who stepped forward, trying to hide her shame. "Nigger girl's age is 31, good with a plow as any nigger buck an' she's even better at cookin'." He took a swig of whiskey and leaned his hand on the naked woman's shoulder. "Girl goes to church and don't commit the sin of lyin'. Hell, every one o' these children here baptized, an' all of 'em strong as oxes. You got carpenter, cow hands, laundry girls, blacksmiths, field hands an' the like," he slurred. He pointed the whip at Charity. "This wench here is a good breeder. Got two three more chillin's in 'er."

The Colonel frowned as Wiley took another swig from the flask, then lifted his single-tailed bullwhip high in the air and stumbled before slicing the leather toward the mass of flesh. Some of the slaves winced, others whimpered, and a few lost their bowels. Another snap and the whip sailed toward the huddled bodies.

The hounds, underfed and tethered to a tree, howled.

He's an idiot, the Colonel thought. His jaw clenched, a flinch with each crack, an urge to pounce on Wiley with each needless release of the lash. The Colonel stared up at the slaves, the chains on their hands, the shackles on their feet. He saw the terrified yearning in their eyes and felt like their eyes were begging for him to buy them.

The slave woman Charity spoke, her voice was almost a whisper. "We real good slaves mastuh. All o' us."

"I'll take them all," the Colonel snapped. "The entire family. Get their clothes back on and remove those irons." The Colored driver began unlocking the chains at once, shackles clanged against the cement. The Colonel saw the mother's knees buckle with relief.

"Thank ya, Lawd."

Bare dusty feet descended the brick platform in the sweltering heat, grabbing up pants, shirts, and sack dresses from the dirt with whimpers and sniffles.

"Single file," the driver barked. He wiped water from his brow as the newly purchased slave family huddled with thirty other purchased slaves. Within minutes Wiley's overseer trotted up on his big horse and ordered them to move toward the Colonel's fleet of wagons. More naked slaves were trudged out. The driver shoved the final batch into position, one behind the other. Each slave turned their bare backs to the Colonel to show there were no scars from beatings.

Each received a good look over from the Colonel.

"Now lookee how limber this big buck here is," Wiley slurred, before sending the bullwhip crashing toward a mammoth, copper toned slave in the center of the pack. The large slave leapt off the block dragging several others with him. Chained together, they scrambled their way back up onto the block, with Wiley whipping at them all the while.

The Colonel gestured for Wiley to get on with it. Weary from the long hot day and the previous days of travel, he was also irritated by the unseemly display before him. He wanted to purchase the large slave and go, but he kept his face blank.

"Let's get on with it," the Colonel said.

Wiley walked up close to the big buck. He stood on his toes and stretched his torso tall as he could. Then he pressed his face inches from the buck's face, stuck out his skinny pink tongue and licked him across his chin. "Got plenty o' salt in 'im."

"I'll have him," the Colonel gestured. "Seven-hundred dollars," he offered without looking up. He took out his wallet and began peeling off bills.

It was an insult, the offer. But Wiley was too drunk off whiskey for reason.

"Seven-hundred it is," he swayed, hand lifted. He steadied himself to collect the bills, just when a scream rang out in the distance.

"Not without mah baby!"

"You git in wench!"

"Not without mah boy! Not without mah baby!"

The Colonel turned toward the commotion and saw near a grove of butterfly vines the mass of barefooted slaves he had just purchased herding toward his wagons. In front of the pack was the dark-skinned woman, Charity, the one with all the children. She was wailing and scratching, screaming something about her baby. The Colonel shifted on his cane and peered in the distance. "What in the hell is going on?"

Wiley shrugged and snatched the cash from the Colonel's hand. "Boy's name is Mingo," he slurred. "The nigger girl's this boy's wife."

Irritated, the Colonel ignored Wiley and kept his eyes on Charity. She was fighting hard, flailing her arms against the slave driver who pushed to get her up in the wagon. She dug her feet into the ground and flung her body back against him. The overseer slapped her across the face and snatched a whip from his bag, pistol swinging at his hip, ready to strike again.

"This is intolerable. Hold it! Stop!" the Colonel called out, with a brush of his coattails. "You there!" he shouted to the overseer, hand lifted in the air. "Bring her here!" the Colonel motioned, demanding the coal-Colored, broad nosed woman be brought to him.

The overseer, a scruffy man with wild whiskers stopped. He spat something the Colonel couldn't hear, and pushed and shoved the slave until she ran past the low hanging vines toward the Colonel. Dust rising beneath her feet, shabby sack dress swaying, she fell at his boots, knees scraping the gravel.

"One more mastuh, there's one mo'," she begged.

"What's your name?" the Colonel asked.

"Charity, mastuh," she said, gasping for breath, her cheeks wet with tears. "He gots mah baby," she sobbed.

"Your baby? Who has your baby?" the Colonel asked. His voice raised an octave. He flipped his cape as if it helped him better understand.

Charity kept her eyes cast downward. Her entire body shook. "Please save mah boy, mastuh," she begged, her husky voice cracked as she grasped the hem of the Colonel's trousers. Her tears wet the tip of his brown leather boots."He took 'im away."

"Shut your damn mouth!" the overseer growled and dismounted from his horse. He gritted threatening words with steps toward Charity. But the Colonel lifted his cane across the overseer's thighs to stop him in his path.

"Kill me if ya have tuh, but don' let mah baby die," Charity returned, ignoring the angry overseer. "Please save 'im, mastah, please! Yah finds 'im in there," she cried, desperate, her lips quivering as she pointed toward a decaying old smokehouse. "One more."

For a moment the Colonel stood silent with Wiley at his shoulder, Charity at his feet. Unsure what to make of the suffering slave woman's claim, he glanced back and forth between the two. Could it be true? He thought he had seen all the slaves. He specifically requested that family members be kept together, yet he knew Wiley had already separated the big buck, the husband from his wife. The Colonel turned, fixed a questioning gaze on Wiley. He sensed Wiley didn't like the matter, was poised to rip the Colored woman's throat out to shut her up.

"Is it true? Is her baby inside?" the Colonel asked, looking Wiley right in the eyes.

At first Wiley gave no answer. He wobbled on his feet as though he might fall, before he drew himself up, and grumbled. "Who cares what a nigger wench says?" he spat with a superior tone. His beady eyes had turned to blocks of onyx. "Our business is done. Y'all kin get offa my property."

Those words didn't sit well with the Colonel. His eyes turned dark, angry at the cruel Wiley. He threw down his jeweled cane at once and snatched Wiley by the neck, causing him to drop his flask. He wrapped his arm around Wiley's throat and twisted his body.

Unable to stand the slightest pain, Wiley unleashed a high-pitched scream. He was like a dog caught in a steel-hunting trap. His legs shook, he tried to untangle his body, but the Colonel's grip was too tight. He fell to his knees, cussed, and begged the Colonel to let him go.

"Not until you answer my question," the Colonel snarled. "Is it true, you drunken fool?" he asked. Wiley pointed his free hand toward the smokehouse, "Spook's in there," he sputtered.

"Where?" the Colonel asked and twisted harder.

"The smokehouse," Wiley grunted.

"The smokehouse." The Colonel's face crumpled with disgust. Anger rose in the Colonel's chest. He twisted Wiley's arm good and hard, before he released him.

"Ain't nuthin' but misery and a waste of time, a year she's been botherin' with that runt," Wiley stumbled to his feet.

The Colonel limped a few steps back, staring at the dirty, stumbling fool. "What kind of heartless soul separates a child from his mother?"

"The boy's blind," Wiley said, rubbing his neck. "What you done ain't right, Colonel, to a white man." He wiped the blood from his lip with his sleeve. "Over a nigger."

"I won't leave a baby," the Colonel growled. He turned his gaze from Wiley and considered the dark slave woman, crumpled on the ground. "Have someone fetch the boy," the Colonel said coldly.

"Fetch 'im yourself," Wiley spat.

The Colonel gave him a long hard look before he picked up his cane and turned toward the old smokehouse. His fine cane kicked up dust as he walked. A narrow dirt path crowded by thick blackberry bushes led the way to the cabin. The Colonel cleared the thorny vines with his walking stick and crushed them beneath his boots. The smokehouse was about a half mile in the distance. He swatted at flies, and trudged up the embankment and down again, and finally reached the area where the small dreary pine-log shack was located just on the other side of the pecan groves. It was closed off and bordered by a bank of trees. It smelled like bacon.

As he drew closer to the door, a pained whimper could be heard coming from inside the shack. The Colonel felt a nervous rush take over his body, as he reached for the rusty knob. He tugged the low-hanging door that dragged against the ground and walked into darkness. A small amount of light seeped in from the cracks; it took a moment for his eyes to adjust. Again there was the anguished high-pitched cry, like a lost kitten's mewl. The sound sent a chill down the Colonel's back. The Colonel moved slowly through the shack, using his cane as a guide. He stopped and listened for the cry; it was coming from the back. He bumped against drying boar, shoulder, and quail, until his boot hit a piece of wood.

The baby's bone-piercing howl rose louder. The Colonel looked down, bent on his cane and saw a makeshift crib from an old dresser drawer by his boot. Looking closer, he found a small, neglected baby with ebony skin in a dirty blanket. The child was covered in urine and bile. Shaking his head, the Colonel gently peeled back the cover. He could see the baby's bones. The Colonel gasped. With his finger, he counted the ribs that poked out dreadfully through the skin. It made his heart wince. "Inhuman, absolutely inhuman," he muttered.

He felt for a dry part of the blanket and used it to wipe the baby's body of feces and vomit. Taking off his frock, he carefully removed the blanket and dropped it to the floor. He picked up the crying baby, who he guessed to be about two. He cradled him to his chest and covered him with his coat. The tiny boy was so light, lighter than a feather. He was trembling in the Colonel's arm. He turned aside his swollen little face and tried to tuck it in the Colonel's chest.

"*Mon Dieu*," the Colonel whispered, as he looked down at the emaciated baby and took in his features. His lids were thick and only the whites of his eyes showed against thin pink rims. He was blind, definitely blind.

The Colonel shook his head. That critter Wiley was going to let that baby slowly cook to death alongside the curing sides of hog and deer! He continued to stand still with the boy in his arms, leaning against the rickety wall, listening to the gentle twitter of birds in the trees behind the shack. He cradled the baby and moved the back of his fingers across the blind boy's cheek.

He shifted the baby's tiny body into the crook of his arm and slowly started to make his way out. A soft sound escaped the boy's lips; he aimed his wet face toward the Colonel and seemed to smile. The Colonel cleared the last row of hanging cow meat and limped toward the cabin door. He saw Wiley staggering just beyond the threshold with glassy eyes, heard him shouting, "Take him. Good riddance, better to put him out of his misery. Nigger'll be a thorn in your side. You'll see."

"Go to hell, you bastard." The Colonel gave Wiley a blistering look.

He shuffled back toward Charity with the boy held tight by one arm, his cane in the other hand. When she saw him with her child, she screamed, descended to the ground, and kissed the top of his dusty boots. Her thick black hair, twined like the soft tendrils of a mop, tumbled past her shoulders. The Colonel couldn't move his feet; she was wrapped around his legs. He leaned down and, while picking up his cane, "Come on now, get up. Here's your boy. You two will stay in the main house for a while, until the baby's better."

"Thank you, mastuh, Lawd, thank you," she said through a waterfall of tears.

The Colonel leaned down and placed the baby into Charity's trembling hands. She clasped the boy to her chest, looked toward the sky and said, "Thank you, Lawd, thank you."

Something in his heart softened, when the Colonel looked at Charity. Tears fell from her eyes and drenched her cheeks. She looked up at him; her expression reached right into his chest and touched him. He leaned over and slipped his hand beneath her arm. He felt her bone as he helped her to her feet and was startled to notice she too was undernourished. The Colonel shook his head, the cruelty of Wiley. He considered Charity for a moment eyes moving fixedly over her faded dusty dress, smudged with dirt. And he noticed a certain beauty she had as she stood with her baby in her arms, dignity and humility in her eyes. She was an exotic creature and very much looked like a native African to him.

He let go of her arm and Charity carried her child back toward the butterfly vines and climbed into the slave wagon. She smiled with tender love at her precious baby, called him Thomas as she squeezed into a corner on the rotted wooden floor. She kissed the baby on his lips and held him to her cheek. The wagon was packed, with fifty slaves and eighteen were Charity's children. Her husband, the big buck, the last slave on the auction block, put his large arms around Charity and his youngest child. He whispered to her, "You done did good, Miss Charity."

The Colonel took off his hat and smoothed back his hair. He limped to his fine carriage. Once he was settled, he called through the hatch to the carriage driver. "See we get that mother some food and water on the way through town, she needs to be strong to feed her baby.

III.

It was before dawn three days later when the Colonel's four-horse carriage and the crowded slave wagons that followed behind galloped down the dark cobbled path toward *Solitude*. The hired horses had been switched out at the posting station ten miles out and the Colonel's fine private horses had taken their place.

Inside the carriage cabin, the Colonel sat on the oak bench seat atop a plush velvet cushion and reviewed troubling letters from his overseers on the failing health of his slaves. A separate stack of bills he knew he could not pay was stacked beside the overseer letters. He sat the letters in his lap and glanced out the window, watching the trees pass. He wondered how long he could keep up appearances. Of winter balls and trips to the country home near the forest of Fontainebleau in Paris, of being one of the most propertied men in Georgia society. Yet *Solitude,* his prize plantation and the most celebrated estate in Columbus, would be the end of him. He sighed and let the window curtain fall.

The carriage tilted on a rut in the road. The Colonel waited for the wheels to steady before pouring a glass of red wine. Feet atop the warm bricks, he squeezed his toes, and began to hum "She'll Be Coming 'round the Mountain," one of his favorite songs. He tried his best to focus on his tune, to keep his mind from thinking about his financial troubles and the troubles that awaited him at home. An uneasy feeling crept through his legs and slowly moved through his body. It wasn't the bills and the bad news about sick slaves that troubled him. He shook his head and sucked in air, knowing he would soon face a hard situation once he arrived home.

He had done it again, entangled himself with a Colored girl.

The sip of wine helped soothe his nerves. The Colonel wondered how Frances was going to react when he arrived at *Solitude* with a slave woman, and her blind baby in tow to serve in the main residence. *"Mon Dieu,"* he said, sorting through his problems by talking to himself. The Big House was his wife's dominion and she personally handpicked house hands. Would she accept the female servant in stride or erupt into jealous curses and throw her parasol at his head? Or worse, retreat behind her English mask of suspicious silence and icy vacant smiles.

"Mulish, thickheaded," the Colonel muttered to chastise himself in the empty carriage, in that habit he had. "What am I to do, send the dying baby to the fields? I may as well have left him with Wiley."

The carriage was only a mile out from the Big House and the Colonel grew tenser with each rotation of the wheels. "I've done nothing wrong," he said with a deep inhale. "It was innocent, helping the slave woman and child; I will not be made to feel guilty. To leave him would be without honor." He shifted his hips on the cushions and pondered; he had made such great progress in regaining Frances's trust. He enjoyed his wife's adoring voice, greeting him softly in the mornings like a gentle sonata. He did not want to lose it again.

The Colonel had finished a half bottle of wine by the time his carriage grunted past the sprawling walnut groves and through the main gates of *Solitude.* The carriage came to a stop and the old slave wagons behind him squeaked to a halt before a row of one-room huts.

He closed his eyes and finished his last glass of wine, as the slaves were herded off the back and driven like cattle toward their quarters. All of Charity's children and her husband climbed out of the last wagon, one by one. But Charity was instructed to stay on board with her baby. There was crying from some of the younger children, as the wagon pulled away and creaked up the winding high hill toward the large white pillars of the Big House.

IV.

A harmonic tinkling from the wind chimes welcomed the cantering horses when they reached the top of the hill and slowed to a stop in front of the carriage porch. Servants rushed with lanterns to meet the Colonel's transport, opening the wagon doors, they set out a footplate for the patriarch to descend. A black cane emerged, followed by a black boot. A young valet, Ensa, proudly dressed in immaculate livery, greeted the Colonel with his singsong West Indies accent. He was tall and quite handsome with high cheekbones, slanted eyes, and skin the color of coffee. He rushed to retrieve the Colonel's wine and his portmanteau from the back seat, while the stable boy tended to the horses.

Though the latter half of the trip passed with some worry, the Colonel was glad to be home. He snapped for the coachman and commanded him to see to it that the slave woman, Charity, was provided breakfast, and then taken to the *grand parlor*. "She and her child are to wait there until further instruction. Prepare the sitting room," the Colonel ordered in a stern voice as he walked past the back of the carriage toward the front stairs leading to the Big House.

Inside the mansion, the bronze chandelier was lit in the great foyer. House servants had seen the master's carriage with its small oil lamps approaching in the distance and had awakened Frances. At twenty-six, Frances was a feminine, genteel creature; petite in stature with big beautiful green eyes, the same deep green as leaves on a rose, and a mole right above her lip. She was well bred with affected manners and perfected fashion.

The mistress descended the grand staircase barefoot–in a flowing pink nightgown and silk robe. Her long dark blond hair was swept to one side and rested down the space between her breasts. She stood waiting for the Colonel in the archway. When the front doors opened, she rushed across the checkered marble floor and greeted him with a warm hug. The Colonel handed his top hat to the footman, pulled her into his arms, and gazed into her emerald eyes. "My beautiful sweet," he said.

Her eyes sparkled as she slid her hands beneath the smooth collar of his coat, up and around his neck. "Welcome home, *mon amour*," she said with another kiss. "Was it exhausting?"

"Tired mostly from the heat, the wine helped."

"And you worked hard and you missed me," she said with a suggestive pout of her lips.

"I missed you more than you know, *ma bichette*," he said in French, brushing her nose with the tip of his finger, drawing her closer to him. "The work wasn't at all pleasant."

"Oh dear, please tell me, what displeased you?"

"Wiley's very much the drunk as rumored," he sighed. "You should see how he's let his father's property descend into ruin," he said, taking her hand. He guided her by the waist down the corridor and into the sitting room where the curtains were drawn.

Servants had already poured wet tealeaves on the ashes in the French marble hearth and with the cinders, all the debris had been gathered in the grate. A kindling pile was quickly built with fresh cinder, twigs, and a backlog. Ensa lit the crumpled paper at the bottom with a match to start the fire for the masters' comfort. The warmth from the flames lapped the Colonel's back as he sat Frances on a burgundy sofa cross-stitched with red and blue roses. He adjusted the pillows and placed them behind her back.

"It brings dishonor to his father's memory," he said.

"It's really that awful at Wiley's property?" Frances went on, before crossing her long slender legs. Another servant entered with tea and handed the platter to Ensa.

"Remember the gardens that were the talk of Muscogee County?" the Colonel asked, as Ensa filled two cups with hot, brown, colored water. "Not one rose, not one lily, just weeds. And his father's once proud Landau sits in front of the mansion, with two broken wheels."

"Oh my, I hate to hear it."

"And he's boarded up all the windows on the mansion."

The maid placed a pair of jeweled slippers near her feet. "You're right, my dear. What a disgrace to Edgar Wiley's memory." She slipped the slippers on and tucked her leg beneath her bottom.

"My father would roll over in his grave if I allowed his legacy to fall into such ruin," the Colonel said.

Frances *tsked* and reached out to him, "You would never let that happen," she said and caressed his hand. "You are a man of your word and you made a promise to him."

"'I will expand the Bethune empire of land, law, and newspapers,'" the Colonel recited his promise dictated by his father. It was a promise all firstborn Bethune males make before the patriarch died. "It's a promise I plan to keep," the Colonel said, taking a sip of tea.

He took his cup and sat in the seat across from her. Suddenly, the bad feeling in the carriage came rushing back. He felt his heart speed up as he prepared to bring up the slave woman and her child. It was an issue that could not be avoided. "*Ma bichette*, there's something I want to..."

"Mary and Sarah won their badminton matches," Frances interrupted without noticing he had started to talk. "Of course Caleb thought it would be appropriate to play Strauss in the middle of his hymn recital, so I dare say half the church thinks him the Devil. In *church*, James," Frances stressed. "When he knows the waltz is godless and forbidden."

"He is a bit wild, our son," the Colonel answered. "But I'm sure it was all in good fun. I'll have a talk with him," he said, taking a sip of tea, his eyes fixed on her beautiful face.

He brushed lint from his pants and affected a casual tone. Since there was a natural pause, he decided it was time to share what he'd done.

"I purchased a new head cook for the house and she'll need instruction on the menus," he said, lowering his voice to that slight tone that was barely a whisper.

"I'm sorry, come again?" Frances set her cup on the serving tray at once, her face a slight flush.

Such an immediate sharp response, her reaction to his statement, unnerved him. The Colonel cleared his throat. "I bought a cook from Wiley."

"Purchased a new? You...you....Excuse me? And you want her to work in the house?" came the soft, high-pitched reply. She sat up straight, her neck elongated, much like a king cobra when ready to strike. The Colonel could see her mind working, her imagination running back to the Virginia plantation to when he had broken her heart over and over again.

"Yes, my sweet. Her name's Charity. I purchased her for the kitchen," he said calmly, continuing to watch her closely.

Her eyes had narrowed, and it took her a moment to put all her thoughts together before her green eyes flashed.

"You...purchased...a head cook without me?" her voice came in a slow choppy whisper.

She put her face in her hands, as if she could not bear it. When she lifted her chin, he saw the warmth in her eyes wash away and in them arose a wave of tiny, barely discernible transformations that indicated seething anger.

"Frances..." he cautioned. "It's not what you think."

"No," she said in a small chilling voice. "I don't want to hear it. I shall *not* hear it."

His eyes moved slowly down. He shook his head, his mind recalling faded, buried memories that hurt them both. Pieces came back to him, the way Frances had lost herself, had flown into uncontrollable rages in those days. Back in Virginia, their mulatto housemaid had borne yet another creamy-toned baby in the servants' quarters of the main house. On that day, Frances stepped into the bedroom off the kitchen to see the newborn. She looked down at the baby and saw the Colonel's cleft chin and his clear blue-eyes looking up at her. She abandoned civility and ran screaming through the mansion, "My house! My house!" and crashed into his study.

"That you would have her here, in my house!" she raged. She rushed toward him shaking her fists angrily, the other quadroon children were browner, she had never said a word, chose not to believe. But the blue eyes, "You think me a fool, *mon mari*? You dishonor me and curse your children with that wench under our roof," she said.

He'd bought *Solitude* to mend the marriage, had moved the family from Virginia to Georgia, to begin again.

Now, the Colonel shook his head, his voice low, "it's not what you think."

"I don't care for more of your lies, James," she said.

Frances stood to her feet trembling, smoothed her gown, and retreated to the *petit parlor,* where she took breakfast and all by herself, drank a full bottle of wine.

The Colonel went to retrieve Frances, after sunrise, after she'd finished eating breakfast and drinking, once she'd had some time for her anger to subside. It was shortly past nine o'clock when he approached the open door to the *petit parlor.* A small parlor located near the rose garden, it was where Frances usually took tea in the afternoon and welcomed more intimate visitors. He saw her sitting in near darkness with the curtains still drawn; only one candle flickered on a small end table.

"A female house servant when we are perfectly staffed, *Monsieur*?" she coldly asked as soon as he crossed the doorsill. She leaned sideways and spat out tobacco juice into a can. The scent of her perfume filled the room. The Colonel drew open the curtains. He could see her better now with the sun spilling in. Her face was flushed from the tears and the wine. She let out a small sigh.

"I know I've disappointed you, but it was my decision to hire her, as we both know we are not yet properly staffed." He stretched out his hand for hers to help her to her feet. "She's waiting in the *grand parlor* for your instruction."

He paused, but Frances let it pass for a moment. She closed the silver tobacco box and set it on an end table, shaking her head.

The Colonel kept his hand extended. "Really?" Frances sighed. The floor beneath her feet began to tremble. Outside, the loud bark of slaves shouting at mules hauling cotton and timber to ships on the Chattahoochee could be heard rumbling past. In the silence, all the noises outside came crashing into the small chamber—the tap, tap, tap of hammers, yodeling roosters, the servants sawing in the shed, and the stream of footsteps up and down the servants' stairs. The Colonel stood there in front of Frances on tenterhooks, unable to unlatch himself, as he desperately tried to search for the right words to alleviate her anger.

"I know I've hurt you terribly, but I assure you, all that's in the past," he said in a subdued voice. "On this, *ma douce*, I swear on my honor, I am above reproach."

He extended his hand to her and waited for her to take it.

She finished off her last swallow of wine, let it trickle down her throat and into her body, let it numb her nerves, dull the hurt, before she reached out and slid her palm on top of his. With a deep sigh, she rose from the settee, and followed him out the door and down a flight of stairs to the corridor leading to the *grand parlor*. Arms swirling about like a string in the wind, heels clapping across the floor, she complained with a stiff contempt the entire length of the walk.

"It's up to me, James. We agreed. You are to purchase the Negroes for the running of the property and I choose which Negroes will work in the house. How could you not consider me?"

Adjusting her layered skirts through the hallway, her emotions simmered, her tone filled with criticism, full of the mulatto woman's memory. The Colonel heard the hurt inside Frances's resentment and saw both flash in her eyes. He stopped walking and turned to face her. He tugged beneath her elbow, his face close to hers. "I do consider you," he said. "Always."

Her eyebrows lifted. "By continually putting me in impossible positions?" she maneuvered her arm from his grasp and started to walk again.

The implication stung, but the Colonel refused to address it, refused to dwell on the past.

"Impossible? How is it impossible?" he asked, trailing behind her.

"How can I assign her duties and responsibilities, when my authority has been undercut? When you chose her. Was she so important that you could not think of my position?" she asked her voice trembled.

"I did think of you…"

"After the fact?"

Shame flickered in the Colonel's eyes, flickered because maybe, just maybe, he had felt a rush of pleasure from that soft grateful gaze, that look of worship on Charity's fascinating ebony face after he'd saved her baby. Nevertheless, the Colonel stepped in front of Frances, hooked his cane on his arm, and placed his strong hands on her shoulders. "What else can I say, how else apologize? I had no choice."

"No choice?" she drew away.

He grabbed her slender hand; his blue eyes bore into hers. "No choice," he repeated. His expression was firm, though he wanted her blessing.

But she withdrew her hand, turning her head and her eyes away from him, as she had done so many times in the weeks and months following the mulatto woman's delivery. "Am I to expect another birth, then…"

"*Mon Dieu*, I know I don't deserve your trust, but if you bear with me, you'll see the boy's sickly and blind," the Colonel confessed. "He was left to die in this miserable boiling smokehouse. His poor mother was crying, begging me to save him. So, *oui, mon amour*. The slave woman does not tempt me, I only felt I had no choice, had I?"

Frances considered his words for a moment in silence. But he knew from the way her shoulders softened, the way the fire had dimmed behind her lashes, she understood the difference, understood his reasons for assigning the woman to serve in their home. She lifted her chin in a gesture of defiance, though he knew she would come to see it his way.

Together, she and the Colonel walked toward the *grand parlor*, where they were greeted by a pleasant blend of floral scents—the delicate fragrance of roses, of sweet alyssums, of lavender wisterias, and perfumed pink lilies—along with the smell of burning candles.

It was a large room with high-coffered ceilings, a fine limestone fireplace, a stunning crystal chandelier and plush rugs from Pakistan and China. Charity was standing there, her bare, dirty feet on the black and white marble floor, nervously clutching her son in the clean blue blanket the Colonel's valet had provided.

"Ensa, why did you not clean her feet?" the Colonel commanded. Ensa rushed out, returned with a wet towel and wiped the dirt from her feet. Charity stood embarrassed, the towel was filthy when Ensa finished.

With a nod, the Colonel beckoned to her and Charity made her way, slowly, in her ragged dress and damp feet onto the Persian rug, past gilt Louis XIV furniture—oversized *tabourets* and mahogany curule stools—past porcelain souvenirs from French castles. She crossed in front of the grand piano. The candles from the chandelier shimmered on a few pages of sheet music, a *notturno*, to be played by mistress Frances after dinner.

When Charity came to a stop, she had Frances's full attention. Filled with suspicion, the mistress walked in a circle around the slave woman. Slow and deliberate, she inspected Charity, arms folded across her chest. "Mhmm," she finally said and "tsked" with satisfaction at the thick wooly twists, the broad African nose, the dark coal Colored skin.

The Colonel watched Frances relax with each shift of her eyes. He knew she took pleasure in Charity's dark skin and large lips—that he found intoxicating—and was relieved the slave had none of the delicate European angles or the long silky hair of the mulattos and quadroons back on the Virginia plantation. He watched her brighten, the same brightness he had seen in the great foyer early that morning when she had met him at the front door. Frances looked over at him and he nodded, eyebrow lifted.

"Well now," she said. Her countenance was less than kind toward Charity, as befitting the slave's station. Without another word she peeled back the coarse fabric that sheltered Thomas.

"*Mon Dieu,*" she whispered upon seeing him. "Poor baby. He's nothing but bones."

She shuddered and looked for a moment at the Colonel, who nodded. The skin between Frances's eyes drew to a crinkle, as she lifted the infant's shirt. "You can see his ribs," she said, peering at him.

The baby was asleep. His stomach rose and fell in short shallow breaths and there were four tiny bones on each side of his chest pressed grossly through his skin. Her gaze shifted to the Colonel and back to the baby again. She stared down at the wasting child and noticed his eyes. "So he *is* blind."

"*Oui.*"

"Where is this blind boy staying?"

"In the quarters with his mother," the Colonel replied. "Don't worry, *ma bichette.* It will be *tres bien.*"

"*Tres bien?*" she repeated, startled. "Why James, he can barely find the energy to breath. Even if he makes it, he won't amount to anything. He'll be a burden," she said, without regards to Charity's feelings.

She turned back to the Colonel.

"It's his best chance."

Frances regarded the baby with a queer look. "If he lives," she said, slowly, "when good families call on us here, what will they make of a blind nigger boy fumbling around and crawling about? We are new to society here." Before he could respond, she turned to Charity, "And what are we supposed to do, *cher, avec cette fille,*" she said, staring at Charity, "who's clearly a field hand and *ce garçon aveugle?* I know it's terrible to consider, but…the best visitors will expect fine-looking servants, *non?* We have daughters to marry."

"Oh the girls will not be spoiled before high society because of a child," the Colonel said calmly, familiar with his wife's premature obsession with betrothal visits. He understood well her vigilance in following the customs required by the landed gentry. He wanted his daughters to marry men with decent fortunes as much as she. The slave woman and her blind child would not hinder that desire. "You get your nose bent out too much, *ma bichette*. With the proper uniform, the new girl will look as fine as the rest. *Et le garçon aveugle*, well…" he paused, his mind back at the sweltering smokehouse, even now he felt chills watching the baby's labored breathing. He looked down at the withered boy with his painfully thin skin and bones. "We must wait and see if he makes it."

V.

A horn wailed for the nursing mothers in the cotton fields to feed. Up the large hill, the sound of Christmas music could be heard coming from the Big House. Shortly after dawn, the Colonel had climbed onto his Warmblood mount and rode to the orchards where he carefully chose the tallest Scotch pine with the fullest branches and ordered the slaves to cut it down.

Now, Ensa was leading the slaves through the servants' entrance to the *grand parlor*. Seven dark-skinned slaves grunted in the winter heat and angled the big green tree, as cones fell to the ground. The men took small shuffled steps and squeezed one by one through the door. The last man at the end heaved a snort as he balanced the massive trunk on his shoulder to clear the doorsill. Ensa guided the men across the room, where they set the tree down. The fragrant evergreen stood fifteen feet tall in the corner of the domed parlor near the opposite wall from the grand piano.

The Colonel, Frances, and the four Bethune children, aged four to nine, gathered around the large tree with eggnog and cookies to discuss decoration plans. Each family member opened cardboard boxes filled with homemade

Christmas ornaments, then began to decorate the strong smelling conifer with fruit, nuts, candles, and sweets the family had crafted together shortly after Thanksgiving.

Taking the left side of the tree, John, the eldest, stood on a ladder—his cleft chin deeper and his hair blonder than his father's. He was nine. Eight-year old Mary insisted on hanging all the glittery stars and gathered each golden pentagon into a pile, her chubby cheeks gathered into a smile when she finished. Caleb, a moody six-year-old who strutted through life with an arrogant indifference in his brown eyes, hung only one ornament—his own homemade stocking, a green boot with his initials stitched in the middle—before retreating to his favorite chair near the billiard table and snacking on sugar cookies and milk.

"Sarah, please stop that," Frances called from the other side of the tree. "It's not ladylike."

Little Rachel giggled at the sight of her older sister climbing the tall ladder. She hung a homemade angel on the lowest branch and exclaimed her frustration when glitter fell off and sprinkled onto the floor.

When at last the Colonel placed the final ornament—a large porcelain angel—atop the tree, Frances rounded up the children by height and took her place at the piano to continue practicing carols for the social season. The Colonel saw the lean, graceful figure of Ensa approaching from the servants' entrance. He knew the moment he looked into the valet's troubled eyes, before he whispered in his ear, that it was bad news regarding the blind baby Thomas. A wretched queasiness swept over him, though he managed to look outwardly calm.

"Dashing through the snow, in a one horse open sleigh," the children sang, Sarah's voice trilling above her siblings, knowing full well she was singing too loudly.

"Sarah, *pianissimo!*" Frances shouted from the piano stool, as her fingers continued to caress the keys. Sarah softened her voice, as the harmonized melody soared throughout the Big House. "You must be ready to perform at all times, *mes enfants*," came their mother's soft soprano.

The Colonel slipped away from the mantle unnoticed, past the *grand parlor's* double doors, through the back hallway and down the creaky servants' stairs. "The First Noel" echoed dimly behind him, as the servant's door shut. The Colonel descended into the basement and limped along the busy hall toward the private servant's room where Charity and Thomas lived—away from the other quarters. Only a handful of sconces were lit in the dark corridor. There was a buzz of chatter and the clinks and clangs of serving dishes. The Colonel walked hurriedly toward the open door, barely noticing the soft tread of Ensa trailing behind him.

This wasn't his first visit. The Colonel had done this at five thirty every afternoon in the weeks Thomas had been fighting for his life, before he grew stronger and meat had thickened on his bones. He had done so, as he was now, before the dinner hour, before he spent time alone in the study with his worries and his cigar. He felt small sneaking about in his own home, sidestepping servants lugging baskets of laundry and hauling trays of dirty dishes.

There was crying. He could hear the crying increase in volume as he neared the private servant's door. His heart dropped. It was a sickly, melancholy cry, and there were footsteps, a soft tread, light thumping pats, with Charity's comforting voice, "Shhshh-shhshh..."

"Master," Ensa called softly from behind him, as he stood at the door. "Saliku says it's not Yellow or Scarlett," he said, relaying the slave nurse's diagnosis. "But we must prepare, master. He's still in a bad way. She thinks he could go tonight."

The muscles in the Colonel's cheeks tensed. An overcast feeling descended upon him. He nodded. He wanted to turn away, but took a deep breath, then pushed the door open. He braced himself for what he would find inside. Charity was pacing back and forth with Thomas close against her chest. She barely turned her head in the Colonel's direction when he entered. He removed his top hat and stood near the door. There wasn't much to the room: a small thin table, bare walls—and a cross with Christ crucified, hanging over a flimsy truckle bed. The Colonel noticed a steaming pot of water with meadowsweet leaves and willow bark the slaves drank to reduce fever.

Charity walked over and sat on the edge of the bed atop a thin cover and sheets, her thick hair wrapped in a scarf. She continued to rock Thomas, tears streaming down her face. From where he stood, inches from Charity's lap, the Colonel could smell vomit on the rag across her shoulder. He balanced on his cane. Charity tilted Thomas at an angle in the blue blanket, so the Colonel could get a good look at him. The Colonel peered closely at Thomas and drew in his breath.

He felt the emotion threaten to crack the mask of serenity he normally wore. The single flame from the gas lantern revealed the baby's bloated stomach. The Colonel took his finger and nudged his thighs, and with his finger felt the lack of strength in his legs. The baby's head lay limp against Charity's shoulder, his entire body covered in sweat. He was so lethargic he didn't move when the Colonel touched him, lightly on his head, lighter on his chest. Thomas looked like a cadaver; if it weren't for his wheezy short gasps and that mournful sick cry, he'd have thought him already dead.

The Colonel reached out, touched Thomas's forehead with the back of his hand, and shuddered. "Dear Lord, the boy's burning up. What happened?"

"Lawd knows," Charity mumbled.

"But...he was doing fine. He was eating, getting stronger, he was getting meat on his bones."

Charity's face tensed and she didn't respond.

"Where in heaven's name is Saliku?" The Colonel didn't know what to do, so he took charge. "Find Saliku," he commanded, calling out the door, gesturing, and cane wagging in frustration. He turned his attention back to the room and looked at Charity. She kept her eyes on her son. Thomas was dripping with sweat and fighting for breath.

"She gone be right back, mastuh," said Charity in a soft voice.

"For what good reason is she not here? Where the hell did she go?" The color in his cheeks burned red.

Before Charity could answer his question, she heard the familiar slow, heavy pounding of Saliku's feet in the hallway. Saliku waddled into the room, a short fat chocolate brown slave with deep-set eyes and tree trunk legs. She carried a bucket of cold ice water with fresh sheets folded on top. She set the bucket down with a thump, shuffled over to the bed, and with her big hands began removing the wet blanket and sheets. She grabbed the clean sheets from atop the bucket, snapped them out, and quickly began to smooth and tuck the fresh bedding into place.

"Come on, set 'im on down, an' take dat blanket offa dat boy." Saliku took a rag from her front dress pocket and motioned toward Charity. "Got ta keep the baby cool and you gots to drink up that water I made," she said, her breaths short and heavy.

Charity placed Thomas on the bed, on top of his blanket, as Saliku dipped the rag into the ice water, twisted it and laid it on the baby's head. His body looked so little, even on the small bed. As Charity filled a cup with the steaming herbs and began to drink, the Colonel pointed to Thomas.

"May I," he asked, indicating his desire to hold Thomas. With Charity nodding her permission, he lifted Thomas from the bed and pulled him gently to his chest.

"I won't give up on you," he whispered against the frail baby's cheek. "You have been through hell and then some." He murmured now in Thomas's ear. "But you are a soldier, my strong little soldier." He turned toward Charity. "I want you to stay with him. Whatever the rest of your duties are tonight, tomorrow, next week, you see to it he is properly fed, and have someone else take care of your labors. You hear me? You see to it."

"But mastuh..."

"I won't hear any of it," the Colonel interjected. "Saliku, see to it, find someone who can cook the meals, make the menus, clean, iron...all of Charity's work. "

"Yes, massuh," Saliku said over Thomas's unrelenting cry.

The Colonel moved closer to Charity and with one hand lifted her chin. "I mean it. Keep cool rags on his head." He made her look into his eyes. "Refill the buckets with ice water. And eat," he said and lifted her chin when she tried to look away. "Eat whenever you are hungry, drink what Saliku made for you, and feed him whenever he will take your milk."

Charity lowered her eyes. She nodded and the Colonel realized the awkwardness of speaking forthrightly about the intimacies of nursing a child. With his handkerchief, he dabbed at the sweat on his forehead. At that moment, Thomas wailed. It was a terrible, weak, dying cry. The Colonel looked down at the sickly sweating baby, and shook his head. He felt his heart sink with a rushing sense of defeat, and right then his faith failed. The Colonel's face shifted. His jaws tightened. He steeled himself, braced himself for the possibility of the worse, for the terrible news that was as sure to come as the blanket of frost in the morning.

The small dreary room, the baby's wail, the slow cloak of coming death, coming despair, became suffocating for the Colonel. He glanced around at the gray closed in walls, the concrete floor, the faint light, and he felt like a coffin was about to close on him. He lay the baby back on the bed. He took a few deep breaths, turned away from Charity and her dying child; felt the sudden need to get away, mumbled an excuse in French, to get out, to get upstairs.

The next few evenings, the Colonel didn't go to see Thomas, though he'd heard his faint cry from the kitchen in the mornings. Now, he sat in his favorite spot on the *settee* in the den, his tailcoat neatly folded over the arm, as he drank a sherry cobbler through a short straw. He set the glass down, trimmed his wick, and then stretched his long boots across the leather ottoman. He leaned to the side and picked up "A Christmas Carol," his favorite of Dickens, and began to read, savoring each sentence on every page.

Nearing the end of the fourth chapter, he kept his mind on the story and away from the dying blind boy. When he finished reading about the last of the three spirits that came to Scrooge, he set the book down in his lap. He rested his head against the back of the *settee,* and thought of shops he would visit to purchase dolls for his girls, anxious to place more gifts beneath the Christmas tree. He was pondering which frock he would wear for the first ball of the season, when behind him, the servants' door creaked open.

For a second his heart stopped. The Colonel lifted his head, saw Ensa with a tray of coffee and truffles, and sighed with relief when he realized Ensa wasn't bringing bad news. The Colonel placed his book on a side table, leaned forward, and lifted his spoon, then let it dip into the coffee cup. He stirred and stirred, then let the spoon rest with a clink inside the cup. He sat back, slowly rubbed his hands in thought, and then grabbed his waistcoat, deciding to make his way to Charity's room.

As he walked past the sitting room, Frances saw him from the sofa and called out to him. He stopped and stood by the door. "James, would you like a bite of Stilton Blue cheese? Mother had it sent overseas from Derbyshire," she said, pointing at a small silver plate, stacked with yellow-green triangles.

"I can smell it from here," the Colonel said with a sniff.

"It's gourmet. All the rage in London. Share some with me, please," said Frances with a flirty flash of her lashes. She looked stunning in a dark blue dress, tightly corseted at the waist, with dozens of layers of ruffles of lace, her décolletage accentuated by a sparkling sapphire pendant, her lips a deep red.

"Not now, *ma bichette,* I'm afraid I still have plenty of work to do," the Colonel lied with a dashing smile.

Sighing, she held up a piece of cheese with her fork. "Then I will savor it all alone," she said with a kiss at the air toward him. The Colonel lowered his head politely, turned, and slipped through the servants' door off the kitchen, down the back stairs to the small servant's room to see about the baby. As he walked through the back hallways, he instructed himself not to show panic if the boy was on his last breath. "Do not startle the mother, James. Be a soldier."

With grave eyes, he walked through the door into the darkness. The room was hot and he ordered a servant to bring another bucket of ice water for Charity.

"How is he?" the Colonel asked, as he leaned over Charity on the small bed to give his usual rub to Thomas on his stomach.

He stroked the baby's belly, fully expecting the boy not to respond. But, Thomas wiggled his stomach beneath his fingers and opened his mouth with an ear-piercing laugh that rose and floated across the room. The Colonel froze with shock. Did the baby just laugh?

Having confessed to Frances that he'd visited Charity's room and the baby wouldn't make it, here he was, and Thomas was full of life. The baby giggled, kicked his legs, lifted his hands, and squirmed beneath the Colonel's fingers. The Colonel was so filled with pleasure that he couldn't find the right words. So he began to laugh. The more he laughed, the more Thomas laughed.

"Do you hear? Do you hear?" the Colonel said at last to Charity.

Tears formed in Charity's eyes and would not stop once they began.

Staring down at Thomas, the Colonel pointed. "I told you little fella, you are my brave little soldier," he said. Thomas smiled and wrapped his hand around the Colonel's large thumb and would not let go. A loud screech began in the corner above their heads, as violins from his daughters' room warmed up, and started to sing through the vent. The Colonel angled his ear and immediately recognized the first few notes from Beethoven's "Fur Elise." Thomas released his grip on the Colonel's finger and began to clap with a big smile.

"Look at him, I believe he likes the music," the Colonel said to Charity. The Colonel felt a flood of relief as he watched the smiling baby.

The blind boy was going to live.

VI.

1905

Warrenton, Virginia

The old Colonel shuffled across the cell's stone floor. His right foot felt numb, but he was appreciative of the curious mixture of odors that filled his nostrils, a mixture of coffee, burning pinewood, and fresh paint. The police officers that had arrested him months ago were long gone. On the orders of a high standing member of Richmond's court, he had been moved to more accommodating quarters, quarters befitting a man of his status. The large room was located behind the jailer's residence, a good distance from the soiled debtors and foul-mouthed Irish thieves in the facility's other barren stone cells. The Colonel's maple rocking chair, a black Knabe piano, a few choice furnishings, and a portion of his library had been delivered from *Elway* for his comfort. All thanks to his old friend, the Honorable Judge Josiah Cobb. Judge Cobb was long retired, but his power was still far-reaching in these parts.

"Hmph," the Colonel grunted as he reached for the pot of coffee, *enslavement.* That was the charge he was cited for. *I took bullets for this land, stared in the eyes of savages for this land.* He clucked his tongue, thinking of the successful Indian campaigns he had led that helped create Muscogee County. Now, here he was, a captive. The Colonel was grateful the judge was lobbying behind the scenes for his release, but he was being held without bail due to an outcry of citizens who were residing in the area with ties to New England.

"Troublemakers. Ridiculous," the Colonel spat to himself. His hand shook as he poured coffee into a cup. He'd intended to live out the rest of his days quietly at *Elway,* but his past had thrust him into public consciousness. The family lawyer was dead, but the Colonel was a southern legend and still had a great deal of influence in Georgia.

The Colonel heard footsteps and the main guard pushed open the heavy door. He was a tall scrawny man with a sloping jaw who checked in frequently to make sure the Colonel had fresh coffee. The guard's father and uncles had served in the Confederate Army; he felt the Colonel, as a pillar of southern life deserved the upmost respect. His footsteps were soft as he approached. The Colonel was looking out the window where he could see purple lilies in the garden. It was unmistakably beautiful and not lost on the old man that he could not appreciate its beauty up close.

"Not alone today, sir," the soldier drawled. "Got a visitor for you."

The Colonel nodded and rocked in his chair.

"Bonjour, Mon Père."

The Colonel lifted his hand and slowly turned to face John as he stood in the dull shifting light by the small bookcase. He quickly took note of his son's appearance. He was dapperly dressed in a crisp black waistcoat and polka dot necktie, but the Colonel could see that his blue eyes had dimmed by the fret of his imprisonment. The Colonel couldn't help thinking *he looks terrible.* A stab of pain rippled through his heart. He knew his son was particularly distressed over the fact he refused to hire an attorney. He refused to give credence to the growing opposition to him by the Yankee rabble-rousers who came into town from their backcountry estates to cause trouble outside. Every morning in his bed, he was awakened by the obscenities. They gathered in angry mobs, taking shifts outside the Old Jail, strains of their bloodthirsty chants seeping through the closed windows.

"Hang him! Let him rot in hell!"

"Slavery is over! Monster!"

There was more movement near the cell door. The Colonel turned his head for a closer look. To his surprise, he saw his son had not come alone.

"Father, this is Matthew Shaw," John said.

Shaw was a young attorney, a graduate of Yale Law, the Colonel was told.

"Shaw. I know that name," the Colonel said.

"You know my grandfather, Jacob Shaw."

Jacob Shaw had fought under the Colonel's command during the Indian campaigns.

"Matthew's never lost a case, *Mon Père*," John murmured thoughtfully.

At that, the Colonel turned his blue eyes toward Matthew. *A deceptively boyish face,* he thought. His head was covered with waves of blondish curls and his dark frock was impeccably pressed. He bowed his head in respect, his baby face hard as flint. The Colonel's mouth tightened in thought, as Matthew pushed his stylish wire-framed glasses back against the bridge of his nose.

"Hmph," the Colonel snorted with reluctant approval.

Matthew stepped forward and got straight to the point.

"Is it true, Colonel Bethune, that you kept Thomas Bethune out of greed, kept him enslaved to make a fortune from his God-given abilities?"

A dark cloud moved over the Colonel's face. *Greed?* Anger rose inside his chest.

"Go to hell," he said roughly. "If it were not for me, there would be no Blind Tom, no Thomas Bethune the Great.*"* Stabbing his cane against the floor, the Colonel struggled to his feet. He stubbornly brushed John away. "Leave me be."

He ambled over to a small window where he gazed at the white flowers of the dogwood trees swaying in the wind. He closed his eyes, and the modest, concrete chamber gradually faded, receding into the soft distant memories of the first time he encountered the frail baby that would grow into the old boy and, for a time, bring honor to the Bethune name.

"Tell me then," Matthew urged. "Help me understand why you still have control over him fifty years after slavery has ended."

The Colonel waved his hand for his son to retrieve the family annals from the crowded bookshelf. "It's time," he said beneath his breath. It was time to begin the recording of his life into the Bethune paternal books. John removed a thick tome from a dark leather cover lined with soft red silk and untied its ivory ribbon. John opened the book and found the page where his father had ended the history of his grandfather's life, and rescued a silver pen from a leather valise. Once he was ready, he nodded to his father.

"Greed?" the Colonel began. "Hardly," the Colonel started, remembering the slave child not a soul wanted, not a soul could have conceived would one day play sonatas and compose concertos for prominent men. "Like an unexpected pearl found in an oyster's belly. His was a story of an unlikely star. If it were not for me, he would not have survived, he'd be desiccated bones in an infested shack— starved and alone."

The Colonel shook his head at the depth of his memories. "It was just a blind sickly baby I saved and then…" The Colonel looked into the eyes of his son, "then we got to know Tom. He was worthless and not I nor any man on this earth could have foreseen the fortuitous path of his future, despite his lacks and peculiarities."

VII

1852

Columbus, Georgia

Charity placed logs on the fire so the large breakfast room would be warm when the masters came down for breakfast. She stacked the extra wood by the grate and stoked the crackling fire with a cast iron poker. It was four a.m. and the dark rain clouds had moved down the Chattahoochee River carrying the storm with them. Charity heard the bells ringing far off from other plantations and the overseer blew the ram horn for the field slaves to start work. She was wide-awake and had already milked the cows, and picked the fresh fruits and vegetables for the day's meals. She yawned. She'd finally gotten into bed at two a.m., an hour later than usual due to Thomas being restless.

After placing the breakfast china on the long dining table, Charity returned to the kitchen and stood for a moment against the beam near the door to think about her other immediate chores. Morning work was grueling and Charity detested the routine. Hauling wood, carrying fresh eggs from the barn, and toting pails of milk, her entire body was aching—on top of very little sleep. Three-year-old Thomas had slipped out of her arms last night after she'd closed her eyes, trotted around the great house knocking over anything that wasn't bolted down, and tried to lift the top of the pianoforte again. Ensa pulled him from the piano stool and carried him back to the slaves' apartments. His familiar sing-song voice woke Charity up with the news. Terrified, Charity's body trembled, fearing the masters would rise and find the *grand parlor* in a mess before she could return it to its proper state.

Now, Thomas sat on his bony knees in a corner of the tiny kitchen, grasping an ear of corn in his little hands; he turned the grain upside down so the tassel was pointed toward the ceiling. He'd been at work with Charity since before dawn, shucking corn near a small wood table cluttered with mixing bowls. Charity rubbed her sore back and peered down at her youngest child. He was taking some of the workload from her aching shoulders, much to her relief.

The kitchen lamps on the shelves flickered softly, the rising sun offering more light through the small window. At the stone hearth stove, Charity put a pot of potatoes to boil over the fire. Thomas was making a mess, tossing leaves all over his shirt and onto the floor. Charity swept the leaves into a pile before putting the bacon in a skillet on the stove. Though at times sloppy, Charity was grateful Thomas had found a skill to perform so the masters would never have reason to send him away. "He done made good of his'self," she whispered to her husband Mingo one sultry night beneath the twinkling sky. "He worth somethin' now," she said, as the slaves danced and sang around the bonfire.

Charity felt like a heavy weight had fallen off her shoulders. At *Solitude,* slaves were expected to work the fertile land from before sunrise to late at night when the sky was pitch black. "Can't see to can't see," the slaves called it. Charity knew the fact Thomas was blind had made room in the Colonel's heart, but he wouldn't be a toddler forever.

"Missus ain't got no likin' for 'im," she confessed to Mingo after church one Sunday. She knew perfectly well Frances didn't care for Thomas living in the Big House. She saw the way the mistress rolled her green eyes and ran off screaming, "that's eighteenth century Louis XIV," if he knocked over an antique vase or toppled one of the silver candlesticks. As Thomas continued to grow from a cute blind baby into a big black boy, Charity couldn't sleep at night, fearing the Colonel's goodwill would disappear like the sun at the end of a long day. She was convinced the mistress would complain about the blind boy, pour salt in the Colonel's ear, and have Thomas sent to the cotton fields to die in the rows.

Most of her children started tasks at age four, sweeping up scraps in the kitchen or picking berries in the orchards. But Thomas was already a hard worker at three. "Thank ya Lawd," she whispered, as he shucked corn. Something about the grinding sound ripping the kernels from the stalk seemed to mesmerize him. Each time he pressed the corn through the hole, he'd place his ear against the machine. Charity guessed he liked the way it sounded, because he always clapped afterward.

Thomas's ability to be of use came by surprise. Charity had been shucking corn in the kitchen one afternoon. When she cranked the lever, Thomas heard the old machine squeak and the *shhucka-shhucka-shhucka* sound of the kernels tearing away. He crawled over, snatched up an ear of corn and shoved it into the shucker. She grabbed his little hands and pulled the corn out of the machine. Then she got it in her mind to teach him.

"Corn is yella, like da sun," she said.

She explained that corn had to be undressed and showed Thomas how to properly prepare the fruit for shucking. She took his tiny hand, slid his fingers over the fruit's ovaries along the stalk and showed him how to pull the foliage away.

It didn't take long before Thomas could strip the corn leaves himself. Charity noticed he had good coordination, grasping the stalk, snapping the leaves. After mastering the corn shucker, it seemed anything that made noise, Thomas could learn: hulling rice, juicing sugar cane, and cracking nuts. One day, in the backyard behind the Big House, Thomas lifted a thick stick to smash the rice. The other slave mothers saw him and fussed, telling Charity she was crazy for allowing him to try it.

"Gone hurt his'self fo' sure."

"Dat boy blind, an' he too little, Charity."

The women went silent when Thomas jammed the stick right into the hole, only the singing of crickets and the slave women's gasps were heard.

The longcase gonged in the dining room, then the tall case echoed the hour through the second floor hallway. It was almost time for breakfast; the masters and little masters rattled about and chatted upstairs in the bedchambers. The house smelled like coffee and hash browns. Charity rolled a large ball of dough in flour, kneaded, then tore off pieces to make biscuits for the little masters. She rubbed her eyes. Not one of her other eighteen children could hull rice or shuck corn at three years old like Thomas; they couldn't get their eyes and their tiny fingers to work together at that age.

So enthralled was she by his early development, Charity was miles away from considering anything other than lack of sight was wrong with Thomas. The boy's tendency to hum and rock back and forth or focus on repetitious tasks for hours on end, did not strike her as odd. She did not blink when he ran full speed to the *grand parlor* whenever he heard music tinkling from the piano or the little masters' violins, having to be pulled away kicking and screaming.

In fact, her mother's love made it so Charity was as blind as her son when it came to Thomas's peculiarities–she was not troubled by the fact that he couldn't talk. Yet every day, some two or three slave mothers worried Charity about her baby boy's lack of speech. Just yesterday afternoon, Charity was in the back of the Big House making soap in the hot sun while the mulatto Sa'diyah and some Yoruban women were boiling clothes.

"How de boy is?" Sa'diyah asked, dropping a pair of the masters' shirts in a big pot. She was a slim, gossiping Ghana girl, with short hair beneath a big floppy hat.

"Jus' fine."

Charity appeared to brace.

"Jus' fine," Sa'diyah repeated in her thick accent. "Boy talkin' yet?"

"Ain't nonya bisness Sa'diyah. That woman crazy," Charity heard Saliku's voice huffing and puffing, breathing heavy in her mind. She had plenty to say about the babbling Ghanaians when Charity would tell her what was going on as they worked in the kitchen. She'd slap her big thighs and her nostrils flared.

The tense hush around the bonfire seemed to go on forever. It seemed like the battling sticks stopped pounding and the blocks stopped banging. Sweat dripping from her temples, Charity continued to pour ashes from the kitchen hearth and fats from the pork into the lye. Lord, she was sick of this question, she thought, wiping her forehead. She didn't look up from stirring the boiling mixture. What she wanted to say–exactly what Saliku told her to say–she couldn't without starting trouble. One cross word and the Ghanaian husbands would get involved, Mingo would defend her and it would cause more mess, so Charity took a moment before answering.

"That chile gone speak when the Good Lawd want 'im ta speak," she said, wiping sweat from her forehead, lips pursed and eyes flashing with anger.

"Amen."

"That's aw right."

"Gawd is good, he gone talk," the slave women carried on after hearing the warning in her stern tone. Charity knew they didn't mean it.

Charity put the biscuits in the oven and focused on preparing breakfast.

Little Thomas sat on the floor blind as a mole shucking one piece of corn after another. He smashed the last ear of corn into the machine, cranking the lever, while rocking as he cranked. The machine grumbled and groaned to his delight. When it was finished, he jumped to his feet and trotted through the kitchen and out the hallway through the back door of the house.

Rubbing her hands on her apron, Charity peered through the small kitchen window. There were clouds out, but no rain, so she let him go without following. Charity never questioned why Thomas could get around without sight and she didn't know why he wasn't talking. But after the Almighty saved him from the smokehouse, she figured it wasn't her place to question anything when it came to her baby boy.

Bending at the waist, Charity peered in the oven to check on the biscuits. She sighed. It bothered her, the different tall tales going around the plantation about Thomas—slaves and idle time was surely the devil's playground. At night, some of the Yoruban women spread stories down in the quarters about the blind boy. "*Onidudu,*" they said, calling him peculiar. While hoeing corn in the afternoons they gossiped about Charity saying she'd gotten a hookworm from dog stool when she was pregnant making his blindness. "No, it was uh spell put on 'im inside duh womb dat caused his blindness." Thick hair glistening with sweat, the Ghanaian mulatto, Sa'diyah, would sway her hips by the night fire after drinking moonshine. From the top of her lungs, she'd swear it was an evil spirit that allowed the blind boy to move about without help.

Charity shifted from one foot to the other in front of the hot stove; the motion eased the throbbing pain in her feet. Her soles were sore and swollen from all the hours of standing. She remembered the night Thomas was born in the barn, the superstitious mid-wife wanted her to kill him. When she refused to kill him, the mid-wife whispered, "The blind boy's sorrow will never bring joy," in her thick Gullah patois. But the old woman had already been proven wrong. Charity took the bread out of the oven and said a prayer for herself and her blind baby son–leaving him in God's hands.

Days later, by late afternoon the skies had turned a dark shade of gray and the angry clouds above *Solitude* brought pounding showers. Sitting on the front steps, little Thomas craned his neck to let the rain hit his face and opened his mouth wide to catch the plops with his tongue. He loved the rain and hummed as the drops hit his skin, ran down his face and arms.

Between cooking, ironing, and folding clothes, Charity tried to keep Thomas inside where the oven fire snapped and kept the kitchen warm. No sooner did she turn her back and he'd bolt from the kitchen. Charity chased Thomas back and forth from the kitchen to the dripping wet steps and back again three times before she gave up and let him sit in the rain and wait for the Colonel. He rocked back and forth for hours, waiting. It was another one of his odd ways.

As daylight began to fade, Thomas heard the clopping of horse hooves splashing in the mud. He stood to his feet and clapped his hands, splashing rainwater in his face. The Colonel's carriage rattled up the big hill and stopped in front of the white pillars where Thomas was sitting.

The Colonel spotted Thomas, sopping wet, and shook his head. *"Mon Dieu,* Tom, get out of this rain, at once."

The Colonel mounted the stairs and grabbed Thomas by his wet little hand. Thomas's face erupted into a smile.

"Charity, you can't let him sit in the rain," the Colonel admonished.

"Yes, massah," Charity said, holding her tongue.

"Come, you mustn't wait for me here when it rains or you'll catch pneumonia." The Colonel took Thomas by the shoulders and guided him to a dry spot underneath the balcony. "If it's raining, you must wear shoes, Tom, remember? And if you must wait for me outside, wait for me here under the roof, *d'accord?*" he asked. The Colonel had a habit of speaking to Thomas as if he understood. He never spoke baby talk, never spoke slow, he spoke to him as he did his own children.

As the Colonel spoke, Thomas responded in his usual manner: bumping his face into the Colonel's leg while nodding.

The Colonel rubbed Thomas on the head.

Behind him, Ensa and the servants watched with envy the kind way the Colonel spoke with Thomas. The way the master rubbed on Thomas's head and was patient; one could see the valet, the coach driver, the butler, all admired the child.

"Come now. Get him dry, Ensa, and take him inside," the Colonel snapped. Ensa nodded and handed the umbrella he was holding to another slave to keep the Colonel from getting wet. Thomas clapped as Ensa wrapped him in a large towel and he was dried off and bundled up, yet again. He took his hand and guided him to Charity who took him back to the kitchen.

VIII.

From the second floor window, Frances let the curtain drop and called over the banister, beckoning her husband to the bedchambers. She'd been watching the scene between him and Thomas on the front porch while in the rain. The Colonel saw the slightly discernible scowl on her face, as he took off his wet coat in the great foyer. He climbed the winding staircase, pecking her on the cheek when he entered the large bedchamber.

"What were you saying to Tom, James?" Frances ventured as he pulled away to kiss her on the nose.

"Nothing that would concern you, my sweet," the Colonel replied, cautiously.

"It's a wonder he doesn't catch pneumonia the way he sits out there in the pouring rain waiting for you," Frances crossed the room and took a napkin from the drawer of her vanity. She blotted her lips then began to apply a new coat of lipstick. The Colonel sat on the chaise longue near the hearth without responding. Tired after a long day between the newspaper and his law office, he tugged off his dirty boots. Removing his high collared shirt, he pulled his favorite robe onto his shoulders.

Still primping, Frances watched him change clothes in her mirror.

The Colonel leaned over and grabbed a handful of nuts from the nearby table. There was cheese and also wine waiting in a silver ice bucket. He poured himself a drink and savored the smell of raisins and walnut that rose from the glass.

"I don't think you should indulge the nigger boy. It's stunting him, distorting things..." Frances said.

"Distorting things..."

"His place."

She lifted her hair and twisted it into a perfect French knot, but a few pieces spilled out.

Tucking the stray and fixing them with a hairpin, she looked for the Colonel in the mirror and saw he was staring at the fire.

"For goodness sakes, James. You're the head of the entire plantation, talking to a nigger child...a nigger child that is...Surely, you've noticed, haven't you?" she asked. "Why even the other slaves have noticed."

The Colonel turned and finally met her gaze in the mirror. "Noticed what?"

She set down her brush. He knew she felt he was being obtuse. "Noticed, Tom," she said, enunciating her consonants, speaking slowly.

"Noticed Tom?" the Colonel lifted his eyebrows. "Noticed what about Tom?"

"Noticed what?...Noticed he's peculiar," she said, turning in her chair to look at him.

"Peculiar?" the Colonel heaved a sigh. He stood, and with the glass in his hand, walked over to the window. The room felt cold, despite heat from the crackling fire at his back. A bleak sensation came upon him. He and Frances were on trains traveling in opposite directions and there was nothing he could do to prevent the inevitable—she wanted to take up the blind boy with him and he had business problems on his mind.

Undeterred by his stiffened shoulders or the smoldering look in his eyes, Frances forged on. "Why you know it to be true, James. *Le garçon est particulier.*"

"Ah," he said. There it was.

"That's all you have to say? Ah?"

The Colonel lifted the thick crimson drapes and gazed out at the twinkling constellation of cotton fields. His wife's tiresome ramblings about Thomas a mere murmur behind him as his thoughts were on his financial troubles and a telegram he'd recently received from the bank:

Please be advised. Stop. I've done all that I can. Stop. I don't know how much longer I can delay your debts. Stop . The time is near, James. Stop.
Gerald

"I've done all that I can." The words echoed in the Colonel's mind, like an ominous moan, drowning out his wife. She had no idea the burden he was under. That telegram. The Colonel sighed. Gerald had made it official; at last, the time was near. His brow began to sweat. He was on borrowed time with the bank: missed loan payments, foreclosure threats on his plantations in Virginia, the past due mortgage on the home in Fontainebleau. His entire life was crumbling before his eyes.

So, he ignored Frances's ramblings about the blind boy and studied the cotton rows below. They were bright with torchlight. The twinkling flames flickered between the stalks of the field hands who were still picking the fluffy white gold beneath the glow of the full moon. Please, let there be a great harvest, he thought.

His wife's drone continued behind him, as he stood staring out at the massive estate he'd bought to please her. He stood there thinking of the trips to Paris for the fashion season to please her, the trips to New York for the theater to please her, and the sittings with the painter who canonized the family in oil above the gilded mantles-again to please her. *All for her, all because of the mulatto children in Virginia.* A sense of failure took hold of him. It was settling in that he was on the brink of losing the Bethune legacy, and there was a tingling sensation in his left hand, tingling in his foot; they could not afford any of it.

The rattle of his wife's voice began to seep back in. The Colonel lowered the curtains and turned to face her, watching her prepare her look for dinner. She turned to her mirror and with her teeth pried open a pin for her hair. "He's three years old, James. He breaks everything he comes into contact with. I think we should send him, and his mother, to the fields. I won't have him ruining the house."

"The fields?" He stroked his chin and took in a breath. "The boy doesn't mean any harm." He moved over to the ornate jade fireplace, where the fire warmed his hands, then turned and stared back at Frances. "I'm inclined to protect him, Frances, you know I am," he said.

"*Noblesse oblige,*" she sighed. "Nobility obliges," she shook her head. "You French and your burdens of helping the helpless."

He lifted his chin with pride. Yes, *noblesse oblige* was indeed in his noble blood. It was in his ancestral heritage from *La Maison des Bethune*, advisors to French kings, to protect those of lesser station. He would never turn his back on a helpless blind child.

"It's simple mischief you're describing, *ma bichette*. Our kids get into mischief, drop things and spill things, don't they now? Occasionally break things, don't they?"

"You equate the nigger boy with our children?"

He squinted at her and tilted his head, a perplexed look on his face. "He's a good boy. He's been through a lot and he's got much more he'll go through. You weary me with such talk. So much fret over a Colored child. *Mon Dieu*, he's blind!"

"He's also strange, James, in too many ways to mention. Besides being spoiled by you, and breaking my precious things, he should be talking by now, like the other Colored children his age. Instead, he makes odd noises, twirls in circles, and spins that stupid tin can all day. We must face the truth. *Le garçon Tom, est un muet, et un arrièrèe mentalè.*"

The Colonel stiffened. A mute? A retard? It took a moment for her words to resonate. The Colonel shifted his weight and the floorboards creaked. He shook his head slowly.

"No, this is the same child you accused of being possessed by voodoo."

"James…"

"…because he could get around without help. It took John to convince you otherwise."

Her eyes met his and her face flushed with shame. It was true, because Thomas was blind and moved throughout the estate with uncanny ease, Frances had been sure he was under some kind of African voodoo spell or some other evil thing. She gossiped with the housemaids about him while they mended her dresses. The Colored maids were convinced of it as well and whispered the boy needed salt in his shoes to ward off the evil spirits. But the other day, she and the

Colonel had been enjoying tea in the sitting room when John banged through the door without a knock or a pause.

"He can see. Tom, can see," he cried out excitedly. He held Thomas tucked beneath one arm, a candle in the other.

"What in Heaven's name are you talking about, John?" the Colonel asked, his teacup and saucer in hand. "You know Tom's blind."

"No, *mon Père*, he can see. Tom, can see."

Frances rose up on the velvet cushion. "Why Tom's as blind as a bat. Has your father given you wine again?" she asked, as she sweetened her tea with a teaspoon of honey.

"*Non, maman*, I haven't had wine. And Tom's not blind as a bat." John brought the squiggly boy closer to his cheek. "He is blind, mostly, but watch."

John moved the candle from side to side. Each time the direction changed, Thomas turned to follow the light, his head moving only when the flame reached the very edge. "You see. It's not voodoo, *maman*, or any such evil thing. He can see a little out the sides of his eyes."

Frances made John show her countless times, before she was convinced.

"See, *ma bichette*. No voodoo. So no more listening to cackling slaves."

Frances looked in the mirror and sighed, before putting the last pin in her hair. Softly, she persisted on the topic of Thomas, "James…for his age, it's not normal. Not even for a nigger child. What will we do when the dimwitted child gets older?"

She stared at him in the mirror, flames from the hearth danced in the glass. The Colonel took in the smell of burnt wood, enjoying the mixture of scents in the room, letting its pleasure carry him away for a moment, before he turned and made eye contact with his wife's reflection.

"He will be useless," Frances whispered, twisting the string of pearls around her neck and the ribbon on her broad skirt.

Without answering, the Colonel walked over to her and kissed the back of her neck. He reached his hands around her chest, lightly brushing the top of her nipples. It was the only way he knew how to subdue his wife. Frances gasped with a soft sound of pleasure, head tilted back, as his hand wrapped around her breast. His sultry eyes met hers in the mirror, enjoying the effect he had on her while he spoke his truth.

"As for *le garçon* being useless. *Oui, ma chère*. We already knew that. He will stay here, in the house." Her eyes narrowed with passion, her breath shallow as he pulled away. She stared at him in the mirror. He squeezed her arms, before planting a kiss on her lips. He was tired, there were far more pressing issues Frances had no inkling about that he needed to address, but he knew passion would bring harmony, if only for a short time.

IX.

Charity placed a pot of sausage next to the grits on the breakfast table. One by one the Bethune children clattered in, breathless, black leather boots scuffing the hardwood floor. The Colonel stood at the head of the table; he grabbed the *Columbus Enquirer* from his chair and sat down. He crinkled and snapped the pages, making mental notes to give his staff at the morning meeting. Frances entered in a flowing violet robe, a sparkling diamond locket around her neck. When she sat at the table, the scent of her elegant perfume overpowered the bacon and biscuits. Heads bowed, the Colonel said grace, and Sarah, when he finished, spiked a piece of bacon onto her fork. "I know who's playing the piano after supper," she teased, licking her fingers.

"Sarah," Frances said, in a warning tone. "It's not a great secret, but in any case it's not yours to tell." Sarah closed her mouth and looked down at her plate. "John performed wonderfully last night and at last it's your turn after dinner tonight, Mary."

"I don't wanna play." Mary frowned. She hated to play the piano.

"Don't be petulant, Mary," Frances snapped.

Mary tightened her chubby cheeks and stabbed her fork into her toast. Though not as striking in beauty as her lean younger sister, Sarah, she had a soft pretty face like her mother's. Head full of silky flowing hair; she possessed a feminine grace Sarah did not.

"I'm sorry if it's petulant mother, but it's true." Mary slumped back in her chair and looked over at her father who shrugged. "Father," Mary pleaded, staring at the Colonel. "Do I have to?"

The Colonel scraped the last of the grits onto his fork and into his mouth, before resuming his inspection of the newspaper. Mary grunted and poked her lips out.

"You do have to," Sarah interjected, green eyes pointed at Mary.

"Of course you have to, silly. For five hundred years the Bethunes have had music after dinner," chimed John, "since Phillip II."

"You will do fine, Mary," the Colonel assured. He patted her on the head, stood, and avoided making eye contact with Frances.

"Where are you going in such haste, my love?" she asked.

"Yes, why so fast, *Mon Père*," Caleb echoed. His youngest son was indeed a defiant child.

"A man's work," the Colonel answered, hoping to quell his wife's curiosity– even though he cringed inside. The work he was set to do was not manly at all. He told the children to be good at school, grabbed his top hat and left the breakfast room to take the carriage ride into town.

It was cold, dark, and raining when the Colonel's vehicle galloped toward *Solitude* later that evening. The scent of baked chicken, ginger, and spices greeted him when he crossed the threshold as Thomas was there grabbing at his legs.

Ensa took his umbrella and removed the overcoat from his shoulders. The Colonel snapped at him to instruct Charity he would not be in for dinner. His face taut, his voice harsh; he was on edge. His fingers felt the bulge of his wallet from the thick wad of cash he'd received from the pawnshop; he was tired from all the secrecy of the day.

The Colonel turned abruptly and brushed past Thomas without so much as a glance. He heard Mary on the piano, a few fluid notes, followed by sudden, uncertain pauses. He felt inclined to stop in and offer a word of encouragement. But he kept walking right past the parlor into the darkness of his study.

He struck a match and lit the candles on the mantle. As the amber flames flared, he caught his reflection in the mirror. He should've been looking forward to Mary's upcoming performance, but he felt soiled. Though he looked the impeccable southern gentleman in his cream frock and starched shirt collar, he felt himself a fraud and spat at his reflection. He'd spent part of the day attempting to collect debts owed to him from other planters; the rest was spent asking for loans. He'd only received a small amount from one of his father's former business partners, just enough to survive another month.

So he'd pawned some more of Frances's jewelry, the wad in his pocket from the dishonest deed was his prize.

The Colonel slumped into his favorite chair, withdrew a cigar from the humidor and lit yet another match. He heard his children's voices from the hallway, looked at his watch and realized an hour had passed. The patter of Thomas's little feet came in from the corridor, and he trounced right into the darkness of the room and stopped at the Colonel's boots.

Little Rachel trailed in behind Thomas. She'd changed out of her school clothes and into a simple dress Charity had made for her. Thomas wouldn't keep his new boots on his feet—more hand-me-downs of Caleb's—and Rachel was chasing behind him trying to get them tied up tight around his ankles. Rachel turned on the gaslight chandeliers.

"Papa, you missed dinner," she said, throwing the study into light. The Colonel reached over the side of the chair and gave her a bear hug. He could see Thomas was impatient from the way he leaned back a bit and bounced on his heels. Ensa entered with a platter filled with nuts, cheese, and wine, the Colonel's favorite pre-supper snacks.

"Calm down, Tom. You look as if you'll burst," the Colonel said.

Thomas lifted his arms straight up in the air for the Colonel to pick him up. When the Colonel didn't respond, he tugged on his trousers and Ensa stepped in. "No," Ensa snapped, and grabbed Thomas by the waist and lifted him off his feet, his little boot tumbling to the floor.

"It's okay. Tom's fine," the Colonel said, pointing his cane. "Let him be, Ensa."

Ensa caught his breath. "Yes, master," he said, setting Thomas to the floor with a slight bow. He stepped back and watched as Thomas pulled himself onto the Colonel's lap, and snuggled his body into the crook of his arm. The Colonel laughed at his boldness. "Indeed, you are spoiled, Tom."

The little ones lifted his mood like a balloon floating on the wind. The Colonel smiled at Rachel, gave Thomas a pat on the head, and thrust the pawning affair out of his mind. He rose to his feet, Thomas on his shoulder like a sack of potatoes.

A few minutes later, the Bethune family crowded through the double doors of the *grand parlor* for the traditional night of music. Charity brought in a tray filled with carrot cake and hot chocolate and offered the treats to the children while Frances lifted the lid on the black grand piano and removed a sheet of music.

The room's furniture was moved around: *settees* and chairs rearranged. The family circled the piano and Thomas grabbed a handful of hems of the little masters' skirts, struggling to squeeze past for a closer listen. John blocked him with his body and lifted him into his arms.

After a while the children, started to sing, one by one. Sarah and John took turns as violinists and after taking bows the moment arrived for Mary's solo. She looked at her father who gave her an encouraging nod, then took her place at the keyboard and adjusted her bursting skirts, the sides of which spilled over the stool's edges. From a stack of sheet music that rested on top of the piano, she picked up two pages and set them in place on the rack.

She drew in a deep breath and in accordance with Bethune tradition, announced, "Ladies and gentlemen, tonight I will be playing Mozart's *Requiem For a Dream.*"

As soon as her fingers touched the ivories, Thomas began to wiggle about in John's lap and strained his body toward the piano. "Whoa there, be careful Tom. Maybe we'll let you touch the piano when you get older," he whispered, tightly clutching Thomas as he writhed with excitement, moved by the music.

The Colonel managed a dutiful smile, but his shoulders started to sag and his cheeks dropped with each pedestrian phrase. Her wayward notes sailed through the large chamber. She began the finale with competence and finished with a great sigh, rested her hands in her lap, a pout on her face.

The Colonel clapped with loving enthusiasm while the rest of the family offered lackluster mock applause and insincere platitudes. But Thomas clapped wildly and leaned toward Mary, struggling for the piano. John laughed as the little boy squirmed out of his arms and dashed toward the piano. John leapt from his chair to catch Thomas, but he was too slow. The blind boy headed straight for the piano stool, only to be intercepted by Sarah who smothered him up and into her arms.

John took it upon himself to usher his siblings off, "*bon soir, Maman, bon soir, Papa.* Come on Rachel, Caleb, Sarah, up to bed." Each child gave their parents a hug, grabbed a candle from the mantle, and went forth to the staircase.

While the Colonel and Frances sat on the chaise longue finishing a glass of wine, Charity blew out a few candles on the table. The Colonel rose to his feet and offered his hand for Frances to follow. She and the Colonel made their way out of the great room, but at the French doors, the mistress paused in front of Charity. "Charity, the children tell me the boy loves rattling around the pianoforte," she said, looking over at Thomas who was on the floor spinning an empty can. "He is not to touch it. It's hand carved and cost more than that child is worth," she said, before catching herself. "Just make sure he doesn't get smudges on it."

"Yes, ma'am," Charity said.

Husband and wife left the great room, climbed the carpeted staircase to their bedchamber where the fire in the hearth was blazing. The Colonel helped Frances with her corset, took off his clothes and put on his nightclothes. His head pounded as he leaned to blow out the candles; the many troubles on his mind had returned with the wooziness of too much wine. He grimly climbed into the four-poster, feather-stuffed bed with thoughts of the diamond necklace he'd pawned, the relief he would feel once it was back in its proper place.

The minutes ticked before midnight. A rapid rain came down in heavy sheets, pounding the windowpanes. Lightning bolts lit up the blackened sky and thunder wrestled the Colonel from slumber. Amid the wind and rain, he began to hear piano music fill the bedchamber. He lay motionless for a moment against his pillow, taking pleasure in the tune. He didn't move any part of his body for a few minutes, until it struck him. Piano music?

He raised his head, reached over to a small mahogany nightstand, and felt for matches to light a lantern. He roused himself to the edge of the bed, inclining his ear toward the heavy bedroom door. Though groggy from sleep, he recognized the piece coming from downstairs. "Mozart's *Requiem*," he murmured. He nudged Frances in her side, but she was not readily roused. With both hands, he shook her by the shoulders. After several shakes, to-and-fro, she sat up, startled, her breast visible from where her nightdress had come untied.

"What is it, James?"

"Do you hear that?"

He grabbed his robe from a rosewood armoire, "What impudence!"

"Well it isn't Mary," Frances said with a yawn. "Those expressive chords..." she swung her legs off the bed and slid her feet into her slippers. "I suppose it could be John." She tied her nightdress and shrugged on her robe. "He's a perfectionist, you know, probably couldn't sleep thinking about besting Mary."

"Well he could've waited for a more decent hour."

The Colonel took up the lantern, and together they made their way toward the spiral staircase and down the marble stairs to the first floor and to the parlor. From the hallway they saw Rachel squeezing her way between taller bodies. In the low slanting candlelight, they saw all four of their pajama-clad children crouched, bleary-eyed, beneath the crystal chandelier.

Still ahead, there was Thomas, drenched from the rain, with puddles beneath the stool at the pianoforte, playing Mozart. The Colonel moved into the darkened chamber. It was cold in the room and the Colonel pulled his robe more tightly closed and wrapped his arm around Frances, who stood stunned beside him. *Tom?*

Surely the flickering flames and the darkness were playing tricks with his eyesight.

John took his hand and looked up at him, the marvel in his eyes. "Can you believe this?" he asked.

The Colonel went to the far end of the grand piano and placed the lantern there. He could not take his eyes off Thomas: his off-focus, pink-rimmed eyes, the crooked curve of his legs too short to reach the pedals, his head leaned back as he played with an unearthly intensity of focus. The sweet sound beneath his fingers, the fluid movement on ivory keys, the notes yielding to the boy's whim or will. The slave boy was in the third movement of the somber mass, at the *Confutatis maledictis*, each consecutive note mounting in feeling, rising in profundity. His tiny fingers moved rapidly, floated lightly above the keys, yet even with his keen sense of hearing, he seemed not to have noticed the family in the room. *Tom?*

The Colonel was shaking his head. Uncomprehending.

Images from the past two years ran inside the Colonel's mind: Thomas in the old drawer, bones and ribs in the sweltering smokehouse, sold to him for free. (Thomas spinning cans and banging pots on the kitchen floor, twirling in the garden, drawn to rain and thunder and the hourly chimes of the grandfather clocks). The way he'd writhe and reach and whine and strain toward the piano when anyone played. *Tom?*

The tiny, undisciplined blind slave child–who broke Frances's fine dishes and spilled expensive wines, the boy who mimicked frogs and was an insult to the senses–that boy, that child, was playing the piano like a trained master-having his way with their beloved pianoforte.

The Colonel stared in awe. As Thomas entered the final part of the *Sequentia,* the *Lacrimosa,* his fingers traveled east and west across the keys. He played the complex *arpeggiated* chords with ease. Ones the Colonel himself could never master as a teenager while studying in Vienna.

That speechless boy, *un muet un arrièrèe mentalè,* was speaking now with eloquence, passion, and charisma. Eyes closed, the Colonel inhaled the fragrant music. The strong, graceful beauty soared throughout the chamber, like an eagle floating along a blue sky.

In a low voice, the Colonel started to sing the *Dies Irae* hymn that accompanied Mozart's music.

"Lacrymosa dies illa. Qua resurget ex favilla..." he sang.

The text spoke of a day of tears, of returning to dust, and God's final judgment, urging the Creator to spare the deceased and pleading with Jesus to grant eternal rest with Him in heaven. Before opening his eyes again the Colonel wondered, maybe it was indeed a dream he was inside. *Tom?*

The blind boy played on, *finger legato,* effortless, at three years old. It was a dream he found himself inside. It had to be, how could the mute, retarded boy do what he himself had always burned to do, but did not have the pitch, the dexterity to do—when he was a young boy studying piano in Vienna? The Colonel blinked several times. Yet, when he opened them, there was Thomas, untrained, strumming his fingers effortlessly across the keys, with feeling, pleasuring the family with the boastful flaunting of his perfect pitch.

Now, the Colonel opened his eyes again and his family was there in the candlelit room.

The echoes of Mozart began to melt away.

The Colonel studied Thomas: head tilted oddly, swaying back and forth like he was his own metronome. Tiny feet, without shoes, covered with mud, his puny legs swinging haphazardly from the piano bench. He looked for some signpost of greatness he may have missed.

There was none.

There was stunned silence as the final notes disappeared, but before anyone could speak or move, Thomas leaned forward and began to strum the piano keys in a frenzy. It was a melody unfamiliar to the Colonel's ear. At once light, buoyant even, then suddenly thunderous such as might inspire fear. The Colonel experienced an eruption of feeling stirred by the imaginative, floral piece Tom played. Finding his voice, something spurred him to ask.

"What is it you're playing?" he called out above the roar of sound and sensation. "Tell me, Tom, what are you playing?" the Colonel insisted.

"Remember, he doesn't talk, Papa." Sarah had stepped close and had taken hold of her father's hand.

"Quiet," the Colonel commanded with a lift of his index finger to hush her. His eyes bore into Thomas, who continued to play. "Tom, tell me what you are playing..."

"What the rain and the wind told Tom," the blind boy answered, faced aimed at his master. There was a collective gasp. Frances was shaking her head in disbelief.

"Tom, tell me what you are playing," Thomas continued, repeating the Colonel word for word. "Tom's playing what the rain and the wind told him," he said, referring to himself in the third person, speaking in full sentences better than any three year old.

Stunned, everyone in the family stood there in near darkness with perplexed expressions, flames fading on melted candle wax. The Colonel's mind reeled. Thomas, talking, Thomas speaking in the third person- it was mind numbing.

"What the rain and the wind told you?" the Colonel said, his words slow. He turned to look at his family. Frances was blanched and had sunk into a nearby chair. "Tom, are you saying this is your own creation?"

"This is the wind," Thomas said, his fingers fluttering through the first rhapsodic movement of his song.

There was no way for Thomas to explain the vision of his music to the Bethunes, the choir of angels singing to him. How the twelve winds of the seventh heaven had whispered the first movement in the form of a fragrant rhapsody rushing across lakes and mountains, across golden-leaved treetops through the falling chants of percussive cadences in droplets against the wagons.

"Thunder, rain!" he shouted, describing the passage where his fingers played *tremolandi* like a gathering storm, which created a thunderous tone on the piano.

The rains had breathed the thematic exposition to him as he was beating the rock outside, so his little fingers made feathery touches, playing light triplets like the droplets that had fallen earlier that night. *"Rainstorm,"* Thomas yelled out. "Tom calls it *Rainstorm*."

"Rainstorm," Frances whispered. *"Rainstorm,"* she said, eyes stretched open, as Thomas strummed out notes, *glissando*, fingers gliding across the keys. Frances sat with her hand at her mouth. Her head shook back and forth while taking in the

sheer beauty the blind boy's fingers produced on her piano, and her eyes began to water. As Thomas finished his new composition, the tall cases struck, summoning him to their bellies, signaling the end of one hour and the beginning of the new. He leapt off the stool and bolted to the nearest large clock at the back of the room. He pressed his ear to its stomach. When the choir of notes faded, Thomas skipped off toward the servants' quarters.

The Colonel shifted his eyes to each one of his family members and each one stood stunned, each one speechless. "Did we just...Did that just..."

"Yes," Frances interjected, nodding with shock. "Yes, we did."

It had been a long night for the Colonel. First, he recorded everything he could remember that had occurred with Thomas, second, he wrote a list of every prominent musical figure he knew. The moment came when darkness gave way to light and morning smiled through the windows. From upstairs, the Colonel heard his wife's high-pitched voice giving orders to the children. He looked over at the longcase clock and it was almost seven a.m. The children yawned and groaned, dragging their feet, and walked past the landing rubbing their eyes.

"Oh *Maman*, I thought my eyes had deceived me last night. It didn't seem real."

"Can we bring him to the parlor and have him play again?"

"Do you think he can do it again?"

The Colonel was so tired his entire body felt numb. Still at the *secretaire* where he'd been writing all night, he stretched his legs. A pile of letters stacked on the left side of the writing table. He dropped his quill and massaged his fingers. It dawned on him, as he listened to the sound of his wife and children dressing for Christmas shopping, that they would never fully process what had taken place in the wee hours of that morning. The Colonel dipped his pin in the inkwell; his hand throbbed as he wrote the last sentence of his final letter. He had written more than thirty letters to medical doctors, psychologists, and renowned musicians all over the world. Each letter began in the same manner:

On this day, December 7, 1852, I have witnessed the most extraordinary sight. A slave boy three years of age, blind and tried in countless ways, playing celestial music in the form of Mozart upon the Bethune pianoforte...

The Colonel set his quill in its inkwell. The letters included an invitation to *Solitude.* He repeated the words over and again while sitting in the gilt-trimmed chair. His eyes on the cream-toned page, he reread the last sentence: "I am requesting your presence at my expense." Hand to his forehead, he estimated his expenses: overseas fares, train tickets, food, and lodging. He slumped, sighed and rubbed his eyes. He couldn't afford it, shouldn't extend such, but couldn't afford not to. He still had cash from the diamond ring and there were more rings and jewels to pawn until his finances set themselves straight.

He signed his name and blew the ink dry on the final letter then began to fold each letter in three and tuck each into its gold trimmed envelope. He would ride into town with the family, do some Christmas shopping, and post the letters. Then he would slip away and make the trip he despised—to the pawnshop.

X.

The Colonel heard the familiar honk of the mail wagon's horn as he clattered down the set of stairs in front of the *Columbus Enquirer* and its columned portico to the busy street. His nerves were on edge as he hurried past the butcher shop and the stone textile mill where black trails billowed from smokestacks toward the auburn sky. The ground shook from the large weaving looms spinning inside and the stench of raw sewage came up from the river. A few weeks had passed since the Colonel had mailed the letters about the blind slave boy and he was anxious for responses. He continued to walk and was a block from the post office when he saw the mail wagon on the opposite side of the street.

Ears cold, he pulled up his scarf, stabbed his cane against the concrete with impatience and went back and forth wondering whether he should have worded things differently in the letters; whether he should have kept the boy's race and status out. What was he thinking, telling white men of letters the boy was a slave? "Stop it," he muttered, shaking his head, blowing into his gloves to warm his hands as he hurried to cross the street, sidestepping a speeding cart with a little trot to make it to the other side. The crowded post office was located inside the general store, a building with two large windows and a door made mostly of glass.

Before entering, the Colonel collected himself and slowed his breathing to make sure his entrance befitted his status. Jonathan Daniel, the clerk, recognized him through the ice-covered windowpane and opened the door.

"Colonel Bethune," he said with a smile. "Saw you across the street." He extended his hand, a tall scrawny man in his thirties with thick curly hair and a bushy brown moustache. He dug in his shirt pocket after the two men exchanged a hardy handshake.

The Colonel took the cigar he offered and moved into the heart of the packed store, boxes and shelves stacked to the ceiling; the main floor was crowded with sacks of rice, coffee, flour, and bundled up customers. Inhaling the pungent perfume of smoke, pork, and beer, the Colonel tipped his hat at the men from the card table who called out "Colonel," as he weaved to the front. Cane beneath his arm, he grabbed a loaf of bread, and waited to reach the counter. When he got to the front the postmaster greeted him.

"Got quite a bit o' mail for you Colonel," the postmaster said. He was a barrel-chested man with a round belly and stood behind the counter with his hands on his hips. He was trying to catch the Colonel's eye, itching for small talk that might lead the Colonel to explain the mass of letters. But the Colonel avoided his gaze anxious to get his mail and find out who had responded about Thomas.

The postmaster placed a small box filled to the brim on the counter. The Colonel peeled off one bill, muttered a thank you, and grabbed the box. He turned on his heels, without waiting for change, and made his way back to the teeming street. The wind was harsh against his face, as he bumped his way through the crowds and jostled the box to navigate the crush with his cane. Cutting through an alley, he made his way into a coffeehouse where he found an empty table. He pulled out the chair, brushed away crumbs, and put the box on top of the rickety tabletop. Still standing, he drew out letter after letter and read them. His shoulders dropped. Every single letter expressed disbelief and rejected his offer. He reached for another and began to read:

Dear James,

Please pardon my cynicism, but the idea of a blind retarded nigger playing Mozart brings to mind Mr. P.T. Barnum's hoaxes, Feejee Mermaids and other freaks. However, since you are a former pupil who has done well for yourself in becoming a highly respected gentleman and since you insist on your honor that your slave is authentic, I, by no means, intend to disrespect your reputation. I will indeed accept your request to make the trip to Solitude to observe him with my own eyes and provide my expert opinion.

Dr. Palanski

The Colonel put the letter down and slumped into the chair, his forehead ached. A frown on his face, he replaced the letter and pulled out another and another again. His coffee arrived, black, with sugar. Each additional letter he opened and read, expressed doubt about his declarations and declined his offer to observe the blind slave. After a dozen such letters, he rose with sagged shoulders from his chair. He emerged from the busy coffeehouse longing for a drink much stronger than coffee as he made his way through the streets and back to the *Columbus Enquirer* to finish his workday.

It was dusk when the Colonel placed Dr. Palanski's letter on top of the scattered papers that cluttered the table in the formal living room. The blue gilded wallpaper caught lamplight and cast rainbows on the ceiling. Frances lounged on the settee working on a puzzle, as the Colonel paced. "P.T. Barnum's hoaxes he says. Feejee Mermaids and other freaks."

"What an uncouth man to write such a thing in a letter," Frances said, the tassels on her short sleeves almost sweeping the tiny puzzle pieces to the ground.

"It is an outrageous claim," the Colonel said to himself. "A slave boy, blind, Mozart. Maybe I am a fool," he took a seat next to his wife. He liked the way she looked with her long slim legs casually tucked beneath the soft layers of her pink dress. She appeared so relaxed and unburdened; her silky hair fell loose about her shoulders, her green eyes were accentuated by a dark green eye shadow that matched the buttons on her dress and the pendant around her neck.

She leaned over and placed a piece in the center of the puzzle that didn't fit, tried to angle and press the piece into a few more spaces with no luck. She turned, swung her long legs to the floor, and wrapped her arms around the Colonel, a soft kiss on his forehead.

"You need not worry yourself so, *mon bèbè*," she said, another kiss on his lips. "We know what we've seen. They will see, these men of letters, when they come to see him..."

"*If,* they come," the Colonel interrupted. "I have a box of rejection letters," he sighed. "I cannot blame them for being skeptical. I certainly wouldn't believe it myself if I hadn't witnessed the slave's exploits with my own eyes. What if he can't really play and it's all..."

"Darling," Frances interrupted. "You sound like me, worrying over nothing. Pessimism doesn't suit you. You've watched him play every night since."

The Colonel's brows furrowed and Frances, snapped toward Ensa who was stoking the fire with a heavy poker. "Ensa, fetch Sarah and the violin she practiced with this afternoon. I need to refresh someone's memory."

"*Non,* Ensa," the Colonel said, stopping the valet at the door. "That won't be necessary."

He remembered what he'd seen with his own eyes, but Frances gathered her skirts and scurried out of the room for Sarah. The Colonel sank back into a large leather chair. He heard the thrum of his wife's voice, followed by bumps and bangs.

"Good Lord, what are they doing up there," he muttered. He stared up at the ornate frescoed ceiling filled with bright strokes of blue and splashes of red among a mass of biblical figures. The painting paid homage to Michelangelo's *The Last Judgement* from the Sistine Chapel and depicted mankind's fall from grace. One hand on his hip, he leaned his head back.

More bumps, followed by more bangs, and the sound of footsteps, a flurry of little feet clopping and bounding down the stairs. "James!" Frances sang out sweetly from the end of the corridor.

The Colonel pulled his eyes away from the ceiling as Sarah dragged into the room, wearing her pajamas, toting a violin in one hand and a teddy bear in the other. Frances trailed behind her, a folder of music beneath her arm. The Colonel sank back in the chair, arms on his chest, and watched curiously as Frances set up a music stand.

"A *sonata* for Sarah on the violin," Frances said. Sarah nodded and opened up the instrument case.

"My darling," the Colonel finally said, as Sarah began to warm up, the room filled with string plucks. "What in the world are you doing?"

"You will see, my love," she said in her sweetest voice, turning away toward Charity who walked through the double oak doors carrying Thomas, arms and legs wrapped around her body.

"Just hold him tight for now," Frances instructed Charity. "Sarah, are you ready?" she asked.

Sarah held her violin in one hand and adjusted the music on her stand before she nodded. She placed the violin on her left shoulder, fingers in third position, and lifting the bow she began to play a beautiful *sonata*. At the first stroke, Thomas began to rock in Charity's arms and kicked his feet against the back of her legs. Sarah played the *sonata* with skill and competence. When she finished the first page, Frances raised her hand for her to stop. "Go ahead, let the boy loose," she told Charity, who let the boy hop down.

"Here, Tom. Remember, how to hold the violin?"

Sarah took Thomas's left hand and placed the violin beneath his collarbone and shoulder. Before she moved her hands away, Thomas tucked the violin beneath his chin and was holding the instrument with proper posture. Before Sarah could say another word, he began reproducing the *sonata* she had just played. When he finished, Frances turned to the Colonel. "You see my love? It wasn't a fluke or an imagination," she then faced Thomas. "Very good boy, Tom," and with a nod to Charity, Thomas was taken away.

"You may go, sweetheart," Frances gestured for Sarah who trudged out of the room.

She sat back, tipped the top of the puzzle box and poured more pieces onto the table, the pieces hit the oak with a rippling sound. "See? Why do you worry about what these men will think about the nigger boy, James? It's of no consequence really, is it?" She leaned into him with pouted lips, her chin lifted for a kiss. The Colonel held his tongue and bent his lips to hers.

Contrary to Frances's declaration, professional endorsements attesting to the slave boy's abilities would mean everything. Musical slaves at social events, amid bottles of Veuve Clicquot and wine from Hocheim on the Rhine, brought prestige to their masters. It was a coveted thing not to have to hire out for music when hosting a party. Musical slaves made their owners more money than other slaves.

Classical slaves made even more profits from loan outs to other plantations for balls and other social events—but a slave prodigy? The Colonel drew in a breath.

Thomas, if deemed prodigious, would elevate the Bethunes to the top of the social ladder. For the best people in Columbus and Atlanta to say, "we're having the Bethune nigger on the piano," would be beyond grand. So the stakes were higher than Frances could ever know; the retarded slave, might be the answer to the Colonel's money woes and the beginning of even grander plans. "I'm sorry, you're right, *ma bichette,*" the Colonel said to Frances, lifting the back of her hand to his lips. "I shouldn't have concerned you with any of this," he said and leaned forward to kiss her on the lips.

He glanced down at his wife's calm expression, thinking he must not worry her with his troubles—it was uncouth. Besides, in the box of letters, he'd received confirmation of his invitation to observe Thomas from an old friend who was teaching music to nobles in Scotland. Until then, he would keep his wife out of his business affairs and do what was necessary to provide for his family.

XI.

This was the last time, the Colonel told himself as he dressed for work that next morning. He buttoned his white vest, before walking over to Frances's vanity. In the middle of a pile of beads, there was a large, ornate jewelry box inlaid with twenty-four karat gold. The Colonel lifted the top. He sifted through the mound of sparkling jewelry, locating a diamond and ruby ring. He quickly separated the rare piece from a strand of pearls that were tangled around it. Once free, a queasy feeling overcame him. Nevertheless, he ignored it. He wouldn't be doing it again, he told himself, slipping his wife's expensive ring into a velvet pouch and into the inner pocket of his frock.

The smell of bacon greeted him as he entered the hallway and descended the circular flight of steps to the first floor. There was the clinking of glass as he rounded the corner to the dining room where Charity had set the table.

Frances had already said grace. The Colonel greeted everyone and ate quickly. He took his last bite, folded his napkin and pushed his chair away from the table. His mind was not on school recitals or the Bethune night of music, but on selling the precious ring in his pocket to pay some bills. "I'm going into town." He kissed Mary on the top of her head as she slouched in her chair, her arms crossed tightly across her flat chest.

"Come, children," Frances stood up. "We must get ready for school as well."

Behind the Colonel there was a rumble of chairs and the scurry of feet on the marble floors through the rooms and up the stairs. The Colonel heard them giggling and tittle-tattling about the torture of sitting through Mary's performance.

Out the mansion's front door into the dim gray light, he looked up at the sky that seemed to be grumbling at him, frowning down judgment on him, and he shuddered. He patted Thomas on the head on the way down the stairs. "It's too cold out here, Tom. Go back in." He certainly couldn't have the boy getting sick before his examinations. Thomas jumped up and bounded inside, as Ensa draped the Colonel's overcoat over his shoulders and helped him into his carriage.

Dust rose from the hooves of the Colonel's horses as they came to a stop at Main Street. The busy street was bursting with Italian, Jewish, and German accents. Just in front of the bakery, Elizabeth Landon and her two daughters emerged. The Colonel descended the coach and dropped his face to avoid an encounter. He could see the pawnshop's garish sign at the end of the block, beckoning him with dangling golden spheres. He'd deliberately instructed the driver to stop blocks away from the shop to avoid prying eyes.

Heading for the curb, the Colonel dodged a buggy, just as the church bells rang from steeples announcing the seven o'clock hour. His steps were brisk. He walked past the bakery and bumped into Mrs. Johnson, a stout woman with a stiff bun who owned a tobacco plantation on the opposite side of town. He greeted her relieved she wasn't the gossiping kind. His heart was heavy. He could feel his dead father's presence, could hear him scolding, "A man doesn't squander, a gentleman doesn't pawn his wife's belongings." He desperately wanted a change in circumstances, to remove the stain of debt, now, only the blind boy Thomas seemed his best option. If he could make a profit from the boy. He caught himself-he shouldn't think it.

He moved in the shadows of the buildings, hoping to go unnoticed. This morning's trip to the pawnshop would make his third in three months.

It was unforgivable, the way he had lingered against the feathered pillows earlier this morning, pretending to sleep while his wife readied herself for her bath. He had peeked out the bedchamber to watch her walk down the red-carpeted hallway to make sure she entered the washroom and then crept about her belongings like a common thief.

After buying cheese at the market, the Colonel walked past the clock shop, toward the storefront with the three golden spheres at the end of the block. Now, he sank beneath his top hat and felt an awful misery. He hoped no one would notice the turn he was about to take–through the pawnshop's doorway.

Just as he was about to duck into the shop, a pretty woman passed by. The Colonel tipped his hat and she smiled. She reminded him of Frances, of the ring, and his lies. He glanced about at the bustling streets and felt as though everyone was averting their eyes–as if they knew his plight, knew about his foolish spending on opera boxes and furnishings from Paris, the summer estates and thoroughbred horses.

Suddenly, his breast pocket felt heavy, like a weight was inside, or more accurately a heavy burden. He slipped his hand inside the lining. It wasn't his ring to sell. Frances would take the children away, leave him, if she ever knew he'd pawned her family heirlooms.

Still, he had to do it. Bills had to be paid. He adjusted his cravat and when he pushed open the door, a shrill bell jangled as he entered the shop. It was a small space chock-full of antique furniture for sale, portraits and landscape paintings, pretty porcelain dolls, figurines, and rare jewelry. The owner wasn't at the counter, so the Colonel walked to the far side of the room, to a pile of once prized instruments. The flutes, violins, and trumpets were piled one atop the other, with price tags shamefully taped to their sides like scarlet letters.

He bent his body to view the guitars and violoncellos that had been put in pawn. In the center of the stack was a small case, a piccolo. As the Colonel reached for the instrument, the pawnbroker, Abraham Simons scuttled out from the back office to greet him.

"Hello, hello, Colonel Bethune," Mr. Simons said. He was a short gentleman nearing fifty. He was balding, with a curved moustache, and wore a decent frock that from the cut, was a few seasons old. "Welcome, welcome," he said in his soft stammering way. "What do you have for me, something nice, yes? Let me see, if I may," he said, pushing his wire glasses up his thick nose, as he circled to the opposite side of the counter.

The Colonel reached inside his frock, pulled out the velvet pouch, and handed the diamond ring to Mr. Simons. "Yes, yes, something nice, something exquisite," Mr. Simons nodded confidentially. He adjusted his spectacles once more.

The Colonel regarded the shop owner with cautious respect. There were very few men he found worthy of it. But Mr. Simons, who hailed from a family of jewelers, had a reputation for fair prices and meticulous records. He was an honorable man who had already proven himself discreet. Not one sordid word had reached the Colonel's ears about anyone from the town's best families— many who'd surely visited the pawnshop, at least on occasion—nor had there been even a whiff of talk about his own visits. Mr. Simons simply did not repeat anything privately disclosed.

He was a rare breed, the Colonel thought, as he watched him rummage through two messy drawers. His spotted hands sifted through wrenches, papers, and rubber bands before rescuing a black loupe. He praised its beauty and excellence of condition. "A fine, fine piece of jewelry, Colonel." Mr. Simons carefully set down the diamond and turned to the Colonel to inquire whether he wanted to sell the ring. "No, no. As the others, I will retrieve it," the Colonel said with conviction in his voice. "I simply need a loan."

"I see, I see, yes, simply a loan."

The Colonel nodded.

Mr. Simons pulled open another drawer and withdrew enough cash for the Colonel to pay down bills and continue with appearances.

The jangling bells on the back of the door were surely placed there to draw attention to his shame, the Colonel thought. He replaced his hat and took a breath before returning to the street.

XII.

Warily, Professor H.S. Oakley observed Thomas sprawled out on the *grand parlor* floor. *Thump, thump, thump.* Thomas banged his head against the far wall opposite of the pianoforte. The Colonel rubbed his forehead and peered down at him, thinking about what he should do. Of all days, all days for Thomas not to cooperate, the Colonel looked down at him splayed out on the floor, banging his head. He wanted to disappear into his study and pretend it never happened. Professor Oakley was a very important associate of the Colonel's who had come to see Thomas perform. Now, the scholar stood in the *grand parlor* watching the blind slave boy with a perplexed look on his face.

"Tom, I want you to stop it," the Colonel commanded and grabbed Thomas by his armpits and stood him to his feet. "Come. Professor Oakley is a dear friend, an important musical scholar and he's here to see you play the piano."

Thomas threw a tantrum, swinging, kicking his legs.

It had all been arranged. The *grand parlor* had been swept, dusted, and the floors waxed. Fresh flowers had been placed on the tables and scented candles lit. The slave looked dapper in Caleb's black slacks, perfectly ironed, and the tail of his black frock hung neatly behind his back. The Colonel smoothed the toddler's pants and pulled him toward the center of the room, toward the piano, but Thomas dragged his boots against the Persian rug, and spun out of his grasp. He ran across the marble floor to a sofa where he started banging his head again.

The Colonel walked over to the large oak mantle, his entire body was rigid as he stood beneath a gilded portrait of his grandfather, the Comte de Bethune. He shook his head and stared across at Thomas, embarrassed. He watched his guest, Professor H.S. Oakley, observing the slave with a bewildered look.

"This boy?" he pointed at Thomas.

"Yes, that boy," the Colonel sighed.

At thirty, the professor was a year older and an inch taller than the Colonel with thick brown tousled hair and a long friendly face framed by bushy sideburns. He had arrived from the University of Edinburgh late last night and had been coaxing Thomas for hours, but had yet to hear the blind boy play a single note.

"Of all days," the Colonel muttered. He stared across the room and shook his head as Thomas continued to bump his face into the cushions. The tension rose and filled every corner of the gilded chamber with each lift and drop of the slave's head. Most days Thomas had to be pulled kicking and screaming from the piano, but not today.

Today, he refused to touch the keyboard or come anywhere near the violin. John's tunes from the flute did not move him to play, nor did Frances on the piano. Mary, Caleb, and Rachel tried, they traipsed into the *grand parlor* and harmonized his favorite songs in the hopes he would accompany them on the forte. Even the Colonel put forth great effort to get him to play. He had chased Thomas to and from the tall case clocks and personally fetched him from the pond and back to the grand piano again, the boy writhing with resistance and contorting his body. He surrendered and let Thomas sit and bang his head.

"It's a disaster. The entire morning," the Colonel whispered to Frances when she entered the parlor to see when the men were taking a break for lunch. She looked stunning in a violet and jade patterned dress. Her corset tight and straight-laced, two teardrop emeralds dangled from her ears, and a bonnet shaded her white skin from the spring sunlight.

Frances smiled, nodded to Oakley, then angled her back to the professor and kept her voice low. "Perhaps taking a break to eat a proper lunch is a good thing then, my love, *non?*" She caressed his arm with a gentle squeeze.

"He didn't travel from the other side of the ocean to have soup," the Colonel groaned.

"Fine, my love. I'll have Charity bring the soup and sandwiches here," she said through a forced smile. "You can't starve him insensible. You both need something in your stomachs."

She stood on her tiptoes and gave the Colonel a kiss. She wiped the lipstick from his mouth with her thumb and gave him a mischievous smile before turning on the heels of her boots and swishing back toward the double doors. Unable to bear watching the ongoing fiasco, the Colonel slumped into a nearby chair and rubbed his eyes.

"Tom, boy," Professor Oakley swabbed his forehead with a worn handkerchief. "You say you see shapes and colors when you play. Is that right?"

"Yes, Tom sees shapes and colors," Thomas said with another bang of his head. His voice rose with excitement, "Tom sees blue! Tom sees Green! Yellow-green!"

"Yellow-green?" the professor lifted his brow.

"Tom sees blue-black-yellow-black-purple-blue..."

"I don't understand, Tom. Blue-black-yellow-black? What do you mean?" Professor Oakley asked, perplexed.

"Tom, boy. You say you see shapes and colors when you play," Thomas repeated. "I don't understand, Tom."

Professor Oakley looked over at the Colonel who took a few sips of iced tea. If only he could make the boy play, but he could not. The Colonel sighed.

"He does that," the Colonel explained. "He likes to repeat what people say."

"Ah," replied Professor Oakley.

The Colonel peered through his fingers. A piece of lint dangled from the back of the Professor's coat. The Colonel resisted the urge to walk over and brush it off. His old friend obviously didn't concern himself with appearances; his oversized suit was unfashionable, slightly frayed about the edges, and missing a button.

"But Tom boy, you can't see," Professor Oakley scratched his head.

The Professor's brow furrowed, his eyes squinted with exhaustion. He was a patient man, trying to make sense of the tiny slave boy, still, these many hours later. Thomas continued to bash his head into the sofa. But the Professor was persistent and asked in a soft voice, "Tom, how do you know colors you can't see?"

Thomas didn't lift his head. Instead, he turned and flopped to the ground, belly onto the floor, and covered his head with his hands. The Colonel glared at him, ruining the press in his frock, his slacks, scuffing his shoes.

"Tom," Professor Oakley asked, gently, bending down with him, hand on Thomas's back. "How do you see colors?"

Thomas lay still and quiet. He liked the professor's voice, saw a warm lavender color behind his lids. Professor Oakley blushed with frustration as he stood and watched the unresponsive child. But Thomas had no way to answer him, to explain that he knew colors from his visions of heaven. That in the heavens there were thousands of intense breathtaking colors that didn't exist on earth; colors like green that were so green they were nearly blue–a green blue–and the colors carried inside them music, vibrations, numbers, liquid, and pure love. How could he, at three, explain that colors in heaven were pure love and held music and liquids?

Thomas's body shook. Worried, the Colonel crossed the room and stood over him as he began to whine, his convulsions grew more intense and anguished from visions.

"There's no telling what he may do next," the Colonel said. "As I explained to you in the letter, the retardation..." He gazed down at Thomas, then over at the professor with an apologetic look on his face.

Professor Oakley nodded, his look thoughtful. He was one of the Colonel's oldest and dearest friends. They had studied composition together at the conservatory in Vienna in their youth and had always held each other in mutual regard. But at that moment, his friend looked distant and wearied. The Colonel was sure by the way he bit his lip that he was thinking him foolish and was sure he now regretted travelling from the university for this epic failure.

The Colonel released an embarrassed sigh. Professor Oakley turned toward him with a bewildered expression.

"And you saw the slave play with your own eyes, James?" he asked.

"Yes, yes, with my own eyes," the Colonel said. "The whole family on many occasions since. Just last night, he played for hours."

"Perhaps it's the time of day. We can wait until this evening," Professor Oakley suggested, "Maybe then the boy will play."

Professor Oakley picked up his leather portfolio from the top of the grand piano. He seemed downcast, his shoulder sank, and the Colonel sensed he was on the brink of dismissing the slave boy's exploits as a fairy tale.

Thomas kept his face hidden beneath his hands and kicked the floor. Just as a tray of soup and sandwiches arrived, he lifted his head and spoke softly.

"Tom can see," he said. "A is red. A sharp is a purple wave with a ninety-six. B minor is lightning. Tom can see," he said and buried his face back into his hands.

A moment of silence followed. Professor Oakley stood still, his face crinkled with a stupefied look.

"Professor Oakley is a lavender seventy-seven," Thomas added. He lifted his head up and down, then hid his face with his hands, and giggled.

The Colonel's cheeks turned red with embarrassment. But it was like someone breathed a second wind into Professor Oakley. "What did you just say, Tom?" he asked. He walked from the piano closer to Thomas. "Tom, what did you just say?"

"His ramblings are sometimes idiotic," the Colonel tried to explain. "But he's only three. My apologies for involving you in such a preposterous proposition..."

But Professor Oakley lifted his hand and ignored the Colonel. "What do you mean, A is red?"

"A is red," Thomas, repeated. "A-sharp is purple."

"Tom, I won't have this," the Colonel chastened. "Behave."

"No, James, let him speak," Professor Oakley shushed the Colonel. He rushed over to the piano stool with his notepad. "This is remarkable."

The Colonel was puzzled as he watched Professor Oakley's eyes sparkle and his face light up at the slave boy's bizarre explanation.

"Did you hear what he just said?" He flipped open his folder, pulled out a small note pad, and began to scribble notes. "The boy is not yet four years of age," he said, his words stumbled out in a rush. "And yet, how is it possible he understands pitches? "

It was a statement and a question all at once. The Colonel's face was covered in a shadow of confusion; he didn't understand a word Thomas had said. Yet, Professor Oakley's eyes, which for most of the day held a cool disinterest, now held warm fascination.

While Professor Oakley wrote down his notes, Thomas jumped to his feet and had begun to twirl. "Number 97 is beautiful!" he screamed. "Number 98 is sad. Number 99 is ugly! Professor Oakley's lavender 77. Lavender seventy-seven is nice."

Professor Oakley looked up and smiled before he continued to scribble in the notepad. Then he pulled out the piano stool and sat down to play. Eyebrows lifted, the Colonel watched him begin a rapid-fire chromatic progression of randomly played chords that were both dissonant and quite difficult. His fingers moved so fast up and down the keys and at times it seemed he was bashing the keyboard with his fists. Just as fast as he had started, Professor Oakley stopped, swiveled on the stool and addressed the twirling slave.

"Tom, can you name the notes I played?"

The Colonel had moved to the cool shade beneath the curtains. "Name the notes," he muttered, incredulous. What had just taken place confused him. He thought the question ridiculous as he slumped against the wall. But, Thomas began rattling off the names of notes.

"D-sharp, A, C, F-sharp, B-C-flat-G-A-B-sharp," Thomas said. He rambled on reciting notes in succession.

Professor Oakley stood to his feet and looked at the slave as if he wasn't of this earth, then he turned to the Colonel, who stood up at once, with an intense gaze.

"How...?" the professor gasped. "How does he know this?

The Colonel's eyebrows lifted and he shrugged. He had no idea whether the notes were correct or mere ramblings, but the professor's reaction seemed to confirm the former. Something in the professor's tone excited the Colonel.

"Tom," Professor Oakley left the piano and stopped Thomas from twirling by putting his hand on his shoulders. "How did you know those notes?" he asked.

Thomas maneuvered from his grasp and began to spin.

"Sol-fa Sarah, in D major," he said, in a high soprano that sounded just like Frances. "Doh, re, mi, fa, so, la, ti, doh!" he sang. "D, E, F, F sharp, G, A, B, C sharp, D. It never changes Sarah, Doh is always C and so on, no matter what pitch you start in, *d'accord*? Okay maman."

The professor turned again to the Colonel who was now at his shoulder.

"My wife gives lessons to the children..."

"Even so, how could he remember? He's only three, yet he named every single note in perfect succession!" He drew his hand through his hair. "Do you understand? This is incredible," he insisted.

"So you see some promise in him?"

"It's more than promise. Remarkable, really, it's absolutely remarkable."

The Colonel blossomed with hope, as this was exactly what he'd been believing for. "What does it all mean, *mon ami*?" he asked as Thomas, pretended to be a frog, ribbitting and hopping around the room.

"It means he has a hyper intuitive relationship with pitch," Professor Oakley explained. He spoke in a rush, his head down while he wrote notes on his pad. "Even the most expertly trained ears, the best in the world, struggle to identify half the notes I just played."

"The best trained ears only identify half? In the world?" the Colonel repeated.

"Yes, yes, in the world, James," Professor Oakley spoke rapidly. He flipped the page of his notebook and continued to talk and write without looking up. "For the slave boy to correctly name all the pitches with unfailing accuracy...I've never seen anything like it in all my years." He paused. At last his eyes met the Colonel's. "The fact of the matter is, it's rare, very rare, only a small group of musicians, only those..." Professor Oakley stopped himself.

His speech was deliberate and when he stopped, somehow, the Colonel knew what he'd been about to say. His eyes widened, but he did not push. The two men stood a moment in silence, as Thomas's ribbits filled the room. The Colonel watched him hop on the cold marble floor, past pillars with rare busts and vases.

Like a typical toddler, Thomas bounced about. Until he leapt and giggled his way to the grand piano, pulled the stool closer to the keyboard, climbed up with a swipe of his tails, and began to play.

Professor Oakley watched the display as if in a trance, moving in close to the pianoforte. He marveled at the toddler's finger placement, mastery over the keys, his choice of song.

"*Rondo Alla Turca?*"

"*Piano Sonata Number Eleven in A major,*" the Colonel confirmed with a smile.

"The eloquence, the intention," the professor whispered. "I'm seeing the unbelievable."

Professor Oakley kept his eyes on Thomas, on his every move, the professor's head shaking with unbelief the entire time. When Thomas finished the last six bars of the rousing close, he applauded himself. "Good job, Tom," he said. "Outstanding, Tom, boy." Then he proceeded to play a few more pieces from Brahms and Bach, before Professor Oakley interrupted. In a few short minutes, he'd gone from oddity, to child prodigy in the minds of both men in the room, though the word "prodigy" had not been said.

"May I play something for you, Tom?" Professor Oakley asked. As if speaking to a superior! The child was a slave. A blind retarded slave and Professor Oakley, a man of letters. None of the latter was lost on the Colonel, who watched with a curious expression.

Thomas continued to play without acknowledging Professor Oakley, engrossed in his music. After a glance at the Colonel, who nodded, Professor Oakley sat on the edge of the stool. In rhythm with the music Thomas shifted his hips and scooted over in two hops, as the professor took more space and began to play with him.

The beautiful music spilled out from the *grand parlor,* attracting the attention of the house servants working on the same floor. The maid, the footman, and valet, suddenly had cleaning to do near the *grand parlor.* From the corridor, Charity too watched Thomas play; she was proud of her son. She took a moment to collect herself, then entered the grand room with a tray of sandwiches and hot soup. Another servant carried a plate of lemon cookies and a pitcher of iced tea. Frances slipped in a short moment later and stood beside the Colonel, beaming up at him.

From the piano, the Colonel saw Charity's eyes flicker with joy as she glanced at her son, rested the tray on the round table near the fireplace and took longer than necessary to set the plates and place the napkins and utensils. She moved them around and back neatly again.

"Good boy, Tom. Good boy!" the Colonel said. He caught Charity's eyes, briefly, and nodded with a smile, as if to say, "that's your son." Charity glanced down, nervously smoothed her apron, and finished preparing the table without another glance toward the Colonel or the piano.

"Gentlemen, I hate to interrupt your business," Frances announced, voice as sweet as sugarcane. "But you must stop and eat. I insist...you'll get sick. Charity, take Tom."

Thomas had started another song. Charity crossed over to the piano and spoke into Thomas's ear. Thomas continued to play and Charity gently pulled him from beneath his shoulders; he kicked and screamed as she angled him away from the professor. She kissed him on his cheek and walked with him smothered in her arms out of the room. The piano stool moaned as Professor Oakley stood, face full of excitement. "Mrs. Bethune and James, I thank you for allowing me the honor of witnessing your talented slave," he said.

"The pleasure's all ours, *mon ami*," the Colonel said, beaming at the professor's words. The homey, wholesome smell of onions from the soup and lemons from the cookies was pleasing. The Colonel, with a quick clap of his hands, bellowed, "Let's eat," and they sat for a celebration at the grand round oak table.

After lunch, the two old boarding school mates passed through the long cool hallway, out to the terrace, and down the stone staircase to the pebbled walkway below. The sun was out and it was a moderately warm spring afternoon with a welcoming soft breeze. Professor Oakley inhaled the potpourri of fragrances from the abundance of fruit trees and flowers.

"Well?" the Colonel's eyebrows lifted. His tone was casual, as he and Professor Oakley stepped from stone to stone along the vast garden pathway. "Tell me, *mon ami*, what do you really think of my blind slave boy?"

"I, I must say, James," the professor sputtered. He pushed aside an overhanging vine and searched for the right words. "It is...It is beyond intriguing."

The Colonel's eyes locked on him. "An interesting phrase...," he said bluntly. He cringed at his own tone, the anxious chill in his voice.

The professor turned toward the Colonel, raised his hands in a gesture of surrender. "I mean that in the very best way."

"Ah." the Colonel nodded with a smile. "Continue, by all means..."

They climbed to the arching cast iron gazebo where the servants had set the table with toast and liver pâte, a brandied gentleman's punch, fresh melons and nuts.

"It's mind boggling," Professor Oakley said. "Was it for you? I'm sure it must have been?"

"I'm still processing it," the Colonel conceded. "I've seen him, over and again, play the piano, play the violin, the flute, each time it is unbelievable."

Professor Oakley took a seat on the stone bench as the Colonel poured punch into glasses. "I'm still trying to digest it all myself," Professor Oakley said. "You see, it's as if your slave's inside the music when he plays." A gentle trickling of water from the fountain seemed to catch his ear. "Doesn't the music seem to come from somewhere? It's hard to put it in words." The professor was a thoughtful man and took his time. "His technique...he's obviously mature beyond his years, but it's not that. There are prodigies, of course we know of, Mozart, Beethoven, Handel. But, it's that he's blind, and..."

"And a nigger," the Colonel added, taking a sip of his drink.

"Yes, yes, there's that, of course," Professor Oakley conceded. He broke off long enough to spread pâte on toast, took a bite and let the crumbs fall where they would. He began again, "When I'm watching him, if I make his race a nonfactor, I must admit I hear something original and deep in the music. He's not just playing notes, you see, it's as if he's channeling it, from the outer spheres where numbers and music and meaning collide. It's hard to explain it all, but he's memorized, clearly, yes...yet he's *interpreting* what he's heard, which is rare, and there's something else..."

"Yes, what else?" the Colonel waited.

Professor Oakley finished his punch, set the glass on the table, and threw his hands in the air. "As a scholar, it contradicts everything I was ever taught. As a musical scholar, purely judging the music, without considering the boy's nature...The nigger's a highly superb musical talent. There's no doubt in my mind." Yet, he hesitated with a sigh. "He is a...he-he...He is a genius. There you have it," he finally released a large breath of air. "A child prodigy for certain."

Something burst inside the Colonel; he rose from the bench. It was the word he'd been hoping to hear, wanting to hear.

"Genius!" He maintained a modest tone. "A child prodigy. Are you sure, *mon ami*? Genius? Are you sure?"

"Perhaps some sort of genetic anomaly," he said, "obviously some mental development implications. But that is not for me to judge. In music alone, the slave boy is a genius."

The Colonel beamed. Relief filled his soul. The fact of the matter was, Professor Oakley in that moment had potentially saved his life. If Thomas could fill his pockets, he would be able to pay off the banks and protect the Bethune legacy.

"I've taught the nobles of Scotland and heard the best young royals in Paris," Professor Oakley continued. "None of my students I've witnessed can play with the passion and skill of that wild, erratic and, unsettling little nigger boy. "

The Colonel stood and patted the professor on the back. "Never mind this punch." He waved for Ensa. "Best bourbon we have, bring it with the crystal glasses." He turned back to Professor Oakley. "We'll make a toast, but before we do, my very fine friend, I have a request."

"Of course. Anything for you," Professor Oakley said.

"If you deem the slave, Tom, worthy," he spoke with urgency. "Would you write a professional endorsement, a testimonial that makes clear the wonders you've seen here..."

"A testimonial?" Professor Oakley interrupted.

"Yes, a professional recommendation. You see, I will need this before you leave, to convince the unbelieving. Those who because of the boy being a nigger, and blind, would be disinclined..."

"Of course, yes, indeed." Oakley eagerly and immediately agreed. "I understand, for the doubting Thomases — of Tom, if you will."

"Yes. For the doubting Thomases," the Colonel confirmed with a smile.

That night the Colonel weaved his way through the corridors of his mansion, unusually giddy. The servants took double looks as he passed by, smiling and nodding, acknowledging their presence. It was just before dinner and he had an uncommon yearning to try his hand on the pianoforte. It had been years since his fingers had touched the ivories. Humming in the quiet hallway, the children upstairs dressing for supper, he all but skipped and clacked his way to the grand parlor like a schoolboy.

Frances's warm arms and the press of her breasts were a nice surprise. She'd snuck up behind him, her shoes dangling from two fingers.

"Are you going to tell me what he said," she whispered, then shrieked as his cane crashed to the floor and he lifted her into his arms, pressed her against the wall with a passionate kiss. He pulled her through the parlor doors to the piano, where he sat her on his lap and lifted the lid.

"James, tell me."

He sat on the piano stool, his foot on the pedal, his frock coat neatly laid across the settee. He kissed her neck. "He wrote a testimonial," he said, against her skin while he strummed the piano with one hand and hummed.

"A testimonial?"

"He called him a genius, *ma chère,* in writing." The Colonel played a delicate tune she remembered from the early days, when they were courting. He was formal then and stood with his chin toward the clouds. "It seems something could be made of the retarded boy after all."

"Well, you're happy, *mon cher,* so I'm happy. I've been worried about you lately."

"Don't you concern yourself about me, *ma bichette,*" he said, pleasantly.

He adjusted his hips, surrounded by music stands and instruments, portraits of noble Bethunes, and the busts of distinguished kings, the Colonel felt at ease. No more lying to Frances, no more skulking around the jewelry box or bringing perfectly fine antique statuettes into town for "repair," he thought. His fingers glided across the keys effortlessly.

Frances climbed off his lap and crossed the room to light a lamp, and then straightened some books that had tumbled. "These just arrived today," she said. She stacked Dumas' *The Three Musketeers,* and *The Count of Monte Cristo.*

The Colonel glanced up and saw the sudden pensive look on her face. "What is it, *ma petite?* Is it my playing?" She knitted her fingers and fussed with a bowl of sweets. He was silent and after a moment she moved closer to him, hand touching his shoulder.

"My love," she said gently without looking up. "It's already March. Aren't we meant to be in Paris this spring? The newest fashions are already being shipped," she sighed. "It seems small, I know, at a time like this, but we've the ball at the Jamesons in a month's time, and I've nothing at all. The dresses are tight at the wrist, this year, with buttons for miles from there to here and my spring dresses are... Oh James," she slipped in beside him and the piano stool. His fingers played lightly on the keys, nothing recognizable, just wandering. "Is it dreadful of me? With all your doings and preoccupations, to ask you now?"

He kissed her cheek and stopped playing to light a cigar.

"To think I'll be so out of style. I'd be a laughing stock as your wife...I wouldn't care much if it were only my reputation. But to think of people saying such things behind your..."

"*Mais oui, mon amour*, make your plans, make them. We will go in proper fashion," he assured her, blowing out smoke. "Soon, as always, *ma petite*," he offered with a kiss and a smile. But a twinge of apprehension tightened his stomach and his heart beat faster. He felt his chest tighten. Soon? He cringed-there was only one way he could make "soon" happen.

She caught her breath. "Really? Really James? I love you, my darling." She wrapped her arms around him, rested her cheek on his shoulder and watched him play. "Paris is so splendid," she said with a soft sweetness. "It will be like always. The *escargot* and fresh *baguettes a Le Grand Vefour*. The *pâtisseries!* And a bottle of wine on the River Seine. We'll take in an opera and visit Versailles," she said rapidly with a twirl of her hair.

"And of course, shop," the Colonel smiled, and nodded, and continued to stroke the keys. She had no idea still of their financial ruin. He realized she would never be able to handle the truth. Why should she? He was born rich, he knew of no other way to live and neither did she.

"Of course, shop," she giggled, leaning in for another kiss.

"New York and then Paris," he said, greeting her lips with his.

The tall case chimed across the great room, interrupting their fairytale. Little Thomas broke through the doors to embrace the belly of the booming clock as it sang the dinner hour. Professor Oakley joined the family wearing his best frock, greeted by an anxious Colonel. The ink was still wet on the expensive paper that declared the talents of the blind slave. Without delay, he handed the radiant Colonel the testimonial before the first course was served, although the Colonel did not know his victory was only for a fortnight.

XIII.

"Genius?" Dr. Frederick Palanski scoffed above the thumping of Thomas's feet against the examining room wall. Palanski's Atlanta office was plain with drab gray walls, miscellaneous medical contraptions, and a large desk covered with loose papers. Two large windows filled the room with sunlight. Atlanta was even hotter than Columbus.

The Colonel fanned and squinted through the sun's rays. "We've already had one highly respected professional provide a testimonial praising his abilities," the Colonel nodded at the letter from Professor Oakley on the nearby table.

Professor Palanski glanced with disdain at the boy, then lifted Professor Oakley's testimonial from the pinewood table. Holding the paper close to his eyes, he read the contents aloud: "Upon hearing the first ten bars of Mendelssohn's Kinderstucke 72, Tom climbed onto the stool with me and began to play the piece faultlessly. I began to further test his abilities." He let the paper fall to the heart-pine floor, where it landed near his boots.

Dr. Palanski was a tall man, fifty years old, wrinkled face spattered with dark brown spots. He was an accomplished musician, a doctor who had forayed into the study of psychology. If he legitimized Thomas, it would be a major coup for the Colonel. But Dr. Palanski's demeanor was brisk, off-putting.

"Did this Oakley fellow test him with his eyes closed?" he asked in a harsh tone, his long fingers pressed against the bridge of his big nose while an assistant picked up the testimonial and handed it back to the Colonel. "It's utterly preposterous. If Professor Oakley were standing here before me, I'd tell him so." He gestured toward Thomas. "I can run tests on this creature..." Gesturing again, one of his assistants scooted Thomas far enough away from the wall so that he kicked without making contact. "But there's nothing here but nature's freakish aberrations."

"But you heard him play last night," the Colonel offered. Thomas had performed on a square piano for a half dozen musical scholars at the estate of a prominent Atlantan, pieces from Brahms, Bach, Mozart, and his own creations. Dr. Palanski was there, frown and all, listening the entire time with skepticism. "I assure you Oakley's examinations were thorough."

"Based on what empirical evidence?" Dr. Palanski snapped. "For all I know, the words written on that paper are pure fiction."

The Colonel's neck turned red and it spread up to his cheeks, as he stared angrily at the doctor. "For that to be the case, Dr. Palanski, Professor Oakley and I would be liars. I came here to try and share with you something quite extraordinary. I will not be accused of lying, much less colluding with the Professor in a more complicated lie."

Standing, the Colonel straightened to his full height and left his cane against the wall. He posed an intimidating figure to most men, but Dr. Palanski was bloated with self-importance, unmoved and unimpressed by his menacing demeanor.

"I've agreed to observe the little nigger, to state the facts as I see them. I need empirical proof that last night wasn't some elaborate mirage."

Dr. Palanski led the seething Colonel into a room abuzz with the ticks and clangs of medical machinery. Thomas followed behind. There were tables filled with instruments, porcelain bowls and glass beakers, tubes and metal probes.

Palanski's team was squeezed in the room, a four-man team from Harvard College. Accompanying them was a Dr. Jefferies–an unpretentious young man with blond hair and honest brown eyes.

Amidst swift nods of introduction, the Colonel shifted uneasily. He watched the interns set up their complicated contraptions while Thomas, on his knees, played with an empty coal pail near the fireplace. Dr. Palanski pulled at his beard and stared down at Thomas as he would a virus through a microscope. He kneeled for a closer look, pulled a magnifying glass from the pocket of his lab coat and pressed close to the slave's skull, examining the boy with the same focused acuity he would a lab rat.

"There's mental defectiveness for certain," Dr. Palanski explained. "A nervous system dysfunction."

"He's a blind child with evident abilities, that's why I'm here, Dr. Palanski."

"He's hardly human," Dr. Palanski snapped. "There's obvious idiocy in the Africanus, as evidenced by the Negroid's pressed cranium and diminutive skull capacity. Do you see his behavior, the twittling about?

"Of course I see it. He lives in the same house..."

"He is wild, born of lesser stock, and practically a monkey," Dr. Palanski evinced, pointing at the blind boy banging the pail on his head.

"But again, doctor, you heard him play. What of his musicality? His potential..."

"Potential?" Dr. Palanski said. He slammed the one thin file he'd compiled on Thomas onto his desk, turned to the Colonel and glared. "It is clear. It is evident to anyone with eyes to see, this nigger will never produce music with any sustained proficiency."

"Or maybe he will," came a timid reply.

"Excuse me?" Dr. Palanski said, turning his hard gaze on the young Dr. Jefferies, now. A tense pause passed between the two scholars as the young doctor summoned his confidence, stood up straight, and set his jaw, refusing to be intimidated.

"I said, maybe he will," Dr. Jefferies reiterated, slipping a glance at the Colonel. "He demonstrates retardation, marked by streaks of what could be dubbed brilliance," he said, as he squatted next to Thomas, held his shoulders firm but gently.

As if a brake lever had been pulled on a locomotive, the noisy room fell silent. The Colonel turned toward the young doctor, raised his eyebrows. "Continue, please."

"Jefferies, this is lunacy." Dr. Palanski ranted.

"Go on, Doctor." Lifting his cane, the Colonel pointed it at Jefferies. "I very much want to hear what you have to say."

"He exhibits streaks of brilliance."

"Definitely not intellectual brilliance," Dr. Palanski interjected in a now measured tone of rebuke. The Colonel's glance travelled from the older doctor to the younger assistant, remembering he had noticed their divergent point of views regarding Thomas in their behavior the night before.

During dinner, Dr. Jefferies had been cordial, but the Colonel could tell from the slight frown on the young doctor's face that he found the whole idea of being in the South, with its swarming insects and penchant for slaves, distasteful. But, Dr. Jefferies clearly had an open mind about the slave boy: he had leaned against the front of the grand piano last night and, rapt with admiration, watched Thomas play.

On the other hand, Dr. Palanski had affected a hardened, stony face. He stood detached, arms crossed, refused to acknowledge a scintilla of remarkability in the boy. Instead, he walked in close to examine the slave's hands and searched beneath the stool while Thomas played. He circled round and round, inspecting the grand instrument from every angle, clearly looking for strings pulled, smoke and mirrors played, considering the entire musical display a deceitful fraud, and a sham.

"I do consider the boy's abilities prodigious," Dr. Jefferies said quietly. With his hand under Thomas's arm, he prompted him up off the floor. "I fully agree with Professor Oakley's testimonial. The boy has genius."

"You're wrong," Dr. Palanski snarled. He stomped his boot. He owned Colored slaves, maids, footmen, cooks, and superstitious nurses with broken, guttural speech; offensive creatures he'd always felt repulsed by. He was turned off by their smell, their dancing and ooga-booga chants and he would never truly ever see them as fully human, much less brilliant or talented at a white man's craft. "The fact is, he is a nigger slave. Negroid stock. The music, if it is authentic, is an accident of behavioral neurology, due to damage in his brain. It won't sustain."

"Do you agree that it can't be sustained," the Colonel asked Dr. Jefferies with a disappointed lilt in his voice.

Dr. Jefferies hesitated and he lowered his gaze. "I can't say for certain that it will last."

Dr. Palanski exhaled a sigh of triumph. "Finally, a sensible conclusion."

"Are you certain?" The Colonel stared at the older doctor. "He's played countless times since I first wrote to you, including last night."

"Don't be deceived by the erratic temporal exhibitions." Dr. Palanski scanned the room to make sure he had everyone's attention. "I'm sure we can all agree on this, at least. After all, this is a blind nigger we're talking about, is it not?"

No agreement came from Dr. Jefferies. He had led Thomas to one of the couches and had given him a tambourine with ribbons with which to play. Now, he sat beside him.

"*Capici Italiano?*" he murmured, kneeling to get closer. "*Hai capito?*"

"What in the world? Dr. Jefferies. He can barely speak English," Dr. Palanski said.

Thomas frowned. He lifted his hands and hit the tambourine against the arm of the couch. He frowned whenever Palanski spoke, covered both his ears, and shook his head. He didn't like Dr. Palanski's voice; it was an ugly yellow-red with dark mean-spirited numbers.

"Tom, do you understand Italian?"

Thomas smiled as Dr. Jefferies spoke.

The younger doctor's voice was warm to Thomas, a grayish-blue, and his numbers were kind and caring. So Thomas stopped twisting the ribbons on the tambourine and smiled.

"Do you, Tom?"

"This is absurd," said Dr. Palanski's with disdain.

But Thomas's odd guttural voice repeated the words, "Tom, do you understand Italian?" *Capisci Italiano, hai capito?*" His voice was low, his tone pure. "Tom speaks Italian," Thomas said. "Tom understands, Dr. Jefferies," he continued.

The Colonel felt a rush of excitement. Dr. Palanski was stone faced, but Dr. Jefferies was animated.

"Yes, *si certo, si certo!*" A faint excited murmur escaped from Dr. Jefferies. "*Grazie per la riposta, Tom. Grazie,*" he said, before he looked up at the Colonel.

"How did you know?"

"I suspected his memory wasn't for music alone," Dr. Jefferies said, "but spoken words as well, as evidenced by his uncanny repetitive auditory skills. In any language he's ever heard, he is probably fluent. It is a trait most prodigies—"

"Stop it," Dr. Palanski cried with a clap of his hands. "This is deception at its highest form. Don't you listen to a word of this, Colonel," he spat, saliva shot from his mouth. "These slaves are quite skilled in their ruses of trickery as a race, and the nigger boy is cut from that cloth, it's clear as can be."

"No," Dr. Jefferies stood up and shook his head, facing off with his old mentor. "It is not a ruse."

"Listen to me, Colonel. You will never be able to harness this so called music into any productive form. The boy is unequivocally a freak of nature. For your own reputation, Colonel, do not pursue this any further." Dr. Palanski handed the Colonel his hat and opened the door into the hallway, the overcast sky visible through uncovered windows. "I respect your military achievements, Colonel, I do. As well as your accomplishments as a newspaperman and lawyer, but you are being sorely misled by youthful optimism. I'm sure Professor Oakley wanted to please you…"

"Come, Tom," the Colonel interrupted.

Thomas heard the shuffle and scuffle of feet and coats and went to the Colonel, held tight to his arm. Dr. Palanski continued as he escorted them out, "I warn you, Colonel, implore you to end this foolishness with the slave." The Colonel lifted Thomas into his arms and held him close.

"All of this could reverse at any time," Dr. Palanski stressed, "there's nothing to count on, and your reputation is at stake. Now, Colonel I bid you good day." With a tilt of his head and nod, he shut the outer door to his office.

Out on the street, with Thomas in his arms beaming up at his face, the Colonel was still somewhat bewildered by the events in Dr. Palanski's office. He continued to walk when a breathless Dr. Jefferies called him from behind.

"Colonel Bethune." He closed the distance and took hold of his arm.

"Colonel, don't go yet, please," the young doctor said, out of breath. "I have something I think may help you understand your slave a bit better."

Eyebrows lifted, the Colonel waited for him to continue. Dr. Jefferies hesitated. "If you'll give me the chance. I think it will help clear some things."

"Please, by all means," the Colonel said. He shifted Thomas to his other arm and leaned on his cane.

Dr. Jefferies cleared his throat. "There was pioneering research done by a Dr. Benjamin Rush, at the turn of this century, on the powers of human memory. Dr. Rush wrote of an African slave, Thomas Fuller, whose mental abilities were like a human calculator. If you told Fuller your age, he could calculate how many seconds you'd been on the planet or the diameter of the earth's orbit— all within a matter of seconds–without use of a pen. He would calculate for leap years, and proved himself an extraordinary Africanus intelligence, not before believed possible."

"Hmm. Curious, but still one case, correct?"

"Yes, but..."

"But not retarded and blind as Tom..."

"No, but it proves that contrary to what my esteemed superior Dr. Palanski claims, Africanus, at least in this one case, is capable of extraordinary mental abilities. In addition to their known musical tendencies" Dr. Jefferies said. "The full spectrum of extraordinary Africanus abilities has yet to be explored."

"Indeed." The Colonel's attention was fixed on the voice of Dr. Jefferies. "Was this Thomas Fuller musical, like Tom?"

"Well, no. Not that we know of," Jefferies said. "But like your slave here, he exhibited areas of genius, yet if you asked him the simplest of questions, he'd barely be able to communicate the answer. In all other facets, he was retarded."

"So based on your assessments," he shifted Thomas again. "Tom is like this Fuller: mentally defective?"

"Yes," Dr. Jefferies nodded.

"But his music, if he can retain it, does evince genius?"

"Yes," Dr. Jefferies replied.

Thomas wrapped his arms around the Colonel's neck, feet around his waist. "So let me understand this. You're telling me Tom is both retarded *and* a genius?" the Colonel lifted his brows.

Dr. Jefferies hesitated, his face became flush, "Well, yes, sir. He is both."

A frown on his face, the Colonel thanked Dr. Jefferies. For good measure he asked the young doctor to prepare a testimonial reporting all that he had seen of Thomas. Dr. Jefferies agreed. The Colonel gave him his address and Dr. Jefferies promised his letter would arrive promptly. The Colonel didn't welcome the confusing news Jefferies shared regarding Thomas as he hailed a taxi to transport him to the train station and the locomotive that would return him to Columbus. "Both." A small fortune spent on an inconclusive assessment. He shook his head and gazed up at the sky that was as hazy as the conclusions about the blind boy.

XIV.

The following evening at *Solitude*, the Colonel withdrew to the terrace, gazed out at the garden, and lit a cigar. He enjoyed the longer days of sunlight that came with spring. Through the trees, winged statues stood guard over the sprawling gardens.

"A blind, retarded, genius," the Colonel mumbled. He drew a long puff on his cigar and blew out a long stream of smoke. He gazed up at the sky where the first star and moon were already out, then watched as the sun sank toward the horizon, it's reddish brown hue taking over before yielding to the moon and the night.

Medical science had no explanation for his slave-boy, Tom.

The Colonel tapped ashes over the terrace railing, watched them fall to the ground. "He is a genius and he's retarded," he repeated. "Hmph." He shut his eyes. It was unfortunate that his money difficulties had become so darkly disturbing that he spent most of his time thinking about them, mulling over the possibility of taking in boarders, or renting pieces of his properties to other farmers, to ease his financial burden. The trips to the pawnshop had not ceased.

"It's quite a mess, James," the Colonel whispered to himself.

His wife, he knew, would tolerate no reduction in their standard of living. Perhaps sensing the threat, she had cooed to him, just the night before, "You give me such exquisite pleasures, *cher*. And I couldn't live without them, you know."

He listened to the sounds of the evening: the whistles, hoots, and caws all around him; he thought about his older sibling, his brother Pierre and sister-in-law Germaine. The two lived in New Orleans near the corner of St. Louis and Chartres streets and owned banjo players who were wonderful adornments at their dinners and balls. Likewise, it was all the rage in Georgian society for the best soirees and most fashionable tea parties to hire the talented Bush slaves, who played church hymns on their fiddles and tooted folk songs on harmonicas. His slave would put them all to shame, if only his genius sustained. The Colonel sighed.

He finished his cigar and flicked the remaining ashes to the soil below. In a mood to walk, the Colonel descended the terrace stairs into the gentle wind from the lake beyond the woods, and for a while strolled the labyrinth of narrow pathways bordered by hedges that circled and twisted around the main property. As he headed toward the back end of the carriage house, he heard a strange squawking. Drawing near, he saw beneath the gaslight, Thomas, jumping about making croaking-like sounds in response to the frogs singing in the nearby trees. The Colonel stood and watched with his mouth twisted, as Thomas flapped his arms and hopped about.

With each stumbling revolution the Colonel's heart sank. What was he thinking? He chastised himself. How would the twirling squawking slave before him behave if hired out–by the Archers who were devoted to the fine arts, or the Randolph's who obsessed over the world's finest wines–for the winter season? He shuddered and imagined the boy barking on all fours across the parquet floor of some grand ballroom packed with society waiting with expectation for a grand rendering of a Bach concerto.

"Tom," the Colonel said. He moved from the shadows and walked closer to Thomas, who pretended not to hear him and kept twirling and squawking. The Colonel squeezed the top of his cane. The silly sweet-hearted boy was retarded. It would be foolish to think anything could be done with Thomas. Dr. Palanski was right, it was not worth risking his own good reputation—and yet he knew the child was talented and found the music he played transporting beyond measure.

"Tom, come along," the Colonel said. He lifted him onto his shoulder. Together they walked around the back of the carriage house, up the walkway past gardenias in bloom and jacaranda trees in blossom. The Colonel carried him through the front doors of the Big House, Thomas squirming so much he was dangling precariously on the Colonel's arm.

"Ensa, ring for Charity."

Ensa pulled on the long tope against the wall and Charity came rushing through the servants' door. "Yes, massuh?"

"I found Tom outside, alone, playing near the carriage house."

"He always runnin' off, massuh. That's what Thomas do."

"Now, what if he got hurt?" the Colonel glanced between them.

Charity cast her eyes down and twisted the towel in her hand. She glanced at her boy, regret on her face.

"From now on, I want you and all the staff, including the maids and footmen, to make sure Tom is never left unattended. He is to have someone with him at all times." He let Thomas go, and he ran to his mother. She grabbed his face, kissed his cheeks, and lifted him into her chest.

"Do you understand? Never alone."

"Yessah, massuh," Charity and Ensa answered in unison. "Won' leave 'im untended," Charity added.

"And I don't want him walking around without shoes," he continued acknowledging Charity's nod. "We've given you plenty of Caleb's old shoes. Make sure he keeps them on his feet. If he takes them off, put them back on. We need to protect him and we need some clothes made for him. Tomorrow I'll see about getting an upright piano in your room to keep him safely occupied. That'll be all." The Colonel saw to it that Thomas was protected, much like a prized filly.

Climbing the stairs to his bedchambers, the Colonel knew he needed more information before he could make a decision about Thomas's future.

A few evenings later, the crack of pool balls and clink of Scotch glasses mingled with hardy laughter and surrounded the Colonel like the merrymaking at a bazaar. It was welcome time away from work and worries, a time of smoke and heavy drink. Within the dark mahogany walls of the gentlemen's club, the Colonel kneeled to assess his options on the billiard table while his opponent, Jacob Bush, puffed on his pipe. Relaxation aside, it had been the Colonel's hope upon departing *Solitude* that the wealthy merchant would be at the club, as he owned two of the best fiddlers in town. The Colonel was eager to pick his brain about their profitability whenever the opportunity arose. Now, as he hovered over the table, was as good a time as any.

"Those Colored fiddlers of yours, they performed at the Augustine's dance the other evening?" the Colonel asked casually; he squinted his eyes trying to get the best angle.

"Yes, indeed," Jacob smiled. A preening fellow with a tear-shaped face and dark curly hair, his corset cinched at the waist. His checkered burgundy pants matched his burgundy scarf and top hat. "Quite entertaining, those two," he continued, "created quite the excitement among the guests."

"That's what I hear." The Colonel took a shot and missed.

A notorious braggart with a few drinks already in him, the Colonel knew it wouldn't take much to get the prideful merchant to tell him everything he needed to know about his musical slaves. "So, you rent the boys out quite a bit?" the Colonel asked, leaning on his billiard stick.

"Quite a bit is an understatement." Jacob put his cigar in his mouth, cued up, and hit his blue ball from one end of the table all the way to the opposite side pocket. "Those two fine niggers are famous throughout Muscogee County for a reason. Mrs. Wallingford–*the* Mrs. Wallingford who famously refused to receive a Duke, no less, for his reputations against tastes–insists my fiddlers are a must have for her spring garden party and has generously paid me double in advance to ensure their attendance."

"*The* Mrs. Wallingford? Double? Quite impressive, indeed. *Mais oui,* the nigger fiddlers are filling your pockets?"

"Bursting my pockets, you mean. Boys bring me almost half as much profit as the shipping business some seasons," he boasted and sank the solid red four into the right corner.

"Almost half?"

The Colonel lifted his brows, a flicker of intense curiosity on his face. "You're the biggest shipper this side of the Mississippi, Jacob."

"I'm telling you James, almost half," he chomped down on his cigar. "Can't keep up with the amount of requests those boys bring in. It's a pretty good deal all the way around. I get rich, in turn, boys get some extra money and I give them passes and let them play the nigger dances. When they aren't playing, I let them visit their gals on other plantations when it doesn't conflict."

The Colonel leaned against his stick thoughtfully. Jacob was one of the wealthiest men in Georgia, famous for good living. Society folks in the know believed he took his father's business to great heights through cunning and sheer ruthlessness, yet here he was declaring that a large portion of his wealth came from two fiddling slaves.

Almost half? The Colonel surveyed the billiards table, intoxicated by the possibilities with Thomas. His associate's words stirred a pot of ideas in the Colonel's mind. The blind boy Thomas, had a talent none of the Colored fiddlers had, a talent for classical fare that was considered more valuable in aristocratic circles.

Jacob's ball bounced out the lip of the middle pocket and it was the Colonel's turn to shoot. He aimed his stick but couldn't block out raised voices at a nearby table behind him. The men were discussing the swirl of rumors taking over Columbus about the banks and he completely missed his ball. "The banks are coming down on planters, demanding payment on debts." The Colonel used his pool stick as a cane and limped closer to the party chattering in the lounge. "Did you hear about Joseph Lange?" a bare murmur in the rowdy room.

"What about Lange?" another voice muttered.

"Got himself in a bit of trouble...."

"Old man hung himself," the Colonel overheard.

It was his turn again. The Colonel's ball was impossibly lodged between two striped balls. His cue ball hit the cluster and sent the balls bouncing off walls all over the table.

Unable to resist, the Colonel joined the conversation. "Is it true?" the Colonel asked, he lifted his stick and rested it against his shoulder. He made eye contact with the refined voice behind him, young Brandon Mingott, a sturdy man with intense brown eyes whose father was a rich tobacco planter.

"Quite true. According to his wife, Margie, they came back from a stay up north to a notice of default and sale on the front door. It was more than Lange could take."

A frown settled across the Colonel's face. How horrible for poor old Lange. It was not lost on the Colonel that one day he could very well mount the stairs at *Solitude* and find a note on his own front door.

On the drive home down Main Street that night, the Colonel mused about Thomas. Maybe in time, he'd grow out of his odd ways. He rested his head back, inhaled the old cigar and fried-fish smells trapped in the fabrics of the carriage. He could not bet all his cards on young Oakley's enthusiasm or on Dr. Jefferies testimonial. There were more Dr. Palanskis to consider than Oakleys and Thomas was too wild, too unpredictable to stake his reputation on. His only hope, the Colonel believed, was time. Perhaps with time, he could invest in the slave boy's talent, but not now.

Against the wail of a steamer's horn, he dismissed all thoughts of Thomas for good and breathed a sigh of relief. The harvest was proving fruitful this season;

he'd rescued all his wife's heirlooms from the pawnshop earlier in the week. Now he was onto making arrangements for the family's trip to Paris. After all, there were shows to see and new fashions to acquire. Life would return to normal, and Thomas would have a piano in his room—to keep him happy and perfect his skills.

XV.

1905

Warrenton, Virginia

He hadn't expected Matthew Shaw to return, it seemed the young attorney had already judged him guilty. The Colonel was finishing his breakfast when Matthew entered the makeshift cell, wet from a sudden rainstorm. John was walking right behind him. The Colonel simply nodded when he spoke to say good morning, while John removed his drenched coat and prepared the Bethune annals.

"Last time," Matthew was saying.

"Last time?" Lost in his thoughts, the Colonel had missed some of the conversation.

"You said you had decided not to pursue anything with Tom, one way or the other, after meeting with the three different experts."

"Ah, yes."

The Colonel took two small bites of toast, crumbs falling on the saucer. He wiped his lips on the napkin and watched the fire turn different colors in the hearth.

"Would you please, continue?" Matthew urged. "So initially, you'd given up on Thomas?"

The Colonel seemed irritated by the question, shifted in his rocker and the wood squeaked.

"You understand young man, status and one's reputation are of the utmost importance, so I did not push for Tom to perform publicly, at first with his nature being such as it was."

He squeezed his cane and rocked in his chair.

"I'd not given up as you say. I could not, given my stature, risk being made a fool of by Tom. I knew his talent." The Colonel hit his cane against the floor. "But I could not tame it."

Matthew moved quickly to smooth over his *faux pas,* noting he'd upset the Colonel. "I misspoke, Colonel Bethune."

"A rather unfortunate problem for an attorney, isn't it?"

Matthew attempted to mask his discomfort. "I know you believed in his talent, because at some point he became very famous."

"For too many reasons to share in one sitting, Tom would have never become famous without my management. But I can't take credit for the initial push. It was the very people I feared for my reputation who seemed to think I was lacking for not acting on what I'd initially contemplated."

He leaned over and picked up a picture on a small table. "This is Tom, when he was about nine or ten years old, after his first concert. But his first concert almost never happened, because of me."

"How is that?"

He closed his eyes. "He was as unpredictable as the wind. For that, I could not, would not risk myself. Not even for the riches that I hoped could possibly result from investing in him, he was still too erratic, banging pans, knocking his head against walls." He opened his eyes and looked at Matthew. "I almost stumbled where most capable people fall, never achieving life's greatest moments, that hole where dreams in life are never reached," the Colonel sighed. "You see young Shaw, I almost did nothing..."

PART TWO

I.

1859

Columbus, Georgia

Nine large jack-o'-lanterns decorated the front of the Bethune mansion for Halloween, evenly spaced between thick white columns. Small candle flames shone through the pumpkins' jagged eyes and crooked mouths. The sound of raucous laughter and the clinks of crystal goblets spilled outside and from the garden, ruby-throated hummingbirds sang their high-pitched *chitit*.

In the *grand parlor* Frances giggled like a schoolgirl, bobbing apples eluded her in a large oak barrel. She was dressed as a princess in flowing layers of lavender velvet with her hair swept up into a bun and a glistening crown perched on top. Her adult guests, dressed as Renaissance courtiers, witches and warlocks, the children as jesters and demons, laughed at her predicament. With a deep breath, she plunged her face back into the water, snapped at apples bobbing against her nose. She snagged one in her teeth and pulled back her head to a rousing applause. The forbidden red fruit dripping from her mouth, she curtsied and looked around for her husband.

Across the room, near the gilt card table where a game of Faro was underway, the Colonel hid his nerves under a large smile. Frances walked over to his side; he tipped his head and took a bite of the apple when she offered it to him. His smile remained, yet he was on edge; he was almost always on edge these days. No expense had been spared on decorations or provisions. The reality of the cost of their life was spinning out of control, but friends in high places had strategically kept the banks at bay for many years—until recently. All his financial troubles had suddenly come to the fore.

Just a few weeks ago, he'd received a disturbing visit at the *Columbus Enquirer* from an old family banker friend. It was a chilly afternoon and he'd just finished going over the details for the next day's edition when Gerald Helm strode into the newsroom past several rows of reporters. A strapping, confident man in his late sixties with striking silver hair and a crisp charcoal frock beneath his overcoat; the look on his face was grim. The Colonel went flush upon seeing him; it was the visit he'd been dreading for years: the Senior Vice President of Georgia Savings Bank and Trust Company. He weaved his way through the crowded office, right up to the Colonel.

Gerald had asked to speak with him privately and the Colonel walked with him to his private office where he drew the blinds. The sprawling room was cluttered with large books and piles of newspapers and there was the smell of burning wood. Gerald took a seat in a small leather chair in front of the Colonel's large messy desk. The Colonel placed logs on the fire in the hearth and braced for the worst. He knew from the grim set of Gerald's jaw it did not please him to conduct a meeting about the outstanding debts the Colonel had with the bank.

"You know I admire you a great deal, James," he said, hands folded, legs crossed. "But there's nothing more I can do in this matter. The bank is calling in your loans."

The Colonel shuddered and his head began to pound. That news coming from Gerald was the worst. He was practically a second father to him, had been James Bethune Sr.'s best friend and personal banker for thirty years. The Colonel knew he'd been protecting him all this time.

"Gerald," said the Colonel, drawing out the "a" in the way he had since he was a child, in the hopes of easing the mood. "Come on *Geraaaald!*"

"Did I not warn you years ago about your extravagances James?" Gerald said, cutting him off. His tone was firm. He knew about the imported settees, his stable of Swedish Warmblood mounts, costly parties, the mulatto slave, and his bastard quadroon children back in Virginia. "Even the wealthiest of men have to learn restraint," he reprimanded.

The Colonel's shoulders sagged; his confidence ebbed like the ocean's tide, but he grasped at hope. "I'm certain there will be a great harvest this season. And when the cotton prices rise, all will be well again, and I will settle with the bank."

Gerald winced. "When the cotton prices rise?"

The Colonel regretted the words as soon as they slipped from his lips.

"Cotton prices haven't risen in years, James," he snapped. "It's no longer an issue of having a great harvest. A lot of good men are suffering from debt on last year's crops and the year before that. I have been given the responsibility, from my superiors, to enforce collections."

"Your superiors, Gerald?" the Colonel asked, his eyes flashed; his voice carried a haughty lilt as he raised his regal cleft chin. He slid a pile of books to the side and sat on his desk. "My father is the reason Cobalt is president of that bank. Has he forgotten that?"

The base of Gerald's neck turned a dark crimson; it was obvious he found the entire episode disagreeable. "He has not forgotten, but he, as well as the bank, is getting pressure from Washington."

"Then perhaps you could simply pressure someone else, Gerald," the Colonel protested.

"James, I pushed for a long term loan out of loyalty to your father. If you do not have the capital to pay your debt, perhaps you should consider liquidating to raise…"

"Liquidating? My father would roll over in his grave if I sold one piece." The vision of Frances crept its way into his pain, he saw her lovely green eyes flash, and her jaws tighten into cold punishing silence before she packed up the estate and sought refuge with her wealthy father.

"There's no shame in making your assets work for you while you are still able."

The Colonel shook his head. "I won't sell one piece of land. That's not an option."

"You could fetch a good price for the Negro piano player," he offered.

"Tom?"

"Is he a good boy?"

"Is he? Gerald! Pour l'amour de Dieu."

"Has he been baptized?" Gerald continued, ignoring him. "Does he attend church?"

The Colonel flinched. "My entire life is at stake and your solution to saving it is my idiot slave? Selling him away from his family?"

His tone carried more edge than he intended. His brain was still stuck on "liquidation." At that moment the enormity of the debts hung before him like two trees forming gallows. The Colonel rubbed his hand across his forehead.

"Sixty-thousand dollars, James," Gerald said with a sigh.

Both men were silent. A sense of dread gripped the Colonel. Hand shaking, he walked around to the front of his desk and slid open the bottom drawer, retrieved a bottle of bourbon. The thick bottle made a small clunk when he set it on top of some papers.

"The bank is placing liens against all of your plantation properties," Gerald said; he set legal papers down on the desk. "Rental dwellings, slaves, livestock, transportation, crops, this newspaper and your law practice. Public auction will begin at the end of the term."

The Colonel nodded.

"The best I can do is give you six, maybe seven more months, nine tops, hopefully by then you'll have your affairs in order." He paused and switched subjects. "I'm told your Negro played here for the news staff last week. I'd love an invite to hear him next time," he said, pulling the belt of his heavy coat tight before exiting the office.

Now, in the crowded breezy parlor, the Colonel shook hands and greeted visitors with a plastered smile that did not reach his eyes. He was on edge about Thomas. Ten years old and a considerable burden, Thomas had disappeared just as guests were arriving for the party. He was expected to perform this evening—everyone in town was looking forward to the debut of the odd little blind boy—but he'd vanished and left a trail of knocked-over chairs and pans and their lids behind. The children were searching for him as Frances distracted guests with party games.

Servants passed out candy to the children and carried platters of sausages and fine cheese. There were a dozen Halloween fruitcakes on a table beneath the mantle each with five objects hidden inside that were meant to foretell the future: a ring meant marriage; a thimble meant forever an old maid; a coin meant wealth; a key would bring a journey; and a button, love.

In front of the well-spiked gentlemen's punch stood Vernon Johnson, his wife Angela, and their two sons. Vernon called over to the Colonel, who recognized his great height and voice from beneath the black stocking mask that covered his face. Two red horns stuck out from the top of his head. "When will blind Tom play, Colonel?" Vernon asked.

"Soon, soon," the Colonel smiled, "we must keep up the mystery."

The men shared a big laugh, but it was all a big stalling tactic. The Colonel stood next to Frances and squeezed her hand. He kept a stiff smile over gritted teeth, dreading the impending embarrassment. He excused himself from Frances, nodded at masked couples on his way out of the parlor, merriment and chatter at his back. Where was Thomas? He joined the children, looking in every crook and cranny throughout the house, as the mansion continued to fill with costumed guests. Sarah searched in the library and had already scoured the bushes where he liked to hide. John had climbed the many stairs, peeked under the beds in every chamber. The Colonel looked beneath the desk in his den then behind the bundled curtains and back in the hallway again.

"Dozens of Georgia's finest families are downstairs expecting first-class entertainment and Tom is nowhere to be found," the Colonel complained to the children.

Invitations had been sent and gossip had been stirring about the wondrous abilities of the blind slave who would perform on the piano, Halloween night. In the years since Thomas had first played Mozart, the slave's reputation had grown throughout Georgia; everyone in the south's high society wanted to witness Thomas with his or her own eyes.

The first to make the request for a private viewing had been the balding General Butler, the wealthy rice and cotton plantation owner from Savannah.

"Might I see this mysterious blind slave who deems himself worthy of Mozart?" he'd asked during a round of lawn tennis when Thomas was four, and the Colonel had acquiesced, but not before explaining the slave was hopelessly retarded, hopelessly strange. General Butler had come for dinner on a Saturday. After being thoroughly delighted for a full evening during the Bethune night of music, he went on to share tales of the classical retarded slave with the other old Georgian families who then brimmed with envy and shamelessly vied for private performances.

"Colonel, about your slave," the requests came at the market.

"Colonel, I hear from the Chief Justice you have a retarded musical slave?" came Governor Brown's greeting during the spring ball last year. The wives, jealous upon hearing of one invitation granted and not another to see the boy, took it out on Frances. The women besieged her with requests across the table at teas, across laps at christenings, and in the cloakroom at parties.

So, after years of feints and parries, Frances and the Colonel had decided to display Thomas to all their friends and neighbors at their annual Bethune

Halloween party. This evening was supposed to be all about the blind slave pianist, only Thomas was nowhere to be found.

Now, it had been a full hour of searching.

"You were to keep your eyes on him. How is it possible the lot of you lost Tom?" the Colonel barked at his children with a stern flourish of his hand, "Find him! Find him now!"

The Colonel didn't see the scowl that had formed on twelve-year-old Caleb's face; he was blocked behind Mary with his bare legs and feathered Indian headdress. It was Caleb, who was hot tempered and pouted often; the foppish one who inspected his custom fit tailcoats with a critical eye, the one who wagered large sums on thoroughbreds, and secretly peeled dollar bills from his father's money clip. In many ways, he was as wild as Thomas.

Caleb simmered beneath the soft gaslights. Biting down hard on the fleshy tissue of his lip, he couldn't help whispering under his breath, "Yessuh, massuh, we's gone finds Tom." And he waited for his father to walk away.

"Are we Tom's mammy?" Caleb spat. He dragged against the wall while his siblings searched. He watched his older brother closely, lids narrowed.

"Caleb," John said slowly. "Tame your mouth. We just need to find Tom." John, now sixteen, could see his little brother was drunk. Caleb always had a flask with him—hidden inside his suit jacket, in pockets he had Charity sew—or hidden in bookshelves and between the mattresses. At the moment, the whiskey obviously clouded his thoughts.

"Don't you see how he treats that nigger slave?" Caleb persisted.

"Shut up, Caleb."

A pulse began moving in John's jaw, but Caleb ignored the darkness forming in his older brother's pupils and continued to talk recklessly.

"Am I the only one with eyes?" Caleb ranted. "He treats that nigger like he's one of us. He displays him before the best families and every acquaintance of import he has. It would be nice, every once in awhile, if he might dote on us as much as he fawns over that blind monkey. Or at least pretend to afford us some small acknowledgment that he remembers we exist."

"Caleb," Sarah tried to interrupt, to calm things down, but Caleb continued with his outburst.

"Our father, favoring a slave," he pointed in the direction his father had walked in. "Placing us beneath the nigger purchased to draw our water and fetch our food! Placing himself beneath the paw of his own servant!"

John lunged at his little brother, shoved him up against the wall, grabbing him by his coat. "Enough, Caleb," he said between gritted teeth. "Or I will be forced to quiet you myself."

Caleb stood his ground, propelled by the whiskey.

"Open your eyes, big brother. Can't you see that our white father, the great Colonel Bethune, cares more about his dumb darkie slave than his own children? Everyday it's about that nigger."

"You're talking foolishly, Caleb, please, hush," Sarah said.

John pressed his arm against Caleb's neck, but Caleb was too filled with drink for any pain to register.

"I'd think you would be embarrassed of our father speaking so highly of his black slave," he spat. "He introduces the blind monkey before he makes introductions to us."

"You're foolish little brother. Just foolish!" John said. He let Caleb go and stared at him with a set peculiar expression. A realization began to manifest.

"Envy, like the worm, never runs but to the fairest fruit," he muttered, quoting Francis Beaumont. "Like a cunning bloodhound, it singles out the fattest deer in the flock."

"What do you mean by that?" Caleb asked.

"Ever since that night he played the Requiem, you've been jealous."

"Jealous? Of that dumb, blind nigger?" Caleb's eyes flashed.

"*Oui, mon frère!*" John got in his face. "Jealous of our blind nigger slave who has little more intelligence than a two-year-old. It's quite pathetic, *mon petit frère,*" John said.

Caleb winced.

His older brother turned to walk away, but the truth enraged Caleb. He rushed forward and pushed his older brother in the back. John's body jerked forward, then catching the balance in his legs, he swiveled around; the two squared off, nostrils flared, snorting at each other like angry bulls.

"What's pathetic is the way you and father grovel over that dark monkey," Caleb said, hands raised, ready to wrestle his brother. "You think you can dress him up in a fine suit and have him play Hayden like a white man? Flaunt him before other fine white men, all the while grinning like hyenas, living piteously through him. I won't bow or cast my pearls before nigger swine, like you and father."

"Caleb, why do you speak of Tom this way?" Sarah interrupted.

Before another word was spoken, John charged forward and wrestled Caleb to the ground, delivering a punch to his gut.

"Brothers! Stop it. Behave!" Sarah said.

John's hand was balled up for another blow; his entire body shook.

"Caleb I saw Clarence Adam and his sister Jillian downstairs," Sarah said. "She told me she couldn't wait to see Tom play."

Of course all the siblings knew Caleb fancied Jillian, a pretty girl in his class, and Sarah was hoping he'd be embarrassed if the concert didn't occur because they couldn't find Thomas. Was his excitement over Jillian greater than his anger and enough to make him want to find the slave boy quickly?

The siblings waited for his reaction, although Caleb was as unpredictable as Thomas.

It was crowded. Half of Muscogee County was at *Solitude* that Halloween and amid the laughter and clinking of dishes, Caleb searched the mansion with his siblings. Thomas was nowhere to be found. Ninety minutes. How much longer could they delay the boy's debut? If the Colonel could pull the hair from out of his head, he would, he thought in complete frustration. "Tom!" he called down the second floor hallway. "Tom, if you can hear me, I want you to come out right now." He softened his voice to signal he wasn't angry.

He waited a moment and considered whether to have John fetch the flute and begin playing around the mansion for Thomas to hear and then he would come. It was a festive day perhaps guests would not view it with suspicion. "We have very special people here and they are waiting to see you play, Tom," the Colonel said. "If you come out, I have cake for you."

"Tom will play," he heard Thomas's muffled voice from somewhere behind him.

The Colonel sighed, turned around and strode back toward a storage closet at the end of the dark hallway. He opened the door and Thomas emerged from beneath a pile of shipping crates, old boots, and Christmas garlands. "Tom will play for the special people," Thomas said. He was lanky now; his head at the Colonel's chest, long thin arms and legs. "Tom likes cake," he said and hugged the Colonel around the waist.

In the kitchen, Thomas dabbed his mouth with a napkin, halfway through his second piece of chocolate cake. Charity had placed a towel across his lap to protect his suit from crumbs and gave him a kiss when he finished.

"You gone go play da' piana, now, huh? Play good like you promised the massuh?" she whispered in his ear.

"Tom's gonna play the piano," he said aloud. Charity helped him out of the chair with a hug. "Tom's gonna play the piano good for master Colonel like he promised," Thomas repeated.

The Colonel escorted a skipping Thomas out of the kitchen, through the corridors, and stopped just outside of the bustling parlor.

"Tom, we're going to walk through the parlor to the piano, don't skip," he said patiently. "Walk, *d'accord?*"

"Don't skip, walk. Tom understands."

"Yes, walk," the Colonel said with a firm grip on his arm. He grabbed him by the hand and the two weaved through the crowd to the grand piano.

"Very good, Tom," he whispered in the boy's ear. A buzz began when some guests noticed the small slave with the Colonel, looking well turned out in John's beige waistcoat and vest. The Colonel had no idea what selection Thomas would play but simply hoped the music would flow as it did when he was alone with the family. Once at the piano, Thomas let go of his hand, sat down on the stool and to the Colonel's delight immediately stroked the first notes to the song, *Angels Hymns from Psalms 95*. "Unpredictable, indeed," the Colonel smiled. Though he didn't know precisely what selections Thomas would play, he did know that it was the Sabbath and expected there would be no classical selections today.

Upon hearing the music, the fine guests stopped playing cards and carried their apple cider and wine toward the piano. In the middle of a charades game, the children stopped, trotted over and sat on their knees. Once settled, the little ones whispered about the idiot musical slave they'd heard about while playing on their parents' yachts, in between dances at balls, and near the card tables at birthday parties.

"Is that him?"

"Of course, silly."

As if in his own world, Thomas fluttered his fingers over the keys. He charmed the clustered crowd of ghosts and goblins with his emotional rendering of favorite hymns, further thrilling them all when he began to sing. The Colonel leaned against a wall and observed the unpredictable slave, hiding his nerves behind a cigar, as the boy played to "oohs and ahs."

"It's as if the instruments have a spirit of their own when the slave plays," Mademoiselle Lucien gushed behind her black-and-gold mask. "His talents must not be wasted."

"Will he play any of the classics?" A voice questioned.

"Of course not, you heathen," another guest jested. "Why it's the Sabbath!"

"Of course, of course," came a chorus of replies with nervous laughter.

"Why have you been hiding him, Colonel?" another voice exclaimed.

"Oh, if we could take the slave with us to perform at our debutante ball," Mrs. Roosevelt cried in front of him, caressing her fur muff, as the melodic sixteenth notes drifted from the pianoforte.

The Colonel tipped his hat to his wife's distant cousin. He wondered how the round woman would fair squeezing her rotund rear through a dirt hole beneath her Greek Revival mansion to retrieve the slave boy from his hiding place in time for her imagined fine event.

Oh, Thomas was wonderful when he was calm, wrapped up as he was in the soothing resonance of his music—smiling and singing—his belly full of his mother's cake. But the Colonel was tense, because the boy could jump off the stool at any moment and dash off into the woods or trot down to the slave fields and beyond. His antics made him an impractical commodity. Thomas finished a song, stood up from the piano and applauded with the guests, who chuckled and whispered. In a blink, he was back on the stool and playing another hymn.

In some ways, Dr. Palanski was correct: Thomas could not be trained. The Colonel doubted these elite patrons applauding him now would take kindly to the boy's peccadilloes, once fees for his services were required. Nonetheless, the Colonel took in the cluster of masked guests applauding every crescendo, and he smiled. Charity too was taking it all in. She had paused from filling baskets with candy at the table near the mantle, her hand over her heart, as she marveled at the city's best people admiring her child.

When Thomas finished his last song, those guests who were sitting, stood, and those standing stomped their feet in appreciation. Frances stood and clapped her heart out. The Bethune children, John, Mary, Sarah, Caleb, and Rachel took up their instruments and began *"All Hail the Power of Jesus Name"* with Thomas accompanying on the piano. The Colonel beamed and felt a sense of pride.

When it was over, the Colonel was bombarded, twisted and tugged at, crowded and pressed all around by masked faces. Pats on the back came with adulation for his slave and unsolicited advice.

"He's a genius, the retarded nigger. Why don't you put him on stage?"

"Outstanding Colonel, you should book the Colored boy at Columbus Hall."

"It's a shame for him to be hidden away at *Solitude*."

"Why do you hoard him selfishly away from us, Colonel?"

"Indeed, indeed," he responded to this one and that one. "But he has gray moods and temper tantrums. He bangs his head against walls, you see, rocks all about and talks to himself."

"Yes, yes, but he plays remarkably."

"Lovely."

"Other worldly if you ask me."

"It's because he plays all the time," Sarah piped in. "He stays in his room and plays on the piano father bought for him, has done for years now, ten twelve hours a day," she said, hanging on her father's arm.

"But it seems he cannot be trained," said the Colonel soberly.

"He doesn't really play on command," John piped up from beneath his cowboy hat.

"A shame, a shame," came the chorus.

A shame, yes, the Colonel nodded as Thomas began a spontaneous piece and the audience stirred once again. It was a piece the Colonel had never heard.

"What is this one, Colonel," Mrs. Jefferson asked.

"He often makes up his own songs," the Colonel replied.

"You don't, say. How marvelous."

"The angels are singing," Thomas said as his fingers danced on the keyboard, summoning the crowd's attention back toward him. "Tom calls this Virginia Gallup."

Murmurs spread throughout the parlor. The music had a light, moving effect and his guests shifted in their chairs, uncertain how to react. The angels are singing? Thomas often spoke of angels, as if they were part of his real world of experience. It seemed the boy sincerely believed his music came from heavenly messengers and he heard their beautiful choruses at all hours of the day and night. Whenever the angels sang, Thomas would run toward the piano no matter where he was on the estate, no matter what hour.

"Can you hear 'em, master?" Thomas asked. The Colonel dropped his head as if to hide from embarrassment.

Thomas scrunched up his face and rocked his head back and forth, while caressing the keys to his own creation. At that moment, he was experiencing the glory of the heavens, the angels were singing in multitudes in brilliant utterances as winds, as bassoons, as bolts of lightning, and his fingers played their melodies. Thomas was lost in the music, his entire body rocked side to side and his feet stomped on the pedals. In spite of his beautiful playing, his appearance at the keyboard was unsettling to those watching; the odd movements–the way his head swayed side to side, backwards and forwards–murmurs rose, the Colonel wished he could disappear as he inched closer to the piano. The moment of shame had come, inevitably. The boy's retardation was inescapable. It manifested in his wild, unorthodox movements.

"Master, do you hear them? Can you hear the angels?"

"No, Tom. I can't hear them." The Colonel stood behind Thomas at the piano and spoke softly, hoping to settle him. "Calm down. Play softly, Tom, like the cake you love. Gently." Thomas relaxed a bit, his body swung less wide. The Colonel slowly turned his head and dared to look up and out at his guests. He saw with relief that their faces were not scrunched as he'd expected, not horrified, but enthralled.

Thomas continued to bounce his feet on the floor, rocked his head side to side and played the final chords. Before he could begin anew, the Colonel slowly lowered the piano lid and whispered. "Charity will give you more chocolate cake now, Tom."

Thomas finished the last phrase, clapped with joy and leapt off the stool. He trundled across the *grand parlor* without taking note of the roaring applause, without taking a bow.

"Gifted, but untamed," the Colonel said to himself as he took the boy's bow.

Watching him trounce off, the Colonel thought Thomas was as unpredictable as the next season's crops. He could not share him on a grand scale with the public, no matter how many people told him to do so. The Colonel departed the throng of Thomas's admirers and joined Frances on the settee where she sat in her still pristine princess gown, the crown slightly crooked on her head now.

They were sipping wine together. The rumble of talk about Thomas had settled down. Suddenly, a man with a thick upward curved moustache stepped up to introduce himself. He wore a gold mask, a black cloak and pants, large black-feathered wings.

"Colonel Bethune," the man said in a thick guttural accent. "An honor to meet you, sir, name's Perry Oliver. You've heard o' me?"

The Colonel set down his glass of wine and stood. "I'm sorry, I can't say that I have."

"I'm a concert promoter? Like to talk to ya 'bout takin' your nigger out on tour."

The Colonel glanced at Frances who was busy talking with her aunt. He looked around and guided the stranger to a more private corner in the busy room.

"You were saying?"

"Ain't man much to mince words, Colonel," the Irishman lifted his mask, looked the Colonel straight in the eye and didn't flinch. "I'm thinkin' we can make some money together, you and me." The Colonel's eyes widened, money? "By all means. You have my undivided attention," the Colonel rejoined, appreciating the Irishman's directness.

"Welp, way I see it, there's a lot talk about the nigger boy. Had to come see for myself an' the way I see it, the nigger boy'll bring in a lot of coins," he said, wiping his mouth with his hand. "Boy's worth 'bout twenty thousand dollars for at least one year on tour."

"Twenty thousand dollars," the Colonel repeated the words slowly. The figure assaulted his senses—that was close to three times the profit his businesses had generated in the past two years! But the Colonel's expression didn't reveal it; he presented a casual tone, as if he were entertaining several offers, cards close to his vest in the hopes of getting a tad more.

"Well, Mr. Oliver, you certainly don't mince words," the Colonel said. He reached beneath his cape for his cigar box. "I appreciate a straightforward man. I'll be honest with you, I know the boy's talented and I've considered loaning him out before. A year..." he shook his head. "We're all rather attached to the boy, you see. He needs a lot of patience, the boy's retarded, you know, good-natured, but ill-tempered at times, and not good at much."

"You mean, except when he's on that piano..."

"Of course, yes, he's phenomenal on the piano," the Colonel agreed with a laugh.

A year, Thomas with a stranger away from family and familiar ground- it didn't feel right. Yet his mind drifted back to Gerald and the ultimatum at the newspaper. He hated to see the boy separated from his mother for such a long time, but ultimately was motivated to look out for the best interest of his own family. The Colonel's eyes narrowed.

This stranger, if real, was offering a small fortune, a way out of financial ruin. But, there were no visible signs of financial desperation on the Colonel's part, as the businessman in him emerged. "I must tell you, there are several promoters negotiating for Tom," he bluffed.

"Well, I'm the only one here," Perry said with confidence.

The Colonel lit his cigar, buying himself some time to think. "Actually, there's a promoter from New York right over there," he said with a casual nod toward a masked gentleman on the other side of the crowded room. "And from Chicago over there." He gestured in the direction of Larry DeGault, dressed as a count in a draping burgundy cape.

"I ain't one for false modesty, Colonel. I'm one o' the best concert promoters there is, heck one o' the best promoter's period outside of Barnum himself. Them other fellas, I ain't never heard of 'em an' I kin guarantee ain't none of 'em offerin' you fifty thousand dollars, plus whatever's left after my fee."

The Colonel choked on smoke and coughed. Oliver patted his back, but he assured him he was fine. The Colonel shook his head, as if to clean out his ears. Did this stranger really up the offer to fifty thousand dollars plus whatever was left after his fee? Was it some kind of twisted trick, the Colonel wondered?

"Did you say, fifty thousand dollars, plus?" he managed to ask.

"Take it or leave it," the Irishman said firmly. "I have it in gold."

It was a staggering sum that would help significantly with his debt. Yet, the Colonel being a seasoned businessman was skeptical. The offer was as unbelievable as Thomas playing the piano in the middle of the night. No male slave he knew of had ever sold for more than twelve hundred dollars, even the most beautiful quadroon girls only sold for two thousand. But this man was offering a fortune to *rent* Thomas. The Colonel reached for a glass of water and took a swallow, his hand shook a bit. What if he was genuine? To think he could wrest himself from financial ruin and make his fortune off his blind, retarded slave, it seemed inconceivable. Every fiber in his body rushed to move his hand toward the concert promoter's hand, however, he didn't want to appear desperate or make a foolish decision, so he finished his water with a casual air.

"Your offer is very intriguing, Mr. Oliver," the Colonel said calmly enough. "Very intriguing, indeed. But taking the boy a full year away from his mother?" the Colonel mused to test the stranger's character, "I'd hate to do such an awful thing."

"Ain't like niggers got the same kinda affection like white folks, Colonel," Oliver said. "She'll get used to it. But heck," he detoured, noticing the Colonel's lifted brow, "with the kind o' coin I'm offerin' ya, yer kin send the mother to visit him once in awhile if yer have a mind to."

The Colonel nodded and quietly puffed on his cigar.

"Well, whaddya say 'bout renting him out?" said Perry Oliver after allowing the Colonel to think for a while. "You're a businessman, so ya know that's a small fortune I just offered ya. Promise I'll take good care of 'im, treat 'im fair. He's a born entertainer."

"There's a lot more to Tom than you know," the Colonel said to stall. "Tom dances, plays the violin, the flute, and he sings as well. He has the ability to entertain in many ways, Mr. Oliver."

"Sounds to me like we should be makin' a deal."

"Wouldn't be right if I didn't tell you, Mr. Oliver, Tom's an uncommon boy. I'm afraid he falls into ill temper, gets his blood boiling, and often throws quite a tantrum. Proper training, I'm afraid has been lost on the boy. To send him off alone...I'll have to sleep on it."

It was a once in a lifetime proposition, but the Colonel was no fool. He wanted some time; he had no idea who this Irishman was, no idea whether his offer was legitimate. "How long will you be in town?"

"In town for Tom, Colonel," he said, bluntly. "I have business in Atlanta, but I ain't sure my offer'll still be good when I return." He replaced his mask and walked back toward the festivities. "Wait," the Colonel called, to no avail, the mysterious promoter disappeared among the guests.

III.

Warrenton, Virginia 1905

In the weeks that followed his arrest, John and Matthew Shaw hoped to convince the stubborn Colonel to fight for his freedom. It was cold enough in the makeshift cell for both men to have on heavy coats when they entered. The Colonel was in a robe, already warm from the hearth's fire. John removed his scarf, pulled up a chair and prepared his quill before opening the family's history book. Though old, the Colonel was certainly not befuddled; his memories were sharp and detailed.

Matthew unpacked a bag of fresh coffee and began to prepare a fresh pot.

"Are you comfortable, *mon père?*" John asked.

"I am old, my bones hurt, what do you think?" the Colonel scowled and turned to Matthew. "I have coffee, plenty already young Shaw, no need to duplicate efforts."

The not so subtle hint was taken and Matthew poured the Colonel a cup from the coffee in the heated pot.

"Did you ever think Tom would become famous?" Matthew looked intently at the Colonel, prepared to judge whether his response was frank or fabricated, as he handed him his coffee.

The Colonel responded, "Being a Bethune, a man of noble birth, I was expected to expand my father's empire and the last reality I considered was Tom having anything to do with it. Now that I am old and dying, I marvel at God, at the manner in which He chose to allow my fortune to grow. It was all so seemingly inconceivable, unfathomable, truly. It was not some master plan of mine."

"No?"

"If you have nothing better to do than to waste time trying to figure my guilt or innocence, then perhaps if you listen long enough you will find what it is you are looking for."

"What is it you think I'm looking for?"

"I know what it is, your judgment comes without intimate knowledge of the way things were. I am not the monster the Yankees outside think I am. The matter of Tom and his fame was not an overnight thing. You have to understand the times, the nature of the boy, you see. Of course by now, I knew he was talented, but I was unconvinced anything could be made of it."

Pushing his feet into the floor, the Colonel began to rock in the chair.

IV.

1860

Columbus, Georgia

November started off gloomy and wet, the ashen sky a horrible infinite gray. The Colonel drew out his cheroot case. He'd never been an indecisive man, but he still had not given an answer regarding Thomas to Perry Oliver, the entertainment promoter. He'd asked around about the Irishman, had summoned a few theater types to *Solitude* to get an idea what the traveling troupe might be like. It appeared the showman was legitimate, a regular promoter at Columbus Hall, and the Colonel thought maybe he might get more for the slave boy than what was offered. But first, he needed to open his pockets and find an expert teacher for Thomas.

He lit his chocolate cheroot from Havana. It was close to noon. Standing alone beside his carriage near the center of town, the Colonel blew smoke and waited impatiently for John and Thomas to exit the vehicle. It was chilly and for once, he wished Thomas would move faster, not slower, but Thomas was in a playful mood.

"Five-thousand, two-hundred eighty feet to the piano store," Thomas said, as he hopped out of the carriage in a heavy black coat without the brown gloves the Colonel had put on his hands moments before. "Five-thousand, two-hundred eighty feet times nine. Nine miles, eight inches to the piano store, John. You tried to trick Tom. You told Tom ten million."

"We have to get there before noon, before he goes to lunch," John said, descending the carriage stairs behind Thomas. He was speaking of the German who owned the only piano store in Columbus, who was also the best piano teacher in the area.

After Thomas's successful performance on Halloween, the Colonel felt he owed it to the Bethune legacy to help the slave perfect his piano skills on the chance he could be exhibited and cover the family's debts. The German on Main Street was the best candidate for the job. The Colonel had heard plenty of stories about the tall, thickset immigrant with a gruff uneven accent and aloof disposition from his son John and friends from his yacht club. He could be rude, members said between puffs on cigars, and dismissive, they said between sips of brandy. But both of his good friends, the Gates patriarch and Jonah Washington, spoke highly of the German's work with their children, despite his lack of social graces.

The Colonel walked swiftly toward the store and sidestepped a puddle. He hated when his boots became muddied. Though he didn't accept Perry Oliver's offer that night, he hadn't dismissed the mysterious promoter. If indeed he decided to make the deal, then Thomas would need a music teacher to travel with him on tour.

"It's an orange day today," Thomas said, bouncing through puddles.

"Tom, this way," the Colonel said, guiding him with his gloved hand.

As the sharply dressed, heavy coated trio walked down the sidewalk, a crowd of townsfolk formed behind them. When they drew near the piano store, the butcher leaned from the doorway of his meat shop.

"Is the nigger gonna play?" he called out.

"Yes, sir, the nigger sure is," John said.

The butcher flipped over the open sign to "CLOSED."

Eyebrows lifted, the Colonel looked at John, but his mind was too occupied to comment. By now they had reached the store and when he glanced around, the Colonel was a bit staggered by the thickening crowd that had formed. He searched the faces and saw Ian Crouch, the shoemaker, Mr. Carter, the baker, and Dr. Boland, one of the richest men in Harris County.

"*Et Bien*, what are these people doing?" he asked John, perplexed.

"Coming to hear Tom play," John said with a slight shrug. "He's been playing here for months and people come to hear him."

"How is it I didn't know about this, John?" asked the Colonel.

"Mr. Friedman lets Tom play on the good pianos in the front now. At first, he'd only let him play on the one in the back, you see. But it got too crowded."

"I see," the Colonel said, eyebrows knitted, as he pushed open the door of the music store and was led into the showroom that gleamed white with marble floors and pianofortes of every size and shape displayed.

The Colonel weaved his way to the German's office at the back of the store and knocked on the open door. Gerd Friedman was on his knees, his breath heavy while polishing a piano piece, white hair bouncing with each circular motion. The office smelled of oil and was cluttered, the floor covered with soft rags, detached keyboards, and piles of tuning pins.

The Colonel cleared his throat. "Mr. Friedman, my name is..."

"Know who you are, Mr. Bethune," Gerd said, without looking up. "Read your newspaper, every day."

"Ah, very fine. I'm here to discuss your services."

"Services?"

"Yes. I'd like—"

"To train that blind darky of yours?" he interrupted. Flipping his rag, he continued to polish the maple wood without looking up.

"Yes. He needs a teacher and you are the best Columbus has to offer."

Behind the Colonel, the showroom was filling with townspeople. So many locals had piled into the store there was almost no space to move. Thomas was warming up on a piano with random runs.

"I'd like to offer you five dollars per lesson."

But Gerd shook his head and mumbled. "No. I can't. I won't be able to do this, sir."

"Six dollars," the Colonel countered. It was a good offer, more than double the money most music teachers made, and would likely require more trips to the pawnshop.

But the German kept at his work, shaking his head. "It's generous of you, Mr. Bethune. I am honored, but I must say no."

"You must say no?" the Colonel asked, his voice frosty.

"Yes. I must say no to this offer."

"*Monsieur*, you are a music teacher and I have made a rich offer, more than fair. Please tell me why. If it's the boy, because he is Colored…"

Gerd stopped polishing and stood up. He mopped his forehead and approached the Colonel. "It's the nigger boy."

Now, the Colonel was getting angry, offended. So he did not want to teach a slave, the Colonel thought. He glared at the German. "Because he's —"

"Because there's nothing I can teach him, Mr. Bethune." Gerd was visibly uncomfortable.

"Listen. Do you hear? Listen to him."

In the front of the house, Thomas played Gottschalk.

"This slave boy. He is superior to me. I cannot train him on the style or technique of playing. He paints pictures with music, sir. It's something no teacher can teach, more than any man can learn."

Silence fell between the two men. The Colonel studied the way the German was watching his slave, more than high regard, it was awe in his eyes.

"Thank you for your time," the Colonel said. "I understand now."

"Do you?" Gerd's blue eyes flashed and his tone was bitter. "Because I do not," he said, looking at the Colonel intensely. "This Colored boy's had no instruction, yet his manner of touch is of scientific precision. Me, I studied the music in Germany, my country. Maybe, I thought, I'd be called to the court and teach princes. But I could not will it into existence. Now to see it in him, this strange blind nigger boy...I feel it is something beyond my comprehension."

The Colonel nodded and turned to leave, but the German's voice stopped him.

"The best thing is for him to hear good music, sir. Take him to Germany."

"Germany?" the Colonel breathed.

"He will hear the best and learn." The Colonel nodded. "Do you know, Mr. Bethune, men work all their lives reaching for what this strange nigger boy already has? When he hears, he will work it out himself, and then he will become more valuable for you. But he needs to hear the finest music. Take him to my country. There's an American girl, a teacher here I recommend to you. She plays better than I can play and she is young, maybe she'll travel with you."

"*Merçi, Monsieur.*"

The Colonel tipped his hat and considered the German's words. He stepped into the crowded room and began to push his way toward Thomas.

It was long after midnight, when the Colonel removed his boots and in his socks, he walked to his closet. In the darkness he grabbed a row of neatly pressed suits, turned and laid them across the bed. He'd been thinking about the German's suggestion for more than a week and had made the decision against

Perry Oliver, for now, and for training Tom, to make him more valuable. A light was burning. Frances had turned on a gaslight and was examining his face. She took a moment to let the information sink in before summoning up the courage to respond. "Did you say, Germany, *cher*?"

"A steamer leaves from here the day after tomorrow," he said, packing toiletries into a leather valise.

Frances's expression was unreservedly confused.

"But you forbade me to go to Paris, now you're suddenly taking a trip to Germany?" Her voice was filled with protest.

"It's for business, Frances, not pleasure," he replied with a tinge of irritation. "I'm taking Tom." He had a lot on his mind, firing an abusive overseer, promoting John to take his place.

"Tom?" she asked with alarm. From her settee, she regarded him with shock in her eyes.

"Yes, Tom." Without looking at her, he piled more suits onto the bed.

"Mon cher, le petit garçon will only break your heart," she said. "He has a great many needs, mon amour. Why just the other day Caleb coughed and le garçon cried in a fit about catching an illness. I don't know whether a trip overseas is such…"

"Enough, Frances," the Colonel cut her off.

Her shoulders back, her tone of disapproval: it was more than he would tolerate.

"What I decide to do for this family is my business."

Frances lowered her head. She recognized the warning sign. Tread carefully or risk an unpleasant row. "It feels we are becoming strangers," she said. She rubbed the pendant around her neck. "We barely see each other. You barely touch me. I need your touch." She tried to soften things by reaching out and caressing him, but he shifted his body away. He wasn't in the mood for her seductions.

He grabbed his best pair of boots. "Tom's music. I may have underestimated his worth. He may be more valuable to us than cotton."

"More valuable than cotton?" came Frances's response. "I see." She looked away.

The Colonel paused, his muscles stiffened at her tone. "You see?" he repeated, his eyes turning hard.

He was irritated by the implication of those two simple words. It made the hairs on the back of his neck stand at attention whenever he sensed a hint of his wife's disapproval, of her deeming him unworthy. "What exactly do you see?" came the question.

"It's just..." She paused and focused on helping him pack while searching for the right words. "James," she continued. "You practically take our children's heads off if they so much as breathe on Tom. First you were consumed with preserving the Bethune name, now that nigger boy is everything to you."

She kept her eyes down, knowing she had overstepped her bounds, but she didn't stop. "What if Tom falls and hurts his head? What if Tom falls and damages his hands? You shackle the children. Caleb resents it, the other children resent not being able to play freely with the child. The children love the boy, but after all you are their blood, their father remember?"

"I won't tolerate condescension from you, Frances." His face hardened, it was as if she'd slapped him, yet he hid the sting of her words. It angered him that his petite silky-haired wife could reduce him to his knees with the slightest disapproval.

Frances sat postured as if she might persist, but the Colonel raised his finger to his lips, warning her to leave the matter be. "Ma petite, I have a great many pressures and I'm doing what is best for you and this family. I'll hear no more of this."

The Colonel still had not told her of the cascading troubles with the bank. He brooded alone in his den at night, sharp pains seizing his chest, but he'd kept from her the critical state of their finances for years and would continue to do so. He had only a few months to save them from bankruptcy.

He let out a long breath. Dare he confess he had doubts himself about embarking on this fool's errand, this risky trip to Germany? It felt like bricks were on his shoulders. He longed to tell her about the financial troubles that occupied his mind, whether he could travel to Germany and back in time to pay the bank. It's inappropriate to burden a lady with such matters, he scolded himself. So he simply fell silent.

And she sought peace. "You are right. I apologize, mon amour. My prayers for you are with my heart and not my lips alone," she said. "I do not want to stand between you and any business opportunities you may have for the slave."

"We leave in two days."

Her lips parted, she wanted to say more, but she could see he was already adrift, his thoughts well at sea.

It was too early for the cocks to crow. Charity crept as quiet as possible past sleeping bodies in the leaky old slave cabin, rousing her children. For a day, her head had been pounding. Her head ached with painful thoughts, wild imaginings of her miracle baby going to ride in a ship across the big waters to play music for European white people. She may never see him again. She shook her head. Her biggest fear in life had been losing her youngest child to malnourishment or a cruel wasteful death. She'd thought she could protect him better than she had Mamankoh, the daughter she'd lost the year before he was born. She'd been a field hand in those days. On that fateful afternoon, her daughter had been in the shade beneath a big cypress tree. Charity was planting in the fields in front of the oxen with Thomas in her belly when she felt that tingling sensation caress her body, felt her daughter's spirit pass by. She looked toward the sky and saw black vultures with white claws circling between the clouds. She made it to the cypress tree, saw her little girl's sallow face covered with flies, and a large snake sliding across her neck. Her screams had pierced through the plantation. "May her soul, absent from the body, be present with the Lord," the slave preacher whispered over her daughter's grave.

"Singin' in the heavenly choir now," the slaves had told her in those dark hours of failed solace.

Charity shook her head, tears falling, as she woke up her children to see Thomas off. She never wanted to hear those words again. Now she had to worry about her youngest surviving a trip across the ocean? Her mind couldn't take it. What if the ship sank? What if he caught a disease and died? Charity felt a heavy cloud drift over her spirit. It was a cruel life. How much more suffering could she take? The thoughts of her master taking her baby so far away from her made her want to stop eating for good and ask God to take her home. "Jus' blow da horn Gabriel," she whispered through tears.

The ram horn would start screaming soon. Charity wanted all her children to make it to the fields on time, but she also wanted them to be able to hug their little brother Thomas, before he went off to sea with the master. She sighed, weary. From the moment she'd learned the Colonel was taking her baby across the water, she had not been able to sleep. "Prepare his clothes, the nicest frocks of Caleb and John, pack plenty of Arrowroot, bread, and cakes he likes," she'd been told. She'd cried and cried in the cold servant's room. The old African woman in the kitchen knew her troubles and offered her a small cock to put in the boy's bag for good luck. But Charity shook her head, no; she didn't want any part of her voodoo black magic. She threw the charm into the fire and prayed the boy would make it across the water and back.

She shook her daughter's shoulders. "Come on now, y'all git up," Charity rushed her shabby clad children. The kids slept in ripped hemp pants and frayed skirts. One by one, all eighteen lined up to hug their baby brother goodbye. Thomas was dapperly dressed in a fine Italian day-suit once worn by little master Caleb. He stood near the front door looking more like a rich white child than a slave.

"Come say goodbye to Tom," Thomas beckoned. The blind boy was excited. He laughed and smiled, oblivious to what lay ahead of him. Some of his siblings were crying but Thomas kept saying, "It's gone be all right. Tom's goin' to Germany. Then Tom'll be back."

"That's it. Now go on," Charity gave her last child a hug and hurried her toward a bowl of pot liquor that would serve as breakfast. She took Thomas by the hand and headed toward the dark path that led up to the master's mansion. The Colonel's fancy carriage was waiting by the Big House, a half-mile away.

In the cotton fields, as the sun rose, Clarence and Sherry stopped picking and stood straight up, risking master John's whip. The two siblings stared toward the Big House. Against the sun's soft rays, Charity gazed from the front steps of the Big House, a suffocating thickness in her throat. She hugged Thomas tight, "Now don' you forget yo' mama and don' forget yo' daddy." Ensa tapped her shoulder. She released Thomas, wiped her tears, and watched as the master's fancy carriage drove her baby boy down the dirt road and disappeared.

V.

The Columbus loading docks were filled with the crack and groan of freights, the bang of hammers, and the click of boots on wooden planks that afternoon. The white sky was slowly beginning to fade, a part of nature's cycle bringing shorter, cooler days. A bustle of passengers brushed past, as Frances stood up on the tip of her heeled boots and kissed the Colonel firmly on the lips.

"I will write, *ma chère*, as soon as we reach port," the Colonel promised with a rub of her pregnant belly. He hugged her close and kissed her forehead. *"Mon ange*, take good care of my child and please don't worry." He turned and motioned to his children. "Come, give your *père* a hug. Be good for your mother, *d'accord?*"

The whistle blew and a funnel of black smoke spat up to the sky. The Colonel settled in among the first-class passengers as the *SS Atlantic* sailed out of port.

Thomas and the teacher the German had recommended, Vivian Amaliè Tutein, were traveling on the bottom deck. As Mr. Friedman, had suggested, Vivian had happily accepted the Colonel's eleventh-hour offer to travel with and train the odd young pianist. A woman of high class who downplayed her looks, Vivian preferred her light brown hair pulled into a bun behind her head and wore men's trousers beneath her dresses. Her attire was not to the Colonel's taste, as she was part of some newfangled ladies movement that was doomed to failure in his opinion. Nevertheless, he'd observed her with Thomas and she was wonderful, an accomplished pianist trained at Columbia Female Academy and then London. She insisted she could cultivate his already extensive repertoire and to the Colonel's delight, she had offered to transcribe the blind boy's imaginations on the piano.

Thus, the Colonel was willing to overlook her incendiary dress since she also possessed the necessary patience to manage Thomas.

Moving closer to the front of the ship, the Colonel gazed out at the retreating landscape of ships and warehouses that marked the Columbus harbor skyline. He could see the bell towers and rooftops shrinking as the impressive-looking ship slowly cut through the Atlantic Ocean toward Europe. Out on the open sea, the sun finally broke through the clouds and the Colonel dug into his pocket for a letter that read:

Dear James,

If the pupil is as great as you describe, then come to Leipzig. He will hear extraordinary music, and I will arrange for the greatest pianists in Europe to try him. Giacomo Meyerbeer, Sir Charles Halle', Liszt, Soltaire, and myself among them. Safe journey and I shall see you anon.

Yours truly, Ignaz

Water swelled and splashed against the ship starboard. The Colonel held the elegant stationery and pondered the future. With finances choking him, he had in his hands one of the most important letters of his life. He took proper care to refold it in a manner that would not damage it. The soft paper was an answer to his prayers and a key to his own secret dreams.

As the steamer ship's horn howled, the Colonel stood atop the large deck and waited to meet the awe-inspiring view of the city Goethe lovingly named "Little Paris." Blood pounded in his veins as the large square buildings with countless windows and soaring steeples came into view: Leipzig. It was breathtaking, an ancient city with sprawling lime trees and colorful daisies. God had spoiled the fertile land with his most gorgeous treasures of nature. The sun caressed the Colonel's body and a gentle wind lapped at his hair. Here he was, at the shore of the city where Mendelssohn conducted the world's most inspired symphonies. He was convinced that the choice he'd made to travel here was the right one.

The timing couldn't have been more ideal. It was the height of opera season, so when the darkness of night descended, the narrow streets were clogged with elegant carriages, the fine vehicles filled with modish patrons adorned in capes and tiers of ruffled gowns. One coach, a hired taxi, rattled at a snail's pace carrying the Americans from Georgia that were properly dressed in their best opera attire. While Vivian explained to Thomas the story of *Il Crociato in Egitto*, set during the Sixth Crusade, the Colonel struggled to keep his head straight. He'd already drunk a full bottle of wine and was feeling a little woozy. The finest aristocrats in Europe would be in attendance. He opened a second bottle of Merlot.

"Half notes or sixteenth notes," Thomas asked about the opening musical sequence while kicking his legs.

The Colonel took a large sip of wine. He glanced at Thomas who tapped the back of his boots against the bottom of his seat. "It is my only requirement, Ms. Tutein."

"He will be fine, Mr. Bethune, I'll see to it," she whispered.

His eyes moved slowly from hers and he lifted the curtain to look at the crowd of carriages. He felt his stomach leap. "Indeed, it's time," he whispered. His heart raced, despite the music teacher's confidence, doubts filling his head: was it wisdom to expect the unpredictable slave boy to sit still in an opera house, to not make a spectacle of them all? It was a nerve-rattling proposition that he couldn't shake as he walked up the stairs and into the venue.

The Colonel smoothed his best serge cape with his gloves. His blue eyes glanced up at the golden ceiling of the world-renowned Leipzig Opera House and his chest swelled with pride. Settled into a good box, as the American guests of the great Maestro Ignaz Moscheles, the Colonel's spirits soared. He peered down at the distinguished Giacomo Meyerbeer as he led the orchestra onstage. Old and wizened, and thin, the revered composer's air was nevertheless regal and his presence commanded awe.

It was a grand sight and sound and the Colonel managed to bask in every note rising from below his tier. However, he could not help that his eyes wandered about, pleasuring in the grand display around him. He smiled to himself, slowly digesting that he was actually in Saxony, the center of learning and European culture. His talented slave, looking very much the product of a well-off man in his expensive opera attire, rocked quietly in the velvet-covered seat beside him.

The fetching soprano sang in high shrills, her voice sweet and silky. Thomas swayed with the music and even began to hum. The Colonel took up his opera glasses and discretely turned his head. In the best boxes sat proud Saxon royalty. He swept the chamber and found Franz Liszt–his blond hair carefully coiffed, his hands audaciously clasping his buxom mistress's hands. Across the house was Sir Charles Halle, the renowned pianist-conductor, the white-haired elder statesman of the arts, the North Star in the heavens, beloved by the English. Oh, what a pleasure it will be to meet such a regal figure, the Colonel thought.

The Colonel lowered his glasses. Relaxed now, he was enjoying the drama of the opera as much as its colorful attendees. Thomas rocked to the music with a barely discernible hum. The second intermission was nearing when suddenly Thomas stood up, his arms flung wide, and he belted out the lyrics, right along with the lead castrato!

A whimper escaped Vivian's lips.

"Tom, stop it, right now!" the Colonel hissed and pulled the boy down to his seat, utterly embarrassed.

A sea of refined heads swiveled and opera glasses shifted directions. The Colonel drew a deep breath. *Mon Dieu!* Everything seemed to move in slow motion, as men gestured and ladies' fans lifted to conceal shocked lips.

"Take him, now!" he barked at the teacher.

The Colonel rose to his feet, lifted the crimson curtain, and squeezed past the box of French composer Soltaire Franco. The Frenchman gave off an imperious air, even in the low light. His ample beak was scrunched as if something fetid was in the air. At that moment, he frowned at the Colonel. Only the Colonel didn't see the disapproving expression, as he was already in the carpeted corridor with Vivian and the boy in tow

It's a terrible mess, he thought. The possibility that he'd risked everything, his reputation, his life, all to travel to Germany for naught crossed his thoughts. How would he pay the bank? It occurred to him his entire life was in ruins.

Outside, Cathedral bells were ringing. The Colonel walked swiftly toward the row of taxis. "Lost. It could all be lost," he muttered. Vivian pulled at Thomas and was having a hard time keeping up, but they made it to the carriage waiting at the corner of Nordrand and the Augustusplatz Square.

"Herr Meyerbeer is a visionary," the Colonel sputtered at Thomas as they climbed the coach steps. "The most revered opera producer in all of Europe. He alone has transformed the entire genre and you ruined, absolutely ruined his masterpiece, Tom," he wailed.

His body shook with anger as passersby found their way around him. A tavern door lay open and inside German artisans played cards with big-breasted barmaids leaning in toward their intentions. The Colonel was disoriented with the despair of shame. German aristocracy was more formal, and more unforgiving than even Georgia's elites. The wine he'd consumed did little to comfort him.

"Don't speak of this to anyone," he spat. Vivian moved Thomas quickly inside the carriage. "Not a soul."

"You have my word," she whispered.

"Because if I hear of it, here or in America, if I hear of what happened here tonight…" He pulled his cape high on his neck. "You will be relieved of your services."

He turned his attention to his slave. "What do you have to say for yourself, Tom?" the Colonel asked in a stern tone.

Thomas responded by belting out another loud, high note.

Vivian let out a gasp, then struggled to hide a smile.

"Sir, I dare say I think it will be all right?" She tried to comfort her boss.

The Colonel scowled, flipped his cape, and climbed into the cab, knowing his entire future could very well lie in ruins.

The next day, rain fell like toppled pails of water and poured down on hard Leipzig's streets. The Colonel sat back in the carriage wearily pinching the narrow bridge of his nose as the memory of the prior evening haunted him–Thomas's howling notes, a sea of fine heads swiveling, the sneering glares. The Colonel sighed and snapped for Vivian to move faster in smoothing out the child's clothes. There was no turning back. No matter how unpredictable, undisciplined, and potentially disastrous Thomas could prove to be, the time was at hand. Maestro Moscheles had sent word: their audience with the Masters was not cancelled.

"The show must go on, mustn't it," Vivian said as she swiped at his pants.

"Tom. Boy, you must be at your best today. There are important men in Leipzig who want to hear your music," said the Colonel. "If you behave. If you will play for these men, I will make you my little concert pianist."

"Tom will be on his best behavior today," Thomas. "Tom will be Master's little concert pianist."

The Colonel tightened his lips and shook his head with a smile. He realized, of course, that the slave's word was as unfailing as a pair of twos in a hand of high-stakes poker. He drew in his breath and tightened the belt on his greatcoat. There was nothing he could do but to trust that God would not bring him to Germany to make a fool of him.

The hired carriage hit a muddy pothole and came to a stop. The Colonel lifted the curtain and peered at the imposing ivy covered building. The Leipzig Conservatorium, massive as a mountain of redbrick, sat proudly against a grumpy gray sky. Music spilled onto the streets from inside the brick walls where trumpets punctuated the high-pitched dance of violins.

The Colonel peeled off some bills, handed them to the driver. The German driver stared oddly at the American coddling his slave, but the Colonel ignored the driver and dismissed him with a nod. Lightning cracked. "Come, Tom," the Colonel beckoned. But Thomas sat still as a corpse, his back frozen against the velvet cushion. "Tom's gonna catch the pneumonia and die," he said. "It's raining."

"*Mon Dieu,* we're going to get struck by lightning. You bring him in," the Colonel barked at Vivian as the sky got angrier and the raindrops heavier. He turned and made his way toward the music hall doors.

Vivian sighed beneath her parasol and bit her bottom lip. She was still learning how to navigate her pupil's behavior. She was a great observer and was vaguely aware of the slave boy's growing ego. "You must come inside the hall with me, maestro. It's getting colder and colder by the minute," she said and tightened her headscarf. "I certainly hate to think of leaving you in the carriage where you might freeze to death."

Thomas began to shift his body forward at once. "Don't leave Tom to freeze to death," he said lifting to his feet. "Tom will come with you. It's getting colder and colder by the minute."

Vivian helped him down the steps and crossed her fingers in the hope all would go well.

VI.

The famed Gerwandhaus Concert Hall proved quite unassuming despite its high arched ceilings. It seemed much too plain to be the pinnacle of the world's most important music figures, yet the chamber was brimming with the crème de la crème of the music world. Famed virtuosos in crisp frocks greeted one another with double kisses, speaking French–the preferred language of the highborn–and offering modest bows.

Seated in the front row before the stage was the esteemed Professor Hautman, director of the St. Thomas School which trained Wagner and Bach. Next to Professor Hautman sat Sir Charles Halle in his somber black suit observing the pre recital ritual with thoughtful eyes. Across from Sir Halle stood the balding Professor Richter, who taught counterpoint at the Conservatory. He lit a thin cigar amid an intimate conversation with the rascal Liszt. And on the opposite side of the room Maestro Ignaz Moscheles stood out from those waiting to see the slave prodigy. He was holding court on a raised stage occupied by two grand pianos. He pointed with a white handkerchief and dictated the final details for the afternoon musical arrangements.

The Colonel recognized every star of the musical heavens; his hands were wet with sweat inside his gloves. He grabbed the tip of his hat, as if to keep from teetering over. He was slightly dizzy, experiencing a nervousness not even the eve of battle could bring. This had been his own dream in his youth, to be in this room, and then it became a dream for his children. The reality was settling upon him now: it was not himself, not even one of his children, but Thomas, his blind and retarded Negro slave, about to make his European debut.

"James, welcome," came a voice from the stage. Ignaz Moscheles spoke in a silky alto and he was smiling. "I look forward to hearing your Negro play," he said, waving the Colonel toward him. Ignaz descended the stage steps and crossed the parquet floor.

The Colonel's former teacher was fully gray now, his caramel visage confirming the rumors of some African Creole descent. Musical advisor to the Rothschild family, revered composer and teacher, Ignaz possessed the carriage of a respected elder statesman. He stood straight with his chin slightly lifted in the air; his presence stamped with that refined air the Colonel remembered from his youth.

While the Colonel caught up with Maestro Moscheles, Vivian made her way through the crush of masters and students toward her employer. She gave a brief nod of acknowledgment to Maestro Moscheles and whispered in urgent low tones in the Colonel's ear who then politely excused himself from Ignaz and exited with the American music teacher to the rehearsal room where Thomas was perched atop a table, swinging his legs.

"Missus Vivian's a Thursday child, has far to go."

"Someone sneezed so he refuses to rehearse," Vivian explained.

A dark cloud crossed the Colonel's face at once. "Tom, you need to rehearse your repertoire."

"Tom got a disease sneezed on him," the boy said with a cough.

"Tom, you do not have a disease. Now come. Stop this silliness."

"Tom got a disease sneezed on him, James."

The Colonel felt a catch in his throat and struggled to maintain control of his temper. He drew in his breath. The mercurial slave was uncontrollable and insolent, destined to humiliate him. He knew Vivian could see his anger and knew she understood the pressure that was causing the vein in his neck to swell. But the situation in the dully-lit cavern was a delicate one, because the gifted slave was also emotionally volatile. Inhaling long and deep, the Colonel forced himself to calm down. He thought for a moment on how to handle the situation and decided to try to appeal to the slave's ego. He described to Thomas the magnificent scene awaiting him in Gewandaus Hall. "The finest musical minds of the last century are outside those doors, who want to see you, Tom. There is a fine piano for you on center stage and those very important people are waiting to hear your music," he managed in his gentlest tone.

"Tom's gonna die."

Sweat formed on the Colonel's forehead, in spite of the cold in the room. He felt his blood pressure begin to ascend. He struggled to maintain his composure. "Tom, we came all the way from the other side of the ocean for this moment. For you to play."

"We came twenty-six million, six hundred and eleven-thousand-two-hundred feet for Tom to play."

"Yes, Tom, for you to play. Do you understand? You must play."

The Colonel was frustrated, but Thomas was in his own world.

"Nothing at last is sacred but the integrity of your own mind," said Thomas, swinging his feet. "Emerson was one of our great thinkers, the Plato and Socrates of our time. Don't you think so Frances? Yes, James. Emerson was one of our great thinkers."

"My entire life is flashing before me and he's quoting Emerson?" the Colonel turned to Vivian, completely exasperated. But she had no answers.

"Tom has pneumonia. Tom's dying."

"Don't keep saying that. For heaven's sake, you are not dying Tom!"

Whatever made him think he could put the blind boy to work? He was moaning, holding the back of his hand limp against his forehead like he was faint.

"Tom, I will not tolerate this behavior. Come, you must warm up."

"Who will come to Tom's funeral?" he whined. "Emerson? He's a great thinker."

The Colonel flinched; he wanted to slap him but Vivian positioned herself between him and Thomas.

"Tom, you are perfectly healthy. Don't you want to play? We're here in Leipzig, Germany," she said, "and there are men of great eminence waiting to hear you play."

"We're in Leipzig, Germany and there are men of great eminence waiting to hear Tom play. No. Tom's dying."

"Dear God! *Mon Dieu!*" *Catastrophique*, the Colonel thought.

"Colonel Bethune, wait," Vivian called after him.

The Colonel barely heard her; he was walking quickly away from the rehearsal room. A plan of action hadn't formulated in his mind. He just kept limping at a fast pace through the rows of arched hallways. When he emerged into the warmth of the Gerwandhaus Concert Hall, stage lights shimmered from the ceiling, he saw Sir Charles Halle talking to Maestro Ignaz Moscheles near the stage. He nodded at Ignaz, then politely asked Sir Charles Halle if he would kindly play a selection on one of the vacant grand pianos.

"But your slave is not here."

"*Mais oui, Monsieur,*" the Colonel said with a mysterious smile. "*S'il vous plait.*" The Colonel gestured toward the piano.

Sir Charles acquiesced. "Certainly, Colonel Bethune. What is it you would like for me to play?"

"Play whatever it is you wish, Herr Charles," the Colonel said, the portrait of calm. His demeanor belied the gnarled knot in his stomach. He bowed his appreciation to Sir Charles, then motioned for the maestro to take his place. Nodding, Sir Charles walked onto the stage, pulled the small mahogany stool away from the piano and took his place. After a brief pause, he began to strum an original piece.

The Colonel heard whispers. When Ignaz asked him what was going on, he nodded and said, "You will see, Maestro." He stood to the side of the stage—feigning confidence and praying for a miracle. The slave boy flocked to music and the Colonel was hoping he'd respond in the same he did at *Solitude* when one of the children began practicing in the *grand parlor*.

As sure as a bee to nectar, Thomas tore into the main hall. He wove and spun about, knocked over a few music stands, causing a stir as Vivian struggled to stay close to him.

Soltaire shifted in his seat near the stage as Thomas knocked over a row of music stands. "Isn't that the creature who interrupted the opera last night." Soltaire whispered to Liszt.

"He's the slave Herr Moscheles spoke of."

"Idiot indeed," Soltaire snorted.

Thomas twirled to the music, bizarre and uncomfortable for the Germans and their guests to watch. Soltaire clucked his lips in outrage. "The boy is a defect" he flicked the air with his wrist in disgust. "Is this a game you're playing on us?" he cried out. He'd seen enough and grabbed his coat, unwilling to endure the insult any longer.

"Herr Soltaire, please do not leave," the Colonel said. "I honor your skepticism. I assure you, Tom is not a hoax, but a fine pianist worthy of your esteemed consideration."

Soltaire turned toward the Colonel and glowered. "Monsieur Bethune," he said. "Do you expect us to believe he's capable of melody?" His outrage palpable. "Do you not see what I see?"

The Colonel did not turn to look. He knew well enough what Thomas was doing.

Soltaire was known as a man of miserable character loathe to admit virtue in any musician other than Mozart. Soltaire watched Thomas's bizarre antics and was repulsed. He clucked his lips in absolute outrage. "Look at him. That boy is a defect, born of jungle parents, whose ancestors lived in the bush of Africa," he flicked the air with his wrist in disgust. "Is this some kind of hoax?" The Frenchman cried in protest. He'd seen enough. Promptly, Soltaire stood up and tightened his heavy coat. He began to leave the hall and Liszt followed.

"I assure you Herr Soltaire..." The Colonel stepped in his way to forestall him. "I will stand in the town square and admit to chicanery if the slave does not satisfy. On my word before God."

Liszt whispered persuasions and Soltaire relented. "If the boy does not perform as reported, I will make sure you are ruined, Colonel."

Now, Thomas broke away from Vivian and pushed Sir Charles in his ribs toppling the piano stool.

"*Mon Dieu!*" the Colonel gasped as Sir Charles fell to the floor. It was mayhem, but the music continued. The Colonel and three other men rushed to help the composer to his feet, but the Colonel was lost inside his own spinning mind, his ears burning with a desire to whip the shameless boy. At that moment while he bent and Sir Charles flapped, it occurred to the Colonel that Thomas wasn't the idiot, he was. The Colonel shook his head. Tom will never be able to harness the music into any productive form. The Colonel regretted his decision to pin his future on the retarded slave boy, but he was left with no choice. He'd been desperate and without alternative, the slave was his last best hope.

The back of his hand to his forehead, the room had gone blank. The audience murmured in their seats and some stood up pointing. But the Colonel didn't see, didn't hear for a long moment in time. He would grab the boy and leave, he thought, leave and never again consider the possibility. "Miss Tutein, take him!"

"Leave him!" came Sir Charles's voice. "Don't touch the boy!"

The murmurs, the chatter in the preferred language of French came to a hush.

"Verbatim et literatim," Sir Charles said with incredulity. "He plays exactly…"

"Word for word and letter for letter," Liszt breathed.

Thomas was playing Herr Charles' original piece tone for tone with the same style and flourish and fluidity!

Liszt leaned forward in his chair, then turned to Soltaire. "Upon one hearing! Do my ears deceive me?" Soltaire gazed ahead as if bored. "A freakish mime," he said. He refused to give the retarded slave boy any credence.

On the stage, Sir Charles adjusted the stool and began playing in unison with Thomas. The Colonel watched from the wings and mopped his brow. "Verbatim et literatim," Vivian whispered behind his ear.

After a horrendous start, the slave boy's beautiful music arced over the room like a rainbow after a storm. He had the audience in his little palm. As the last notes faded beneath the twinkle of stage lights, Sir Charles began an unfamiliar tune.

"Do you know this music?" The Colonel asked Vivian as the unfamiliar notes filled the hall. She angled her ear, then shook her head.

"I know his music well, sir, but this piece I do not know."

The sonata was strange to the ears of all who were seated in the Great Hall, completely unrecognizable in every sense, and extremely complex. Young Thomas didn't miss a beat; he immediately began to play in perfect harmony with Sir Charles, note-for-note, phrase-by-phrase, movement-by-movement. Gasps erupted around the hall. Harmony, perfect synchronization on an unknown song! His feats before the European crowd were unending. It gave the Colonel a great feeling to hear the audience's reaction and to witness his slave's music mesmerizing on the learned German crowd.

Notoriously impatient with unworthy musicians, the incomparable Liszt sat transfixed. He moved to the edge of his seat, his eyes locked on the American slave boy. "Secondo?" he said, in complete shock. "My Lord. Only Mozart is reported to have performed such feats."

Whispers flowed in waves around the concert hall when the realization of Thomas's prowess dawned, for the slave boy was displaying incomprehensible virtuosity and creativity. Head lifted heavenward, his fingers moved with agility and strength, body swaying side to side, the slave appeared to be in a blissful state, his face filled with pure ecstasy. It was one of the best performances any of those elite musicians had ever seen.

"This is outstanding," Liszt said. He rose to his feet.

"Le Negre Mozart!" A voice yelled from the back of the hall.

"Le Negre Swan!"

A tingling sensation surged through the Colonel's body. Le Negro Mozart? His chest swelled with pride as the music drifted to his ears. The sonata was indescribably lovely. The murmurs throughout the hall continued to ripple as the realization of Thomas's genius spread.

"*Le Negre est un miracle,*" Ignaz whispered. He motioned to the Colonel. "How long do you have here in Leipzig," he asked. "I would like to train the boy." The Colonel told him they could only spare a few days, as he had pressing business back in the states.

The illustrious Moscheles's eyes lingered on the stage before he stood from his chair and applauded the American slave.

"Bravo! Bravo!" He exclaimed. As each note progressed, the entire audience of the Great Hall rose to their feet with applause. Filled with emotion, stomping the cold floor, they chanted the slave's name "Tom! Tom! Tom!" until the floors shook.

Overwhelmed, the Colonel felt as if he had passed and his spirit was looking down on the stage from the heavens. The explosive reaction from the audience sent a sensation through his body that made him feel like he was floating. Gazing at Thomas, he was reminded of Schumann: "To send light into darkness of men's hearts—such is the duty of the artist." For the first time since arriving in Leipzig, the Colonel smiled, for the hearts of the greatest virtuosos of Europe had just been lit.

In the midst of this great ovation, Liszt looked over at the frowning Soltaire. "Herr Soltaire, what do you think now? Still think him a mime?"

The Frenchman spoke in a low voice. "The world has never seen such a thing as this blind boy," Soltaire managed to say. The Frenchman's eternally hardened face dissolved into a softened shell of shame. The Colonel watched the French composer's emotions: he could tell that Soltaire knew he'd just experienced a performance unlike any he could ever replicate.

"Nor will it ever see anything like him again," Soltaire continued. "After seeing this half-civilized plantation Negro's greatness–granted him by heaven, I will never play the piano again from this day forward," Soltaire said resentfully. He nodded to the gentleman around him, to Liszt, to Ignaz, and down the row to several professors, before tightly pulling his heavy coat close to his skinny frame. Soltaire and the German piano teacher in Columbus, would not be the first classical pianists to quit upon witnessing Thomas, nor would they be the last. The Frenchman proudly lifted his chin and walked away.

The Colonel climbed the steps leading up to the stage. He went to Thomas and rubbed the top of his head. "Excellent job, Tom. Excellent job."

The Colonel and his slave were surrounded at once. Liszt was the first to greet them.

"Fine playing! Herr Tom. Superb," the Hungarian said.

"Tom, this is Maestro Franz Liszt, a pre-eminent pianist," the Colonel said, making the introductions. The slave's teacher had already briefed Tom on the background of all the maestros and professors who would be in attendance. Thomas extended his hand to the virtuoso.

"Hi, Maestro Franz Liszt, Tom knows Maestro Franz Liszt," Thomas said. "A Tuesday baby. Full of grace."

"I don't believe I knew it was a Tuesday!" Liszt said with a smile, shaking his hand. "How could he know that," he turned to the Colonel.

"He has a mind of days and dates," the Colonel shrugged.

"Quite brilliant, he is, this slave of yours."

Ignaz had meanwhile ordered wine for the occasion and Liszt reached for a glass. Thomas was enamored with his new admirer and was in a talkative mood.

"Maestro Franz Liszt, born Tuesday, October twenty-second in eighteen eleven, Raiding, Hungary. Maestro Franz Liszt was influenced by Paganini," Thomas said.

"I'm very impressed, Maestro Tom. What else did they tell you about me?"

"Maestro Liszt was carrying-on and ran off with his mistress the Countess d'Agoult."

He gave a small giggle, as Liszt nearly spit up his wine. Ignaz graciously stepped in before any other words could be uttered, before Liszt could so much as exhale. "Herr Tom you are brilliant," Moscheles said. "I will love to train you more. Tell us, where did you learn to play?"

Thomas was silent for a few moments. "Tom," the Colonel nudged him, "Maestro Moscheles is speaking to you. He wants to know where you learned to play such beautiful music."

"God taught Tom," the slave said as the crowd closed in.

"God?" Sir Charles asked to a ripple of murmurs.

"Yes. God taught Tom before Tom came into this world. God taught me."

First there were murmurs, then a burst of cheers and applause.

Maestro Moscheles saw the earnest conviction on the slave's face. "Yes, Thomas," he said, joining in the applause. "I believe He did."

Thomas giggled before the adoring throng; he bowed and clapped his hands for himself.

"Yes, God, through the angels," he said.

"There you have it," Liszt chimed in. "He plays with the angels!"

"May I present to you one Thomas Greene, ladies and gentlemen. Thomas Greene Bethune." The Colonel bowed with Thomas, and Leipzig roared their appreciation for the blind slave boy.

A party was held in honor of the Colonel and his Thomas at the estate of Ignaz Moscheles. Near the center of the room, the two men smoked their pipes and sipped a pure Cabernet Sauvignon once gifted to Ignaz by the Baron James de Rothschild himself. They filled their glasses liberally and toasted to the momentous day.

Thomas had so ignited the passions of the many musicians, at the Great Hall that afternoon, that musical challenge was the order of the night. "Our illustrious young Tom from America will do us the favor of another turn at the piano followed by me!" Liszt announced to rousing cheers and the echo of, "Me, then me, then me again..." Liszt joked, in the room of gilded jade and Oriental rugs.

Thomas played song after song and the transformed crowd sang praises, thronged about the piano and pushed to be closer to him—*tsked* and shushed others nearby. "Quiet now, quiet, let the boy play."

Aristocrats, top students of music, and famed musicians of the time, all watched rapt with fascination as Thomas played his very best. The party swirled around the talented blind slave and his wonderful, angelic sound. Much drinking, dance, and raucous merriment ensued with women in fine silk gowns who pranced-and-preened and flirted with the Colonel. At the sight of an unlaced bodice, he laughed and took a step back while playfully grabbing his heart, but such immodesty was a welcome change, and he appreciated the *joie de vivre* of his European peers.

Late in the party, as the lingering guests gave Thomas another round of applause, the Colonel looked at his former teacher with gratitude. Moscheles gave him a congratulatory nod. "Come, there are more guests who want to meet you, James."

Ignaz led the Colonel away from the ladies. From left and right, the Colonel was bombarded with requests for Thomas to play more selections. "*Le garçon* must come to Paris, *Monsieur* Bethune, *le garçon* just has to play Vienna." Bejeweled hands in rubies and diamonds turned him, this way and that, and he was flattered. He bowed to one potential benefactor and then the next, but morning was dawning and he worried about Thomas. It was a wonder the child's fingers hadn't gone numb from playing for so many hours. His health was a concern. On occasion, at *Solitude,* Thomas had performed too extensively and he'd become physically ill with body spasms and severe headaches.

"We must have the slave play in Strousburg."

The Colonel took the small stage beside Thomas and he graciously declined. "The boy is finished for the night." As the Colonel motioned for Vivian to remove Thomas from the piano, which often involved a crying tantrum, Maestro Moscheles stepped out to address the crowd.

"Herr Thomas Bethune," he said, lifting a glass of wine. "He plays with the angels."

The music stopped and the drunken elite gave their final applause. From that point on, it was rumored that a higher power dwelled inside of Thomas and that power played music with angels in the presence of Almighty God.

At dusk two days later, the Colonel's hired carriage galloped past Castle Church where Martin Luther ruptured the Catholic belief system like tumbling snow from a mountain. Strains of the St. Thomas Church Boys choir could be heard in the distance. The carriage driver tugged the reins left, guiding the horses down the narrow Berliner Street, eventually driving toward the docks and ocean steamers scheduled to sail west to Liverpool, then onward to America. The Colonel looked at his pocket watch, pleased Thomas was able to train with Maestro Moscheles for several hours. But time was of the essence. The Colonel had no minutes, no hours, no more days to waste. He had to get back to Georgia with Thomas and save the Bethune family empire. He sat back in his seat and lifted a wicker box to his lap. Sifting through mail, he found the gold-stringed envelope. He untied the missive for the second time and smiled. The note was the sole reason he had journeyed with the slave to Germany. He caressed each sentence with his hand while reading the testimonial:

"I, Ignaz Moscheles, uphold that which I know to be sound art and in Thomas Bethune I know of no parallel case in musical history. What God wants to express through melody or what a man's soul yearns to speak, this boy knows. He is marvelously talented by nature and I have pleasure in stating, he has the joviality of Haydn, Mozart's aria and Chopin's floridity."

The Colonel finished reading the testimonial and turned proudly toward Thomas. "Maestro Moscheles has written glowingly of you Tom," said the Colonel beaming.

"How does such praise from one of the world's great composers make you feel?" Thomas didn't answer. Preoccupied with the sound of the horses' hooves against the cobblestone, he made clopping noises and rocked back and forth in his seat. Of course he was simple, a mere boy incapable of grasping that his performance at the Great Hall was as valuable to his master as the gilded doors of a king's palace. But the Colonel knew it was done. Once the testimonials he'd received about Thomas from Moscheles and the other European luminaries in Germany appeared in the *Columbus Enquirer*, the Colonel knew many of the other distinguished American patrons of the arts would embrace the slave boy. Nodding to himself, the Colonel nestled back into his seat and re-read Moscheles' letter, savoring the experience like a cheroot smoked in leisure. He knew what was he would do upon his return to America.

VII.

Charity balanced a tray of sandwiches, lemonade, and cookies in the low-lit hallway. She vaguely heard the rushing footsteps behind her. She hadn't been still longer than a few seconds when Angela, one of the pretty quadroon girl's who lived in the attic, came up to her.

"Miss Charity, you better go an' see about your son," she said. She helped Charity balance the food on the tray and as she made her way toward the private servant's room, Charity was startled to hear her son's screams.

"Tom don't know Perry Oliver! Tom ain't goin'!"

Near the stairs that led to the second floor drawing room, Charity paused, and peered down the corridor. She wondered what had her boy so worked up. At the end of the hallway, she saw his teacher Miss Vivian pleading with him to open the door.

"Tom, please, we have to get you packed."

A queasy feeling swept over Charity's body. Packed?

"Lawd, no," she whispered and tears sprang to her eyes as she set down the tray, clutched her belly.

"Tom ain't going! Tom wants to play music with the birds."

"Tom, there are birds where you're going," said Vivian in a tone that indicated she was losing patience.

"Tom wants to play with Columbus birds! Green heron birds, Great blue heron birds! Red-headed Woodpecker birds! Columbus birds!"

The drawing room bell rang impatiently and Charity wiped her face, picked up the tray and hurried up the stairs. Her legs were heavy as she entered the drawing room where a light breeze blew the curtains from an open window and daylight streamed in. Charity set the tray of lemonade and cookies onto the table in front of the Colonel and his guest, Perry Oliver. The Colonel was busy counting bills and shiny coins from a mound of gold while his guest, the Irishman with the curly moustache and foreign accent talked.

"The man above has a sense of humor don't he?" Perry Oliver said. He wore an old ill-fitting brown suit and a matching feathered fedora. "A blind dumb darky genius. Yer gotta love it." He belched and let loose a rough, loud guffaw.

"Tom will take delight in going on a tour of the States," the Colonel said. He leaned back and crossed his legs. "He does love to play."

Charity's hands trembled as she poured lemonade into the crystal glasses, but neither man noticed her sudden dejection. Tour of the States? Her eyes began to brim with tears.

"We'll add some showmanship to his performances. Tricks the slave can do on the piana and what not. Give him a name..."

The Colonel stopped counting bills and glanced up. "A name?" he asked, eyebrows lifted.

"For promoting the shows and things of that nature."

The Colonel shifted. His entire body seemed to coil like a rattlesnake and he drained his brandy glass. "It seems to me Tom Bethune would suffice quite nicely," he said.

"Well, that's fine for him playing in the backyard an' at weekend parties for your friends an' all, Colonel. But for the big stage the nigger's gonna need something more catchy."

"Tom Bethune isn't catchy?"

"I'm a showman, Colonel, and a businessman," Perry Oliver said and crossed his legs. "A damn good one on account of me mother."

The stage name, he explained was essentially a matter of P.T. Barnum. The ultimate showman and master marketer had success attracting attention in major cities with acts dubbed General Tom Thumb and the Man-Monkey. "We've got to have something catchy for the slave to fill seats."

"Go on."

"We'll call the boy, Blind Tom," Perry continued, producing a flier with Thomas's image on the front. He handed it to the Colonel.

Charity cringed. *Blind Tom?* The stage name sounded low in her opinion. Her son's name was Thomas, not Tom. Blind Tom sounded like Uncle Tom, like her son was some kind of circus clown: Blind Tom. Charity hated the white man's stage moniker for her son.

"Marvelous Blind Tom, the untrained plantation Negro," the Colonel said reading the flier aloud. He puckered his lips in contemplation, made a noise indicating he was considering it, and then nodded, deciding the moniker worked.

"Blind Tom...Bethune of course," the Colonel added.

A glint formed in Perry Oliver's eyes. "Of course, Blind Tom Bethune. All the world will know he is your slave, Colonel."

He picked up his crystal glass of brown liquid off the table, nodded to the Colonel, and drank it in one swallow. Vivian, standing unnoticed in the wings, took advantage of the pause in the conversation to make her presence known.

"I'm sorry to interrupt, Colonel."

She didn't have to say another word. Her eyes told the story. The Colonel rose from his chair, excused himself and followed her out of the parlor. Charity refilled the white man Perry's glass with whiskey, picked up an empty serving tray, and quickly made her way out the drawing room behind the masters.

"Did you try giving him some fudge cake?" the Colonel asked as they walked. "That usually calms him."

"Yes, before he locked himself in," Vivian said. "Apparently he overheard a conversation between you and Mrs. Bethune. He knows you're not accompanying him on the tour and he's very upset," she said. The Colonel's brow lowered. "I've far too many business ventures to run traipsing around the South with Tom. It's impossible."

"I understand, sir. He locked himself in an hour ago, said he doesn't want to leave the birds."

As they walked down the stairs and into the servants' hallway, Charity trailed behind them and stopped near the servants' stairs. The Colonel made his way to the private servant's room at the end of the corridor and tapped the door with his cane.

"Tom it's me, I want you to open the door."

"No, suh, massuh! Tom wants Columbus birds."

"Tom, stop it now. Mr. Oliver is upstairs waiting for you. Now, open the door."

There was a loud bang and a thump, as Thomas began throwing items against the door.

"Tell Mr. Oliver Tom ain't going!"

"Of course you're going, Tom! You'll get to play the piano. You love to play the piano."

"Tom don't want to go!" He smacked the door with his hand. Charity stood transfixed. She had to prepare lunch, but she was terrified—she knew her son and when Thomas started yelling and crying, he thought he could get away with it, because white people didn't think he knew any better. But she saw the Colonel counting all that money and she knew not even he would stand to let a slave interfere with his pockets. "Lawd," she whispered.

"Dammit, Tom, listen to me!"

"Dammit, James listen to Tom!"

Charity gasped and Vivian turned away. Their eyes met, before Charity had a chance to avert hers. The Colonel jiggled the knob and banged on the wooden door.

"Tom, I made a deal with Mr. Oliver and I must honor my word!"

"Tom's staying to play with the Columbus birds!"

"*Mon Dieu, garçon,* you need to get your attitude right. You're acting like an imbecile! Like a complete idiot!"

"James," came Frances's gentle voice. "Why are you insulting him?"

It was rare, the mistress coming down to the servants' quarters, her bright ruffled dress in stark contrast to the drab walls. Charity backed further down the hall and around a corner, out of view.

"I heard your screaming and Tom's screaming through the vents in the *petit parlor.*" Her honeyed voice cut through the tension in the hallways.

"He won't come out of the damn room."

"It's not his fault," she offered calmly. "He doesn't understand what's going on."

The Colonel's eyes flashed. "Yet he understands enough to lock himself in the room?"

"He's probably very scared," she reasoned. "He's just a child. You know how sensitive the boy is. You didn't even talk to him about it."

"Talk to him?" the Colonel released a sound filled with frustration, "about business? My business, *ma bichette*?" He turned from her and spoke through the door. "Tom, if you don't cooperate, I'm having your piano taken away."

A loud thud shook the door. "Don't take Tom's piano away."

"Then open the door."

"No."

"Then, Tom! It will all go to hell!" the Colonel said. He stormed past his wife, down the hallway, past Charity, and disappeared around the corner. Charity's lip quivered, the master was upset unlike anything she'd ever seen.

"I assure you this is an anomaly. He's rarely sick, rarely at all," the Colonel was saying to Perry Oliver. Then offered rather unconvincingly, "Now, you must stay for dinner," as Ensa pulled opened the double front doors for him to exit. The Colonel glanced down at the satchel filled with bills and gold in the Irishman's hand. "I'm sure he'll feel better in a few days."

The Colonel managed a sorry smile.

Beyond the portico, the plantation bells started to ring. The chimes signaled to the field slaves that it was time to begin burning the cotton stalks to kill the boll weevil eggs. With a tip of his hat, Perry declined dinner and bid the Colonel *adieu*.

From the doors, he watched Perry enter his Landau. He made sure the vehicle had pulled away, waited patiently, as it got smaller and smaller, then vanished from sight. He turned and strode through the house, stormed out the back doors calling to all servants within earshot, "Bring Tom to me. One way or another, get that boy out of his room."

In the unseasonable heat, the Colonel peeled off his coat and threw it to the ground.

Auction will begin at the end of the term. Those words echoed over and over in the Colonel's thoughts. The slave going on tour was his only hope in a desperate, desperate situation.

"Bring him out! Bring him out now!" he barked at John, his lead overseer. He was manic in motion and shouted loud enough for everyone on the plantation to hear him. He stormed into the fields, under the blazing sun, snapping cotton stalks with his long determined stride.

"What are you doing, James?" Frances raced behind him, kept pace - stride for stride - unimpeded by her rounded belly, she tugged at his sleeve, her Victorian bustle dress swooshing about. But slowing him down was like trying to stop a raging bull mid-charge.

He blocked her attempts with one swipe, "This doesn't concern you, Frances!" he snarled.

An old man stopped shucking corn, a mother stopped nursing, wood-chopping slaves stopped chopping, field slaves stopped picking and stacking, the children stopped separating seeds, and a mammoth slave pounding iron against an anvil in the shed, stopped mid-swing. It seemed even the bells, ringing miles away, stopped ringing.

"James, what are you doing?" Frances asked. The panic in her voice suggested she had a clear understanding of his intentions. He blocked her attempts with one swipe, "This doesn't concern you, Frances!" he snarled.

Tom plays with Columbus birds. "That idiot slave!" He mumbled. Thomas had angered him like never before. His wife and her expensive needs angered him. The bank angered him, it all raged in his mind. His jaw tensed and his lips tightened. The thought of anyone owning even the smallest piece of his family property: it sickened him and he felt queasy. He would take a torch and burn it all to the ground, piece by piece, *Solitude, Elway,* all of it, before he sold one bit.

"I want him out here, now!" he barked and pointed at the whipping post.

Frances was absolutely frantic. Her breaths came short and shallow; she desperately tried to keep up with him, her movements fast and frenetic.

"This isn't your way," she pleaded, raising her hands.

The Colonel marched forward, blinded by untamable rage.

"I will not tolerate his insubordination," he said, as if he were talking about anyone other than the simpleminded slave.

"He doesn't know any better!" Frances shrieked.

He stopped, and turned to her. "Fifty-thousand dollars, Frances! Do you want me to beg like a pauper to our friends to keep a roof over our heads?"

He rolled up his sleeves and in the distance saw the backdoor of the Big House and Thomas being dragged out.

"But James...When has money ever been an issue..." Beside herself, Frances stuttered and the Colonel watched as his wife tried to digest his meaning. She shook her head and her brow furrowed, but when that sweet deliberate innocence formed on her face, he lost it. "What more could we need..."

"Wake up, Frances!" the Colonel barked, "If the slave doesn't go on tour there will be no *Solitude* no *Elway.* The bank will take everything." He stopped, the Big House more than a half a mile away, the whipping post within sight.

Stunned, her words barely a whisper, "How did this happen?"

"I refuse to let all that I've built crumble to protect a peevish slave."

He continued toward the whipping post and ignored her inquiry.

Charity had come down from the house and now watched from the porch of a slave cottage as the overseer prepared the bullwhip. Paralyzed with fear, she stood frozen, but for the rag she wrung with her hands.

Satise, a little bit of a slave with charcoal skin and long thick hair, stopped making lye water for the new soap and made her way over to the porch. Hand on her arm, she tried to get Charity back into the kitchen, but Charity twisted out of her grasp, her eyes fixed on her son.

Clarence, Barry, Sherry, Theron, Daria, Anita and a bunch of field hands, shadows against the sun, gathered on the horizon. Charity couldn't make out their faces, but she knew they were her children.

"Lawd," she said, snapping out of her trance. She dropped her rag and ran down the steps of the porch, across the grass and through the garden. She intercepted her oldest child, the muscular, copper-skinned boy named Clarence.

"Go back, go back!" she yelled, screaming and crying and pushing and shoving. She forced her eldest boy to turn around and made him and the others head back to the fields. And they turned away but for Anita who cried and pressed to intervene. Anita pushed toward the whipping post, defiantly, until the hand came across her face with a loud pop, as Charity smacked her and screamed for her to stop before she got herself lashed to death. Sobbing, Anita turned away and went with the others.

"Lawd, please, Lawd, spare my baby," Charity prayed as she ran back toward the whipping post. She trembled and sobbed as she watched her blind son being tied to the post. The master knew the boy's ways, knew he was special. Why? Charity wondered. She wanted to scream at the master and rip her son away from that pole, but terror kept her from opening her mouth, from lifting any muscles. On Wiley Jones' plantation, she'd seen slaves severely beaten with bricks soaked in gun powder, their legs snapped in two, even killed for daring to get in the middle of a white man's punishment, so she didn't make a move, but stood perfectly still and said a private prayer. Charity stared as Thomas's wrists were bound with leather straps, the school bell ringing in the distance. She felt Malver's hand on her waist, Germaine's hand on her shoulders, but the eyes of her spirit were on God, begging him to intervene and touch the master's heart.

"Papa! Don't do it, papa!" Sarah screamed. John and Sarah ran through the fields to their father.

The Colonel's mind was set. "Get him in place," he commanded.

"Father, please," John and Sarah, begged in heavy breaths. Faces covered in sweat. Tears streaming.

Thomas's innocent voice pierced the veil of anger.

"Master Colonel. The big clock's gonna ring in twenty-seconds," the blind boy said, unaware of the desperate nature of his situation. He giggled as his suspenders were dropped off his tiny shoulders.

"Look at him, father," Sarah screamed. "He doesn't even understand what you're doing."

John glared at his father. He gritted his teeth and his nostrils flared.

"Father, no."

The Colonel stood rigid, in part from determination in part from pride. He was the patriarch of the entire plantation, over the slaves and his family, yet now his own flesh and blood was in stark opposition of his will.

Frances stepped close to him and spoke softly. "He worships you, James. If you do this, he'll never trust you again."

"Master Colonel's mad at Tom," Thomas said from the post. "Master's gray white. Tom'll make master blue. Tom'll sing," Thomas said innocently, and started singing a drinking song he knew in German that his master liked. Everyone, slaves included, looked around, uneasy, and more tears were shed.

"You can't do this." John had tears in his eyes. He was overseer for God's sake.

The Colonel lowered his head.

"Release him," he gestured toward John.

Without making eye contact with anyone, the Colonel walked back toward the Big House. He headed straight for the cellar, where the whiskey and rum were stored.

VIII.

A bugle's wail rippled across the cotton fields. The chorus of slaves singing, the bang of hammers, and roosters crowing all indicated morning. Yet, the curtains were drawn in the Colonel's den, and he was slumped over his desk, empty bottles littered the hardwood floor. Several days had passed since the whipping post and finally the persistent knocking at the door had stopped. Still, Frances's whisper rang in his head, "He worships you, James," and through the break in the thick French doors he'd heard different voices fading in and out.

The worst feelings came when he heard Thomas's tiny plea, "Master Colonel, please," as he hit his head, pounded his fists, pulled on the handle and called out. Charity had tried to peel the boy away, but he'd kicked-and-screamed and held onto the doorknob. The little slave boy sat outside the den's door hoping the door would open, weeping himself to sleep. Each sob brought another tip of rich wine or sweet whiskey, as the Colonel sank deeper into self-condemnation. How the boy could miss him after what he'd done, his stomach knotted.

Now, his wife's sweet voice pierced his haze. "James." Though the liquor had made his body numb, he felt the warmth of her soft hands as she peeled his fingers off the mouth of the glass and set it on a table out of reach.

The Colonel was so clouded in his consciousness, his vision so blurred, he hadn't noticed the turn of the knob, hadn't noticed her standing quietly by the door studying him. Now, she swirled her hair up into a bun and pinned it in place. She looked lovely in her summer dress of white cotton tapered at the waist.

She pulled open the drapes to the east window, flooding the den with afternoon light. "You've been in this room long enough," she said tenderly. "It's time to stop punishing yourself, *mon cher.*"

She looked him over from his hair, tangled and greasy, to his feet, covered in soot. He knew he was a mess and from the scrunch of Frances's nose, gathered that he smelled. She told him in a firm, but loving manner, "It's time for a bath, *mon cher*, a shave, and to get you dressed. You will join us in the parlor." She prompted him up with the back of her hand on his shoulder, walked him out of the room toward the bath, where the water had already been heated over a fire and poured into a cast iron tub.

Later, when the Colonel arrived in the warm glow of the parlor, the piano music trailed off and the singing stopped. He cleared his throat and crossed the black and white marble floor. The Colonel felt like Quasimodo in *The Hunchback* as John eyed him warily. Nevertheless, he steeled himself against the knot forming in his stomach, determined to restore merriment back to the home and reestablish normalcy. He stood to his full height and spoke in a light tone.

"Where is our wonderful Tom?" He said, while lighting a stogie, trying to muster as much nonchalance as he could. His children met his buoyant query with tense, stony silence. Color rose in his face as he looked around the room at his solemn family, arms crossed, lips in pouts. His children didn't respond to the familiar question, heads averted, stubbornly intent on not playing along. From behind the plush curtains came a recognizable snicker—Thomas was in his usual hiding spot, his ashen toes peeking out from beneath the fabric.

The slave's joy both encouraged and shamed him.

"Our delightful Tom should play for us, tonight," said the Colonel, face flushed.

Sarah stepped up to break the ranks of resistance, "I think our wonderful Tom has left us, Father, and I'm afraid he's taken his wonderful music with him," she said.

"We can't possibly have our evening entertainment without him," the Colonel chimed with a relieved smile. "Tom is the best pianist in the universe."

Thomas began to shake with laughter, ecstatic to hear blue, to hear the warm welcoming timbers of his master's voice. The Colonel's vibrations shone behind Thomas's eyelids in cobalt and indigo, bright inviting rays amid all the purple in the room. He bounded out from behind the curtains, sweet and happy, unperturbed by the whipping post; his innocent giggles lighting the mood of everyone in the room. The Colonel stepped in close behind Frances. He wrapped his arms around her, and took in the sweet mingling of perfume and perspiration on her neck as Thomas took his place at the piano.

He placed his tiny fingers into proper position, but before he struck any keys, he aimed his face toward his owner. "This here song is for Master Colonel, so he kin get his attitude right."

The Colonel smiled and the parlor filled with laughter.

In the empty kitchen Thomas sat at the table, humming, as the Colonel cut a slice of chocolate cake, put it on a saucer, and placed it in front of him. Thomas sniffed the dessert, a habit he'd begun around the age of three, then picked up the sweet treat with both hands. The Colonel tied a napkin around Thomas's neck then took a chair beside him.

"Tom," he started, his voice soft with shame. "What happened the other day, it will never happen again. Never..." He paused and searched for the right words. "I will never lay a hand on you and I will never allow anyone to lay a hand on you."

"Mass'll get 'em," Thomas said without looking up.

"Yes, I will. It's just..." he paused at the racket Thomas was making, rocking in his chair. Thomas took pleasure in the sound of wooden legs hitting against the brick floor. "Tom, please listen," the Colonel continued. "You need to understand. We'll lose everything, Tom, the piano will go, there won't be any chocolate cake for you in this kitchen. You and your family, *Solitude*, all will be sold away, if you don't go on this tour with Perry Oliver. I have faith you will go with him and be great Tom."

"Massuh has faith Tom will go on tour with Perry Oliver and be great."

"Yes, that's exactly right Tom. I have faith you'll go on tour and be great."

"Faith is the substance of things hoped for," Thomas said, chewing on his cake, "the evidence of things not yet seen."

"Yes, that's right, Tom. Yes." The Colonel's eyes brightened; he regretted manipulating the simple-minded Tom, but was relieved he seemed to understand he had to go.

"But Tom only plays with Columbus birds! Red-headed Woodpecker birds, Green Heron birds, Blue Jay birds. Columbus birds!"

The Colonel's lips tightened and he sighed.

One week and one Columbus bird later, Vivian carried the wire birdcage toward the carriage. The Red-headed Woodpecker sat patiently in the cage waiting for her to feed him. Stride for stride beside the music teacher walked a fragile Irish girl named Annie that the Colonel had hired. Not more than fifteen, with old rags for clothes, she had hair that looked like it could use a good brushing. It was Annie's job to bathe the prodigy, clothe him, brush his teeth, and monitor his behavior while on tour. Vivian would only serve as his piano teacher.

From the terrace, Frances with the children watched Thomas load into the carriage. On the side of the coach, embossed in gold, read: "PERRY OLIVER'S TRAVELLING TROUPE." Frances turned toward the mansion's front door, expecting the Colonel to join the family, but he was nowhere in sight. She glanced back at the promoter's carriage, without a look at young Sarah who was at her shoulder. She spun around and went inside the house, lifted her layered skirt, and hurried up the staircase to the second floor.

She made her way down the corridor to the study and knocked at the door before turning the knob to peek in. The Colonel was at his desk, going over paperwork. "Sorry to interrupt," she said, looking at her husband. "Darling, are you going to come and see Tom off?"

"I can't see everybody off, every time somebody decides to go and leave," he said without looking up. He let the folder he was holding drop with a thud onto the desk.

She studied him a moment–his eyes downcast, his tone sharp–and quietly retreated. She knew what that set jaw really meant. He had a special bond with the boy and didn't want to see Thomas go. Meanwhile, Charity stood by the shed wilting in the sun like a wearied plant. Tears dried on her face in the hot autumn air as she worked to pump water into a bucket, but the pump felt as heavy as a pile of hay. While her other children were working in the harsh fields picking cotton and dropping seeds behind the oxen, each Bethune child stepped forward and gave Thomas a hug before he was led to the coach.

Earlier before dusk, before the masters had come down, Charity had dressed Thomas and held him tight. When his teacher arrived, he hadn't needed to be pried away. Charity was sure he didn't understand what was happening. His attention was focused on the woodpecker, captivated by the caged bird's drumming.

Now, Charity held the water pump lever in one hand and grabbed her stomach with the other; she felt the worse kind of hurt in her gut. She'd cooked a goodbye dinner for Thomas the previous night and packed weeks of his favorite foods–pickled vegetables, butter-less cake, bread, and bacon–into a large basket. After a backbreaking day of serving, she'd walked barefoot with Thomas a half mile down the tree-thick path to the family's one-room hut in the slave quarters for a goodbye dinner. Thomas was held by one hand, and she carried warm cake, bacon, and some extra potatoes in a separate basket for the informal farewell. A fire was lit in the hearth and piles of hay and cotton sacks were used for chairs. Charity had spread out the meal she'd cooked on a small table and Thomas's brothers and sisters wrapped their thorn scratched hands and calloused fingers around his tiny waist. No one mentioned what was happening. They didn't know quite what to do with Thomas, dressed as he was in fine, white-folk hand-me-downs, with smooth hands and shoes on his feet. So they danced with him and feigned a celebration.

Charity cried by the hearthstone that night and shook with grief. Her mind was paralyzed with thoughts of what would happen to her son once he was out of her care. To the master, Thomas was no better than any other piece of property for them to do with as they pleased, and there was nothing she could do to protect him.

"God works in mysterious ways," Mingo reassured her by the fire, "Now don't you cry…" he said as he walked her back to the Big House with their son on his shoulders that night.

"God works inside Tom, mama, now don't you cry," Thomas said, leaning left and right on his father's shoulders, so Mingo had to hold him tight. Charity smiled and wiped her tears.

Now, she watched as Perry Oliver's carriage began to move. She squinted into the sun. No one had bothered to offer her the last goodbye to her son, nor any details regarding where he was going, or how long he'd be gone. But she'd overheard little master John say Thomas was bound to the show-business man for one year, to perform across the southern states, and then some.

The carriage pulled away, the clatter and squeak of wheels, the slap of leather. Charity dropped the water pump lever at once, ran through the grass and across dirt, alongside the carriage until her legs tired, fearing she would never see or hear from her son again. Tears drenched her face and her head shook back and forth with despair. Living with the unknown was the worst kind of slavery, worse than physical bondage itself. As far as Charity knew, that was the last time she'd ever see her son again.

Up at the Big House, from inside his study, the Colonel let the curtains fall, once the coach disappeared into the distance.

IX.

"Where's Master Colonel?" came the question from Thomas, days later, as the turtleheads brushed up against the carriage windows. The vehicle rocked. Vivian steadied herself, grabbing onto the side of her seat. Her temple was throbbing. It seemed like every second on the minute the talented prodigy was asking for the Colonel. Although she was familiar with his quirks after the Germany trip, Vivian was at her wits' end, sore from the bumpy ride and exhausted by the slave's incessant behavior. They hadn't yet travelled one hundred miles and Thomas was still asking the same question he had asked when they pulled away from *Solitude*.

It seemed he was seized by a dawning dread that his master had abandoned him and Vivian nor the teenager Annie, knew what to do.

"Where's Master Colonel?"

"Tom - "

"Where's Master Colonel?"

"Tom, I told-"

"Miss Vivian, where's Master Colonel?"

"Tom, I told you - "

"Master's back at *Solitude*," he said cutting her off. "Why's master not with Tom?"

Vivian sighed. The forest of weeds was so tall and thick the only thing she could see on either side was a sea of brown and green stems with whitish-pink flowers. She decided to ignore Thomas, as he was not only missing his master, but it seemed he simply enjoyed hearing his own voice.

Finally bored of asking the same question, Thomas started mimicking carriage noises. Vivian reminded herself to cut small pieces of cloth to stick in her ears for the rest of the tour. She shifted her body and lost herself in the fantasies of *The*

Golden Christmas, a *Romeo and Juliet* inspired love story set on a Charleston plantation.

Annie sat next to her and hummed while knitting a shawl. Without warning, she began a sprightly little ditty. The young lady was clearly tone-deaf. Vivian looked up from her novel, resisting the urge to cover her ears. Annie carried on, singing every note off-key. Until Thomas stopped making wagon sounds and turned his face to his attendant.

"Hush up, Miss Annie. You oughtta be ashamed making such a horrible noise. Tom would rather listen to the wheels turn."

Annie sucked in air. She crossed her arms and looked over at Vivian expecting her to intervene, but Vivian held back a giggle and went back to reading.

After a few days journey, the carriage finally connected with a large caravan of coaches, cloth-topped wagons, and open-topped carts carrying show animals belonging to Perry Oliver. The enormous troupe of elephants, juggling monkeys, and sideshow acts, was scheduled to perform a "one night stand" in the big city of Atlanta and was a half-day's journey away.

That night, the tour set up camp at a remote inn in the middle of nowhere, just outside the city limits.

Perry put his wallet back in his coat pocket. While the rest of the troupe made camp off the trail in the woods, he'd purchased a nice room for himself and one for Blind Tom under his teacher's name. At the end of the hallway, Vivian and Annie smuggled the Negro boy into the room.

Tired from travel, Perry Oliver laid on his bed to sleep. Above the drunken laughter and bursts of song outside near the tour wagons, there was noisy confusion inside the rooms next door. Thomas was in the midst of an earsplitting tantrum. Through the thin walls he could hear the slave boy stomping about, crying over and over, "Where's Master Colonel?" Perry lifted his head to listen. The slave seemed to be tossing furniture around in the room and did not want his attendant to come near him. His attendant apparently had attempted to clean and clip his fingernails and accidentally cut him. "Master Colonel, she's botherin' Tom!" he screamed from the top of his lungs.

Perry rolled out of his bed and hurried to the adjoining room in his bare feet.

"What in tarnation is goin' on in here?"

Annie had a look of defeat on her homely face. "It's all right, Mr. Oliver. He just needs to get used to me is all."

"It sure as hell doesn't sound all right."

"Give us a bit of time." Vivian took over, kneeled beside Tom, and grabbed hold of him. "Tom, the Colonel's at *Solitude*. Remember I told you? Annie's here to help you and you have to let her help." She set an oil lamp on a table next to several candles. "The Colonel is expecting a letter from me telling him how well you're behaving."

Thomas struggled out of her hold and resumed pushing the bed across the room. "The bed's s'pposed to be against the window."

Perry Oliver watched, incredulous. "He's not supposed to be here. You've got to shut 'im up."

"We're trying, sir." Vivian turned back to Thomas. "It's going to be okay, Tom. I have a surprise for you." She dug into a large suitcase. "I've got the harmonicas the Colonel bought for you, Tom." She opened the leather box with six different harmonicas.

Thomas reached out his hand. "Miss Vivian has my harmonicas from Master Colonel," he said with a sudden smile. She removed one harmonica and placed it against Thomas's chest. Thomas calmed down at once and began to play. Perry lifted his eyebrows and Vivian shrugged.

"Master Colonel," Thomas called out, lowering the harmonica. "Come listen to Tom. 'A quite lovely rendition of Brahms, Tom.'" He mimicked the Colonel's deep voice.

A confused look crossed Perry's face. He asked, "Why's he doing that? He possessed like they say?"

"No, he's not possessed sir," said Vivian. "He's missing his master."

"The bed's s'pposed to be opposite the window," Thomas complained.

"Put that bed back where it was," Perry insisted.

"He needs things where he wants them, sir. Tom's picky about how things feel and smell and such. "

"I don't care what he likes," Perry said, "shut him up."

Persistent, Vivian continued. "It's important for you to know how he is. Right now, he's missing his master and doesn't know how to manage his feelings. Controlling his environment is one way to control his feelings," she said, "he has very specific ways, like Tom won't play on Sundays, the Colonel told you that I'm sure. And he needs his piano here, Mr. Oliver. He needs to play his piano before he can sleep. Is someone unloading it?"

"Unloading a piana? Most ridiculous drivel I ever damn heard," said Perry. "My men are off the clock now. He should be sleepin'. You should be too. Now keep that boy quiet."

"But he must have his piano," the music teacher stepped toward him, insisting. "The boy plays at least twenty songs before he'll even consider sleep. Often nighttime is when I transcribe his compositions."

He put his hands on his hips and stretched himself to his most threatening height. "There ain't no way on this side a hell I'm gonna have my men unload a piana for no darky for one night."

He shut the door and started to walk back to his room. No sooner had he taken a few steps than he heard screams and crashing of objects against the wall. He turned back around and stormed in. "Make 'im shut up!" he demanded in a low voice, ears covered by his hands, absolutely vexed. "He's gonna get us tossed out!" He spat out through closed teeth.

"I'm afraid I can't do anything, Mr. Oliver," Vivian said, only taking a brief moment to look up before returning to her favorite book. "He won't quiet down, until he has his piano."

Annie stood in a corner with her hand to her mouth.

"Tom, you hush now."

To that, Thomas started screaming.

Thick with frustration Perry relented and pointed at Annie. "For the love of God, fetch a couple o' stage hands an' git that boyo his piana!"

The music teacher looked up from her book, as Perry stormed out, and sighed.

"Master Perry's fifty-nine."

Vivian looked at him with a puzzled expression. "What is fifty-nine, Tom?"

"Fifty-nine's an ugly number," he explained.

Vivian's brow furrowed. It was a bad sign.

X.

Hail was drumming down the slanted roof of Atlanta's main performance hall like stones in an avalanche. The onslaught of frozen rain created the potential threat of postponing the concert as there was a question surrounding the turnout. But dozens of the city's most notable families stood in line to purchase tickets despite the horrible weather, and the show was sold out.

Inside the swarming dressing area, dozens of stagehands and performers prepared for the show. Annie stood in the center of the fray holding a new frock coat, trailing Thomas as he paced back and forth in an agitated state. Annie begged him to stand still, so she could finish getting him dressed for the show.

"Tom won't wear it," Thomas protested.

Thomas angled his ear toward the high ceiling. Above the twang of banjos onstage and the yellow sound of Annie trying to talk to him, sleet slammed against the roof's wood shingles and he liked its rhythmic thrum.

"Listen, do you hear that, Miss Annie?" he said with a clap of his hands, as he paced near the back of the stage, just out the way of the jugglers. He stretched his right hand to the wall and weaved a crooked path past mimes and dancers. He dragged his hand across the thick velvet of the stage curtains. "Where's Master Colonel?" he mumbled as he made a shucking sound with his boots against the floor.

"Mr. Tom," came Annie's voice. The yellow tones of her voice bounced up and down and Thomas liked the way they skipped in pirouettes behind his lids.

"Where's Master Colonel?" he asked again, brushing past other performers, then made a sharp turnabout.

"Mr. Tom, I been tellin' ya…"

"Tom, the Colonel's back at *Solitude*," he cut her off. He twisted his body out of her reach because he refused to put on the new frock she wanted him to wear.

"Miss Annie, where is Tom?" he said from a dark corner.

"We's in Atlanta at the concert hall, Mr. Tom. You need ta stand still, please," she begged.

"Tom needs ta stand still."

"Yes, Mr. Tom. There's an awful lot of people here to see ya. I need ta git you dressed for the show."

"Tom's not playing the piano today," he said, moving away from her reach.

"But you have ta perform today, Mr. Tom," she said, her voice turned more and more yellow. "Everyone's performin' and you, you're makin' your big debut in Atlanta."

"Tom ain't makin' a debut in Atlanta. Today's the Sabbath. God said keep it holy. Exodus thirty-one seventeen, 'it is a sign between me and the children of Israel'," he said.

"Mr. Tom, Mr. Oliver's makin' his way over. Please let me put your jacket on."

"Why isn't he dressed?" came Perry Oliver's voice in a sharp tone.

"Master Oliver's purple fifty-nine," Thomas said and moved away. He paced back and forth. He felt a rush of tension. There was a purple cloud swelling up behind his lids.

"I been tryin' to get him ready, but he says he ain't going on stage," Annie said.

"What exactly do ya mean?"

"On account it's the Sabbath," she said.

"How does he know it's the Sabbath? Did you tell him?" Perry asked.

"No, sir. He knows the days, automatic," Annie said.

"Tom, put on your coat," Perry demanded.

"Ezekiel twenty-twenty," Thomas muttered, "'And hallow my sabbaths,' that's what it says fifty-nine." He had managed to step out of his ankle boots and was walking in his socks.

"We have a sold out crowd, most waiting to see the nigger musician. Where in heavens' name is his teacher?" Perry asked.

"She went ta get Tom some special cake," Annie said. "Mr. Bethune gives him fudge or corn cake before he goes on stage."

"I see," Perry said, spying the slave boy's growing mid-section. "That explains his expanding girth. Fine, the boyo wants cake. He'll get cake."

He marched toward a table crowded with congratulatory flowers and baked foods for the performers. He spotted cake, cut a slice, and returned to offer the dessert to Thomas. "I got cake," he said. "Tom, here's some chocolate cake. Come boy, eat."

There was a swirling purple cloud stirring up behind Thomas's lids, the imagery disturbed the slave. Perry Oliver, as a purple hue, was not inviting. He was cold and unattractive like his accent that floated in the ocean of the musician's thoughts as a menacing, destructive iceberg.

Meanwhile, the concert hall was packed together like buildings on the streets of Prague. The audience was abuzz with anticipation, as grandly dressed patrons endured Perry's many novelty acts while awaiting the performance of the blind slave prodigy.

Mike the Midget waddled by Perry in a cowboy hat and spurs. "About ten minutes for the nigger, Boss," he said.

Perry let out a loud groan. "Jiminy creakers. Get that black monkey on stage!"

"Shhhh! He understands you perfectly well, you know," Vivian said, arriving with cake in hand   .

Perry nodded, turning his attention back to Thomas. "Here's some cake, boyo. Come on. Eat up so you can play the piana."

Thomas walked over, took the cake plate out of Perry's hands, and took a big sniff and a bite. Tasting butter, he sent the saucer crashing into a wall. "Tom hates it!"

Perry flinched as the dish shattered into pieces, his initial shock disintegrated into a sudden swell of anger. But before he could speak, Vivian spoke, as Thomas was screaming.

"Why'd you do that?"

"She said the boyo liked cake," Perry said, looking at Annie. "I give the piss-ant bugger cake!" he said in a raised voice, trying to speak above Thomas who was still squelching.

"Make him shut up," Perry shouted.

"It's too late. He hates butter," Vivian said. "We packed butter-less cake."

Perry Oliver threw his hands up. "I don't give a flying fig. I want that spoiled slave boy on that stage. Give him the cake for Christsakes!"

With his mouth full of sweet chocolate cake Thomas mumbled, "God said keep it holy. Tom can't play." He spat the cake out.

Perry took out his pocket watch. "You've got three minutes to get him on stage."

"Mr. Oliver," she started. "You moved the performance date. I warned you about Sunday..."

Perry leaned toward her, his face red. "He's a slave! He'll play whenever I say he'll play!" He glanced at Thomas who was standing with his arms crossed. "What he needs is a good whupping," he said with resolve. He took a step toward the slave and Thomas yelped at the top of his lungs. Vivian stepped in between Thomas and Perry. She raised her hands against Perry's chest.

"Since time is of the essence, perhaps you should try complimenting him."

"He's a nigger for godssakes! A blind retarded nigger. You've indulged the boy. He's spoiled, I tell ya!" Perry was fed up. He lifted the boy and carried him kicking and screeching.

Perry stopped and dropped the boy. "I should whip the little bugger. *Cad e seo*! He's ornery. He's obstinate..."

"I'm afraid there's nothing we can do to make him play," said Vivian turning to Thomas. "Tom apologize, right now."

"*Cad e seo!* No, Miss Vivian. Tom don't like fifty-nine, Tom won't play!" he said and trotted away.

Perry stood with his mouth open and rolled his eyes. He started to say more, but shook his head. He spotted Mike the Midget sauntering back in and waved him off. "Get Franscesca back on stage," he called, "now. Right now!" His eyes bore into Vivian. "Whatever happens now, it will be that nigger's fault...."

From her reaction, Perry knew the music teacher was aware of Atlanta's reputation. This was a very serious and dangerous situation. Atlantians, even the most refined, could be a rough and tumble bunch. The *Southern Confederacy* newspaper was rife with tales of events that ended in gunfights and duals.

On the stage, Mike the Midget stepped out to address the sold out audience, an audience who'd come to see the blind slave-boy prodigy. He wrung his hands, mustered up his courage, and announced Francesca Panini for an encore. The crowd began to murmur at once and within minutes a scattering of boos could be heard. A general restlessness brewed as audience members realized the Negro prodigy Blind Tom was not performing. All of a sudden, a man rose, full of beer, and yelled out.

"Where's the blind nigger genius?"

"Yes, we came to see Blind Tom!" came a woman's high voice.

"Where is the nigger prodigy?"

The mood in the makeshift concert hall quickly began to sour and the murmurs grew louder.

"Blind Tom isn't performing?"

Balled up fliers began sailing toward the stage. Then the sophisticates began throwing anything on their person; quills, used makeup cases, empty tobacco boxes, and crumpled concert programs. "I want my money back!" Men in their best coats stood to their feet, gloves pointing at the stage, their murmurs becoming crescendoed shouts. "Blind Tom! Where is the Negro genius?"

From behind the curtain, Perry watched seventeen hundred patrons rise up in a rage. Chairs were tossed into the orchestra pit, bottles thrown at the stage. The concert hall fell into chaos. Ladies gathered up their bustle dresses and frantically pushed their way toward the exits.

Perry screamed above the fray and ordered all the performers to their wagons with instructions to head for the next town. He scanned the busy room and saw Vivian slip out through the back door with Thomas. He weaved his way through panicked performers and show hands lugging props. Outside the crowded concert grounds, he caught sight of the teacher with Annie–the women moved swiftly through the shadows, holding Thomas's hands on each side, and hoisted him up the stairs and quickly into a waiting carriage. Once the pianist was safely inside and the doors securely shut, the horses galloped off, disappearing into the darkness.

XI.

Perry heard a faint sound of piano music beyond his hotel door. The Stonehurst Inn was a secluded two-story lodge located inside a thick of trees seven miles safely outside of Atlanta. He groaned, tossed and turned in the thin blankets, exhausted from nightmarish images of the concert hall brawl. He'd barely made it out with his entertainers and stagehands alive and the idiot slave was playing like Beethoven in the next room!

He felt a sickening pain in the gut and his head pounded; the pulses so severe he couldn't sleep one more wink. He reached to the floor beside his bed and located his flask of brandy, then closed his eyes and let the liquid relax his mind. It had been a complete catastrophe: the patrons screamed for refunds and the mayor demanded payment for the ruined concert hall–all told about four-thousand-dollars! His head throbbed. He was already out a fortune just renting Tom!

In the dimness of the room, he reflected. From a business perspective there was a bright side: the shows had been sold out. He knew without a doubt a lot of money could be made from the retarded Negro-if the slave would actually perform.

A lingering aroma of burnt candles hung in the atmosphere. Perry leaned back against the pillow. It was an amazing sight to see ticket lines stretched for blocks-*if only the darkie would play.* To make matters worse, he couldn't motivate the slave boy. If he stepped anywhere near the slave, the boy would throw a tantrum, screaming at the top of his lungs, "Him wants to beat Tom! Tom, don't like him, Tom don't like fifty-nine!" The slave's words echoed in his mind.

"Fifty-nine," Perry muttered, "what the hell is fifty-nine?"

Though his head was raw and he wanted to go back to sleep, the tinkling of piano keys filled his hotel room. It was three o'clock in the morning, and Perry dragged down the hall to the last door where Thomas was playing the piano. As he approached, he heard Vivian talking to the slave.

"Go back, Tom," she said, "and play it again and explain it to me."

Perry opened the door without notice and saw the music teacher sitting at a small table transcribing on lithograph paper. Annie was in one of the beds, apparently asleep, and Thomas was on a chair at his upright piano. The curtains were open and a full moon shone bright through raindrops on the windows.

"Tom played a sixteenth note. Triplet begins in A minor."

"It's a beautiful song, Tom."

"The moon looks like this through the rain, Miss Vivian. Tom calls it *Water in the Moonlight*."

"From what I described of the moon through the wet window?"

He nodded, his round head topped with what looked like beaded wool. "Tom calls it *Water in the Moonlight*," he said again, strumming the piece. "*Types de tonalités*. Tom sees pretty blues and *circle of fifths*. A rhapsody carried by light blue brown winds, Miss Vivian."

Vivian smiled and adjusted the music so she could transcribe the next few bars. "You explain your music in such beautiful terms, Tom." The music was warm and melodic. Perry stood quietly, hesitant to interrupt the moment, sensing the slave's soul was in a place where time and space didn't exist.

"It's three in the mornin', does the boyo ever sleep?" he finally asked.

"Sometimes," Vivian said before returning to her page. "When he's inspired, he can stay up all night." Perry nodded and looked over at Thomas.

"He's fifty-nine," Thomas said with a frown. His fingers came to a sudden stop. "Master Perry's fifty-nine. Fifty-nine's an ugly number," he explained.

That number again. What did it mean? Perry knew the boy didn't like him, but his odd expressions. He sighed and motioned for Vivian to step into the dark hallway.

"He looks ill. Is he eating?"

She shook her head. "I'm surprised he's even playing. He hasn't had a bite of anything since yesterday morning."

"It don't matter that the boyo don't like me, but the boyo's gotta eat."

"I'm afraid, he's making himself sick, sir."

Returning to his room, a powerful realization took hold of Perry, as he sat on the edge of his bed. The spoiled slave was never going to play one note for him. He missed his master. A tremor passed through Perry's body. He had a lot of gold riding on Blind Tom and he had to do something, the only thing within his power, to get the slave to play. As the date for the next set of shows drew near, he could not promote "Blind Tom" on the ticket if the spoiled slave was never going to play for him. He padded over to a small desk and lit the porcelain oil lamp. Beneath the light's faint flicker, he began writing an earnest letter to the Colonel.

Dear Colonel Bethune,

It is from dire straits I write you. I am asking you to join the tour, as Tom is not good. The Negro is difficult. He screams without stopping, calls out your name, will scarce take a bite of food. The tour has been a catastrophe, already. He refuses to play, his first show resulting in a riot and great loss of money. The boyo's spoiled rotten and in need of the lashing. I'm at my wits' end on what to do. If the idiot slave doesn't play, he's as useful to me as tits on a bull. Please come with haste and meet us at our next stop in Charlotte or I will be forced to require a full refund, in gold, and then some for damages and so forth.

Perry Oliver

It was mid-evening when Perry Oliver picked up the letter that had been waiting for him at the Charlotte post office. He opened it and saw it was from the Colonel:

Dear Mr. Oliver,

I am in receipt of your letter. I am coming immediately to North Carolina. Do not lay hands on Tom. He is too simple of mind to understand the severity of consequences for his actions. And perhaps I have indulged him a bit too much. I implore you, honor my wishes and refrain from any physicalities with him.

Colonel James N. Bethune

He let out a sigh, as Blind Tom was not improving and it seemed the boy's health was declining each day. He was relieved the Colonel had written and was willing to rectify the matter, personally.

XII.

Two weeks later, there was ice on the ground outside the small Charlotte hotel, but the sun was shining inside Thomas's room through the open curtains. Annie placed a bowl of chestnut soup on a tray for the ailing slave who was sitting up in a tiny bed, but he weakly shook his head at the broth and pushed the chunky liquid away.

Soft light from the window fell on Thomas's cheek and mingled with the pink tones of Vivian's voice. It was a chilly winter afternoon, despite the sun. Thomas was on his back beneath two layers of sheets and three thin covers, a hot water bottle on his chest. He slipped his long fingers from beneath the blankets and raised them toward his face, then turned his head.

He heard water as his teacher dipped her hands into a bowl and a trickle of drops when she squeezed the rag, then felt the comfort of it as she laid the cloth on his forehead.

Thomas had been in the small bed the entire time they'd been in Charlotte. His empty stomach groaned, but he refused to eat. Not even the smell of chestnut soup could get him to part his lips. Though his stomach grumbled louder with each passing second, he shifted his hips and moaned.

"Tom's gonna catch stroke and die," he lamented. "Isn't that terrible? Tom's sick. Where's Master Colonel?"

"Mr. Tom, ya gotta eat now," Annie said from beside Vivian, her voice heavy with concern. She tucked the thick flannel around his neck. Her skirt rustled as she turned in the chair. "I'm afraid he's gone waste away, Miss Vivian."

"Annie's right, Tom. I know you miss your master and miss everyone back at *Solitude*, but you have to put something in your stomach," his teacher said.

"Tom don't want soup. Tom wants massuh Colonel," he said, once again rejecting proper nourishment.

"We want you to get better, Tom," Vivian said, leaning on the bed. "I know this is difficult..."

Thomas lifted his chin and tried to block out the shuffle of Annie's feet across the floor. He wanted to focus on the pleasant solid green of his teacher's voice.

"Tom, remember all those great men of music who gave testimonials about you? You are a great pianist-composer, the world needs to hear your beautiful music," she said, moving the bowl beneath his nose. "You have to eat so you can have strength to play."

The tiny room was cold. Thomas shuddered and rubbed his dry legs with his foot. He turned his head and shoved his hands beneath his bottom to keep them warm.

"Here Tom, open your mouth," Vivian commanded.

She blew on the spoon in short puffs and shoved it toward his lips, while Annie lifted the covers and placed warm rocks wrapped in a blanket beneath his feet. He raised his hand to his forehead and mumbled, "Tom can't eat. Tom's sick, Miss Vivian. Tom's got pneumonia and he's gonna die."

"You're here, on tour, and you're making yourself sick by not eating and you need to stop this, right now," she said. "You must eat something and get out of this bed so you can play your music. You owe it to Colonel Bethune and to Mr. Perry Oliver who purchased your services. And what about all the people who've paid to hear you sing and play all the instruments you know how to play?"

His body sank limp beneath the layer of covers, his lips parted just wide enough to release affected moans.

Vivian let out a long sigh. "Tom, I stayed up all night praying and worrying about you," she said wearily. "I know you miss the Colonel and what you have is a terrible case of homesickness, but this can't continue."

Through the thin glass, a familiar timbre could be heard right along with Perry Oliver's.

"Where is he now?"

Upon hearing the Colonel's voice, Thomas threw the covers from his body and leapt from the bed, knocking over a bucket of water. "Tom's right here, master," he yelped, as Vivian and Annie scrambled to find rags to wipe up the liquid. "Here Tom is." There were no signs of lethargy. New life had suddenly filled the prodigy when he heard the vibrations of his master's voice.

"Tom, calm down," Vivian said.

The door opened and before the Colonel could cross the threshold, Thomas rushed to him and wrapped his arms around his legs. "Massuh Colonel!" He held on as tight as he could, his cheek smashed against the Colonel's overcoat, the smell of his cologne strong in his nose.

"I'm here Tom, all is well. I'm here," the Colonel said with a laugh and a reassuring pat on his shoulder.

"Massuh Colonel's here. Massuh Colonel's here!"

"Yes, I am, Tom."

"Massuh Colonel's here, not at *Solitude,* Miss Vivian." He started to twirl.

"Sir, he hasn't had a thing to eat in three days," Annie was telling the Colonel.

The Colonel directed her to go to his coachman and have him take her into town to buy proper food for the boy. "Buy only the choicest meats and vegetables," he commanded, taking his place on a nearby chaise. He was determined to set things straight and in quick fashion.

"Tom, come now. You must eat your soup."

Thomas sat on the bed and obediently took the spoon the Colonel offered. Spoonful after spoonful, he ate the entire bowl and then later, Annie brought pork chops, yams, and black-eye-peas from the kitchen downstairs, and the Colonel joined Thomas in a small feast.

"That's right. Eat up," he said, relief in his blue-yellow voice.

The Colonel drank bourbon and Thomas had cobbler for dessert.

"Get that black monkey on stage!," Thomas mimicked. "Mr. Perry was gonna beat Tom," he said solemnly.

He felt the Colonel's hand on the top of his head; it felt warm.

"I promise you on my father's grave," the Colonel whispered in his ear. "A hand will never be laid on you, Tom. Never."

Thomas finished his food and licked the plate. Then, he hopped from the bed to his piano and played for the first time in days.

The Colonel walked past the commotion at the box office outside of Charlotte's music hall. A line of impatient patrons pushed, shoved, and shouted to get tickets to see Thomas before the show sold out. Though a chill had set in, the Colonel was glad the gales had tempered, so dust was no longer whipping against the finely dressed crowd on this important day.

In the foyer, on the high wooden walls, were bright-Colored posters heralding Perry Oliver's variety show featuring a large photograph of "Blind Tom" in which he wore a black frockcoat and was seated at his small black upright piano. He paused a moment to inspect the artwork for the show, and with a tug helped himself to a poster.

"Welcome, welcome," said Gabe Ledoux, the florid concert hall manager, as he collected money in exchange for tickets. The large curls in his hair bouncing like a southern belle's, exposing the gold hoops he wore in each ear. There were rumors circling Columbus about him, still he turned up faithfully at church every Sunday with rouge cheeks and ringlets in his hair. "Enjoy, enjoy," he said cheerily, his lips a deep ruby.

Orchestral music began to spill into the foyer. The Colonel walked toward the main theater, opened the tall double doors and walked between the dark aisles toward the lively stage. He stopped in the center and scanned the six hundred seats at round tables in the two-story hall and smiled to himself. It wasn't London's Canterbury Music Hall. It had no grand entrances or archways, no grand chandeliers. Still the Colonel felt a deep sense of pride to see Thomas at the center of the stage on the throne of his piano stool leading a thirty-piece Negro orchestra through rehearsals.

Gabe bounded toward him. "Lovely Colonel Bethune, may I tell you, Tom is a splendid act," he gushed, his hands moving in wild expressive circles. We're turning people away." The whole town is aching to see him. The tickets have wings, just flying out the door. " He fluttered his hands, leaned in and whispered, "Tell me. How's he doing it?"

"I beg your pardon," the Colonel responded, confused.

"How's it done? I promise, fingers crossed, I won't tell a soul," he said, his pale fingers crossed.

"How's what done?" the Colonel asked. He peered past the manager at Vivian, who rushed from musician to musician and back again to Thomas explaining the repertoire.

"I've been listening, and I've been watching and I can't figure it out. What's the magic trick behind the slave's playing?"

"There is no magic, it's..."

"Secret, I know, I know. All the magicians must keep their tricks hush hush," he winked and bounced off saying, "but I will figure it out. Figure it out I will."

The Colonel shook his head and watched him disappear through a set of side doors.

"Don't think me queer, Colonel," Perry's voice came from behind with a slap to his shoulder. "But I sure could kiss you for joinin' us on tour. I've always made a pretty pence, but the enthusiasm out there, crowd's already wrapped around the corner. Not sure I'm convinced, but his teacher said the boyo's ready."

"You can see with your own eyes," the Colonel said. "Certainly all will go smoothly from here." The Colonel glanced at his pocket watch. "One hour until show time."

With mugs of beer in hand, the Colonel and Perry settled at the table nearest to the pit in front of the stage. Charlotte's finest filled the aisles waited outside the hall doors. The curtains retreated and the Colonel and Perry sat through the last piece of the show. The two men talked above *Hadyn's Symphony No. 94*. The piece began softly with the famous unexpected fortissimo chord and continued nicely toward the second theme. The Colonel beamed, until suddenly Thomas slammed his hands into the piano keys sending a hideous noise throughout the hall. A collective gasp escaped from the Colonel, Perry, Vivian, and Annie.

"*Mon Dieu!*" the Colonel said.

"That A is wrong," Thomas barked, his tiny dark face aimed toward the oboe section. "Why'd you do that? Why you wanna hurt Tom's song?" Thomas said and rose from his stool, his arms flailing in the direction of the woodwinds.

The Colonel climbed the stage stairs and limped quickly in Thomas's direction. "Tom, calm down."

Before he reached the piano, Thomas, charged the oboe section and knocked over several music stands. "He hurt Tom's song!" Thomas yelled, banging his head into the Colonel's shoulder.

"He didn't mean to hurt your song," the Colonel told Thomas. He lifted him up and turned to the oboist with the boy kicking his feet. "The child doesn't know any better," the Colonel said to the musicians. "He's sensitive about mistakes."

"Why'd he want to hurt Tom's song?"

"Tom, listen to me." The Colonel carried Thomas back toward the piano. "He didn't mean to hurt you or your song," he said and set him on his feet while grabbing his shoulders. "It was merely a mistake. Not everyone can play without mistakes."

Waving toward the oboist in question, the Colonel urged, "Play. Play the notes again."

The shaken oboist, a young man of about twenty with fair skin and a face full of freckles, nodded and played the sequence of notes again, this time, in the correct keys.

"See?" the Colonel said. He kneeled to speak to Thomas at his own level while the entire troupe watched in shock. "It was an unfortunate mistake, Thomas. It happens. Sometimes, the other musicians will make mistakes. He didn't intend to hurt your song."

Thomas smoothed his suit jacket and nodded. "It was a mistake. That's all. He didn't intend to hurt Tom."

"Exactly, Tom," the Colonel sighed. "You must not get so upset and leave the piano in the middle of a performance. It was a mistake."

"A mistake."

"Yes, Tom, a mistake." The Colonel's face was red, though he was relieved that Thomas had climbed back onto the piano stool, hands poised above the keys.

"Why'd he make that mistake on my song?" he uttered as he resumed playing the sonata.

Perry joined the Colonel by his side. Before he could speak, the Colonel said, "He'll perform. Just leave him be." The words came, but the Colonel didn't believe them himself.

The Colonel had lost track of time when he heard his name called from behind and turned to see the bookish stage manager.

"Show starts in ten minutes, gentlemen."

The half dozen mimes wiggled past the closing curtains and Mike the Midget walked onto the stage, clapping. The Colonel and Perry made their way to the hallway and down the stairs to the backstage where excited performers bustled, bumped and slipped past one another. "Welp, Colonel, this is it," Perry said, a beer in his hand, and the Colonel took his place near the side of the curtains. "Nervous?"

The Colonel wiped his wet palms with his handkerchief. During a break in the morning rehearsal, he'd informed Perry he wanted to introduce Thomas to provide the boy with a sense of comfort. "He will respond better to me than Mike the Midget," he'd said.

"Don't care if ya have ta sit next to the boyo on the stool if that'll get him to play," Perry said, accepting the Colonel's idea at once.

Now, the Colonel's mouth was dry. He took in all the workers prepping for the next performance. The Negro musicians filed toward their sections in brown suits, holding violins, flutes, trumpets, and oboes. Stagehands carried wood chairs and arranged them in a crescent shape, while the stage manager shouted orders. "Look out, move please!" he yelled to make way for the black upright piano with the red trim. The instrument was rolled out and positioned in the center for Thomas.

Vivian guided Thomas over to the Colonel who was standing by the curtains. "He's ready, Colonel."

The Colonel kneeled down to talk to the young boy. "Remember what we rehearsed, Tom? When I say...Now, Tom boy, play. You will play."

"Now, Tom boy, play," Thomas said. "Then Tom will play."

"Yes, yes, that's your cue," the Colonel said with a rub on top of his head. "It's just like the night of music in the *grand parlor*. If you do well, there's chocolate cake waiting for you when you finish."

"Yay," Thomas said, clapping. "Tom, will do well and Tom will have cake."

The stage manager rushed over and motioned the Colonel toward the stage. "Come, come, it's time," he said, and then turned to Vivian. "Get the boy to the piano."

Holding his hand, Vivian guided Thomas to the small stool.

"Shoulders back, project your voice," the stage manager instructed the Colonel, nudged him along and lifted curtains for his entrance.

The Colonel smoothed his frock and took one last glance at Thomas before he stepped around the thick drapes and walked to the front of the stage. He stepped into the pool of moody footlights and the crowd quieted upon noticing him. He cleared his throat.

"Fine ladies and gentlemen, I'm Colonel Bethune and I thank you for your esteemed presence this evening," he said. "Tonight, I present to you Blind Tom Bethune, an untrained Negro pianist, hailed as a retarded genius and a prodigy by the most respected music scholars in Europe."

The audience applauded unaware of the thumping sound behind the curtain.

"Tom will begin with an original composition *Imitation of a Sewing Machine* conceived at the foot of his mammy while she mended a hem," said the Colonel, turning toward the curtains. "Now, Tom boy, play," the Colonel said.

Quickly, the stage manager pulled down the strings to open the heavy curtains, but Thomas did not start to play. He just sat there, rocking; his feet hit against the body of the piano, producing a rhythmic thump. Murmurs arose in the audience. Patrons leaned forward to see what was making that noise.

"Now Tom, play boy, *Imitation of a Sewing Machine,*" commanded the Colonel, his brow in a sweat.

"I want my money back!"

"Boy's more untrained and retarded than genius!" someone yelled, causing a trickle of chuckles.

Perspiration fell, the Colonel felt dizzy with embarrassment. He wanted to run. But in that moment, where he could flee, Thomas spoke.

"Tom knows *Imitation of a Sewing Machine.* Tom will play."

A smattering of applause came from the floor and upper seats in the balcony. As the song began, a flurry of chords filled the hall and much of the audience gasped at the beauty of it. A wave of relief came over the Colonel. Perry had spent quite a bit of money to rent out the hall, taking a risky gamble on the erratic slave. If the slave had failed to perform it would have been a disastrous financial loss. He exhaled, taking in the concertgoers sitting in the shadows side-by-side, not one empty seat in the house. In the prime seats were ladies of good family with their gentlemen chaperones.

Thomas gave them more than they could've imagined. He sang popular hymns, played the flute, and demonstrated his prodigious skills on the violin. Challenges from musicians were accepted from the audience that required recreating unknown tunes, all with Perry's encouragement from the stage. "Would anyone else like to test Blind Tom's skills?" he shouted with glee.

The Colonel had seen his share of crowds roused by inspired performances, spurred to outbursts by liquor and spectacle, but in all his years, he'd never seen an audience experience pure awe. Some patrons stood up from their chairs, a few ladies gathered their purses and rushed from their tables holding their hats exclaiming Thomas was filled with a spirit, still others could not refrain from calling out "bravo," long before he'd finish a piece.

With each song, relief came over the Colonel as he peered through the side curtain and saw the smiles, the whispers, and the transfixed faces moved by the beauty of the performance. He stood there in the wings, watching his gifted slave in front of all those people and took a deep breath, overwhelmed with joy. It was a success.

Two hours later, Thomas depressed the sostenuto pedal with his tiny foot—bringing Meyerbeer's *Le Prophete* to a sweet end. The crowd stood to their feet with roaring applause, spoons clinking against glasses for a five-minute ovation. Thomas turned on the piano stool, smiling and clapping his hands together in self-praise that generated chuckles.

"Bravo, Tom, bravo!" the Colonel cried. Annie brought the saucer of special chocolate cake. "Cake, Tom," the Colonel called to him and Thomas scuttled away from his piano for a pat on his sweet cotton head and a great forkful of cake.

Amid the crush backstage, the Colonel felt the letter in his pocket from Frances and wished she and the children could've been with him to share the occasion. Pats on the shoulders from the mayor and handshakes from prominent slave traders, the women in the crush were also aflutter, fanning themselves, having been titillated by Thomas's passionate music and the sensual energy it generated.

"There's his handsome master," the Colonel heard from one of the perfumed beauties when he passed by, her fragrance enticed his nostrils like a doe's pheromones luring a buck. The woman batted her eyes and boldly climbed into the Colonel's arms before he could fully pass. She forbiddingly placed one hand on his waist, the other softly on his shoulder.

"Daria Bernice Scarlett," she whispered in his ear, her chest lightly touching his. "Your Negro protégé is magnificent, Colonel Bethune," she breathed.

As the Colonel examined her, all thoughts of his wife and her letter in his pocket vanished. Warmth exploded through his body and his breaths shortened. He was about to respond when a hand pressed his shoulder.

"Colonel, come. Someone important wants to meet you and Tom." Perry pulled him away and whispered in his ear while pointing across the thick crowd, he hurried him down three steps through the staging area to Thomas and his teacher.

"Come, Tom. There's someone who wants to meet you," the Colonel said. He guided Thomas by the hand to a slender, grandly tailored German with dark hair parted on one side and crescent-shaped eyes.

"William Knabe, of Baltimore," he said. The piano maker and owner of the illustrious William Knabe & Co."

"It's an honor Mr. Knabe," the Colonel said with a nod of respect.

"You are the man of the hour, Colonel Bethune, with the most fashionable Negro in all of Georgia," William said in a thick accent.

"Fashionable indeed," the Colonel smiled.

"I'm here fine sir, because I received a message from a countryman of mine, a man from your hometown who extolled the virtues of Thomas on the piano. From what I saw this afternoon, he was quite right in his glowing assessment," William said.

"Thank you, sir. Tom say hello to Mr. Knabe."

"Hello, Mr. Knabe, the piano maker," Thomas said.

Mr. Knabe cleared his throat and leaned toward Tom. "Young man, you play music with subtlety and grace. It was a pleasure experiencing your talents and I have a special surprise for you," he said.

"I cut a grand piano for you. Strong from mahogany with pins of hard rock maple. Designed and built it with my own hand, Thomas. What do you think of that?"

Thomas clapped with what seemed to be the sincerest appreciation. One of William's sons, a tall, slender teenage boy in a tailored tan suit with a diamond-studded wrist watch, walked toward the corner of the room near a set of ladders. With the help of a few workmen, he carefully lifted a large tan cover, revealing a beautifully carved black grand piano with ornate legs, and an elaborately designed music desk with stunning gilded accents.

It was a remarkable sight. Gasps of excitement erupted around the crowded backstage; eyes turned to the back wall and conversations stopped, as everyone admired the more than seven-foot long instrument.

"The great Thalberg plays his compositions on a Knabe as well as Gottschalk, Tom," Mr. Knabe added. "And now so will you, you will play your fine music on a Knabe, as well. The best for the best."

"Tom's the best," Thomas clapped. "The best for the best." He walked over to the piano and caressed the instrument with his hands.

"Tom, thank Mr. Knabe for his wonderful surprise."

"*Ich bin Ihnen sehr dankbar!*" Thomas said, using the German he'd learned from the piano storeowner in Columbus. "Tom thanks you Mr. Knabe the piano maker for your wonderful gift."

Hand at his chin, the Colonel erupted into laughter, as did the entire room.

"*Gern geschehen,* Herr Tom!" the reserved German laughed, much taken with Tom. "*Gern geschehen!*"

The hour of five came and Thomas performed the last of four shows. After each show, the Colonel stood offstage, receiving congratulations from important strangers, accepting gifts: toy trains, stuffed animals, and chocolates for Thomas with promises to bring the slave back for return performances. Perry was paid his profits and he in turn peeled off bills for the Colonel. A beam on his face, the Colonel slipped one hundred dollars from the concert into his leather wallet. "Quite a hefty profit, Colonel. High tide for ya."

The Colonel smiled and drew his great coat tight.

A weary road manager approached from the stage's back door. "Your carriage is ready, Mr. Bethune." The Colonel nodded and began to walk toward his carriage for the trip to the local inn. He took one last look at all the "Blind Tom" posters.

Early the next morning, when the shops along Tryon Street lay asleep and the rest of the inn slumbered as well, the Colonel emerged outside of his room and walked to the parlor where a wood fire was burning. An octoroon slave woman who looked Italian, with blue eyes and milky skin, brought him the *Charlotte Journal* and a tray of hot oatmeal and coffee. He sat near the flickering flame, unfolded the paper, and caught his breath. There, on the front page was a picture of Thomas:

"The musical slave Blind Tom was in town yesterday, proving to be a genius thrusting all our conceptions to the side. Only ten years old and without sight, he still sees more than you and I on the piano, informing the fine citizens of Charlotte that there's a musical world of which we know nothing about and he in fact knows all."

The Colonel folded the paper with the intention of keeping it, and felt for the first time that Thomas might indeed bring fame and fortune to the Bethune family.

XIII.

The Christmas season arrived and a blanket of snow lay over the southeastern states. The snow was up to nineteen inches in parts of Chattanooga—the tour's sixth city and 30th show—when Perry Oliver's wagons trudged into town earlier that morning. The shops were decorated with ornamented trees and strings of garland adorned windows, while scarf-wearing carolers serenaded shoppers.

The theater in mid-town Chattanooga was a white brick building with arched entrances topped with rows of rounded windows. Inside, carpeted stairs on either side of the house led past red drapes to the balconies. Noisy performers rambled about the stage in sparkling costumes. The set was dressed like Venice, Italy. Costumed dancers rehearsed past a small bridge and a gondolier that appeared to float atop a wooden platform and performers practiced their entrances through traps and elevators in the stage floor.

The Colonel stood outside the wide backstage door next to three white-faced clowns and a jester, his brown heavy coat buckled tight around his waist. He was exhausted; the trekking from city to city, the fast pace, was taking its toll on his body. Perry Oliver had warned him about lack of sleep and encouraged him to drink an awful smelling root concoction the slaves liked to make over the fire. He had refused, and now he regretted it–after all the rough carriage rides and sleepless nights of tossing and turning in smoke-filled hotels.

The intense tour included mostly three-day city stays. But the aggressive schedule also included "one night stand" performances that required the troupe to perform multiple shows, then pack up and move to the next town before nightfall for multiple shows the following day.

The banner announcing the Chattanooga Christmas parade hung across Main Street and was the only reminder which town he was in. The Colonel finished his coffee, set the cup on the building's ledge, and stuck his hands deep into his pockets to keep them warm. He was pleased with the publicity and the string of sold out shows. Yet, the Colonel was concerned the heavy travel and lengthy encores would eventually wear Thomas down.

"These challenges, must he do them after every show and encores?" he'd asked Perry backstage after the last show in South Carolina. The muscles in Perry's face bunched into a frown. "I paid quite a coin for the boyo," he said, sucking on a toothpick. "Think I've earned the right ta do with him on stage as I please, Colonel."

At that time, the Colonel sighed, but the strife between he and the promoter over the length of Blind Tom's performances grew. The encores involved hours of long exhibitions that included dancing and singing popular tunes, as well as audience challenges from music professors, amateur musicians, students, and local teachers. Each challenger would take the stage to play the piano, flute, or violin, requiring Thomas to reproduce entire works upon a single hearing. On several occasions, while the raucous crowds herded out thoroughly delighted with the show, the Colonel would lift a limp Thomas into his arms and carry him to the hotel. This angered him.

Now, the fifth show of the day was coming to a close.

Mike the Midget waddled onto the stage. "Fine folks of Chattanooga…to Tom all sounds are a delight and I invite to the stage anyone who has a mind to test the harmless idiot. He will recreate any piece of music of your choosing, don't be shy and don't be afraid."

Six sandy-haired white male students from Tusculum College took the stage to test Thomas with hymns and parlor songs. The young men were of average talents in voice and on the piano, but nevertheless entertaining. Little ten-year-old Thomas pushed his way onto the stool with a shove to his opponents who exaggerated the contact with wild hand gestures and even mock falls to the stage floor. This lighthearted exchange went on for nearly an hour, and the Colonel couldn't help but smile from his leather cushioned chair, the college boys were good fun.

But several hours later, the Colonel's legs were sore from sitting so long. Sweat dripped from his scalp and he dabbed his forehead with his handkerchief then peered through the footlights at Thomas. Sweat was pouring down the boy's tiny face and wet spots had formed beneath the arms of his black frock. It was his tenth challenge of the day, but Thomas played as if it was his first song of the day and made the piano sing as if it were a choir.

At last, Thomas climbed down from the stool and bowed. The side curtains rippled, and Mike the Midget waddled onto the stage to dismiss the weary crowd. Suddenly, a voice shouted above the fading applause.

"I believe the boy to be a hoax! I present a true challenge for Blind Tom," he said, lifting his leather portfolio in the air, "to test the claims regarding the powers of his memory."

"He's been tested enough!" a voice came from the crowd.

"Twenty-six pages of my own composition…"

The audience booed in protest.

"Never before performed in public!" the man insisted in a raised voice.

Perry took center stage. "Ladies an' gents! Please," he said, adjusting his Glengarry hat atop his head. "If the man from Ohio does not believe in the true talents o' "Blind Tom," 'tis my duty ta see he leaves satisfied!"

"Absolutely not!" the Colonel shouted. He punched his cane down and hurried onto the stage. "It's unconscionable! He's more than earned his keep for the day and one more challenge is unnecessary," he spat at the promoter.

He was furious. "And you," he turned, pointing his cane at the man in the audience. "I am Colonel Bethune. Just what is it you trying to prove, *Monsieur*?"

A suspicious smile spread across the man's bony face. "You contend Blind Tom can perform any piece upon one hearing. I have my piece here, to test him. Perhaps the others," he paused, the words caught in his throat, "were plants, sir."

"Are you calling me a liar, *Monsieur*?" the Colonel asked in an ominous tone, stretching to his full height. "Well, Tom will not play," the Colonel snapped. He glared down at the man before turning away to the piano. "Come, Tom, it's time to go."

"Tom will play," Thomas said, refusing to move, feet swinging from the stool.

"Tom, no. Come," the Colonel said. He hooked his cane to his arm and grabbed Thomas from behind by his armpits.

"No, Tom will play!" Thomas cried. He kicked, screamed, and wiggled with all his tiny power. "Let Tom play!"

With a sigh of resignation, the Colonel gazed at Perry. "The boyo wants to play, Colonel." The Colonel nodded, reluctantly.

Pages clutched against his chest, the thin man mounted the stage steps and took his place at the piano. Thirty minutes, forty minutes, then an hour passed. It was an excruciating solo, not particularly difficult to play. A pedestrian melody and as the man played on, Thomas tapped his foot and rocked back and forth. The audience chuckled as Thomas pranced along the front of the stage, flapped his arms like a bird, then placed himself on the floor with his back to the audience—his cheeks resting in his hands.

Finally, the man brought the song to an end. Thomas jumped to his feet, pushed the startled man off his stool and played the same song with beauty and grace to a rousing ovation. On the way to the hotel that night, it all happened so fast. Thomas was skipping hand-in-hand between Vivian and Annie when suddenly his fingers slipped away and he was on the ground, his body thrashing with violent quakes and foam dripping from his mouth.

The Colonel stroked Thomas's head. "It's okay, Tom," he whispered. "Someone get a doctor, now!" He glanced at Vivian and the attendant and snarled at Perry. "His blood is on your hands!" Perry stood by and watched in horror, as Thomas shook in the snow until suddenly the quakes stopped.

The Colonel rose; he lifted Thomas's limp body into his arms, speaking softly to him in French. He clutched him to his chest and walked back toward the music hall.

Beneath gaslight, "Breathe, Tom," Dr. Malachi urged. In a black overcoat and black trousers, the doctor examined Tom's stiffened body on a table in the music hall's prop room. "Tom, squeeze my hand," said Dr. Malachi.

Thomas's tiny fingers remained limp in Dr. Malachi's hands.

"His brain has been dreadfully strained. It cannot process the information it receives from the cells causing an epileptic seizure."

"Is he going to be well?" Vivian asked.

"It's hard to say for certain," the doctor said. "However, with the proper rest, at least a week of bed rest, maybe two, he should recover. He certainly cannot perform before then."

The low-lit room suddenly seemed brutally cold and the Colonel's bones were freezing beneath his overcoat and frock. His head ached. Though he'd cursed the professor from Oberlin College, the Colonel knew from the downward bend of Perry's head and the way his eyes stayed on Thomas, the promoter understood he held him responsible.

The doctor offered his residence for Thomas to rest. "Got plenty of room Colonel for you and your servants," he said, peering at the Colonel. He urged the Colonel, who was carrying the limp Thomas in his arms, to accept his offer as they neared the hired wagons.

It was a kind gesture. The rest of the Perry Oliver troupe had already loaded the wagons and driven the horses toward Memphis. The Colonel paused. As a general rule, he didn't accept generosity from anyone. "Show me an offer of charity and I'll show you the strings," his father liked to say. However, in that moment, with Thomas wilted in his arms in dire need of much rest, he nodded his consent to the doctor. He climbed the steps to the rented vehicle with Vivian and Annie close behind.

From the carriage window the Colonel stared out at the half moon and the distant stars piercing through the dark navy blue sky. The horses' heavy feet clopped against the cobblestones leading up to Doctor Malachi's sprawling property. His home was an impressive-looking three-level structure along Nakajack Lake; a white house featuring several small arches above circular windows and small fenced verandas with steeple-like facades.

Later that night, after a hot dinner with the doctor and his wife, the Colonel stood undressing near the center of the stale second-story bedroom. Thomas was long asleep in a room down the hallway. Two brass lanterns atop small corner tables cast a warm tranquil light and wood crackled in a large iron stove. The Colonel peeled off his wool morning coat, hung it in the closet, and unbuttoned the white shirt the seamstress had made for him. He stood in a pair of long johns inhaling the quiet serenity, the soothing peace of the tiny flames that popped and turned a blue, yellow, and white hue. He stared down at the embroidered black and white coverlet for a long time before he pulled back the layers.

Only now, as he tugged his boots away from his feet in the warm winter room, did he think about the dire consequences of what he'd allowed to happen. The memory of Thomas convulsing in the snow foaming at the mouth haunted his thoughts. "He could've..." he stopped and shook his head; it was a horrible, horrible stain on his conscience. He was furious with himself as much as Perry. He sighed and listened to the whir of crickets, the cadenced tock of the wall clock. Turning on the soft mattress, he pictured the stone hearth in the *grand parlor,* Frances pregnant in a feather stitched cotton nightgown and the children who loved the slave like a brother stood in their pajamas, and he was telling them that Thomas was dead. The thought made him cringe.

He shut his eyes and then lifted his heavy lids to the painting by Rembrandt Peale that was hanging on the wall beautifully lit in soft golden hues by the gas lamp. His thoughts turned to more selfish matters. He experienced a sinking feeling. He still owed ten thousand dollars to the bank and had not received word back from his letter to Gerald on whether his payment was sufficient to stave off an auction. His debt hung over his thoughts like a dark cloud. He had no one who could help him, so he certainly couldn't afford to lose Thomas; the slave boy was still his best hope for wresting his family from public humiliation.

When at last he blew out the flames, he prayed that somehow, some way Thomas would have a complete recovery and he vowed he would never let such a thing happen to Thomas, ever again.

XIV.

The rain was still pouring down, and the Catawba River had flooded and washed away the trails leading out of the Holy City, so the troupe had set up camp near the woods. A Daguerreotypist was passing through town with his magic box on his way to New Jersey and stumbled upon the tangled cluster of Perry Oliver's show wagons parked outside of Charleston. A tall, svelte man in his twenties, his frock stylishly cut, and brown hair in perfect waves. He was charming and brightened the dreary days by offering to make pictures at a discount.

"I can give you magnificent Daguerreotypes available in every style," he had said of his mysterious box and pitched a tent in order to ply his craft.

It was early morning when the Colonel arose after a long night of billiards, bourbon, and music. He entered the camera tent with a large black umbrella dressed in one of his best suits with a healthy Thomas in tow and Annie dragging behind him. She too carried an umbrella along with the slave's black boots to keep them clean of mud.

The Daguerreotypist was just setting up near the black Knabe piano that slaves had carefully covered with blankets and carried for the upcoming picture.

"Your piano's here, Tom," the Colonel said, his gold cufflinks sparkling.

Annie finished tying Thomas's boots and released his hand. He jaunted over to the gleaming instrument, up onto the stool. Annie wrapped her umbrella, took out a rag and brushed lint from his black waistcoat while he strummed the keys.

"Bonjour, Monsieur Bethune," said the charming photographer in the mauve frock, gently cleaning the camera lens with a cloth, "what a beautiful piano to make art with Blind Tom, *oui?* This is perfection. I will make you the perfect picture."

The Colonel nodded and smoothed the vest beneath his frock. Handkerchief to his nose, he noticed the strong smell of lime and iodine in the makeshift studio.

"The smell is a small price to pay for the privilege, the honor to create art, *non?"* the Daguerreotypist said of the pungent stench that hung in the damp air.

"I believe we agreed upon quarter plates for five dollars a piece, *oui, Monsieur?"*

"C'est correct, Monsieur, c'est bon," the Colonel agreed.

The Daguerreotypist lowered the brown muslin fabric behind the box, removed plates, manipulated chalks, and then adjusted the camera on the wooden tripod. The makeshift studio was well decorated with velvet curtains, leather armchairs, silver candlestick holders, and carved mirrors. The Daguerreotypist opened the tent door and light rushed in with the wind.

"It is better, much better this photograph I will create of you, the slave, and the piano. Better than the usual black cloth table, boring lamp, and the stiff pose in an armchair."

He motioned for the Colonel to move closer to Thomas.

When the Daguerreotypist slipped the thin copper plate into the box, the Colonel felt his heartbeats quicken. Unlike the many beautiful, but lifeless interpretive portraits over the mantles at *Solitude*, this photograph would capture their living presence. The Colonel's imagination was lit; he realized the images made that day would exist and be admired long after the souls of he and his most talented slave were carried up to heaven.

It was the perfect time, the perfect light, as if the dark skies had parted on cue. With a clap of his hands, the Daguerreotypist slid black the flap and slipped a bronze-framed plate into the camera case. After counting down, he snapped the picture.

A dark dreadful sensation overtook the Colonel after he left the Daguerreotypist. The light thrum of rain against his tent's roof and the fiddlers fiddling a few yards away didn't help. The pleasure from the morning photos had faded, as he stole a glance at the letter from the bank on top of the small walnut dresser. It could be good news, he told himself without moving, and then again it could be the worst.

He squeezed his hands together and avoided the letter. Walking over to the desk he picked up his soft leather billfold that was next to the flickering candles. Pulling out the bills, he began to count the profits from the "Blind Tom" concerts. He placed one bill on top of the other, $1600 from the past month. That was a great deal of profit for untold days, a godsend, but it wasn't enough to cover his outstanding bills. He shoved the stack back into his wallet, picked up the letter, and took a deep breath. As he pried open the cream-colored envelope and slid out the soft sheet of paper with the bold cursive writing on it; he read the first disturbing sentence:

Dear James,

It is with the deepest regrets that I am writing you.

The words stung. The Colonel set the letter down on his lap and rubbed his forehead. His hand shook. A part of him felt no need to continue, but nevertheless he picked up the missive and continued:

I must urge you to take immediate action regarding your estate. The bank will most certainly not grant an extension on the loan. Ten thousand dollars is due in sixty days.
Gerald

He sat numbly and stewed with visions of his world unraveling. An auction would be posted in his own newspaper. To avoid the humiliation, he'd have to sell two-thirds of his slaves at *Elway,* and that would be a disaster during picking season. There were many outstanding bills arriving each month, $7800 from the cabinetmaker, $450 from the florist, $620 from the butcher, and the contractor on his second plantation in Virginia had yet to send the bill for construction there. He rose from the cot, his stomach knotted. Crushing the letter into a ball, the Colonel tossed the stationery onto the floor. It was indeed the worst-case scenario. After all the favors his father had pulled for the president of that bank. "Ungracious," he yelled out in the vast tented space. "My father recommended you to the board and you do this to me?" He pounded his fist against the dresser. It sickened him, the lack of respect for his father's memory.

He steadied himself and sat on the cot. In many ways he was a strong man, but even men of strength face doubts when confronted with the uncertainties dealt by the unstable hand of life. It was suffocating, the long hand of the bank. The Colonel knew what he had to do.

It was mid-afternoon when the Colonel entered the low-lit confines of Perry Oliver's square-shaped tent, two-thirds the size of his own. It was a mess. In the middle of a small cot sat a half-eaten lunch plate with roasted squirrel, mashed potatoes, and green beans. The lamp on the shelf glimmered, shining light on various half-empty liquor bottles. The floor was covered with dirty clothes, dishes, and piles of old newspaper reviews of the tour.

The Colonel stepped over a pile of shirts and waited for Perry's attention. Perry stood near a small table wearing a beaver coat and whistled while he poured brandy into a tin cup for the Colonel. "Looks like you could sluice ya gob a bit." A musty smell seeped from his armpits when he handed the Colonel a drink before motioning for him to sit in the lone chair near the bed.

"Please, have a seat my friend. Something's blowing in the wind with ya, huh?" he asked in his characteristic pointed style accompanied by a slap on the Colonel's back. His hand was heavy and felt cold, even through the Colonel's overcoat.

"*Oui, mon ami.* I have a business proposition, regarding the boy Tom," the Colonel said with equal frankness as Perry lit his cigar for him. He knew Perry was a man who liked to get to the point, so he got right to it. "The boy is selling out every show in every city."

"The boyo sure is," Perry said. He stood near a lantern and used the flame to light a cigarette for himself. "I tell ya, Colonel, he's living up to everything I thought he would be and more," he said, blowing out smoke. "The highfalutin folks in these towns love the idea of a blind, retarded nigger playing classical tunes like a fancy European."

The Colonel smiled. He leaned back in the chair and crossed his legs, encouraged by Perry's observations.

"In light of Tom's overwhelming success," the Colonel continued. "I'm sure we both have mutual interest in seeing that his contract is extended."

Perry cleared his throat. "Well Colonel, that's what they call puttin' the wagon before the horse ain't it? The boy Tom is a hellava fine draw, but I ain't made my canaries back on this go round."

The Colonel nodded and took a draw from his cigar. Of course the promoter was right. The Colonel felt like a pair of hands tightened around his neck, but he proceeded.

"The numbers are climbing, are they not? It's fair to say, we both know you will recoup your investment along with a most hefty profit before the tour's halfway finished," he persuaded, tapping ashes into a can on the floor.

"That remains to be seen."

"Well, suppose I told you I've been contacted by the Oliver Ditson publishing firm," the Colonel said. Oliver Ditson was one of the biggest music publishing firms in the country. He pulled a contract from the pocket of his overcoat, unfolded the pages, and handed the papers to Perry. "Two of Tom's songs are going to be published."

Perry took the pages and skimmed the paperwork. *"Rainstorm and Water in the Moonlight."*

"Now you know this is unprecedented for a Negro. Yet, the president of the company, a gentleman named Isaac Crawford, approached me with the offer back in Charlotte and he's assured me there will be more. This increases Tom's value some, wouldn't you say?"

"Well, I *say* Colonel," Perry said, shaking his head. "That's mighty fine, mighty fine o' Tom getting published and all, and I'm pretty darn sure I'll make my coins back an' then some."

"That you will," the Colonel said. He was relentless; his eyes were fixed on Perry and he smiled, thinking the two were on the same page.

"But my mammy taught me not to count my canaries before they hatch," Perry said. "We'll just revisit this happy conversation once my birdies are singing on the right side of the ledger." He drank down his bourbon and finished with a belch.

Suddenly, there was no more room for discussion, so the Colonel rose from his chair and went back out into the overcast day. The gray clouds seemed to hang lower, seemed to move in menacing circles and the ground seemed to sway. A mixture of the hard drink Perry had given him and anger spurred the Colonel to take a long walk. Hands shoved into his pockets, he saw black slaves, draped in blankets and ragged overcoats hovered around a large log fire deeper in the woods. A slight wind rustled the trees, but he wasn't cold.

Of course he could cobble together a couple of thousand dollars from friends, but most of his associates were indebted to him from successive years of failed crops. Like him, they too had missed mortgages—rich in pride and land, but poor in cold hard cash.

A stiff breeze came and with it the smell of honeysuckle. The Colonel walked back toward the caravan of wagons. His boots sloshed in front of his cane. He walked aimlessly along a muddy back trail, driven by the drums, the grouse's drums, *gélinotte huppée* his uncles called them.

The talk with Perry couldn't have been more disastrous.

"Damn it," he spat. Though he tried to block it out of his mind that inevitable visit from Gerald and the bank, dread hovered over his heart and permeated every inch of his body.

Perhaps he should've set his pride aside he stewed, while stepping to avoid a puddle. Maybe he should've simply asked the showman outright for a loan or some kind of advance on profits. He walked against the wind, ignoring the chilling cold. He owed it to his family, to those who came before him to do whatever it took to retain every piece of Bethune property. Though it angered him, these thoughts.

"Groveling to an Irishman, an Irishman! Father would disown me," he muttered, defiantly.

His head was hung so low he didn't notice the dapperly dressed Negro leaning against the carriage with the fancy boots and a silk stovetop hat.

"My pa always told me, the only thing down there is lost hope and anguished souls," came the mysterious man's rich drawl.

The Colonel stopped and drew back, startled. He recognized that face.

"Keep your eyes up. Up there is promise and eternal joy," said the Negro, eyes pointed toward heaven, flashing a wide smile. His was a modest southern drawl and the Colonel knew at once some white person had educated this slave. He eyed the man warily, a slave who dared speak to him as an equal.

"Don't want no trouble sir," the caramel-hued Negro said with the tilt of his hat accompanied by a small bow. "Tabbs Gross the name. Freedman from Cincinnati," he said extending his well-manicured hand.

"Ah, *oui*," the Colonel grunted. He was quite possibly the most handsome man the Colonel had ever seen, the Negro freedman. He was tall with a dazzling smile, hair smooth and wavy. He had long lashes and green eyes. The Colonel knew there were plenty like him in New Orleans where his older brothers lived, *gens de couleur libres*. They were beautiful people, with dreamy mocha-Colored women who were graceful in taffetas and expensive silks, and reigned over the quadroon balls. Plenty of Colored boys in Parisian frocks with jeweled cufflinks roamed the French quarters in leather riding boots with heads held high. But there were certainly very few free slaves casually roaming about the countryside where he came from.

"I've seen you before," the Colonel started. He paused, staring at him, trying to remember. "In Memphis and I think I saw you again in Charlotte."

"You are not mistaken, *Monsieur*," he said. "Indeed, I've been watching the young boy."

At this, the Colonel stiffened, suddenly wary again. A free Negro keeping watch of his slave? Suppose he was some kind of abolitionist that wanted to take the boy and escape to the North?

The freedman bent down, struck a match on the side of his boot and offered him a cigar; the Colonel took it with a nod and sat against a soggy log. He appreciated the breeze coming over from the river and nodded without speaking when the strange man lit the cigar for him.

"I wandered through the camp and one of the slaves told me you'd gone for a walk."

Turns out the freedman was a very rich man who'd been liberated by his dying white father and had acquired his wealth from touring Europe with original illustrations of *Uncle Tom's Cabin.*

"I didn't know what to do with my newfound freedom," he was saying. "Just started walking away from my daddy's plantation and came upon a brook. Found the illustrations sitting on top of a trash heap, picked them up to see what I could get. Serendipity's what they call it."

"So what is it you seek with me?" the Colonel asked, losing patience.

"Why folks call me the Colored P.T. Barnum, sir," he said, smiling, flashing those perfect white teeth again. "I'd like to purchase Thomas's freedom and the freedom of his entire family if you would so oblige me, sir."

The Colonel's entire body went rigid. "Purchase Tom and his family?"

"Yes, sir. I have a down payment."

"A down payment?"

"Exactly what do you regard as an agreeable down payment, if I consider this offer?"

"Ten-thousand dollars seems a fair amount to me."

"Well, that's certainly a good starting point," the Colonel said, trying his best to hide his excitement. "Though fifteen seems more appropriate."

"Maybe even more, sir, but I only have ten-thousand with me."

This handsome green-eyed mulatto from the middle of nowhere was walking around with thousands of dollars for a down payment? It seemed like it was all part of an elaborate dream. But the Colonel felt his lips lift into a crafty smile, hand extended.

"Colonel, I know a Colored man can't bind a white man to a contract, but I believe you're an honorable man who would understand my want for peace of mind."

Tabbs produced papers to document the down payment for Bill of Sale. He carefully unfolded the paper for the Colonel to sign. With no intention of selling Thomas or ever seeing the handsome freedman again, the Colonel signed the parchment. Then he walked over to the man's gilded brown wagon, where he was paid in cash.

Later that night, stagehands strummed guitars and there was singing and clapping around the campfire. The Colonel left the warmth of his tent and joined them. Light in his heart, he wrapped himself with a blanket next to Perry near the fire, and laughed with the rowdy performers drinking tin cups of beer. He sang along to parlor songs that Thomas played on the banjo. As the flickering flames warmed his face, he took out the Bill of Sale, unfolded it and tossed it into the fire. He gazed at Thomas, joyously plucking the banjo. The slave was his savior. He thought about the wonderful deal he'd made earlier that day and heard Tabbs' voice in his head. "I believe you're an honorable man."

The Colonel caressed some of the gold coins in his pocket and watched the contract burn to ashes. The green-eyed Colored stranger must've thought him a fool. The corners of his mouth lifted, and he leaned back against a soft cushion of blankets, taking in the ladies swaying their hips like Egyptian Bedouins. *"Tu est the fool,"* he whispered. He took a swig of beer, the liquor numbed his senses, and the fire warmed the bottom of his boots. He'd never sell Thomas or his family, but he would make good use of the gold with the bank, he thought with the flip of a coin.

XV.

The road leading to *Solitude* was a spectacular sight with an army of fancy carriages backed up for a quarter of a mile, all with embossed invitations to the Bethune's Winter Ball. The Colonel leaned on his cane in the foyer, looking dapper in his white vest and fitted black frock. It had been only a few months since he and Thomas began the tour. In their short absence, the hostilities between the North and the South had boiled over, with rumblings of southern states leaving the Union. Now the season's respectable social affairs, like the fine ball that night at *Solitude,* were used as camouflage for covert meetings.

The notable couples strutted into the mansion, checking their umbrellas, walking sticks, and heavy coats with the butler. The Colonel lit a cigar. Moving from the foyer, he walked down the candle lit corridor, the smell of coffee and biscuits drifting in from the refreshment room where Charity was serving hungry guests. He continued into the grandeur of the large ballroom, walking beneath its frescoed ceiling and large-tiered shimmering chandeliers.

The parquet dance floor was crowded with twirling couples performing practiced steps to the Viennese Waltz. Near the center of the grand room, Thomas sat at his black Knabe piano in a new black frock, playing Strauss with ease, the elite crowd luxuriating in the marvels of the now famous slave. Amid the turns and smiles, there were no signs of the trouble percolating down the hallway in the *grand parlor.* A servant offered the Colonel champagne; he took a glass, and watched with joy the noisy festivities around him.

He searched the crowd for Frances, who was a few months away from delivery of their child; she'd had Charity sew a special light burgundy maternity gown that was cut above the waist so that her large stomach was hidden behind rows of muslin and lace. But it was difficult to spot her, so he decided to leave the floor and try from the balcony.

The first dance ended and the couples crowded off the floor. John escorted his dance partner over to a crush of pretty women holding their cream-colored dance cards. He was to dance next with the pretty Rebecca Fantin, daughter of rich family friends who owned a textile mill. Rebecca was standing near to him on his right, but when he started to walk over to take her gloved hand, his eye caught a striking woman across the room. She wore a dark green satin dress and was standing near the grand piano, watching Thomas. She took his breath away. Her auburn hair was swept up into a bun of curls that descended into a waterfall of swirls down the back of her long neck. His eyes sparkled with a rush of desire.

The trumpet blared, summoning couples back to the ballroom floor for the second dance of the evening. The music teacher, Vivian, guided Thomas back to the grand piano, but John was frozen by love at first sight. Who was she? What town did she come from? He found her the most beautiful woman at the entire ball: her petite rounded shoulders and the hinted form of her breasts peeking from the v-shape plunge of her dress.

So lost in the vision of the strange woman, he didn't realize he was blocking couples on their way to the dance floor, nor did he realize he'd lost contact with his partner until a golden-haired school friend nudged him in his shoulder.

"You're showing bad manners *mon ami*," Jake Garrett whispered.

"Keep moving, big brother," Caleb muttered on the way past.

John's cheeks burned and he gave a sheepish grin while scanning the sea of black frocks and wide ruffle dresses for his dance partner. He located Rebecca just in time to get into proper position, her gloved hand in his, gently gliding her back with a soft step forward. She smiled prettily at him, but he was absolutely captivated by the girl on the opposite end of the dance floor. He tried to find her in the swirl of taffeta and lace, his head twisting left and right to catch sight of her.

The stern-faced floor manager, skirt lifted, made her way over to cue the orchestra, while Vivian stood near the grand piano to make sure Thomas began at the appointed time.

Finally, four dances later, the stunning girl was introduced to John in the refreshment room. Eliza Stutzbach, from New York. Eliza, he formed her name on his lips, silently. He lifted her hand and kissed the back of it, the sweet perfume of her skin tickled his nose. Older than he by some years, she had the prettiest green almond-shaped eyes and her pale skin was flawless and soft as cotton.

"Eliza, will you dance with me?" he asked, offering his right arm. She placed her hand in the crook of his arm. His back straightened with pride, the turn of heads made him smile as he escorted the unfamiliar auburn beauty onto the floor.

"Did your father know he was a talented nigger when he purchased him?" she asked.

It was an innocent query to John's ears; after all, most of the guests were fascinated with the famous musical slave. As they spun about, John told her what he knew of the day his father brought the blind slave boy to *Solitude* and continued with more stories of Thomas's antics. Eliza laughed easily, her head thrown back. She kept her body close to his, pressed her chest against him, bent her knee inside his knee and lingered there, her eyes holding his, for one long moment. A tingling rush seared through his body. It occurred to John then, she wasn't some innocent girl pretending to be a woman; she *was* a woman. No doubt, she would be at the center of his dreams that night, hands buried deep beneath the thick quilts, pleasure culminating in ripples of fantasy.

John with Eliza joined the others on the edge of the ballroom. They stood close and watched the other couples, when suddenly there was a crush of teenage ladies surrounding them, giggling and asking questions about Thomas. The blind slave was the star of the afternoon, making John the *fleur des pois* of the ball, as his young master.

"Does he leave his body and come back like they say?"

"Does he bite?"

"Is he a sorcerer?"

"Of course not," John said with a twinkle. "At least not during the day."

A playful slap came against his shoulder. "I don't believe any of the silly rumors about Tom and witchcraft. He's an awfully talented nigger," Eliza said.

"Would you ladies like to meet him?" John asked. His offer was meant for Eliza, particularly.

"Yes, please, it'd be mighty nice," came the chorus of replies.

John gave a bow and gestured for the ladies to follow him.

"Are you for certain he doesn't bite?"

"*Oui*, I am sure, *mademoiselle*," John said, before coming to a stop in front of the grand piano. "Tom, there are some lovely ladies who would like to make your acquaintance. Say hello."

"Tom says 'hello,'" Thomas said. He leaned back on the piano stool and lifted his face toward the women.

The ladies found him charming, petting and stroking his face. Some drew in their breath after running their hands through his thick wooly hair.

"He is real," one swooned.

"Why, he doesn't bite."

"Why, he's not a devil at all."

The young ladies pulled, and pressed, and kneaded the slave like raw cookie dough. And Thomas giggled and shifted on the stool, relishing the attention.

"Would it be possible for him to play a song for us?" Eliza asked, as she gently brushed John's shoulder.

"Of course. What would you like to hear?"

"*Old Master*...No. *Run Nigger Run*! Does he know that?" Eliza said her voice rising with excitement.

Tom knows *Run Nigger Run*," Thomas said and began to play, delighting the girls.

When the trumpet called for the dancing to resume, he grabbed Eliza and guided her onto the dance floor, abandoning the list of women his parents' outlined for him. He led her, his hand wrapped about her small waist.

"Why Mr. Bethune, you should be ashamed," Eliza said with feigned offense.

His cheeks burned, as he thought she was referring to his hand on her waist. But as he lifted his hand, she quickly intercepted it and put it back in place.

"Tell me then, how is it I've transgressed?" John asked.

"No bow of greeting, no request for my dance card."

"My apologies, *mademoiselle*," he said, gracefully guided her into a turn. "May I have the pleasure of dancing with you, my lady?"

They both laughed.

"You're dangerously close to tearing my dress."

"I'll mend it myself," he said, pulling her closer.

"You're a naughty boy for one who supposedly descends from royalty," she said, her voice low, tantalizing. "And owns the greatest Negro in all of Georgia."

"I'll show you supposedly." He led her into an exaggerated spin. "You my lady, are the belle of this ball."

From the balcony, the Colonel narrowed his eyes. "He's lost his mind," he muttered. He'd been watching John frolic shamelessly. Such a blatant display of familiarity was not in good taste. The Colonel recognized a woman whose innocence was long gone. He knew her kind. She was ill-bred, a woman who luxuriated in the favors of men. How did she get an invitation to the ball and why wasn't the dance manager monitoring their number of dances? They were already on dance number three. Surely John had reserved a quadrille or polka with one of the families of old name, perhaps the Mercer daughters? The Colonel looked at his watch, then turned away from the railing.

He had important business to attend to in the *grand parlor*, business he was not looking forward to, but he was displeased with the direction the evening was taking for his son. He sighed. The Colonel couldn't deny the charms of a loose woman, his son was beguiled by her.

The Colonel walked through the French doors of the *grand parlor* into the cloud of smoke. "There's our host," belted Governor Joseph Brown in his booming voice. A heavy-set man, he cut a startling vision with his thick, white-as-snow-beard that provided stark contrast to his youthful features. He was holding a glass of bourbon in one hand and slapping the Colonel on the shoulder with the other. "I heard your slave, Tom, was the toast of North Carolina, Colonel."

"Governor, what you heard is correct," the Colonel said with a smile.

"I look forward to making my way to the ballroom later on."

"Please do," the Colonel said. And facing the room, he nodded with a slight bow toward a dozen serious faced men scattered about. "Gentlemen."

Some of the black-frocked men, professors, lawmakers, merchants, and bankers, stood near the flaming hearth smoking cigars. Others were drinking brandy around the game table.

"Colonel, you know Senator Jefferson Davis?" a familiar voice said from behind.

Judge Cobb introduced a tall and distinguished looking man with deep set, piercing eyes. The Colonel was surprised to see such an important man in the center of his *grand parlor*.

"Senator Davis, yes, of course." He'd met Jefferson Davis, a West Point graduate, some years earlier at a theater production in New York.

"Colonel, I was telling Judge Cobb, that many of us have family ties to the American Revolution and served this country faithfully in the war against Mexico," said Senator Davis with a thick Mississippi accent.

Servants entered and offered trays of chocolates, cookies, and punch. Charity too moved about the room with red wine, the Colonel and Jefferson Davis each removed a glass by its stem.

"The Yankee papers are letting that Negro, Fredrick Douglass, run amok," Senator Davis was saying and his eyes flashed with grave seriousness. "He's spreading lies about the way our slave property is treated here." He tilted his glass. "We need your help, Colonel."

"Indeed, the North has drawn a line in the sand, Colonel, and we must have strong men willing to stand up for the South," added the Judge.

"Of course. Anything I can do," the Colonel said. "What is it you gentlemen have in mind?"

Senator Davis exchanged a serious look with some of the other men in the room. "We need you to announce a call for secession in your newspaper."

"Secession in the *Columbus Enquire*?" reiterated the judge.

"Secession?" the Colonel managed to whisper. A sense of dread spread over him. He had hoped this moment would never come. But his parlor was filled with a dozen of the most powerful men in the southern states and they were all in agreement.

"Our own country, Colonel," the Governor said.

It's suicide! The Colonel thought, but didn't say. He sat back in his chair and pressed his fingers against his mouth, as if contemplating. The government would never allow the Southern states to leave the Union without war, and a war would be horror.

"Jefferson, here, would run for President," the Governor was saying.

The Colonel took a deep breath before speaking. If they persisted with a decision to secede, there would be no turning back. "Gentlemen, I understand your concerns, however, we cannot let our emotions get the best of our wisdom."

"You own more slaves than any of us, yet you'd consider yielding to the Yankees?"

"Colonel, you have the most to lose."

"Which is why I think, as responsible men, we must proceed toward the future with a degree of prudence," the Colonel said.

"We must act now or the North will see to it our way of life is ended." Having heard the reluctance in the Colonel's voice, Senator Davis had already begun making his way back toward the ball. He paused just before reaching the doors. "It's as inevitable as the sun setting in the west. Sooner or later, everyone will have to choose sides. Even you, Colonel, with your fancy slave prodigy," he said.

"Mr. Davis," the Colonel stopped him, "Choosing sides is not in question, but whether or not we're at that wretched hour. Has it come to this so soon?" He glanced around the room at the slow, resolute nods.

"Every one of us in this room believes on the graves of all those we love, the time has come," Judge Cobb said.

The Colonel stood up. "Then I assure you, I am with you, my brothers of the South." He walked toward Senator Davis, "and I will declare it in the *Columbus Enquirer.*"

"Well done, Colonel," Jefferson Davis said. "When you get a chance Colonel, you'll have to see my new dog. It's a Chin, an impressive looking creature given to me by our ambassador from a kingdom called Japan."

XVI.

A few miles outside of Philadelphia, the whooshing hum of a horse drawn reaper could be heard coming from a sprawling winter wheat field. Thomas and the Colonel rode on the back carriage of the machine while Perry Oliver and the entire troupe waited. Arms folded in the cold, and irritated, the performers spat curses and complained near a dirt road. While the tour had stopped to patch up a few broken wheels on some of the wagons, Thomas became fascinated by the sounds the cutting machine made and threw a tantrum until the Colonel agreed to let him take a ride.

"Again," Thomas yelped, clapping, having great fun despite the frosty weather.

"Tom, everyone is waiting for us," the Colonel said over the reaper's thwack. "We must enter the city so you can rehearse."

"Again," Thomas insisted. The Colonel shook his head, but acquiesced. If it pleased the slave, then the six-mile journey into Philadelphia would have to wait, even if it irritated Perry Oliver, the performers, and stagehands. "Again. Yes, why not?" the Colonel said, pulling his knit hat lower to warm his ears.

Perry watched the reaper take another turn beneath the pastel sun and shook his head. The tour was already a half day behind schedule on account of a stagehand's passing from the quinsy. The body had started to decay, so there was no thought of carrying him back to South Carolina, but a casket was built and a reasonable grave dug.

Perry snacked on blackberries and grumbled beneath his breath when the Colonel and his slave finally sauntered up to their carriage.

"*Monsieur* Oliver," the Colonel said, having heard every mumbled word. "While she's a very lovely little lady, I think we both know audiences are not flocking to these great halls to see Francesca or the juggling monkeys."

The oft-cheeky Perry went to open his mouth, but nothing came out.

In every city, the tour had added extra shows to accommodate the demand in ticket sales, thanks to the retarded prodigy. It was a powerful rebuke: the other acts were mediocre copies of P.T. Barnum's road show and Perry knew it. The talented blind slave boy was one of a kind. Proving to be a major draw, Perry could hardly keep track of performance requests.

Now, for the first time ever, the Perry Oliver Travelling Troupe was on its way to the North before the summer season. Shortly after the Bethune's winter ball, a music hall representative from the city of Philadelphia had sent a query specifically requesting shows by Blind Tom. Though he would never admit it, the Colonel was correct: Blind Tom was the main attraction. The Colonel, however, knew the slave's value and did not need his affirmation.

"Philadelphia is awaiting us, *Monsieur Oliver*. We should be on our way," the Colonel said cheerily, and he dismissed him with a triumphant nod.

The Colonel took in a deep breath of fresh air, the belief he was actually here in the "City of Brotherly Love," needed to sink in. He blew into his gloves. The Philadelphia Academy of Music, on the corner of Broad and Locust Street, was one of the finest musical facilities in the world. No city was more critical to Thomas's reputation as a legitimate concert pianist than Philadelphia. The Colonel was apprehensive and excited all rolled together; no amount of happiness exceeded what he felt today except the imminent birth of his sixth child.

He gathered his collar around his neck and turned toward the front entrance. The power of the place didn't fully register until he was looking down on the three thousand-seat-facility, from the third balcony. Hundreds of oil lamps were mounted on the *palcoscenico* and one thousand oil lamps were positioned around the theater waiting to be lit later that evening. His eyes drifted across the hall, past its massive crystal chandelier.

Violins screeched from the orchestra pit. The Colonel marveled at the acoustics, then his mind quickly returned to the day's significance. In the South, the slave presently enjoyed regional fame, his name on the glossed lips of ladies during tea and well-coiffed gentleman at the clubs. But Philadelphians had a passion that burned for the arts. If dazzled by Thomas; the cultured citizens of Philadelphia could lift Blind Tom to international acclaim. Poe wrote from his house here. Strauss and Tchaikovsky headlined here, opera divas sang on its stages, and the best composers sailed across the sea to its ports. It was *the* must-stop city for the world's most prominent international performers. To say Philadelphians were cultural snobs would be an understatement and the city boasted the most skeptical newspaper critics in the country.

Now, the Colonel was completely lost in his thoughts, when he noticed Perry Oliver negotiating the rows of seats in front of him.

"Have important visitors here, Colonel," Perry Oliver said, making his way up the carpeted aisle to greet him.

"Mayor Richard Vaux and Ian McAllister," Perry said. "These two gents are the reason we are here and they plan on attendin' both shows tonight."

"I'm overwhelmed with great appreciation at your city's kind invitation," the Colonel said, receiving the mayor's thick cold hand, and then the slim wet grasp of his companion.

"Friends of ours in Memphis recommended, no insisted, we wire Mr. Oliver and bring Blind Tom to the great city of Philadelphia," Mayor Vaux said. "Blind Tom has caused quite a stir here. We expect he will live up to it," said Mayor Vaux.

"I assure you, he will not disappoint," the Colonel replied.

"We know good music," Mayor Vaux said, "and the Coloreds, they know good music as well."

"And I am aware of the daggers your newspapermen's pens can throw. Fortunately for all of us, Tom likes to please. Expect the highest caliber, the highest," the Colonel promised.

"Or off with your heads."

The mayor laughed, looked at his watch and excused himself.

"So whaddya think Colonel?" Perry asked the Colonel as they took in the magnificent gilded hall. "Not bad for a failed Irish potato farmer, eh?"

"Not bad at all," the Colonel said. "They are more serious about their art here than I imagined. If Tom's not up to their high standards they will serve his head on a platter."

"Like John the Baptist. No doubt about it," Perry laughed, though his voice took on a low, wistful tone. "But if the boyo kin win over this city, we'll be sittin' fat and pretty in the North. I've personally paid a handsome sum for the most celebrated musicians and some scientists ta be in attendance. I'm a bettin' man, Colonel, an' I got my money on the boy."

Vivian bit her bottom lip. She'd never seen so many diamonds and gold earrings, feathers and firs, top hats and capes. She peeked from behind the stage curtain, in awe of the lavishly dressed patrons. Sparkles from the jewelry twinkled in the gaslights like a constellation in the midnight sky.

Blind Tom was the last act, the reason the Philadelphia Music Hall was filled to overflowing. Though she could feel the audience's excitement, Vivian felt queasy. She glanced back at Thomas, on his hands and knees, looking for a spider.

"Please do well," she murmured to herself. Of course by "do well" she meant: "please stay at the keyboard," "don't hop off the stool," "certainly don't roll on the stage back and forth." In Nashville, during a performance of Haydn's concerto for pianoforte, he'd made such a spectacle of himself, crawling on his knees on stage. Although the crowd seemed to enjoy the unorthodox interruption, his antics certainly weren't what Philadelphians were after.

She took a breath to calm herself.

Thomas was oblivious. He was in a playful mood. As the set dressers pushed backdrops off the stage, he rocked back and forth in his shiny black boots: heel, toes, heel, toes, and was making a plucking noise by snapping his tongue against the roof of his mouth. Vivian took one more glance at the sold out house, the eastern gentry was lined in boxes on the second tier along the curve of the house and prime seats across from the stage. She'd grasped the importance of this performance long before the Colonel cornered her at the changing post the other evening to ask whether he'd memorized the new piano quartet by Brahms. "Make sure the boy is ready," he'd said.

"Miss Vivian, Tom's gonna play *The Reaper,*" Thomas said behind her.

"It's going to be lovely, Tom," she said of his newest composition that was inspired by the ride he'd taken in the field with the Colonel. "Come, it's time for the piano." She led him onto the stage to the grand piano. The Negro orchestra settled into chairs and the Colonel took the front of the stage and announced Blind Tom.

The Colonel lifted the red curtain and entered the promoter's box, settling into the seat next to Vivian. The music teacher tilted her hips and leaned toward his shoulder. "He's playing beautifully," she whispered.

He felt a pulsating excitement for Thomas, as he gazed down at him playing on the large stage surrounded by candles and multicolored gaslights. He looked around the hall. In front of him was the dark, curly-haired, Senator Albert Colquitt, wealthy from lace making. He was with his graceful wife Delilah, and apparently quite drunk from the way he seemed to be groping her.

In the box beside Senator Colquitt was the fair-haired Olé Bull; the handsome Norwegian violinist, who'd learned of the slave prodigy from Liszt.

"Travelled all the way from California by rail to be here tonight," the Colonel whispered to Vivian. Bull's esteemed presence made the Colonel's stomach dance with nerves.

But as he peered down onto the glowing stage, through the flickering lights of colors, reds and blues and yellows, there seemed to be no reason to worry. It was beautiful; the music Thomas was playing, full of passion, flowing seamlessly beneath his fingertips from his original compositions to those of the classical masters. And looking up at the Colored section, all were on their feet, leaning over the sides for a closer look, excited and proud to see one of their own on the big stage. Indeed, Thomas was brilliant. He hovered over the keyboard, as if he yearned for the audience to hear the angels he heard. See the visions of heaven driving the expression of each note, each movement, to be transported with him into the remarkable wonders of his creative mind.

On his final song, Thomas lifted his hands from the keys and the last note began to fade away, his foot on the damper for maximum affect; the final notes lingered in the air, echoing throughout the large hall. When the reverberations finally faded, the crowd stood to its well-heeled feet. Serge capes flowed, curls bounced and silk dresses swayed, as palms met together in a deafening, thunderous applause.

The claps were all around him punctuated by the feverish stomping of boots against the hard wood floors and shouts of appreciation. Then Vivian beside the Colonel as they walked through a door and down to the stage said, "They love him."

Another hoarse voice came from behind the Colonel's ear. "The boyo did it. He won Philadelphia. It's done," Perry whispered.

"Yes, Mr. Oliver, it is done, isn't it?" the Colonel said. Perry smiled and produced a cigar. "To Thomas Bethune," he beamed.

XVII.

Senator Colquitt held a lavish party that Saturday with Thomas at the piano. Neither the Colonel nor the women by his side saw Lord Harrington walking toward them through the crush, brown hair glistening from pomade. Anxious to meet the Colonel, the elusive baron broke the circle and did not wait for proper introductions to be made. Instead, the normally aloof Englishman with his straight hair parted on the side, took it upon himself to extend his hand to the Colonel with a hearty greeting.

"It's a pleasure meeting you Colonel. Lord Harrington," the baron said. "I have a refined musical palette and last night was an evening of first-class entertainment."

"Thank you Lord Harrington," the Colonel said with mirrored grace and a slight bow.

"The slave boy is quite a fascinating enigma. Is he a mental defect?" Lord Harrington asked.

"To try and fully understand him is futile," interrupted a heavily accented voice from behind the two men. "He is a solveless riddle," said Olé Bull.

"Mr. Bull, it's an honor, *Monsieur*," the Colonel said, shaking the virtuoso's soft hand.

"Colonel, no man alive possesses musical powers as great as your Tom," Bull said. "Not even my dear friend Chopin."

"Gentleman," Senator Colquitt interrupted, "do you mind if I borrow the Colonel?"

The party was in full swing when the Senator walked the Colonel down a hallway and the two men slipped through a back door where a slave stood holding two overcoats.

"I'm afraid it would cause too much suspicion if we donned our coats inside," the Senator explained, guiding the Colonel toward a private garden path. "Our friends in Georgia, in Tennessee, and Louisiana have asked me to talk to you. This entire matter is a disaster for the South," Senator Colquitt said gravely.

"I have always stood for Southern Unity, Senator," the Colonel said, lifting his chin.

"Make no mistake, Lincoln is a serious threat. I may live in Philadelphia, but my heart will always be in South Carolina with my childhood home. If Lincoln wins the election against President Buchanan, the South will protect itself and seize the Capital. It's a critical time, Colonel. The South needs you. You must act."

He realized it was indeed inevitable, as Jefferson Davis said: The South and the North were on a collision course that could not be halted.

"As I've made clear, I will always serve the South."

The Senator smiled. "Good, good. Then come." He gestured for the Colonel to follow him out the garden gate. They walked a quarter of a mile to a large barn. Inside, there were two covered wagons with four men standing beside them, armed with rifles. Amid chickens and sheep and horses, the Colonel saw a flurry of cloaked activity. Senator Colquitt stopped and stood aside while field slaves tossed large burlap sacks into a wagon, disappearing after the last bag was loaded.

Walking over to the wagon, Senator Colquitt motioned for him to follow and quickly explained. "There's quinine, ether, morphine, and the like," he said, speaking hurriedly. "The South must be prepared. Your slave's concert tour provides the perfect cover. Continue to travel on the tour with Tom. No one will suspect you of carrying contraband.

"Someone will contact you on the tour. Don't worry about when or where. He'll find you and he'll ask if you're a friend."

The Colonel nodded.

"And, Colonel, I must warn you…be cautious with Tom," he whispered. "You mustn't accept any more invitations from free states on this tour."

"But, why?" the Colonel's mind raced. Why would the senator bother to mention his slave?

"There've been rumors of a plot out of Washington to kidnap your blind slave."

"That's preposterous." He tried to take a step back, but Senator Colquitt still had hold of his shoulders. The Colonel shook his head in confusion. "Kidnap, Tom?"

"We have sources in the Yankee camp," Senator Colquitt continued.

"Showmen?" the Colonel asked.

Senator Colquitt shook his head. "He is a profitable attraction and that's a powerful motivator, but no, not showmen…"

"Abolitionists?" the Colonel whispered.

The senator nodded. "Word of the remarkable boy has spread. He's more valuable for their movement than Frederick Douglass. He could raise the profile for their cause as well as bring in all the money needed to finance it. Once you leave here, keep him in the South. You and your slave are in danger, now. Even here, this afternoon."

The Colonel shuddered. He was in enemy territory. Philadelphia belonged to the Quakers. The religious sect was well organized and well financed, many were ardent abolitionists. They were not his friends, but his mortal enemies.

"May they burn in hell," the Colonel growled. He would not ever be made to feel shame for his Divine right to own slaves. "They will regret they ever conceived of such a plan."

Seething, the Colonel walked with Senator Colquitt back toward the mansion. His thoughts raced. Was it true or simply a wild rumor? Would God give him the blind boy to care for, then allow him to be used as a pawn in the unrest between the states? "Over my dead body," he said, in a low growling voice, stabbing the back stair of the main house with his cane.

Senator Colquitt opened the back door. Upon entering the warmth of the grand house, the Colonel followed his host back to the crowded living room. Soon the humming of light-hearted banter surrounded him, but the casual manner he had earlier was forever stowed away in the shadows of the Colquitt barn. Now, he stood rigid, away from the open doors, his back at the large hearth. He sidled closer to the window, scanned the room, peering at the pale faces, the brown and blue eyes, all the while keeping track of Thomas. He nodded graciously, but his eyes shifted quickly. He was in soldier mode; someone in that room was spying on Blind Tom and he was on high alert. Amid the giggles and chatter, he surveyed every powdered and bearded face at the party, searching to see which smiling guest seemed suspicious.

A few days passed. Though he'd warned Vivian and Annie not to let Thomas out of their sight, the Colonel hadn't told them or Perry the seriousness of the problem. The teacher and his attendant had murmured yes, but always kept him close, for the most part.

Outside Pittsburgh, the Colonel kept a revolving pistol next to his bed. He pulled off his heavy boots and sat down to read Dickens by the oil lamp when he heard music and smelled wild goose roasting. Ill at ease, he decided to check on

Thomas and make sure he was safe. He pulled his boots back on and set out through the dimly lit camp. He trudged through the labyrinth of tents, checking each one, his temper rising. When he finally found Thomas's tent, all was quiet and calm, but when he waved his kerosene lamp by the cot, he saw it was empty.

Annie was hard asleep in the the next cot. "Where is Tom?" the Colonel demanded.

"Tom?" Annie mumbled in sleepy confusion, her eyes struggling to focus. "He's in his bed, sir."

"He is not in his bed. I told you to keep an eye on him. Get up, now. We have to find him," he said.

He moved swiftly out of the tent, loudly calling out, "Tom! Tom!"

Perry could hear the Colonel's calls for Thomas from his tent and emerged holding a tin cup of liquor. "What's going on, Colonel?" He was a little cloudy from the rum and struggled to focus.

"Tom's missing," the Colonel said without slowing. "Tom! Where's a flute or a violin? We need an instrument, quickly."

Vivian was exiting her tent, pulling on her overcoat; she had been awakened by the noise. The Colonel raced to her, grabbed her by the shoulders. "Have you seen Tom?"

"He's in the tent with the musicians, is something wrong?" Vivian said in her prim calm manner.

"You left him with the musicians?" He held her gaze with an icy glare.

Vivian hesitated. "He usually plays with the musicians until the early morning and certainly I planned to retrieve him as I always do, sir," she said.

The Colonel rushed toward the sound of harmonicas and fiddling. He stepped inside the low-lit cavern. The musicians were drunk and didn't stop. The Colonel approached a thickset man with rotted teeth who was strumming a guitar. "Have you men seen Tom?"

"Tom?"

"I'm told he was here playing with you."

"No, we ain't seen that blind nigger for a while!" The thickset man said, laughing.

"Maybe he seduced some young darky with his séance music," a thin banjo player with stringy hair offered, before taking a puff from a hashish pipe. The men descended into liquor-induced guffaws. But the Colonel's eyes caught fire. Suddenly, he was across the room, grabbing the thin man by his shirt and slamming him against a pole, his banjo crashing to the ground. The Colonel twisted his arm and pushed him into the pole again.

"Mr. Bethune!" Annie called out. She glanced around at all the musicians afraid her boss was outnumbered.

But not one of the musicians moved a muscle. They were too afraid to take the Colonel on, some out of fear of the military man, others out of fear for their jobs.

The Colonel threw the helpless banjo player to the side and considered stomping him with his boot. He scorched him with his eyes before turning toward Annie. "Are you too simple to understand the most basic instructions?"

Annie cowered and her face turned red with shame.

The Colonel stormed out.

"The slave's been missing about two hours," Perry said, twigs snapping beneath his boots. "So considering his blindness, it's doubtful he's traveled more than three miles by foot, twenty miles if by horse."

The Colonel's expression was grim as he crunched through ice and wet shrubs. Maybe he should have shared the threat regarding Thomas's safety with the others. Those wretched abolitionists were going to have a field day with Thomas as their banner for their ignoble cause. He stopped for a moment to catch his breath and just when he was feeling too tired and mentally spent, a voice came from the darkness.

"I found him! He's over here!"

Relief swept over the Colonel. He navigated the brush toward the raised voices.

"We've got him! Colonel, he's over here."

"I'm coming!" the Colonel called out.

When he reached the spot where Thomas was found, he saw the boy was mumbling some kind of tune. The slave had his arm draped around his rescuer and was using him for support.

"Thank God!" he said. The Colonel hugged the slave boy with uncharacteristic vigor, only to discover he was soaking wet. The Colonel tilted the oil lamp downward and shuddered. Thomas had no boots and his black toes had icicles forming on them-frostbite was surely setting in. "*Mon Dieu*, we must get him back to camp before he catches pneumonia."

"He's all right, Colonel, 'ceptin for a few scratches on his hands from some thorn bushes. But if I didn't know better, I'd say the lad was drunk and in need of a deadhouse."

Indeed, as the Colonel took off his scarf and wrapped it around Thomas's feet, he noticed the slave's curiously merry mood. The Colonel steadied Thomas and they made their way back toward camp. "Who got this boy drunk?"

There were plenty of stares and complete silence. "Listen to me," he said to the crowd of onlookers. "If any one of you scoundrels have the mind to mess with Tom again. If I see so much as a scratch on the boy, I swear by the Almighty in Heaven, I will kill you."

It was a universal warning and from that point on, the stagehands feared the Colonel.

Thomas slept on a cot inside the Colonel's tent that night and for the three nights the tour was in Pittsburgh. Each night the Colonel tossed and turned. The slightest noise jarred him awake; he would hold his breath, in his mind the noise could be cuffs dangling from a belt loop, boots crushing rocks in the faintest, stealthiest motion. He sat bolt upright and drew his pistol, crept across the floor of the tent and surveyed the premises.

As the days passed he tried to keep his daily routine normal, to behave as usual so as not to arouse undue curiosity, but his mood was overcast. Thomas was a sensation in every city, but there was much turmoil behind-the-scenes. A recent letter he'd received from Frances held both delightful news and cause for concern:

My dear husband James,

Our beautiful daughter, Naomi Jocelyn, was born two days ago, January 19, 1861. She has your gorgeous blue eyes and my golden brown hair. She looks as if she'll have Sarah's lean frame and I think she's going to have Caleb's temperament, she's a fiery one already. I am recovering well and spending my days in bed upon Dr. Bardot's orders. Charity is taking good care of us, as if we were her own. In other matters, I have upon your insistence inquired into John's doings in regards to Eliza Stutzbach and I forbade him to see her. He is beguiled by the girl and continues to sneak off to write her. She is not appropriate for him at all. I'm told she suddenly appeared on her poor aunt's doorstep after some scandal with a married man in New York. When here, she walks alone after twilight. What proper lady conducts herself in such an unbecoming manner? I know he is a man now, but I told him he must untangle his affections as he is betrothed. He should focus on overseeing the workings of the plantation in your absence. But I'm afraid he is a stupid boy in need of your guidance. I've stooped to using Ensa to picking up the post and diverting her letters for him to me. I hate to be deceptive and feel terrible watching him mope around, hoping to hear from her. He is our oldest and we've made such great plans for his future. I am in agreement with you that he must not throw away all that he has to offer by shaming the family over some clever immoral social climber. It's embarrassing and quite beneath him. He calls me a prude when it comes to that indecent girl, but he must learn the world in which we live can be a very cold and cruel place. It has its rules and exchanging love letters with the black sheep of a mediocre family is unacceptable. It's too bad you were unable to be here for the winter concert. Mary volunteered to perform a violin trio with Sarah and another girl from the Academy that turned out quite lovely. I'm so glad to hear Tom's working out well for you and that his new compositions continue to display signs of brilliance. After all these years, to think that our little blind slave possesses such musical gifts still manages to amaze me. I miss you so, my darling. I anxiously await your return.

Love, Frances.

With all that was going on, he feared there would never again be simple, good times. Since the warning at the Colquitt barn, the Colonel had grown indiscriminately suspicious and thin tempered. A man on edge, worried about enemies on all fronts.

XVIII.

Around the hour of nine, laughter, chatter, and banjo music spilled out from a lively Pittsburgh bar located near the harbor. The Colonel sat on a stool at the crowded bar. Leaning forward nose-to-nose with Perry, he slammed his fist onto the counter.

"New York? *Monsieur,* New York was not in our contract. I won't hear of it!"

"You won't hear of New York, Colonel?" Perry was astonished. "It's as important as Philadelphia was for the boyo. Why would I turn down a solid offer like this? It's only a five hour journey from 'ere, we take the rail an' a couple o' ferry boats an' we're there."

"It's not what we agreed! Philadelphia, Pittsburgh, Baltimore, Richmond." The Colonel dug in his heels; he didn't fully trust the promoter and had not told Perry about the kidnapping plot.

"He's under contract to me. I kin do as I please with 'im!" Perry shouted. He was livid with the Colonel for his resistance. "New York City is the most lucrative tour destination to date. They're salivating for Blind Tom." He held up a fistful of telegraphs as evidence, showing the Colonel he was receiving wires at nearly every engagement requesting multiple performances for the slave.

"Go ahead, take the tour to New York," the Colonel seemed to relent. Perry's eyebrows rose and he nodded. "But I will be forced to sue you, if you take Tom."

"Sue me? Why won't you let the boyo go?" The Colonel watched the tips of Perry's ears burn red. He knew he was being unreasonable. As a businessman it was inconceivable to skip over New York.

"I'm sorry, Mr. Oliver, but I can't explain why. As wrong as it seems to you, Tom will not go to New York."

"Well it don't make a darn lick o' sense, Colonel. This ain't like you. First you want to renegotiate the boyo's contract for more money, and now we kin make a killin' in New York an' you say no. What's going on with ya?"

Red-faced, Perry sat up straight on his stool and sighed. He shook his head, downed one last gulp of whiskey and slammed the shot glass onto the bar. "Fine," he said, accepting defeat. "The boyo won't go to New York." Reluctantly, he agreed to take the tour from Pennsylvania back south to Baltimore, and then Richmond, Virginia as planned.

The Colonel averted his eyes from Perry's angry gaze and slid a few coins on the counter to pay for their drinks. Rising from his stool, he pushed his way past smelly, wobbling customers and strode out of the bar.

The next day, Perry pulled back the curtains on the carriage to let in the early daylight. He sat with one foot tucked in a groove along the side of the backseat and sorted through a basket of mail, still stewing over the Colonel's refusal to allow Blind Tom to perform in New York City.

"Doesn't make any sense," Perry muttered, picking up a piece of mail.

The sun peeked through the crack in the curtains and fell on the stack of letters on the seat next to him. Perry held a separate stack on his lap, mostly warm missives from professional organizations, music hall promoters, and private citizens wanting to hire Blind Tom for intimate concerts, private balls, and charity events.

"The fine Holy City of Charleston is requesting additional shows," he said, tossing the letter to the side, while Vivian across from him, hurriedly scribbled the information down on her notepad.

"Baroness de Pontalba in New Orleans is requesting Tom for her spring ball. Her tastes are Verdi and Weber." He tossed the letter across to Vivian, then paused upon picking out a piece of mail with soft gold lace trim and the Great Seal of the United States. He slid his finger across the beautiful cream stationery, then leaned forward and opened the trap at once, shouting at the coachman.

"Stop. Stop the horses! Stop the horses!"

"Mr. Oliver, are you all right? What is it Mr. Oliver?" Vivian asked.

But Perry didn't answer, didn't hear her voice. As soon as the horses clopped to a stop, he stood up. The coach driver opened the door and he climbed down the stairs onto the frozen path. Hurriedly, he made his way past the first three wagons to the Colonel's golden carriage and knocked on the door.

When the Colonel opened the latch, Perry met the sweet smell of candles burning. Annie sat next to Thomas on the seat opposite of the Colonel, her stringy blonde hair pulled beneath a cream-Colored bonnet.

"What is it, Mr. Oliver, is something wrong?" the Colonel asked.

Perry held out the fancy envelope from Washington.

The Colonel took in the Presidential Seal and reached for the missive. He lifted his brows.

"The White House, Colonel."

Perry hovered near the flickering candle, biting his nails, anxious to hear what it said, as the Colonel read. The Colonel rested the missive on his lap and sighed. Perry couldn't stand it.

"For the love o' Jesus, Joseph an' Mary, Colonel," he blurted, his Irish brogue thickened with excitement. "What does the damn thing say?"

"We've been invited by President Buchanan," the Colonel said, his words as dry as a faucet running out of water. "It seems the President would like Tom to perform at the White House," the Colonel whispered.

"Invited by the President you say?" He said with a grin, looking up at the sky. "The White House! Now folks in the North will see what we already know. Our boy Tom is a miracle. Right Tom, boy?" Perry said, turning toward Thomas.

"Mr. Oliver's fifty-nine," he angled his small head away from Perry. "Fifty-nine's an ugly number."

The Colonel rubbed his face with his hands. He could be travelling to his death by allowing Thomas to perform in the Capital, but he would forever regret forgoing such an honor.

"Tom?" he said. "This is an unprecedented honor. President Buchanan wants to hear your beautiful music and has invited us to the White House in Washington City."

Thomas angled his head toward his master and smiled.

"President Buchanan wants to hear my beautiful music," Tom said. "Tom will play his beautiful music for President Buchanan in the White House."

"Yes, yes," Perry said. "Yes you will."

But Thomas didn't acknowledge him. Instead, he kept his head down and made bubbles with his lips. "Tom, Mr. Oliver's talking to you?" the Colonel asked.

Tom stopped smiling at once. "Tom don't like 'im."

Perry returned to his own coach and the Colonel leaned back against the green crushed-velvet seat. He could be travelling to his death by allowing Thomas to perform in the Capitol City, but he would not be able to live with himself if he forewent such a great opportunity.

So, he set aside his worries, refusing to think about enemies, spies, or kidnappers and marveled at President Buchanan's invitation. For in the history of America, no Negro had ever been invited to perform at the White House, and

God had chosen Thomas to be the first. Nodding to himself, the Colonel closed his eyes, savoring the honor while listening to the horses' hoofbeats.

Once camp was set that night and the fires were aflame, the scent of roasting wild rabbit mingled with the scent of burning wood. The Colonel decided to visit Perry's tent. Reasoning it would be financially foolish for the Irishman to conspire in any plot against the talented slave, he told Perry about the threat of an abolitionist plot to take Thomas.

"Kidnap? Kidnap the boyo Tom?" he whispered, lowering the whiskey glass onto the small table next to his bed. His voice was raspy from a lingering cold. He rubbed his rough hands against the stubbles on his chin. "That explains New York."

"It would have been unwise to risk any more time in the North. But President Buchanan's invitation…well, I've come up with a plan to protect him."

Perry lifted a kerosene lamp off the floor and angled the flame so he could see the Colonel better. "Damn Yankees get ahold of him, my investment's shot ta hell."

"That's not going to happen."

"Them Boston boys are sure ta be packin' and ta shoot any fella in their way."

It was a grim reality. Every family south of the Mason-Dixon knew about the mean anti-slavery network spreading misery like cancer through the veins of the South. Stories of abolitionists, who snatched slaves in broad daylight and hid them in secret networks, had the South on fire. The Colonel despised these lawless invisible men who smiled in the faces of their southern brethren, then stole their property and set them free.

"Remember, we, too, have guns, *Monsieur*," the Colonel reminded Perry.

"Colonel, there's plenty o' money to be made with the boy in the South," he hedged. "Maybe we oughtta bolt an' skip Washington. Ain't worth the risk."

A sigh escaped the Colonel. Washington was neither free nor slave territory. It was an unruly wild district with its own rules regarding the laws of the land.

There were free blacks with registration papers working all over the city, doormen and messengers, blacksmiths, cooks, and barbers, many even owned land. The free Coloreds walked with their top hats held high, though they had curfews at night. And abolitionist advocates and slave trading predators circled about them at all times. Still the dangers, though many, were not enough to discourage the Colonel from bringing Blind Tom to the White House. His mind was made up.

"Tom has been with me since he was a baby," he said, his stare hard and determined. "He is a Bethune, and I'll be damned if I let some lily-livered abolitionists threaten me. Just tell me which men you trust that you can spare."

In the dim glow of candlelight, Perry thought carefully about his crew, then whispered the name of four good hands. "Are you certain of these four men?" the Colonel asked.

Without hesitation, Perry affirmed his choices. "Trust 'em with my life, Colonel."

He thought a moment, then the Colonel nodded and, leaning in close, shared his plan with Perry. Though the Irishman wasn't a warrior, he was a natural fighter, a hardened man who'd traveled rough terrain with rough men.

"Instead of going together to Virginia, some of the troupe will travel ahead," the Colonel said. "The caravan will split up again, at the border." Perry nodded, agreeing to the plan.

XIX.

Hoarfrost hung from windowpanes and sheets of ice covered the Potomac River making it nearly impossible for ships and riverboats to navigate in or out of port. The bridges and black ice made already slippery roads more dangerous, causing the coachman to drive off course. The moments of steady riding never lasted long, but finally the carriage rolled into the city. The Colonel felt a rush in his body. Here he was triumphantly entering the "City of Magnificent Distances" with the most famous, sought after slave in the land.

Washington City was a rural town surrounded by woods, empty fields, and dirt paths with pockets of small neighborhoods several miles apart and then, the most spectacular stone buildings would suddenly appear. It was like a mirage, these dignified white structures with large domes, triangular marble pediments, and high arching windows that served as symbols of liberty, freedom, and dignity for the Union.

Adjusting his boots on the warm bricks, the Colonel looked across at Thomas asleep on the seat across from him. He gazed at the unremarkable-looking boy. He was so ordinary in appearance, and yet, had no trouble performing masterfully before thousands of fans like he did last night in Baltimore. Now, he was going to perform at the White House. The Colonel couldn't help but wonder whether President Buchanan's invitation might be a part of some nefarious ploy to get Blind Tom to the capital. Yet, even as he pondered the hidden dangers, his thoughts returned to the historical implications of Thomas performing for dignitaries in Washington City.

The Colonel's carriage veered off from the main road. A nerve pulsed in his temple, as the horses made the turn. He leaned forward to open the trap door and ordered the driver to stop.

"Yessuh," the short dark servant cried. "Ho, Nelly, Ho!"

The Colonel instructed Annie and Vivian to stay with Thomas inside the carriage until he returned. "Do not allow him out even to use the bathroom." He opened the vehicle door and gave the driver instructions to walk back to the main road where he would see Perry Oliver's vehicle waiting for him, then took over the driving. The multiple reins were unfamiliar, but he took hold of the soft leather and released them with a snap.

The cold wind whistled across the dark Potomac as the carriage rumbled along.

After three miles, he recognized the description of a boulder and copse of dogwood trees at a sharp bend in the river. The Colonel wondered how he'd become an operative for Senator Jefferson Davis's new country when no war had been declared.

He pulled the carriage off the main path, behind a thicket of snow weary trees, and climbed down from the high seat. He paused a moment to listen and make sure he wasn't being followed. Retrieving his compass, he aimed it in the direction of the coordinates.

By the edge of the Potomac, he drew his binoculars from inside his overcoat and kept them trained on the horizon where there appeared to be a small brown vessel moving slowly toward him. After a nervous moment or two, he discerned it was a canoe, and then that there were two men inside it. They angled their long oars and silently steered toward the Colonel, then, threw a rope around an overhanging branch and pulled the boat to shore. The taller of the two, a thickset man at the helm, alighted from the boat and twice waved both arms over his head in wide arcs – the signal to the Colonel.

Certain the men were his contacts the Colonel, emerged from his hiding place. His heart beat double time as he descended the hill.

"You a friend?" the large man asked.

"Yes," the Colonel said with caution.

"Bob Mudd?" he asked.

"Bob Mudd, yes," the Colonel nodded.

"There are some odd fellows in Philadephia," he said.

The Colonel relaxed.

"Indeed. Colonel James Bethune," the Colonel extended his gloved hand.

"Captain Nehemiah Wright. An honor to meet you, sir," he grabbed the Colonel's hand with his big paw. "You have something from Senator Colquitt?"

The Colonel handed him an envelope the Senator had given him in Philadelphia. As if on cue, a heavy wagon rumbled to a stop at the top of the hill.

Nehemiah nodded at the man in the boat, who climbed the bank, and a group of men jumped down from the back of the wagon and scrambled down the hill.

"Colonel?" Nehemiah lifted his brows.

The Colonel motioned for the men to follow him the short distance to his hired coach where thick burlap sacks were tied to the roof. The men quickly removed the ropes and tossed the bags of medical supplies on their backs, then lugged them up the hill and threw them into the back of the wagon. With barely a word exchanged, the job was done and the wagon thundered back into the darkness.

Nehemiah turned to the Colonel, "Be careful out here. If free soil Lincoln wins the election, there's sure to be trouble in the Capital," he said pointedly. Spinning on his heels, Nehemiah scuttled back down the embankment. He hurriedly untied the rope from the tree and tossed it into the boat. Within minutes the canoe was gliding back down the Potomac. The Colonel made his way back to the carriage. He peered in to see Vivian, Annie, and Thomas fast asleep, then climbed to the driver's seat and headed back to the city.

Shivering black bodies trudged slowly through the soft, tiny flakes that fell in thick drops onto the cherry blossoms of Capitol Hill. Half clothed in rags and bound together by heavy iron chains, the Colored slaves clanked a sorrowful melody of misery in the cold morning snow. It was an odd sight to onlookers beyond the shackled servants to see the young slave boy, Thomas, with white servants waiting upon him, fussing over his wellbeing.

On the sidewalk, Annie held an umbrella over the twelve year old Thomas's head, to her own neglect, her pale face covered with flakes, while his music teacher retied the strings dangling from his wool overcoat. Vivian pulled the ends of the strings tight, making a perfect bow, checking it one last time to ensure he made the right impression for the Bethune family before the distinguished gentlemen of the legislature. The Colonel stood in front of the trio near the Capitol steps and nodded his approval. Vivian tugged on Thomas's top hat, so that it sat perfectly upright on his head, before reaching out and grabbing his tiny hand.

The Colonel turned in the drizzle and planted his ivory-handled cane on the next step, then led them up the stairs. The Colonel had called his eldest son John to join them, to help in protecting Thomas, so he and Perry Oliver followed close behind. There had been so much buzz and press about Thomas's White House performance that there was no hope of slipping quietly in and out of the city. Everyone in the party, but Thomas, was on edge. He giggled, taking the Capitol steps with two footed hops and skips.

"The Capitol's home to the House and the Senate," Thomas said like a parrot, taking another hop.

"Yes, Tom." Vivian smiled, lifted her skirts and followed close behind him.

Once inside, the Colonel tipped his head back discreetly and took in the soaring marble rotunda. Its wide circular sandstone walls were surrounded by an intricate frescoed band with ornate carvings, the large dome was adorned with layers of fine pictures depicting the revolution, and historical paintings hung proudly from the walls. Something stirred inside as he gazed at his surroundings—the beauty was awe-inspiring.

Thomas was a sight in his black frock suit and matching new hat from Smith's on Seventh Street, and there were whispers and stares, even fingers pointed. White servants with foreign accents met the group in the foyer and escorted them to a reception room, where coffee and sweets were offered. The visitors were then led through marble hallways on a tour of the elegant high-ceilinged building, before being led to the noisy second floor stairwell to the raucous House of Representatives.

"Colonel Bethune," William Pennington greeted his guest. "It's an honor to host you and Blind Tom," he said. "He's caused quite a stir in the Capitol. As you know, it is rare indeed to find agreement on the Hill, but even the worst of enemies are in agreement over their excitement for Tom's music tonight."

"Tom, say hello to the Speaker of the House, Mr. William Pennington."

William bent down toward Thomas.

"Mr. William Pennington," Thomas said in his boyish voice. "Speaker of the House, born May 4, 1796. One-hundred-twenty-fourth day of the year. The Speaker is a Monday child, fair of face."

Thomas extended his hand. Mr. Pennington's smile froze at the odd prologue and his eyebrows lifted.

"Thomas is merely saying hello, Mr. Speaker," the Colonel offered with a wry grin.

William smiled and engulfed the small boy's black fingers with his large pale paw.

"Hello there, Tom," he said. Then without waiting to meet the others in the group he motioned for them to follow him to the House chambers where dozens of otherwise dignified men sat shouting at each other from handsome wood desks arranged in a wide descending semi-circle. Many chewed tobacco and spat onto the carpeted floor. In the midst of this political theater, finely dressed ladies sat in the front rows, visiting and flitting about as if they were at the opera.

As the Colonel and Thomas drew near the charged inner chamber, ushers greeted them and to the Colonel's surprise, guided them past more tall columns of marble to reserved seats near the front of the House. In spite of all the boisterous turmoil, Thomas's presence made a stir.

On a raised platform stood Stephen Douglas, a distinguished, smartly clad, short gentleman with black hair and a thick hefty nose. "As I said in Illinois, 'if you desire Negroes to vote on an equality with yourselves, and to make them eligible to office, to serve on juries, and to adjudge your rights, then support Mr. Lincoln and the Black Republican party!" he bellowed. A riotous applause erupted around the chamber, met with an equal wave of opposing grumbles. "Now, I do not believe that the Almighty ever intended the Negro to be equal of the white man!"

"That's sure as hell the honest to God's truth," cried a thick southern voice from the center of the hall. For a moment, it appeared the debate would die down, until a voice shouted:

"To what god are you referring? Lucifer?"

An eruption of noise lifted from the tiered chamber again, hissing and loud voices. The Colonel lightly applauded, and some gentlemen stood up from the balcony level screaming fire down at Douglas, so loud it cut through the baritone and alto of voices.

"Where is the Coloreds' freedom, their liberty, their Pursuit of Happiness!" a long, rangy gentleman bellowed resentfully. His voice was so loud a bear would surely run away from it.

"Yes! Where's Blind Tom's freedom? Blind Tom should be free!"

Everyone in the chamber seemed to rise from his or her seats and talk at once. The Colonel rotated his head to see whence the mention of Tom. He tried to take in every bend and nook of the spacious room, but the voice was lost in the crowd. The fine clad gentlemen were acting like wild savages. A junior representative swung his fist and punched a senior lawmaker in his nose and the chamber erupted once again as members scrambled to pull the two men apart.

Turning, the Colonel saw John gathering up Thomas and felt Mr. Pennington's tap on his shoulder; a group of ushers crowded around him, urging him toward the doors, with assurances and apologies.

John and Vivian called after the Colonel, but he did not slow down as he raced with the boy down the Capitol's steps.

"Come Tom, faster." He dragged Tom along as fast as they could move toward the Wilton Hotel, while Thomas quoted Douglass. "Now, I do not believe that the Almighty ever intended the Negro to be equal of the white man!" Thomas shouted. "Tom, hush, you're creating a spectacle," warned the Colonel. He didn't look back as he entered the hotel, determined to get Thomas safely to his room.

He avoided the sweeping oak staircase in the front lobby, instead he slipped through a side door, up a set of backstairs with Thomas's hand firmly in his, heart beating wildly from fear. Just get to the room, he thought. Past a servant wiping down the walls and up three more flights to the fourth floor. Walking down the gas-lit corridor toward his room near the middle of the hall, the Colonel stopped cold when he heard, "Damn Yankee thieves!" A woman cried pitifully.

"As the general manager of this hotel, I promise you, we do not condone this. We will do everything in our power to see to her return," said the older gentleman with salt-and-pepper hair. A crowd formed around the fine looking lady in a feathered hat.

"I don't believe you'll do any such thing! Damn Yankees!" she screamed.

John was already there, hurrying toward the Colonel with Perry at his shoulder.

"Some guests say abolitionists lured several Colored maids away," John told the Colonel with a grave look on his face. The Colonel's eyes widened.

He squeezed Thomas's hand and escorted him to his room. When Vivian arrived, breathless and worried, the Colonel informed her of the thefts and reminded her. "You must keep a proper eye on Tom, don't leave his side unless you are sure you've left him under the watch of John, Mr. Perry, or myself. There's no honor in Washington City. Not for another man's property, they hold nothing sacred."

Vivian hugged the sleepy boy against her side. The supper hour was spent going over a security strategy for Thomas. The men huddled together and decided to split the evening into three shifts, four hours long. During each patrol, one man would walk the dark hallway throughout the night looking for anyone who appeared suspicious, anyone who approached Thomas's room.

The day of the White House performance, the Colonel cinched the pistol beneath his frock while exiting the carriage onto Pennsylvania Avenue. He looked up and down the snowy street, eyeing the posters announcing the concert performance of "The Magnificent Blind Tom." He waited for Annie and Vivian to emerge from the carriage with Thomas. Soon the street would throng with carriages and crowds of Washingtonians excited to see the boy in concert.

"Stay close together," the Colonel cautioned.

"Tom's performing for President James Buchanan at the White House," Thomas said with a hop down the carriage steps.

"Indeed you are, Tom," the Colonel said. He looked down at the excited boy. He was indeed a boy like any other, the Colonel thought, childish and common, except when he sat down at the piano, placed a violin beneath his chin, or a flute to his lips. At the front doors of the White House, the Chief Usher was waiting to take Thomas through the main entrance down the red carpet to the Blue Room, where he was scheduled to perform. Before walking through the doors beneath the blue Presidential Seal, the Colonel turned to John, "stay alert," he warned, "don't allow for any distractions."

John nodded gravely as they entered. There was a vast blue Persian rug, blue chairs, and lush blue and gold satin drapes that opened up to a view of the south lawn. The Colonel instructed John to guard the two large doors on the north side of the parlor. Perry moved a chair onto the platform. He and the two broad-shouldered hands he trusted were overseeing the final preparations for the concert. They repositioned chairs for the orchestra and set music stands in place, but their primary job was to keep close to Thomas's performance area and protect it against potential ambush.

The Colonel noted six doors circling the oval chamber. In a gilded mirror he saw Vivian guiding Thomas, explaining to him the layout of the space. She passed a large blue marble-top table and walked up six steps to the raised platform, where a Chickering grand piano was perched like a conceited swan. Climbing the stool, Thomas lifted the top of the piano and began to tune the large instrument.

An hour later, the political patrons began to enter the Blue Room and ushers escorted the guests to their respective seats. The Colonel knew some famed distraction tactics and braced for some kind of rumpus: a loud argument, scream, or a sudden rush of movement toward the stage.

It wasn't until President Buchanan arrived and the last of Washington's chic *beaux mondes* had settled into their sapphire chairs that the Colonel could appreciate the oval room designed in the French Empire Style. He took in its gilded furniture and the French chandelier with acanthus leaves. When the house lights lowered and Thomas completed his first piece, the Colonel relaxed. There was little likelihood of an attack during the concert. The danger would come in the frenzy upon its conclusion.

He allowed his eyes to close, as the sweet resonance of a flute soared solo above the orchestra. The instrument's notes drifted eloquently along various ascending themes like a leaf carried by the gentlest of winds. And then a mellifluous falsetto began singing Rossini's Cinderella *Non Piu Mesta*. All of it, the flute, the singing, was of course, young Thomas, playing classical composers as well as original harmonies whispered to him by the trees—his full range of talents on display.

The Colonel glanced over at the President. James Buchanan was a cultivated, delicate man, sitting in the front row on the edge of his seat. From the moment the concert began, not once did the fair-haired Commander-In-Chief seem to even blink as Thomas pressed the mouth of the flute back to his lips.

During Bach's delightful *Allegretto in F* the Colonel felt someone watching him. He peered through the low light toward the South Portico, where Perry had positioned two of his men, but didn't notice anything awry. He looked in the opposite direction, his hand inside his jacket, palm around his gun, but when he turned his head back he saw a woman in pale pink wearing a large millinery standing beside the blue satin curtains. She had a heart shaped face and a dimpled chin, and she smiled back at him, lowering her eyes demurely, as if she were too shy to hold his gaze.

Desire shot through the Colonel, and the lovely music became a faraway footpath to his inner yearnings. *She's the most beautiful creature I've ever seen*, he thought. His curiosity was aroused and, losing all sense of good manners and the potential dangers around him, he openly beheld the mysterious woman. Applause erupted and the lady in pink giggled and nodded toward Thomas. The Colonel blushed, his attention crashing back into focus.

The sun had set by the time the enchanting *Symphony No. 8* by Beethoven was nearing the end of the fourth and final movement, the *Allegro vivace*. The music faded to nothingness. President Buchanan stood to his feet, followed by the entire audience with deafening approval.

The Colonel, John, and Perry, stepped close to Thomas, let him take a few bows, and escorted him off the stage, away from the crowd.

Unaware they were being watched.

XX.

"From the lady," the old Negro bartender at the Willard Hotel said after the Colonel finished greeting the Count. Then the bartender nodded toward the sender, past the china stacked with shrimp toward the red velvet chairs. The Colonel turned and saw the lady in pink with the dimpled chin watching him. She tilted her head in acknowledgment then melted into the crowd. A lady sending a gentleman a drink? It was an unheard of gesture. Preoccupied, and aroused once again, he'd forgotten the line of congressmen, senators, and their families waiting to meet him, and to meet his slave, until he heard a woman clear her throat.

"A pleasure," the Colonel said without yet turning his head to the next person in the reception line. He was trying to keep the pretty lady in pink in sight, but his vision was blocked when John stepped in the way. The Colonel's smile stiffened at once when he saw Eliza beside him. He'd all but forbidden John to see the woman.

"What's she doing here?" the Colonel whispered through a stiff smile.

"Eliza's my wife," said John, matter-of-factly.

The Colonel went rigid. A queasy feeling came over him. He struggled to maintain a cordial smile. He glared at Eliza. That tall classless woman with her auburn hair pulled back in a bun, pearls dangling from her neck, was John's wife? A marriage without his blessing? And Frances, did she know and not tell him? The Colonel had not foreseen this.

"I'm sorry you and mother don't approve, *Mon Père*," John leaned in and whispered, "But I'd like you to at least be affable to her."

Eliza joined the party and John stood beside his father. They both shook hands with all the Blind Tom admirers. But the Colonel was not there in mind, only body. He'd always thought John too level-minded to forfeit the social advantages of a merger with a fine family, but he'd obviously overestimated him. He was a fool in love. That whore—and the Colonel had no doubt she was a whore—had somehow manipulated his oldest son into marrying her. If true, it was a disaster. John was in breach of promise. His hand had been contracted to Tiffany Mercer of the tobacco farming family. The Mercers had already transferred property-they'd be humiliated.

"You dishonor me, *et ta mère*," the Colonel said under his breath, shaking his head.

Now, the Bethunes were exposed to litigation and social shame. He strained above the shoulders of the merchant standing before him to see Eliza's ring finger. She raised her hand to brush her hair and he saw a sparkling Tiffany diamond; it was a large jewel, fit for a monarch. He frowned at once. It was new! It didn't matter that it was expensive. The new jewelry confirmed his suspicions that her family was of a lower class, unable to provide a proper heirloom.

"Father," John said, speaking through a stiff smile, as if there was not an ocean of distance between them, "Will you try for me and be nice to her?"

The Colonel shook his head, the lights bright against his skin beneath the chandelier. He missed his old life. Missed his newborn, the nights of music in the *grand parlor,* missed the picnics amid the fragrant jasmine and pine smell of the gardens and the peaceful brooks at *Solitude.* He missed tea with his beautiful wife and the eldest son who had once upon a time followed his commands. He didn't know how many hands he shook while thinking. This moment was too horrid to digest and troubled his stomach like a bad piece of veal.

"*Mon Dieu,* how could you?" the Colonel whispered through a gritted smile.

"It's done, father, why won't you please accept it? You must accept, I am a man. I make my own decisions," John said.

He looked like a little boy, a child who had no idea he'd just invited a serpent into their midst. The Colonel turned, jaw clinched at the thought of his son's stratagem. He'd taken advantage of the White House occasion to tell him. He knew it would be utterly inappropriate for him to address the matter, especially since President Buchanan was making his way over, accompanied by his niece and de facto First Lady, Harriet Lane.

"Mr. President," the Colonel said, pushing the issue of John out of his mind.

"Colonel Bethune. Allow me to present my niece, Harriet Lane."

The dark-haired Harriet Lane possessed broad masculine features. But she carried herself with a sophisticated and feminine air which combined with her red-brown tresses, near violet eyes, tight corsets, and plunging necklines, made her quite appealing.

"It is my deepest pleasure to meet you," the Colonel said, kissing the back of her hand.

"Colonel, the accounts of your Blind Tom don't do him justice," said President Buchanan. The Colonel noted the feminine twist and flips of the President's wrists. He knew of the tawdry tales of a male companion who lived in his home, referred to in the private clubs as "Mrs. Buchanan"; nonetheless, the Colonel afforded him the upmost respect.

"Thank you, Mr. President, for granting us such a special honor."

"The honor is ours. A most amazing performer, certainly the rarest ever to entertain us here at the White House." And bending toward Thomas he said, "Tom, you are an exquisite treasure."

"Thank you Mr. President Buchanan, the fifteenth President of the United States."

"You're quite welcome, Tom," President Buchanan said, laughing. "And thank you for that divine performance."

"Mr. President, fifteenth President of the United States. Fifteen is a composite number."

"Yes, yes, Tom, it is a composite number, isn't it? You are quite the mathematician."

"Composite numbers are dull like poetry without metaphors," Thomas said.

"Tom," the Colonel gasped. "Forgive him, he's...," the Colonel was flustered.

President Buchanan responded gallantly. "He is quite delightful," President Buchanan laughed. "A retarded genius, indeed," he said to the Colonel's relief.

President Buchanan turned to one of his many aides, hovering nearby.

"Secretary Cass, I think Blind Tom should perform for our Oriental guests when they make their visit to the White House."

"Yes, of course Mr. President. I think that's a wonderful idea," said Lewis Cass, a most serious man with a permanently furrowed brow.

"The Japanese control an island kingdom east of the Oriental country of China," President Buchanan explained to the Colonel. "They practice...What's the word?" He paused and turned again to his aide again.

"Sakoku," Cass answered.

"Yes, Sakoku. It means 'closed to foreigners.' We are encouraging the kingdom of Japan to open up their country to trade with America, by sending some of our biggest Navy ships and establishing our heavy military presence off the coast of their beaches," he said with a light laugh, reaching for a glass of French wine from a servant.

"A delegation from the island kingdom of Japan is making their first visit to the West in three weeks. And we're going to show the Orientals our superiority in technology, engineering, science and the arts. I think it would be fine diplomacy to have Blind Tom represent our country."

A rush of pride seared through the Colonel's veins. "It would be another great honor, sir," the Colonel said without hesitation. But the Colonel knew by accepting President Buchanan's offer, he had given his unseen enemies an opportunity and advantage.

The next day, the newspapers celebrated the musical gifts of Blind Tom. In the hotel over ham and eggs, Vivian read the articles aloud to Thomas. Thomas clapped. "Tom plays with a grace and heavenly capacity," he repeated. The Colonel lifted from the bed and struck a match, gazing across the room. Thomas had changed, he thought. Though blind and retarded, the slave boy was proving as susceptible to swells of ego as any highly sought after celebrity. He'd always had temper tantrums, but he first noticed it in Kentucky, how he held his nose high and seemed to strut at the keyboard. He was a star and knew it. Indeed, Blind Tom was a national treasure now, the boy more famous than the Negro Frederick Douglass.

The weeks went by faster than the Colonel anticipated, day and night, three performances per day. The Colonel felt a twinge of conscience about the added White House concert and finally discussed the matter with Perry a few days before the last show in Charleston, West Virginia.

"You sure about this, Colonel?" Perry said in his tent over a plate of grits and fish. "We don' have ta risk the boy just because Buchanan wants ta show off ta some Orientals." His voice trailed away. He scraped at his plate.

Here they were, safely in the South, the Colonel thought. Now, he was dragging them back to Washington City where tensions were even worse than when they left. He supposed Perry was a bit scared and couldn't blame him. There was a very real danger in returning; this concert meant the potential shortening of all their lives. That godless tyrant, Lincoln, was gaining momentum while anti-slavery attacks were getting more brazen and violent. But the Colonel stood firm. "I gave my word. I committed to Buchanan, but I understand if you choose not to go."

Perry put down his fork and his eyes flashed. "Got too much invested ta bail out on ya. Blind Tom's still contracted ta me. We end up facin' some snatch boys, they dyin', not me."

The Colonel nodded and took a puff on his cigar. "You're a good man, Perry."

"Trust me, Colonel. I know what this means for my pockets," he said.

"A man after my own heart," the Colonel smiled.

Though extremely dangerous, the second White House concert for the Orientals would provide a very lucrative payday for them both.

XXI.

Washington City, D.C.

On the way to the Willard Hotel's bar, the Colonel felt Perry's hand on his shoulder. "Hear the news?" The Colonel narrowed his eyes and studied his face. "Lincoln's won over Indiana last night," Perry said. "Got a standing ovation after his speech."

His head began to pound. Senator Colquitt's warning echoed in the Colonel's mind. "Make no mistake. If free soil Lincoln wins the election, there's sure to be trouble in the Capitol." Now, it looked as if he was going to win the Republican nomination and if so, he'd carry all of the free states in an election.

The Colonel's thoughts immediately drifted to Thomas as he turned back toward the elevators and intercepted John in the lobby. "Be as discreet as possible. Go get our luggage, carriage, and guns ready," he instructed. "We will leave immediately after the concert."

As soon as the concert for the Japanese concluded, he wanted the group to make their way back to the South at once. If anything happened at the concert, John was to grab Thomas and they would all meet on Charles Street near the Washington monument to regroup.

Already, there were thick crowds outside the hotel hoping to glimpse the exotic Oriental delegation: seventy-seven sword-bearing Japanese in full native Samurai dress, slanted eyes, and long ponytails. The frenzy caused by the presence of the massive Oriental delegation made the Colonel even more concerned about the complexity of keeping Thomas safe. Armed soldiers were stationed throughout the hotel and there were masses of people blocking the roads.

It took two hours to make their way the few blocks to the White House. When the Colonel and his entourage arrived inside the Blue Room, he gave strict instructions. "Be vigilant. Keep your eyes on Tom at all times." Pointing at the two stagehands, he barked. "Go to the back of the room and take up posts on opposite sides. You tell anyone who tries to move you that you have orders from the Colonel to stay at your post."

In the receiving room, Thomas sat alone humming and eating a piece of perfect chocolate cake while the procession of Samurai loudly made its way down the hallway toward the Blue Room. They marched in a sing song rhythm, metal wristbands and swords clanged like clashing cymbals. Led by a retinue of military officers, the warriors passed by in full dress uniform then followed by a parade of footmen, politicians, local aristocrats, and the press.

From the table, Thomas noticed the nervous tap of his master's fingers against his cane. "Master Colonel's yellow," he said between bites. "Don't worry, Master Colonel. As per the President, we're going to show the Orientals our superiority in technology, in engineering, science and the arts," he said triumphantly.

Thomas had been on his best behavior the entire trip to the White House as if he understood the importance. The Colonel patted him on the head. "Come, Tom, it's time to go play for the Japanese and our President."

It was mid-afternoon when the concert got underway. The Colonel was studying the audience with a weary expression like a fatigued soldier scouting terrain searching for the enemy. He surveyed every guest through the ambient pools of chandelier light looking for suspicious faces. Meanwhile, the Samurai sat cross-legged on the blue Persian carpet, delighting in every detail. Thomas looked happy beneath his ermine cape at the grand piano. His animated face hinted at the majestic visions he was experiencing: beautiful, luminescent angels surrounding him right there in the Blue Room, magnificent beings with enormous wings, floating about — their voices lifted in song.

The beginning of the program went superbly. Nothing seemed off or out of place in the venue. No suspicious faces. No outbursts or diversions. The Colonel found a moment to enjoy the show. But halfway through the concert, Nehemiah slipped into the vacant space beside the Colonel. "Colonel," he said softly. "I've come to warn you. Lincoln wants your slave."

"Lies, surely," he whispered. "You know there's been talk here, *Mon Dieu*, there were rumors about President Buchanan–"

Nehemiah gave him a cold hard look. "We have people in the Lincoln camp." His voice was a harsh whisper. "An offer of five-hundred-dollars to the man who gets him."

"That's a fortune for most men."

"Colonel, you must take action. He has a plan to use your great slave to move the nation to rally behind the cause to free all slaves. You must leave swiftly, this evening, don't linger a moment longer than necessary. And don't take him back to your Virginia plantation, neither to Georgia. Not if you want to keep him.

Lincoln's boys are most likely watching the front entrance, so find another way out. I'll see you at the meeting place."

Perry tapped him on his arm. "What's going on Colonel?"

"The taxi in the front won't do," the Colonel told him.

"You want me to have it moved around to the back?"

"No, we're being watched." The Colonel whispered in his ear, directing him to meet at the monument.

"On Charles Street?"

The Colonel nodded. "I'll get Tom. Take Vivian, John, and the attendant with you as a decoy. Send another taxi to the back. If something happens and we're not at the monument within ten minutes of you. Don't wait. Take the women and see to it they make it home safely."

Thomas was across the room at the piano with a smile on his face as he massaged the keys of his *concerto* with no clue as to the danger he was in. The end of the concert came and the audience was standing, the floor of the room vibrating with applause. The massive Samurai delegation standing and bowing. The Colonel mounted the steps and took Thomas's hand ready to collect him and depart but, not surprisingly, President Buchanan insisted on presenting Thomas to the Japanese. As the Colonel stood with a stiff smile, bowing to the Samurai, his pulse quickening with the desire to flee, he began to inch his way toward the Blue Room exit with Thomas by his side.

A hasty exit was impossible; everyone seemed to press against them, pushing in different directions, laughing and chatting about the evening. Voices came from all around. "Colonel," they called after him. "Blind Tom is splendid." He pulled Thomas close and edged forward, brushing against the wall, then down the carpeted hallway. The crush seemed to thicken. It felt like all of Washington was pressing around them. He knew the streets in front of the White House were packed with carriages and onlookers.

When he caught sight of the taxi through the doors of the east wing, he paused and hid with Thomas in a nook. An excited crowd filled the intersection, there were horses and wagons, but the hallway and the walkway outside the door was empty. It seemed the coast was clear. His heart was thumping so he was sure any enemy within miles would locate them. Grabbing Thomas's hand tightly, he stepped out the door onto the cemented walk to the grass. He didn't see anyone- not John, not Vivian, not even the security hands.

It was nearly eleven at night when the Colonel entered the double doors of The Willard. He was upset. Things were already not going as planned. They were supposed to leave immediately after the concert, yet Vivian and John were still checked in. The concierge handed him a message. The Colonel looked at it: "Father, please come to my room at once." The Colonel frowned. It was unlike John not to follow orders. He made his way toward John's room, stopping first to drop Thomas off with his teacher. He then knocked several times on John's door and waited a moment.

The door had barely opened when he noticed the look on his son's face was unusual. He let his father in, walked over to the lit fireplace and stood beside his wife, Eliza. John was distressed, the Colonel saw it in the sag of his shoulders, the heavy emotion in his eyes. An intense dread poured over him, even before he noticed the tear streaks on his son's cheeks.

"What is it, *mon fils?*" he asked, walking in closer. Before John could answer, Eliza pulled away and with a brief nod to the Colonel excused herself from the room.

"It's mother."

"Frances?"

His mind spun in circles and a violent pain shot through his stomach. His arms went numb and his legs started to buckle, seconds before John nodded the unspoken.

"Frances?" His voice was barely a whisper and he stumbled back, stunned. It was as if a bullet had been shot through his body. He was not expecting to hear that name. Not that name. Any name, but not that one. He was braced to hear his uncle's name or even one of his brother's names, but not that one. Not Frances. He felt like he was falling, like a feather drifting from the comfort of its nest, slowly, somberly toward a compassionless earth. For a moment, there was complete silence. No birds twittering or crickets singing. The flames even seemed to hold their breath.

"My peace is gone, my heart is heavy," the Colonel whispered. Frances loved Goethe and for the first time he understood the height, the width, and the depth of those words. His heart was met with unfathomable rivers of pain. His legs began to shake.

It was simply a man who collapsed in John's arms that night and shed his tears. Not a war hero, not his superior, or his father. Simply a man of flesh and blood, whose core was rocked by the death of the only woman he ever truly loved. John had never seen his father cry before.

"Malaria," John whispered.

"I fear our God is punishing me," the Colonel mumbled.

"Come father, sit," John said gently and guided him over to the bed. "You know she was not well."

Frances was sickly after the birth of Naomi. She had one of Charity's daughters serve as the wet nurse; and her enthusiasm for riding the Warmblood mounts around the plantation had waned, she no longer knitted near the hearth, and was always too tired for tea with friends. She retired to her chambers early, slept in late and spent long afternoons alone in the *petit parlor.*

"She wrote this for you," John was saying, handing the Colonel a letter.

It was her final, handwritten note, and the Colonel clutched it against his chest before opening it. He took a deep breath, exhaled and started to read:

My dearest James,

by the time this letter reaches you, I will be gone. I want you to know, you are the beat of my heart. Although my spirit is on the precipice of paradise and shall soon leave this body, my love will always be with you. Take care of our children. I wish for you to live your life my love. Please continue our night of music for I will be there, in the heavens, singing along with all of you. Remember my favorite poem of Raymond's? "Life is eternal, and love is immortal; and death is only a horizon; and a horizon is nothing save the limit of our sight." It is my earnest hope that you do not pine for me long, for it is only a temporary goodbye, as I will see you all again, beyond the horizons. I am at peace with God's Will my dear love. Je t'embrasse.

Frances

Tears fell, tumbling down his cheeks. "I must go to her," the Colonel said in a whispered, choking voice.

"Father, we shan't travel tonight," John said, his voice a firm tone. "Thomas needs to sleep. You need rest. One more night won't hurt. Then we shall leave first thing in the morning."

The Colonel wanted to speak of all he'd done wrong. Of the bad choices, the casual affairs, but John cut his thoughts off.

"*Mon Père,*" he said, softly. "You will ask for forgiveness and He will forgive you. Mother would want that. She is in a better place."

A rap came before dawn after the Colonel had finally fallen into a heavy sleep. Startled awake, he reached for his pistol, stole to the door, and asked who it was.

"Bob Mudd," came the answer.

The Colonel carefully cracked opened the door, confirmed it was Nehemiah, and let him slip in. "You have to leave tonight, Colonel. It's serious the threat you're facing. They intend to take Tom while you are in Washington City."

Stealing down the corridor, the Colonel banged on Vivian's door while Nehemiah kept watch. John and Eliza made their way down the hallway. Vivian,

Annie, and Eliza went down one stairwell, and the Colonel sent John to clear the front of the hotel, then led Tom out and across the street toward the Foggy Bottom neighborhood. Uneasy, he weaved his way through back alleys littered with trash, in the hopes of escaping undetected. It was the safest route, the dark passageways. They were all to meet in their original place near the unfinished Washington Monument and flee the city.

As he limped at a fast pace through the scent of urine and past old moonshine bottles, the Colonel felt a gnawing foreboding in his stomach. The closer he got to the hill, the more his breaths shortened in his throat. Just as he passed Washington's statue, there was rustling in the bushes. He froze and pulled Thomas close, ready to switch directions, but it was too late.

Suddenly, a powerful click cracked near his ear. "Don't move."

He looked left and turned right, but there was nowhere to run: seven men surrounded the Colonel. With Thomas in one hand, his cane in the other, there was no way he could reach for his pistol. His face flamed with rage. "Stay back!" The Colonel scowled at the men and swung his cane helplessly. "Get back! He belongs to me."

"Turn the boy over Colonel."

"You can't have him. Not in this life," the Colonel clutched Thomas tighter. "This is my property!"

"Watch yourself now, Colonel." The man growled. He had a scar on his cheek and a venomous smile. "Don't get yourself killed."

The Colonel took a few steps back and a hand fell heavy on his shoulder. When he turned his head, a fist smashed into his jaw. Thomas whimpered. The Colonel felt the crack of a rifle butt on his face. He held tight to Thomas, until another blow to his stomach brought the Colonel to his knees.

"Get the boy, Mitch," one of the men growled to the wide man with the scar.

"You can't have him, damn you," the Colonel groaned. He grabbed the bottom of Mitch's pants leg with his free hand. A foot came down and crashed into his side.

"I have gold," the Colonel moaned, a trail of red dripping onto the white snow. "If it's money you want, I'll pay double." He squirmed on the ground like a worm in water. "Whatever you want I'll give you. On my honor, but don't take the boy. He's of no use to you…"

"Ain't yours no more, ain't yours to give," Mitch said roughly.

The Colonel heard horses' hooves and felt a boot on his back before the men vanished into the night. For a few minutes, he lay alone in the cold snow, bleeding. He didn't think it through. He shouldn't have gone off alone with Thomas, should have had John and Perry beside him, what had he been thinking?

Large poplar and fig trees lined the east wing pathways so no one from the street could see clear enough to help him. Finally, he rose to his knees and felt around in the snow for his cane, the demons had disappeared as quickly as they'd appeared. Probably headed north with Thomas, the Colonel thought, and he didn't fire one shot to stop them. He cursed the kidnappers, praying for them to die a slow, painful death, on their way back to hell.

He stumbled through slush toward the noisy crowded intersection. He needed to make it over to High Street where Nehemiah was waiting below in the canoe. But he was too weak and fell, hitting his head on the ground. Blood streamed from his temple, burning his eyes and a rib jutted painfully against his chest. He stared up at the starless night sky, amid the stench of raw sewage, sunk in desolation. He'd failed Thomas. He'd given his word he'd never let anything happen to him. His limbs were numb from the cold. He'd been looking forward to seeing Frances in three days, but Frances was gone, and he couldn't leave Washington City until Thomas was back in his care. Slumped among snow and wet leaves, he heard the wail of cows, before everything slowly went black.

XXII.

The light stung the Colonel's eyes. Blinking rapidly, he lifted his elbow to block the sun coming in through two large windows that touched the floor. His ribs were sore and there was a bandage on his jaw. His eyes slowly adjusted. He noticed he was lying on a queen-sized bed in a large bedroom decorated with hand-carved Victorian furniture. A chandelier hung from the vaulted ceiling and perfume from candles and flowers filled the air. He lay there, confused; he didn't know where he was. He thought perhaps he was at the Willard Hotel. Just as he was about to ring the bell for room service, a vaguely familiar dark-haired woman bent forward and caressed his hand. Her palms were so soft, her skin the color of milk.

He struggled to speak, disoriented, he wondered who she was. His mouth was open, but he couldn't get any words out. His throat felt like raw meat and his tongue was covered with a thick, yellow film.

"Shhh, it's okay. Just relax," the woman said in a soft, refined voice, patting his forehead with a damp rag. The warm rag felt nice against his skin. "My dear sir, I'm so relieved you're awake," she was saying. "I was frightened half to death. You've been dreadfully ill."

"Ill?" He rasped, squinting in the sunlight; his brain was still foggy. He tried to place her face and that silky voice.

"Apparently, you took a terrible fall and hit your head. You broke a rib, Colonel, and you lost so much blood before the pneumonia came."

"Where am I?" He struggled to sit up, but pain shot through his ribcage, and the pneumonia had made him wobbly as a doe's newborn fawn.

"You're upstairs on the second floor of the White House."

The White House? He tried to lift up, but pain stabbed through his side. As he gazed at the woman leaning over him, he remembered her. Those violet eyes, this was Harriet Lane, the President's niece. She took the wet cloth and gently wiped his forehead. "Myself, the President, and the staff have been praying for you these past eight days."

Eight days? The White House? His next thought wasn't Frances or his children, but Thomas. Suddenly it came rushing back, the rough men, the beating. Thomas. *Noblesse oblige.* The Colonel grimaced. He'd failed to protect the child and broken his promise. "I need to find Tom. I gave him my word I would never let anything bad happen to him—"

"Shhh," Harriet dabbed his forehead again. "You just need to eat your soup and rest." She lifted a pink porcelain bowl of soup. The Colonel was hungry and weak, but he didn't move even though the creamy food smelled like heaven. It wasn't his intention, this ill-bred behavior, but he wouldn't allow the President's niece to feed him like some helpless child. As if reading his mind, Harriet gently lowered the bowl onto the table.

Relieved, the Colonel used all the strength he could muster to lift onto his elbow. He squinted from the pain and struggled to reach for the spoon. He took a slurp of the brown liquid and swallowed the warm broth before speaking. "How did I end up here?"

"One of our ground servants found you," she answered, against the sound of his spoon clanking the bowl. "You took a nasty fall near the rhododendrons. You were bloody, going in and out of consciousness, mumbling about Blind Tom and—"

"Tom." The Colonel struggled to sit up and grabbed Harriet by her wrist. "It wasn't the fall. Something terrible has happened," he said. His voice was a hoarse whisper.

Harriet stared at him, her face full of confusion. "Colonel, you must lie down and rest. You hit your head—"

"No, you must listen to me." The Colonel glanced at the blond haired servant discreetly moving about the room; he stood at the hearth, stoking the fire, barely making noise. Harriet sensed the Colonel wanted to speak with her alone and shooed the servant off, then nodded to the Colonel. "Please, tell me what's troubling you, Colonel," she said as the servant moved away carrying a wicker basket of dirty cloths out of the room.

When the door snapped shut, the Colonel spoke.

"I gave Tom my word that I'd never let anyone or anything hurt him," the Colonel managed, reluctantly. He considered the matter, then shook his head. "It would be ungentlemanly of me to take that awful night up with you. But you can help me, if you can keep what I ask of you secret. You see, I'm sure there are spies in this house."

"I will not betray your confidence, Colonel," Harriet said, gently, reaching her hand out to touch his. "Am I not here?"

The Colonel drew in his breath with serious consideration. Indeed, it was highly inappropriate for her to be alone in the room with him. "*Mademoiselle*," he began. "What I'm about to tell you is disturbing. Lincoln has sent men to kidnap Tom. You say it's been eight days, so there's no more time to waste. They've taken the boy away from the South, I'm sure of it. Sometime soon, they plan to use him to forward the abolitionists' campaign. You've seen the boy, Miss Lane, a genius on the piano, but he's hopelessly lost in the real world. I don't have any idea how they will care for him."

Harriet looked off toward the window, as if the sun could wash away the darkness of what she'd just heard. "Kidnapped, Blind Tom?" she said softly. "That's mad. The President and the Secretary of State were just saying the other day how Blind Tom has taken America by fancy," she went on. "He's certainly the most valuable entertainment we have." Harriet took in a breath, as she considered the obstacles. "It's been eight days, Colonel. Finding Blind Tom with so much time that has passed..."

"Unless Lincoln and his bandits exploit him as planned" the Colonel slammed his fist into the bed and slunk back against the pillows.

"He hasn't been in the newspaper. The men who took him must have him hidden away." She exhaled. "Is there anywhere you can think of they may have taken the boy?"

"No," the Colonel shook his head. "That African Lincoln wants to make a spectacle of Tom."

He struggled to get up, desperately, so he could begin the search for Thomas, but he was too weak. He lay back in the covers, a swell of emotion on his face.

"I need to get a message to my son, John," he whispered.

"Your son? Your son is travelling here. We got word to him a few days ago. He's been delayed for sure because of trouble in Baltimore. Ruffians, the worst kinds of heathens have taken over the streets, destroying roads and burning businesses there. They have made travel nearly impossible on account of Lincoln."

"My son will help me find Tom."

"Colonel, I'm sorry for what has happened to Blind Tom. It's a horrid thing Lincoln has done to you. In this last week, the city has become dangerous. Our citizens fight in taverns, throw bottles, and shoot at one another in the markets. The streets are filthy with violence between rebels and those who support the Union."

Listening to her, the Colonel clenched his jaw and turned his head. He sank deep into the pillows and clutched tight at the sheets. A wave of horror rushed over him. Frances was gone. He'd not made it home to prepare the funeral, and his children must think themselves orphans indeed. Thomas confused and distraught wherever he might be, John travelling alone in a country tearing apart at the seams.

Harriet watched in silence, then readjusted the covers, and leaned close. "You must get your rest, Colonel. By the time your son arrives, you will have regained your strength, and then you can do all that is in your power to recover Blind Tom.

But first, you must do away with your troubles and eat. I won't have it any other way."

Too weak to protest, the Colonel nodded. Harriet dipped the spoon into his soup and he opened his lips to receive the food. The Colonel chewed a chunk of chicken and allowed Harriet to feed him the rest of the soup. The only sound was the repetitive hacking of the gardener's hoe outside the large room's open window.

"Get some rest," Harriet said after his last bite. "You are a very wise and courageous man, Colonel. One man, even with a weapon, cannot defeat many when caught unaware. You did what was right for the boy at that moment. Don't trouble yourself about it, now. It's in God's hands."

She rose from her chair and picked up his tray.

"The fewer people who know I'm here—"

"You are in the Prince of Wales' suite, Colonel," she said, cutting him off. "You will have plenty of privacy. No one will be allowed to enter – only myself and your son John, when he arrives. I will speak to our servant, William, and secure his discretion."

XXIII.

It was disorienting, the way the floor and ceiling kept switching places. The Colonel lay in the canopy bed and gray light spilled through the curtains' cracks for untold days. Only Harriet came and went with silver trays of tea and soup. Little by little the Colonel regained his strength. By the time John arrived, he could sit up without assistance and within a day, he was walking and anxious to draft a strategy to find Thomas, though time was against them.

John, having put Eliza on a train to her cousin's, sat on a divan next to the Colonel's chair. The two discussed in hushed tones how to organize their search efforts. "The hounds found no scent," John said. "They must have taken him away through the river. I'll go down to the wharf and ask about him there."

Harriet entered the suite in her splendid blue evening dress, hair twined with two glamorous braids. "I expect you are making plans to recover Blind Tom?" Harriet asked when the door shut. John continued to stare at her warily, until the Colonel nodded that it was okay to speak freely.

"Do you know where you'll start?" Harriet asked.

"It's coming on three weeks, he could be anywhere by now," John said. "He could be in Pennsylvania or as far away as Maine. Or he could be hidden somewhere here in the city."

"Wherever he is, the men who have him will want money, will they not?"

"I offered them gold, but they scoffed. You know I'll pay whatever I have to pay to get Tom back or kill whoever I have to kill," the Colonel said with a growl.

As the clocks chimed, Harriet cut her visit short. She had to return to her hostess duties in the drawing room, where diplomats buzzed with members of Congress and the Supreme Court. She stopped short of the double doors and turned back toward the Colonel. "If you hope to leave unnoticed, the next two hours provide the best time to do so discreetly as everyone will be occupied with dinner."

The Colonel gave her an appreciative nod.

"Please be watchful, Colonel. It's not safe. There are spies all over the city and there are many Union sympathizers who would get a perverse joy in hurting a proud southern man."

"I well know the dangers of Washington City, dear Miss Lane," the Colonel answered. "Rest assured, I'll take the necessary precautions for my son and myself. As you know, there are more than Union sympathizers in this city."

"Of course, Colonel," she smiled. "When you leave here, take the northeastern staircase to the first floor, past the President's dining room. Then proceed down the back roadway, behind C street," she told him. "It's Saturday night. The residents there will be far too drunk from moonshine to notice you. You'll need your handkerchiefs for the stench."

"Thank you, for all the ways you've cared for me, and please don't worry."

Harriet looked out the window, across the lawn. "Abraham Lincoln has yet to take office and already, he's managed to make quite a difficult mess of many things hasn't he?" She turned to face the Colonel, drew in a breath and spoke quietly, "There have been whispers that have come to my attention, but I hesitate to share them for fear of sending you on a goose chase."

"Please," the Colonel urged. "Any bit of a clue that could help us…"

"Again this evening, I heard a rumor about abolitionists hiding out at the Dully Plantation, Richard Bland Lee's winter property in Northern Virginia, though he is on business in London."

"That's not far from some property I own." said the Colonel.

"They took him across the Potomac," John blurted. "That's why the tracking dogs found no scent."

"You're familiar with the area then?"

"Yes, very familiar."

"The mistress of the home, Mrs. Darcy Lee, we attended boarding school together. I'm told she's at odds with her husband's politics. Perhaps you can use me as an excuse to visit and maybe find some clue to the whereabouts of Blind Tom. But you must arrive before 9 p.m. or it will be improper for her to receive you."

Emotion swept over the Colonel, at the thought of Thomas being near. The Colonel barely remembered leaving the room, or walking with John to the stables and mounting the horses. Late evening turned to night and the two men road through light snow and rain toward the Virginia border.

It was nearly nine o' clock when they reached the bottom of the knoll in the county where the Dully plantation was located. The Colonel was dead tired when at last he motioned for John to stop. He pulled his horse to a halt in the thick of trees a half mile from the large house. The Colonel snuffed the flame of the lantern out, and stepped down from his horse, leaves brushing his face, the stem scraping his skin like tiny nails. He rubbed his aching neck and was tethering his horse when he heard a noise. He stiffened and reached out, touching John's forearm to signal silence. Father and son crouched low. The Colonel aimed his pistol.

"Don't shoot," came a whisper. "Bob Mudd."

"Nehemiah," the Colonel whispered.

"Yes." Nehemiah dismounted his horse. "I followed you."

"Tom," the Colonel started. "He may…"

"I know. I've been watching this house. There are four to five men inside at all times."

"Do they have guards?" John asked.

"No. Abolitionists survive by blending in," Nehemiah whispered. "Guards would draw suspicion."

"If Tom is there, how will we get him out?"

"The men play Faro, every evening and drink into the night. They are all surely drunk by now."

Colonel led them toward the large house then motioned for John to cross over to the domed front porch. John climbed the stairs and knocked lightly on the door. A tall, handsome slave opened the door, and kindly greeted John who told him he was the cousin of Miss Harriet Lane, a childhood friend that attended boarding school with Mistress Darcy. The slave fetched Darcy Lee, an attractive, fair-haired woman in her early thirties with a friendly face.

"Sorry to call upon you so late," John was saying. "My uncle and I left Washington, our carriage broke down a few miles out and I remembered my cousin Harriet Lane saying she had a schoolmate in these parts."

Cautiously, Mrs. Lee widened the door. "Harriet?"

John noticed her gaze had travelled to Nehemiah, so he turned toward his companion. "This is Jeremiah Learner, my uncle, Mrs. Lee. We're looking for a musical slave…"

"John," Nehemiah cautioned.

"Uncle, she seems like a nice woman." John ignored Nehemiah's warning glare and pressed forward. "Mrs. Lee, we heard he might be somewhere around this area."

Mrs. Lee's eyes widened and the blood drained from her face. "I don't know anything."

"I'm sorry ma'am," John sputtered. "We're not suggesting anything by asking. It's just Tom's like family and some bad men stole him from us when we were in Washington City."

Mrs. Lee hesitated, still unsure. "Is the child Tom, blind?"

John nodded. "Yes, yes ma'am. We are worried about him. Do you know where he is?"

"I knew this day would come," she said. "Before my husband left for England he came home with the men and I heard a child crying, calling out for his master. He told me to have the servants bring hot tea and leave him be. But I stayed in the hallway, behind the parlor. There was quite a ruckus as the men tried to subdue him. I heard one of the men say 'be careful the boy is blind.' He put up quite a fuss."

Excited, John turned to Nehemiah, who stared at Mrs. Lee with distrust. "It's good to know he's still his old self," John said.

"A hard-faced man came in after the others and demanded money from my husband. My husband was only doing what he thought was right for the boy's kind."

"Ma'am, he belongs to me and my father."

"The man, I believe his name was Mr. Mitch …"

"Mitch?" John repeated. "That's the man who brutalized my father and stole our Tom."

"Well, I heard him say Lincoln backed out, wanted nothing to do with taking the blind boy. Then the men were yelling back and forth and the boy was crying out, repeating everything he heard. Mitch said the boy was still valuable and he wanted to take him down south to sell, but my husband wouldn't let him."

Leaning in, Mrs. Lee looked John in his eyes, she whispered, "The blind boy, is he Blind Tom?"

At that moment, Nehemiah stepped forward with his hands to his lips. "You don't want your guests to hear you."

Mrs. Lee glanced back toward the parlor; the men were loud and clearly full of whiskey and other hard drink. Chairs scraped the floor and glasses slammed against tables. Nevertheless, she adjusted her voice again. "My husband told them not to do anything until he returned from his trip to London. The men stood arguing until my husband proclaimed that no one had a right to the boy but his birth mother and father."

"Where is he?" John asked. "Is he in the house?"

"He's upstairs in the guest suites," she whispered. "They keep one man outside of his door at all times. They have no idea what to do with him."

"We should go get him now," John said to Nehemiah, but Mrs. Lee lifted her hand.

"You cannot. There are half a dozen men here. Even drunk it's too dangerous to risk, as the upper guest rooms are on the west side of the house and you'd have to go through the parlor."

"We can take a half dozen men," Nehemiah said.

"Without bloodshed?" Mrs. Lee raised her eyebrows.

The jangle of bells rang out from the hallway out of John's sight.

"More whiskey!" Hoarse voices demanded with the ring of a bell.

"We've talked long enough. One of them may stumble out."

"We won't leave here without Tom," John said.

"I told my husband and my brothers keeping the boy would cause us nothing but misery," Mrs. Lee said, wringing her hands at the waist of her coat. "It's not right keeping him here." She stared at John as if afraid to meet Nehemiah's gaze. "Come back around three, they should all be asleep from drink, including the guard. Wait for me at the back of the house, I will bring him to you."

Her tone, the earnestness in her eyes: the men knew she could be trusted.

"But how? If Tom doesn't know you, he won't go with you," John said.

Just then, slurred voices could be heard behind her, along with stumbled footsteps.

Mrs. Lee's face tightened with fear. "You must go, before you are discovered." Her bottom lip trembled. She was insistent, shaking her head before John could speak. Her swan-like grace taut with panic; she turned swiftly and shut the heavy doors.

Hours later, they crept quietly toward the back of the estate and waited for a few minutes before the Colonel rapped lightly on the oak wood door with his cane. Mrs. Lee cracked the door open, with a finger to her lips, she motioned for them to enter and led them swiftly through a narrow back hallway.

"Mr. Mitch and my two brothers are still awake playing a game of high stakes poker," she explained softly. "Three are asleep on the sofas. I went upstairs and saw the night guard, asleep in front of the boy's door."

"We must get Tom out, tonight," the Colonel whispered with a sense of urgency.

"I must let you know, Mr. Mitch was bragging to my brothers about a foreign promoter willing to pay top dollar for Blind Tom," Mrs. Lee told the Colonel, as the ring of keys she carried, jangled.

She lifted the lantern and guided the men up a flight of stairs, each careful with their steps, so as not to make noise with their boots. At the landing, the men followed her down a long, dark hallway with high ceilings. A heavy draft carried with it the familiar smell of cigar, a smell that seemed to blanket the entire house.

"The guest suite has a second set of doors. If we are quiet, the guard will never hear us," she whispered. "Promise me. My husband nor my brothers can ever know I helped you. They would never forgive me."

"You have our word," the Colonel said.

Mrs. Lee lifted her finger to her lips again, just before stopping at a large oak door.

"It's already unlocked," she whispered.

She pulled the door open. The steady breath of sleep could be heard as well as the distant sound of drunken voice and the shuffling of cards. Beneath a mountain of blue blankets, Thomas slept. The Colonel bent over and spoke softly in his ear, "Tom, I'm here."

He rocked and made weak yelping noises, then wrapped his small arms tight around the Colonel's neck. "Massuh Colonel," he murmured, sleepily.

"Shhh," the Colonel cautioned. "I must get you out of here."

Nehemiah stood by the suite's double doors, listening to the sleeping guard's uneven breath. The Colonel tightened his free arm beneath Thomas's bottom. He turned and followed the light of Mrs. Lee's lantern out of the room.

Mrs. Lee led them into the study, past the fireplace to the French doors where she unhooked the latch and pushed the right door open wide. "Hurry," she whispered.

Through the windows, the Colonel heard laughter; Mitch and his card-playing partner seemed to be at the end of their game. "Like taking candy from an ugly baby," one of the men laughed. The Colonel shifted Thomas in his arms.

"Go," she urged.

"You have righted a wrong," the Colonel whispered, "Thank you."

The Colonel crossed into the brisk night air and Nehemiah slipped past Mrs. Lee with John not far behind. Mrs. Lee blew on the flame, throwing the study into darkness.

The Colonel was at the edge of the landing when he heard heavy footsteps in the house behind him. A man's voice, slurred. He froze, and hid behind shrubs at once. Then Mrs. Lee's gentle voice sounded, "You are delusional from brandy, Jessie. Everyone is asleep."

PART THREE

I.

Kentucky, 1863

The Bonnie Blue flag flapped in the wind high above a Confederate camp near Carter's plantation. The camp's medical tent was littered with the mangled bodies of fallen Confederate soldiers. They were simply boys, many younger than the Colonel's own sons, uniforms soiled and tattered in blood. In the distance, still more soldiers hoisted rifles onto their shoulders and were marching toward the bluffs.

As the icy winter had given way to the blossoms of spring, the world into which Thomas was born no longer existed. Blind Tom was now fourteen years old and America was at war with itself. Within months of Lincoln's election, seven states seceded from the Union and the country fell into the throes of a violent and bloody civil war. Perry Oliver had taken his riches from Blind Tom and sailed back to Ireland; Vivian and Annie returned home to their families.

Thomas was going to play for the troops, to raise morale, but the Confederate camp was a grim site for a concert. The air was noxious from mounds of burning flesh and waste set afire in the fields. The Colonel held his handkerchief to his face as he walked through the long line of wounded men waiting for medics. Orderlies were helping stock mobile field hospitals, while soldiers carried in more sick comrades. What he'd seen in the war against the "red man" was tame compared to the carnage of mangled bodies that lay in these fields. At his side, Thomas skipped along and mimicked the moans. The Colonel stopped to look for the concert stage and held Thomas tight by the wrist. He allowed a couple of soldiers to pass, pulling Thomas into his greatcoat to protect him, but the growing boy twisted out of his grasp, excited by the rhythmic beat of the soldiers drilling in the fields.

A sergeant's voice barked above caravans of wagons transporting shipments of artillery along a man-made trail. There was all kinds of loud machinery. What the Colonel perceived as utter chaos in the Confederate camp took on the shape of a melody in the field of Thomas's mind. The shuffle of boots and the bang of rifles, a symphony, the clopping of horse hooves, poetic opera, the shucking of corn in the makeshift kitchen, a sonata. The Colonel held Thomas tight as he bounced and tugged at his greatcoat, trying to pull him toward the fields.

But something was distracting the Colonel. It wasn't the cadenced sound of soldiers marching in the fields or the loud barking voices. His eyes struggled to identify the figure in the distance, a man standing near the large poles that indicated the staging area Thomas would perform. The Colonel lifted his hand to his forehead to block the glare of sun from his eyes. Yet, it was not a trick of vision: there he was: Samuel Clemons, with his bushy walrus moustache. The writer known as Mark Twain had made the trip to Kentucky to see Thomas play again.

His heart raced as he led Thomas through the narrow walkway past the officers' tents and over to the gated concert area. The Colonel lifted the latch with his free hand, the other hand holding Thomas and his cane. He felt Thomas's fingers pulled against his, but held on tight. The Colonel had explained to Thomas that he would be performing for honorable men, brave men, who were fighting in the war for the South, and the boy was excited.

"Tom's playing for important men of honor. Men of the South," he announced.

The Colonel gathered his composure as Twain approached.

"We meet again, Colonel," Twain said. Hat in hand, Twain ran his fingers through his mane of thick wavy hair. He was tall, with dark, piercing eyes framed by thick eyebrows. He wore a brown frock spattered with rain; mud clung to the top of his boots. Twain had already attended three shows in Memphis and three shows in Knoxville. His presence that afternoon in Virginia made it official: he was a fan of Blind Tom, genuinely enamored with the slave.

It had all happened by chance. Twain's fascination had taken root after an unexpected meeting on a train. Late one winter night, Locomotive No. 201 of the Charleston Railroad, chugged south from Nashville. The Colonel was in the smoking car, having finished his cigar, and was taking a nap. Thomas sat behind him, in the back of the car, against a window. Hat over his face, Twain was asleep, unbeknownst to the Colonel, in the very front of the same smoking car. The train's whistles blew in short bursts and Thomas, excited by the sound, began to clap, whistle, and screech. Twain's eyes flipped wide open. He sat up straight in his seat and lifted his hat from his face. His eyes glided across the empty seats of the cab, before landing on the podgy slave. The Colonel woke up when he heard grunts and saw the back of Twain as he stormed out.

"I'm trying to sleep," Twain complained to the Steward. "And there is a barbarian making all manner of crude noises, driving some kind of viewless express train!"

The curtains rustled and Twain peeked in, pointing at Thomas. "Do you see what I mean?" he snorted.

"Yes, sir," the Steward responded.

"Tell me why this impossible boy is riding in my smoking car?"

"Mr. Twain, sir," the Steward said, "that's Blind Tom, the famous concert pianist. His master must be in the loo."

The Colonel flinched. Upon hearing the Steward address the stranger as Mr. Twain. Sitting up straight, he peered toward the front of the cabin for a closer look. The writer stuck his face in the cabin, staring at Thomas with a mixture of shock and intrigue. "That corpulent annoying child is the great Blind Tom?" He'd said, staring at the tall, overweight slave.

Twain didn't notice the Colonel as he entered; his brown eyes were locked on Thomas.

Blood seeped to the Colonel's face. He had to acknowledge, as he glanced toward the back of the cabin, it was true, Thomas was podgy. Though the boy had grown several inches while on tour, his face and waistline had become swollen like a soufflé from the daily bribes of cake and candy for his cooperation at the piano.

"They say he plays like Mozart," the Steward said. "He appears in Memphis tonight."

The Colonel stood up from his seat as Mark Twain passed down the aisle and, now, he introduced himself. "Mr. Twain, I am Colonel James Bethune, the owner of this slave."

Mr. Twain's eyes sparkled. He invited the Colonel to sit and speak with him.

"Tom, come there's an important man who wants to meet you."

Thomas used the back of the seats as a guide to make his way to his master. His boots were shiny and his suit well-pressed. The Colonel noted how Twain peered across at Thomas, curiously. He watched Twain's expression, how his eyes filled with questions as he took in the blind slave's air of confidence, belied by his obvious idiocy.

"Tom, this gentleman's name is Mark Twain, he's a famous writer," the Colonel said, breaking a bar of chocolate in half and stuffing it into Thomas's hand.

Thomas took a small bite and smiled. "Hi, Mark Twain, you're a famous writer," he said. "Mark Twain. Tom, this gentleman's name is Mark Twain."

"Come, sit, Tom," the Colonel said.

Thomas slid into the seat next to his master and the Colonel rubbed his cottony hair.

"Now, Tom, let Mr. Twain see how well you sing and play the harmonica."

Thomas finished his chocolate and dug into his pocket. He began an upbeat Negro spiritual that he'd once loved to perform for the Bethune children at *Solitude*. The music was accompanied with claps, stomps, and a beautiful deep voice.

"Well done," said Twain.

"Tom, now imitate Stephen Douglas and his speech on Capitol Hill," the Colonel directed.

Thomas replaced his harmonica and summoned Stephen Douglas's bellowing voice.

"Now, I do not believe that the Almighty ever intended the Negro to be equal of the white man," Thomas said, reciting the entire speech.

"Wonderful! Bravo, Tom!" Twain applauded.

After asking as many questions as he could think of, and listening to Thomas's delightful feats of musical mastery and memory, Twain announced he was going to abort his trip west – to meet up with Charles Dickens–and would instead travel to Memphis, so he could witness, with his own eyes, Blind Tom in concert. Memphis, the first of six concerts Twain attended–truly enthralled.

Now, here he was in Richmond, surrounded by the wounded and dying, waiting to witness Blind Tom once more.

"It's settled upon me," Twain said with his hand on the Colonel's shoulder. "I will see Blind Tom as many times as I am able during these troubling times. Consider me your devoted servant."

A short time later, Brigadier General Wade Hampton, C.S.A., stood at the center of the makeshift stage addressing hundreds of battle-tested soldiers.

Hampton was a tall man with a face overwhelmed by a kinky, bushy beard and a moustache that curled up at the ends. He was the richest planter in the United States and owned the most slaves of anyone in the Confederate Army.

"We appreciate your heroism and your zeal in fighting with dignity and honor for the Confederate States of America! Because of your fearless service–your dedication to carrying out God's Will, and your loyal service to the Confederate States of America, we are proud to present a very special guest," General Hampton said. "Please welcome the internationally famous, classical Negro pianist, the Marvelous Blind Tom!"

The soldiers erupted into thundering applause, as the curtains pulled apart revealing Thomas. Thomas began in a dramatic fashion, hammering Beethoven's powerful Fifth Symphony, its short staccato opening punctuated by its rousing final note, lingering at the end of the stirring motif. The familiar rousing start caused the soldiers to burst into frenzy. They clapped and slammed crutches against the back of seats. The whooping and ruckus served to inspire Thomas.

The slave entertained the troops for more than an hour. When he was finished with the last song, Thomas stood to his feet and soaked up the enthusiastic applause. He walked toward the front of the stage and then stopping, said: "God bless the South! God Bless the Confederate States of America!"

The troops exploded into wild cheers and chanted his name. "Blind Tom, Blind Tom!"

Twain stared up at the gangly boy with his expanding belly, the face aimed up at the clouds he couldn't see. The sky seemed like it had messages for him. Twain set his pen to his leather-bound notepad and, took in the weatherworn faces, wounded men brought out on cots, soldiers hardened by battle, all applauding a Negro slave's divine music. For these broken men, Blind Tom was the bright North Star.

"Maybe the angels do sing to him," Twain whispered.

His thoughts drifted back to that first concert he'd witnessed in Memphis.

The Colonel had stood on the stage and gave the command for the slave to play, but the boy didn't start on cue. Instead, he'd rocked, puffed, and neighed like a horse without touching one finger to the keys. It was the oddest display he'd ever seen. He'd put his hand over his mouth in shock. Yet, it was all very riveting, watching the boy's master speaking in an urgent voice in the wings.

A wild primate, that's what Blind Tom looked like in his eyes, initially. But the fact was, when finally he played his music, it was magic, it was inspired. That night, in his hotel in Memphis, all Twain could think about was Blind Tom. The image of his black face taut with passionate delight over the piano, had etched itself in his mind. And taking nips from his favorite bottle of Old Crow while at the desk in his hotel, he dipped his pen in ink and wrote deep into the early morning. Thomas had lured him into a web of contradictions. Never in his life would he experience another boy – a blind child and a slave at that – who could perform with such genius. He'd grown up around slaves, his uncle owned plenty, and sometimes his father borrowed a few hands to work the land. In his travels, he'd witnesses some amazing slave musicians, but none with the perfection of Blind Tom. That's why he'd made the trek to Knoxville and Memphis, then Virginia instead of California to mine for gold or Missouri where he could offer his riverboat expertise to the Confederate army. No, joining the fight against northern aggression with his brothers would have to wait. Now, he gazed up from his notebook.

"Encore, encore!" soldiers screamed.

Thomas stood still and proud with his head tipped back toward the heavens. He returned to the piano. His fingers moved feverishly over the piano's keys. The boy was about five-feet-six inches in height, awkward, stout, and clumsy, but his fingers, while on the piano keys, tripped in a mature flurry; on the violin, he soared with the elegance of an eagle.

That night, with candles lighting his tent, Twain wrote. "It is a fact Blind Tom is not the slave, but the master when he is center stage. He lorded his will over the emotions of his military audience like an autocrat. He swept them into his path like a storm; he lulls them to rest again with melodies as tender as those the rest of us hear only in dreams."

Twain blew on the ink to dry it. With his chin resting in his hands, he reflected on the relationship of master and slave. From what he'd witnessed, the rumors were true: Blind Tom was the Colonel's biscuits and gravy. That while other slave owners were suffering from the ravages of war, the Colonel was thriving. He ate fine chocolates on yachts. He drank Veuve Cliquot in the suites at the track while watching his thoroughbred horses-purchased with profits from his beloved Blind Tom-win races. The slave was his best championship horse. And what did that say for the rest of the South and its future?

After the concert, General Hampton poured bourbon into a pair of small glasses, while Thomas played with a bandalore in the corner of the tent. Handing a drink to the Colonel and one to Twain, General Hampton lifted his glass for a toast.

"Colonel, thank you for Blind Tom's services," he lightly tapped his glasses to theirs. "The nigger's been important to our cause, Colonel. Inspiring our troops all over the south to win this war against the godless Yankees and boosting our boys' self-confidence across divisions."

"Your men are brave," the Colonel said. "It's my honor to serve the Confederate States and Tom is available for the troops whenever you need him."

The sentinel's bell rang somewhere. A few minutes later, the rushing clop of horse hooves outside of the tent could be heard. A courier pulled his horse to a stop before a captain who approached General Hampton's tent and handed the commander a dispatch.

"This just came in," the captain said. "We defeated the Yanks at Manassas! Long live the South!" he shouted, running outside of the tent. "We defeated the Yanks at Manassas!"

The Colonel offered another round of drinks, as a roar erupted and shouts reverberated throughout the camp. Soldiers and officers spilled from their tents as news of victory spread. The boys left the fields of drilling to celebrate. Rifles were thrust in the air and a series of artillery bursts echoed for miles. "To the death!" came shouts.

"Long live the South!"

Beneath the dimming sky, the Colonel heard the sound of trumpets. Bells began to ring and rifles continued to blast.

"We will go to hell across lots before we give in to the Yanks!"

Later that night, loud pops and explosions filled the night sky: colors, whites, reds, greens, and blues lit up the heavens. The Colonel watched the celebration from the door of his tent, with Thomas celebrating each victorious blast.

At last, Thomas was asleep when he wrapped himself tight in his overcoat and stepped out of the tent. Distracted, the Colonel had only limped a few feet before tripping and losing his balance. The edge of a dirt hole caught his boot and he tumbled to the ground with a loud, crunching, breaking of bone. An intense pain shot through his ankle, an ache so excruciating he blacked out.

II.

1863

Richmond, Virginia

It was a who's who of Richmond society in the parlor of Congressman Elijah Wishborn's mansion. The fundraiser was so crowded the Colonel could barely make out any faces. In the center of the parlor, Thomas sat upon a stool at a burgundy piano draped with a Confederate quilt; and a quartet of musicians on violins and flutes accompanied him through a list of Richmond's favorite songs. The popular slave's appearance had garnered more than $2500.00 for much needed army supplies for the Confederacy and some of the ladies close to Mrs. Wishborn were still in the drawing room counting money.

The Colonel grabbed his crutches from the wall; he wasn't going to let a broken ankle dampen his spirits. The victory at Manassas was the focus of many conversations, and bells rang out again and again against peals of laughter. His son, John, had gone against his wishes and joined the war. Nevertheless, he fought with courage, and the Colonel was anxious to see his son with his own eyes. He drew a cloth from his pocket, and as he was wiping his damp brow, he noticed the silky-haired lady in pink with the dimpled chin that he'd seen at the White House. She wore the same large pink hat- he'd recognize her anywhere. She smiled at him, lowered her eyes demurely, and held his gaze.

"Colonel Bethune," came President Jefferson Davis's voice from behind.

Distracted, the Colonel turned to greet the Confederate Commander-In-Chief.

"Mr. President. Congratulations on the victory at Manassas."

"I want to thank you Colonel for your great service to our country. I'm told Blind Tom has raised thousands of dollars for the Confederacy," the President said, before continuing in a more serious tone. "I have a niece who is president of the Hospital Association in Mississippi. She tells me they are in desperate need of funds for operating costs, medicine, and medical supplies. Perhaps Blind Tom could give a benefit concert there?"

"It would be an honor, Mr. President," the Colonel said. "I'll see that it is taken care of at once."

As the Colonel adjusted his crutches, a familiar face approached. Dr. Jefferies from Boston. The Colonel hadn't seen him since he had tested Thomas at *Solitude* more than a decade ago. Though graying at the edges, he still looked youthful and his brown eyes retained their kindness.

"Surely, Tom won't remember me, Colonel," Dr. Jefferies was saying. "You know I continue to tell every colleague who'll listen, Tom is the most gifted musician I've ever encountered."

"He will most certainly remember you," the Colonel assured him.

"He was barely three when I examined him and he's what, fourteen now?" Dr. Jeffries asked.

"He never forgets a voice." Hobbling on his clumsy wooden crutches, the Colonel led Dr. Jeffries over to Thomas. They waited patiently while the pianist finished the song he was playing.

"Tom, there is an old friend here to meet you. Do you remember Dr. Jefferies?" The Colonel asked.

"Yes, sir, Massa Colonel. Tom remembers Doctor Jefferies," Thomas said.

"Hello, Tom," Dr. Jefferies said. He pulled a chair up close to Tom's chair. "What exactly do you remember?"

"Tom, *hai capito Italiano? Capici? Che cosa e che stai giocando.* Tom do you understand me?" He said, repeating the words Jefferies had asked him so long ago. "Perfect Italian. He's three!"

Dr. Jefferies laughed. "Why Tom, you have remarkable powers of memory!"

Thomas angled his face toward his first professional believer.

"Dr. Jefferies of Boston. Tom never forgets. Tom's a genius," Thomas said with a grin.

"Yes, yes you are, Tom," Dr. Jefferies laughed. He patted his soft shoulder and turned to the Colonel. "This war is truly wretched, Colonel. My brothers have run off to fight for both sides."

"Families write me of the horrors. Their farms have been burned, they have no money for wood, much less food or rent. There are only so many benefits Tom can play. A limit to what we can do, but I try to fulfill as many as I can."

Dr. Jefferies nodded solemnly. "Our politics differ, but you have my empathy."

"God has given me Tom, and if his playing can help provide for supplies, then it is my duty to do as much as I can. Even in the absence of his music teacher and attendant. I travel alone with him."

"You're an honorable man, Colonel. And what of your family in Georgia?"

"I worry about them. They're provided for, food and shelter, and protection, but I'm so often far from home now. Tom is, of course, a great part of their security. The money he makes us is a mysterious blessing. God's ways…"

Suddenly, he frowned. Out of the corner of his eye, the Colonel caught a glimpse of his least favorite person. He'd hoped the lack of news about her had meant she'd disappeared or fallen deathly ill and out of his son's life.

"Father-in-law," Eliza said in her cloying sweet way. The Colonel clenched his fists as well as his jaw. "Someone is requesting your presence," she told the Colonel. The Colonel nodded and bid *a bientôt* to Dr. Jefferies and hobbled behind Eliza to the crowded drawing room.

He noticed on her wrist a beautiful ruby bracelet, a family heirloom of his late wife. She must have whispered to John her yearning for it. Fuming, the Colonel lifted his crutches across the threshold into the parlor and there in the center of a crowd was his eldest son. He stood on the brick hearth, his arm in a sling.

"The Yankees left Washington whistling and singing," he was saying. "But when we were finished with them, those boys weren't whistling or singing a whit!"

"That's right! We sure did lick 'em!" A private shouted.

Upon shifting his gaze, John stopped his fantastical story. "Father!" He stepped down and pushed his way through. "I've missed you, *Mon Père!*"

The Colonel smiled with pride. "Go on, son, I don't want to interrupt," the Colonel said. "Continue with your story. Go on. I want to hear all about it." He nudged him back toward the hearth.

The Colonel took a seat while John proceeded to retell every aspect of the great battle. He spun tales until the wee hours of morning when the tolling of bells, several farms away, alerted guests to the dawning day. The soldiers, officers, and their ladies bowed graciously to their host and descended the stairs to their carriages. The Colonel leaned on his crutches once more and together they made their way to the guest room, where John continued his war tales, with Thomas at his feet. History was recorded in more than one way that evening, for Thomas knew the battle's surges and swells by heart and his creative mind was sparked.

Artillery blasts marked the opening phrase of Thomas's original composition, *Battle of Manassas*. Boom! Clack! Clack! Cannons roared and soldiers marched in unison in a piece composed out of the victorious stories shared by John at Congressman Wishborn's. The red and white Stars and Bars flag of the Confederacy fluttered in the breeze and emboldened regiments were seated enraptured in rows beneath the flag. It was a proud moment for the Colonel, Thomas performing for President Davis.

The Colonel sat in the front row, nibbling on warm cornbread, the crumbs tumbled onto his overcoat. He sat back, expansive, and brushed his pants. No one noticed his *faux pas* as all eyes were fixed on the large stage set up behind the White House of the Confederacy.

The soldiers whispered among themselves and scooted to the edge of their seats. The battle weary men, young and old, tried to figure out how Blind Tom was making the piano sound just like cannon fire! Near the front of the stage, President Jefferson Davis, his entire cabinet, and their wives sat similarly perplexed.

Thomas was in rare form. The Colonel was caught up in the memory of walking across the dank smokehouse, picking up the soiled baby Thomas, so tiny and fragile. Now, here he was watching the teenage slave perform his proud masterpiece to the pleasure of the South's President and military regiments. The uniformed men yelped and whooped with pride at Thomas's skilled reproduction of their victorious battle. What amazed them most was the slave's precision, for he had captured every detail of the fight in music.

The first movement was an ambitious recreation. Thomas represented the Southern Army leaving home as they marched to their favorite tune, *The Girl I Left Behind Me*. The song began lightly, like a halo of dust carried by a slight breeze, *pianissimo*. It was subtle in the distance, soft, and innocent. Only to grow louder and more threatening to portray the Confederate army's approach to Manassas, complete with a growing, increasingly grave motif of drums and fifes: boom, clack, boom, boom, clack-clack, signaling the impending conflict.

The Colonel had managed to stand. He looked out into the sea of amazed faces.

The second movement began with pure brilliance. The *allegro* portrayed the Grand Union Army arrogantly marching out of Washington to the blithe and disrespectful tune of *Dixie*. The musical phrase reflected John's report that the U.S. troops, swelled with arrogance, had left the capital singing loudly in anticipation of a swift and convincing Union victory. The mere tinkling of the popular Yankee melody had infuriated the waiting Rebels and now, as *Dixie* swelled the troops watching Thomas began to shout.

The slave's fingers moved rapidly, tenderly, across the piano keys, punctuated by flurries of rising and falling sixteenth notes. Thomas was creating sounds and tones that emulated other instruments, making the piano sound like a piccolo, an oboe, making sounds on the piano no one thought humanly possible – all in an elegant retelling of the greatest victory of the South's new country.

As the troops cheered, the Colonel was convinced he'd just heard the angels Thomas spoke of so often. He heard their high-pitched voices singing, ministering to the military men of the South, healing their wounds, and bringing them fresh courage to fight on. The Colonel shut his eyes, enchanted by the music harmonizing in his heart. A thought struck him: Thomas was like the Chinese *Bombyx mori moth*, an unsightly blind insect, insignificant in appearance, whose offspring were a fiercely guarded secret for thousands of years. Spies were killed, traders hunted and executed, all for that tiny unlikely creature which was responsible for producing the finest, smoothest, and most expensive silk known to man.

Thomas was his Chinese Bombyx mori moth.

Later that evening, the Colonel was relaxing with a glass of sherry in the drawing room of the Confederate White House when he received disturbing news from Davis.

"Detectives working for Lincoln have been stirring up insurrection in our cities for weeks. Today a half dozen slaves working on fortifications at Marion Hill secured refuge, after expressing their desire to enlist in the Union Army," Davis said disdainfully. "They seek to destroy our property and our peace. I've instructed my men to retrieve the fugitive slaves.

"But you must leave tonight, Colonel."

"Leave?"

"My men sent word this afternoon. There are men asking questions about Blind Tom's performance schedule."

"This is ludicrous. We're in the middle of war now."

"You've raised a lot of money for the Confederacy. The North would like to use him for just that." Jefferson Davis lifted his hand and the servant opened a door. Two soldiers dragged in a badly beaten man, fresh blood dripping from his lip.

"This man's been paying prostitutes to solicit our men to help capture Blind Tom."

For a moment, the Colonel did not hear anything else in the drawing room. He exhaled, clasping his cane; he stabbed it into the floor as if he wanted to break it against the marble with the force of his palm. President Davis waved the man away and handed the Colonel a healthy glass of brandy.

"Blind Tom was exceptional today, Colonel. My men were thoroughly inspired," said the Confederate President. "Go to London, Colonel. It's not safe for you or your slave here. I've arranged for your passage across the ocean at the end of the month. That gives you enough time to return to your home, see your children in Georgia, get things in order. By then perhaps we'll have a better handle on winning this war."

Something stirred in the Colonel's heart, a blurred weariness as he thought about his family back in Georgia, of running from Washington, running from Virginia. Though tired of running like a deer during hunting season, he did not struggle with his decision. It would be foolish not to heed the President's advice and slip out of town with Thomas under the cover of night. He nodded and finished the rest of his brandy.

Later, when he yawned for all to see, he had no plans of sleeping once he reached his suite. He entered, lit a few candles, and crossed the cold wood floor to grab the clothes hanging in the closet. At that hour, when he was sure the Union investigators were unlikely to discover his departure, he helped Thomas out of a first floor window, then slipped through himself.

A few Rebel wives he'd supported with cash knew of his plans for escape prepared a travel basket with freshly baked pies, cakes, biscuits, and fried chicken. He could not have foreseen the container of food would be his last southern style meal for untold years.

III.

1863

Atlantic Ocean

Thomas was too excited to sleep. The threes were falling softly now, but the sixes slammed against the ship and howling wind caused the cabin to rock from side-to-side. Deep yellows and waves of red spread across the heavens with trumpets roaring *staccato* above the ships creaking, "Hail as large as ostrich eggs," Vivian whispered. Thomas began to hum. The hail against the steamer's hull, the wind and claps of thunder, all made a beautiful chorus of timpani drums and felt a composition begin to form.

"If by some miracle we make it to London alive, Tom, I am looking forward to visiting the Queen at Buckingham Palace," his teacher's yellow voice interrupted his emerging rhapsody. "Her name's Queen Victoria, Tom. She's quite easily the most powerful woman on earth," the teacher whispered. "A woman of higher social rank than your master. Even higher than President Buchanan. She's royalty and she wants to hear your beautiful music, Tom. It's another great honor."

He felt her arms tighten around him, her warmth made his body warm. " I will teach you a new piece from Haydn, and you will mesmerize her court Tom, I know you will."

Thomas smiled. He kicked the cabin wall with his boots. "Tom will perform for the Queen of England and mesmerize her court. Tom will play his beautiful music for the queen."

"Good, Tom, I know you will," whispered Vivian. "I will tell you a story I once heard about her and maybe then you'll sleep."

At half past noon, the Colonel kneeled to pray at Westminster Abbey. On bent knees, he snuck a peek into the shadows. A note had been left in his cabin, on the steamer crossing the Atlantic. He'd been directed to come to the famous church on this day, at this hour, but there was no one waiting for him beneath the statues of Moses and King David, as the note had suggested. When the worshipers next to him began to stand, he leaned on his cane and stood to his feet, then crossed his body in the same manner. Once mass concluded, he lingered in the sanctuary, his head angled toward heaven, spending time with God. He lit a candle for his father and one for Frances, wandered the empty aisles, and after a long while gave up hope.

Finally, he exited the cathedral into the wet, brusque London air. He walked along Suffolk Street dejected and confused by the false call. He opened the door to the carriage on Great Smith Street, behind the Abbey where ruffians, prostitutes, and ragamuffins crowded the fetid alleyways. Climbing the steps into the cab, the Colonel stopped short. Folds of green and purple taffeta filled the cabin. Beneath an ample brim was the beautiful and familiar face of the woman in the pink hat. That beautiful woman from the White House who showed up again at various concerts, then disappeared, always in pink, always out of reach. Until now.

"Come, Colonel Bethune. This is the right carriage," she said. He hesitated and she spoke for a second time. "I assure you, I don't bite...unless upon request. Belle Graham," she said, extending her hand. "Your slave and his teacher are safe."

Holding her eyes with his, he took her hand. "I never forget a beautiful woman," he said.

"Nor I a courageous man." She took out a lavender and gold case and offered an exotic cigar to the Colonel.

She was well-bred, with a small mouth, high cheekbones, almond-shaped eyes. Her waist was small and her corset could barely hold in her breasts. President Davis was shrewd in using her for Confederate missions, the Colonel thought. Realizing he had lost himself in the charms of her beauty, the Colonel forced himself to speak.

"Mr. Benjamin and Mr. King? I received correspondence to meet them here at the Cathedral."

"The Secretary of State and Mr. Thomas King are on their way to France to meet Napoleon."

"With victorious results we hope."

"For once the French are getting it right. They can be dull-witted. No offense to your lineage," she said eyeing him casually to see if he was a man quick to take offense.

The Colonel knew she was assessing him and responded coolly. "None taken," he said. "Today's French are not noted for their acumen."

He lifted the long brown cigarette to his nose and sniffed, before settling into his seat. Biting off the tip, he spat it onto the carriage floor. Belle leaned in with a lit match and lifted it to his cigar, in such a way that he could not fail to glimpse the ample rounds of breast.

From her cleavage, she retrieved a folded letter.

"When you meet the Queen, it is President Davis's desire that you use the opportunity for the benefit of the South and appeal for recognition of the Confederate States as a sovereign country," she said.

The Colonel lifted his brow. "Is she amenable?"

"It is sometimes easier to be wise for others than it is to be wise for ourselves," she said, approximately quoting Rochefoucauld. "You're an accomplished military officer, you know the science of strategy Colonel. Make her amenable."

"*Oui, madame*," the Colonel answered, nodding his acquiescence.

She leaned forward with a glimmer in her eyes. "Are you amenable to all of this?" she asked suggestively. "Even the wealthiest of men are feeling the impact of the war, yes?" She reached out and softly stroked the side of his beard with the back of her hand.

"Do you fancy that you flatter me or do you presume to know me?" the Colonel breathed.

"One cannot truly know a man from accounts or chance observances. But one can certainly infer a man from the way his soul speaks through his eyes. You're a man of excellent manners, unyielding in your disdain for the nonsense of men. A man who associates with men of rank, a thinker, but not without humor."

The Colonel's breath caught in his throat when she touched him. His eyes drifted to her lips and he drew her closer. "You have Tom here, whom I hear is bringing in quite the profits," she said. "But, if we can't persuade England or France, then, that, too may be taken away, yes?"

The Colonel thought he answered yes but wasn't sure. He leaned in and took her lips and then, for weeks, continued to take her.

IV.

Bells tolled, marking the nine o'clock hour. The Colonel stood on a small bridge in his finest dress coat overlooking the Tyburn stream at Buckingham Palace. Trumpets blared and cymbals clashed behind him as an English military band performed in the garden. The royal levee had begun promptly at eight o'clock that morning. Liveried soldiers in tall furry hats marched across the lawn in formation. The Colonel felt an unexpected nervousness as he struggled to remember the many royal protocols. There was the protocol from President Jefferson, protocol on addressing royal servants, protocol governing the proper etiquette for presentation to Her Majesty. It was daunting trying to remember it all.

He adjusted his white gloves, watching the trickling flow of the water in the stream, and his face brightened when he caught sight of the Lord Great Chamberlain approaching. The sixth of the 'Great Officers of State', he was dressed in black breeches and a black silk long coat with golden stitching down the front. The Colonel caught his breath. The Chamberlain informed him he'd been summoned to court by Her Majesty the Queen. The stoic Chamberlain provided no explanation, but began coaching him, once again, on the precisions of court etiquette as he escorted him into the palace.

The Colonel was curious as to why he was being summoned, but refrained from asking. His mouth felt dry as he entered the Grand Hall with its soaring arched ceilings. He took in a deep breath as he stood by the white marbled statues in the Guard Room, where guests awaited entry to Her Majesty's Throne Room.

As he waited for his audience with Queen Victoria, the knot in his stomach tightened. He composed his thoughts by taking in the beauty of the red carpet along the white marble staircase. Gilded frames with portraits of the Queen's ancestors lined the stairway, and his eyes were drawn to Queen Victoria's grandmother, the mocha-hued Queen Charlotte, with her distinct Negroid features–there was a resemblance to his bastard daughters in Virginia.

Overcome with a sense of dread, the Colonel considered the possibilities-all were unnerving. Soon the Lord Great Chamberlain gestured for the Colonel to approach. The heavy golden doors protecting the Monarch's Royal Court were opened. Across the threshold, the Colonel's eyes beheld the grandeur of the gilded Throne Room. It was a large chamber with dozens of splendid crystal chandeliers, golden candelabras, and gilt friezes. The floor was covered in a rich red carpet and gilt molding and framed walls of crimson silk.

The Queen's court teemed with hundreds of attendants: pretty ladies-in-waiting, the Mistress of the Robes, noblemen and women of every rank–all in elaborate and brightly colored clothing. And guarding the Queen's court were dozens of ornately dressed soldiers.

Her Excellency Queen Victoria sat on the golden throne of England beneath a silken canopy. Cradled in her arms was her prized Pekingese. The royal dog, a gift from one of her military officers after British forces seized the Forbidden City and the aunt of the Emperor of China committed suicide. The Pekingese barked and the Queen hushed the fluffy dog.

It was all so lavish and grand, the gold, the silk, the velvet. The Colonel's brow began to sweat; he hoped his nerves did not show.

Queen Victoria tracked him with a piercing stare as he walked in steady, measured steps, toward her royal presence. He stopped several paces before he reached the throne, just as he had been instructed by the Lord Great Chamberlain.

"Colonel James Bethune from America, Your Majesty."

The Colonel walked forward, bowed before the Queen and kissed the ring on her hand. "Your Majesty," he said without lifting his eyes to hers. Then he stood and stepped back, waiting for her to address him.

He noted the once pretty teenage queen had become thickset with heavy jowls, in middle age. She had the look of a well-fed Doberman pinscher, with piercing eyes as blue as a clear noon sky. Dressed in all black, there was an understandable melancholy about her, given her perpetual mourning over the death of her beloved husband some time ago. Though he'd been warned the Queen was opinionated and strong-willed, she seemed remarkably shy in manner. When she finally spoke, he was struck by the exquisite sweetness of her voice—like honey dripping from diamond-shaped combs.

"Colonel, I sent for you because I am deeply fascinated by the news of Blind Tom's musical abilities."

"It is my honor to bring him to your court, Your Majesty."

"I look forward to his performance this afternoon in the Picture Gallery. However there is a small matter regarding the pianist's repertoire," she said.

"I serve at your pleasure Your Majesty." His voice was calm and confident, until she brought his world crashing down.

"As Sovereign, I am responsible to God for the lives of men and I take that honor most seriously. Therefore, I will not allow *The Battle of Manassas* to be performed in my court- though I'm told it's a wonderfully promising piece. Nevertheless, it may put my impartiality toward your war in America into question. And thereby place my country in the midst of undue tensions with the Union."

The Colonel reeled. Somehow, he managed to nod and bent at the waist, much deeper than he had upon entering and mumbled:

"Your Most Gracious Majesty. Please accept my sincerest apologies. The piece will be removed at once."

Queen Victoria's half-crown sparkled in the lights of the chandelier. Without another word, the Colonel began backing away along the imported marble floor. In adherence to protocol, he was careful not to turn his back on the Queen and offend the Crown of England.

With one royal diktat and the wave of her hand, the Queen had squashed any hopes the Colonel had of persuading her to the Southern cause. The censorship of his country's most beloved musical piece was undoubtedly a bad omen. For Queen Victoria was not just a crowned figurehead, but a powerful and influential voice in the British Empire and one which held great sway over the decisions of England's Prime Minister, Europe as a whole.

He mulled over the event for the next few hours. But the morning passed quickly before the Colonel and Thomas were escorted down the palace's marble walkway into the Queen's Picture Gallery where the royal art collection hung on patterned cherry walls. At the far end of the long room sat Queen Victoria, on yet another gilded chair, still cuddling her petite Pekingese, still under the watchful eyes of her bejeweled ladies-in-waiting.

The Colonel sucked in his breath.

All eyes were on the Americans as they promenaded through the gallery toward Queen Victoria. Thomas's frock and black pants were newly purchased and tailored for the occasion. He held the Colonel's hand and walked slowly. Many royals filled the chamber: the Duchess of Kent, the Queen and King of the

Belgians, the King and Queen of Prussia, and the Queen of Spain. Directly beside Queen Victoria stood her goddaughter, Sarah Forbes Bonetta, a beautiful African princess exceedingly loved by the monarch.

"Bow before the Queen, Tom," the Colonel whispered, when they were the appropriate distance away. He prayed Thomas would cooperate. He bent at the waist and to his relief Thomas too bowed gracefully, just as Vivian had taught him. "Your Majesty, I present to you Blind Tom Bethune," the Colonel said. "Tom, greet Her Majesty, Queen Victoria."

"Greetings, Her Majesty, Queen Victoria," Thomas said. "Tom will play beautiful music for the Queen."

The stoic Queen gazed down at the blind slave and her somber cheeks began to rise into a smile. "Why, Tom, I am quite eager to hear your beautiful music."

Her Majesty's voice was a sweet pink color with tinges of brown that indicated deep sadness to Thomas. The teenage slave decided he liked the Queen and sensing the melancholy in her heart, he sought to lift her spirits.

"Your Majesty, it is Tom's pleasure to play his beautiful music for the beautiful Queen. Tom's eyes have never seen such beauty Her Majesty. Tom hopes to make the beautiful Queen happy."

Stunned, the Colonel shuddered, but to his amazement, Queen Victoria's body started to shake and she erupted with laughter. After the Queen's mirth was displayed, the rest of the Royal Court joined in the merriment, also smitten with the slave.

"Why thank you, Tom," Queen Victoria said.

She turned to her goddaughter and whispered that she found Thomas charming. Then, as the entire court watched, the Queen gathered up her dress and, breaking protocol, rose from her throne, her fluffy Pekingese in one arm. She offered her bejeweled hand to Thomas and escorted him to the grand piano. The Queen assisted the prodigy as he climbed onto the stool. Once settled,

Thomas shifted his hips, lifted his hands above the keys, and began his repertoire not with Haydn, as planned, but with the thrill of Beethoven's Fifth Symphony.

The striking opening chords of the beloved piece set the tone, warming the hearts of the royal crowd. Thomas wanted to please the Queen, he played with technical brilliance; his honey-toned harmonies, refined and designed to impress Queen Victoria. Not long after his playing began, the crowned heads and aristocrats began to whisper: a report spread around the gallery that the Negro's musical genius had not been exaggerated.

At the piano, Thomas tilted his head back and forth with the music and at one point during the repertoire, stood on the stool to play backwards. The normally solemn Queen was so ignited with appreciation; she applauded and openly shared her delight.

"Gaetano Donizetti, Tom. Are you familiar with his creations?" Queen Victoria asked, in her simple manner, well after his repertoire for the day had been completed.

"Yes, Your Majesty. Tom knows Gaetano Donizetti."

"Bellini, Tom, do you know Bellini?"

"Tom knows Bellini, Her Majesty," he said of the Sovereign's favorite composer.

When the last note faded, Queen Victoria rose from her gilded chair and gestured for Thomas. The Colonel smoothed the back of Thomas's frock.

"Tom, I have had the pleasure of hearing many great composers," Queen Victoria said. "I have never witnessed such artistry and perfection as yours. Your music is heavenly."

"Thank you Your Majesty. Tom's music is heavenly."

"I have something special that I had made for you, Tom." She gestured to an attendant who handed the Queen an eighteen-karat gold-trimmed violin. "This is for you, a gilded violin."

Tom clapped his hands wildly. "Her Royal Majesty has given Tom a gilded violin. Thank you, Your Royal Majesty."

V.

After Buckingham Palace, the invitations poured in for Blind Tom at the American's London hotel. News of Thomas's exceptional performance for Queen Victoria was on the front page of *The Times* and every other daily paper in London for weeks. Blind Tom was the hottest ticket in London and was called back to Queen Victoria's court on several occasions. The Colonel and Thomas were carried in fine carriages to large estates and castles in the city and nearby countryside. For every performance, Thomas was in fine form, but the flood of requests was beginning to wear on them all.

Now, the morning sun flitted in through the open curtains. Thomas was pacing in and out of the sitting room. The Colonel ignored Tom's grunts and groans, nestled on the divan in his robe, smoking a good cigar and trying to read the morning paper. The reviews were still good, but the Colonel was distracted and had been for days. The Queen's rejection of the *Battle of Manassas* had curtailed any political discussion and the possibility of winning her to the cause of the Confederacy. Most nights he'd lain awake, gazing out the window of the hotel bedroom, calculating how he might win another audience with Her Majesty.

"It's not as disastrous as it seems," Belle said as she entered the sitting room, kissed his forehead, and stroked his hair. She took a long drag from her thin cigarette and ignored Thomas's rustling about behind the divan.

Suddenly, Thomas threw his harmonica against the wall.

"Tom, enough."

"Tom needs his piano," Thomas yelled.

"We don't have your piano here," the Colonel sighed.

"The angels are singing. Tom needs his piano."

"Wait a moment, Tom boy," the Colonel set down his cigar and shuffled about some trunks and boxes, withdrawing two instrument cases from the pile. "When the angels sing, Thomas will not cease pacing," he said to Belle – who sat in an upholstered chair watching the domestic scene, her robe not quite closed, indifferent to her exposed breasts.

"There's the lovely flute from the Duke of Edinburgh, Tom, or your gold violin, presented by Her Majesty, Queen Victoria!"

"Yes," he cried, his arms outstretched. "Tom would like the gold violin from the Queen Victoria." He took it and ambled through a doorway into the suite's parlor.

Though the golden violin was priceless, the Colonel's piece of mind was more valuable.

Belle made room for him on the large chair and he joined her. "Maybe you'll have better luck with the Emperor," she said. She looked at the Colonel from the settee, as the melodious sounds of the violin began to eddy past her ears. Her eyebrow rose. "He's prodigious on the violin?"

"As well as the French horn and the flute," the Colonel answered, distracted. "The Emperor, you were saying? You're speaking of Napoleon?"

"Yes. While riding together last weekend, he spoke expansively of the South," she said. "I told him of Queen Victoria's deep pleasure in the slave boy's music, and he was intrigued. I suggested he invite Blind Tom to his court, and I imagine he will."

"I imagine he will, the invitation from you while astride a great mare."

"He is much more amenable when we are riding."

She examined his face to assess his thinking and shook her head. He still managed to have a naughty sense of humor, though his life and the lives of generations of those behind him were dependent on the South winning the war. "In all things it is better to hope than to despair," the Colonel said, adoringly.

"Ah, Goethe." Biting into a heart-shaped chocolate parfait, Belle curled into his broad chest and purred like a kitten.

On occasion, after too much wine, he'd get beside himself and prattle poetically about their future together, though he knew theirs was a hopeless romance. "I look forward to speaking with the Emperor," he lifted her chin and kissed her lips.

Later that evening, Thomas sat by the window making loud kissing noises and repeating what he'd heard that morning. "You are a beauty beyond compare," he said, and smooched more kisses.

"That's enough Tom," said the Colonel.

There was a knock at the hotel door, and the Colonel hurried to open it, hungry and expecting room service.

"*Le Colonel James Bethune?*" The man bowed and spoke with formal dignity in French. "*Oui, Je suis le Colonel Bethune.*"

The man changed to English with a strong French accent. "His Royal Highness, Emperor Napoleon Bonaparte the Third requests your presence and the presence of your slave, Blind Tom, at the Tuileries, to perform..." The man stopped when he recognized Belle, and he gave her a wisp of a smile "...at his masquerade ball."

"Tell His Royal Highness we would be honored."

VI.

1863

Paris

Dressed as a knight in shining armor, the Colonel placed his helmet on the seat of the carriage outside the Grand *Hotel De Louvre*. Belle sat beside him, dressed as Makeda, the dark Queen of Sheba, munching on chocolate covered strawberries. Thomas sat beside Vivian, on the opposite bench, and they rode through the narrow cobbled streets toward the *Palais des Tuileries*.

Belle licked chocolate from the strawberries. She was exquisite in a flowing jade dress, cut low revealing an inch of her breasts. Her silky hair was swept upward with jeweled stickpins that held a complex maze of braids in place. The Colonel admired her feminine refinement and defiant courage.

Her life was as much at risk at that moment as his. The masquerade ball was more than a lavish party, Napoleon's castle was a magnet for assassins and some were sure to be Union agents.

Once past the iron palace gates, the Colonel and his entourage ascended the stairs to the main entryway. Vivian and Belle were separated from the Colonel and Thomas who were conducted to a separate quarter of the palace where a small apartment was provided.

"Tom, stand still." The Colonel held a black silk matador's cape he was trying to wrap around him. He stepped forward, but Thomas moved away. "Tom, let me put on your cape."

"Massa Colonel wants to hurt Tom," Thomas said, stepping back and ducking beneath the cape like a small bull. He slipped around a small tea table and evaded his master.

In his heavy armor, the Colonel couldn't maneuver fast enough. The suit clanked and creaked as Thomas fled from him. "Tom, it's a costume, I'm wearing, making this noise. It's my costume for the Emperor's masquerade ball. This cape is your costume." He said, frustrated. "I cannot but stress that you're performing before important diplomats, members of the House of Commons, a number of sitting monarchs, not to mention the Emperor of France, Napoleon the Third, and his wife the Empress, do you understand?" He asked wearily.

"I cannot but stress that you're performing before important diplomats, do you understand?" Thomas repeated and spun in another circle, then started to run and smacked into the side of the table. The Colonel folded the cape over his silver arm. It was taxing wondering whether the slave prodigy would cooperate.

"Don't mimic," the Colonel said.

He was worn out. Perhaps it was the late night soirees, perhaps fatigue from the hard sea voyage weeks ago, or the uncertainty of the South's victory in the war. Whatever the cause, the Colonel closed his eyes and imagined that Thomas, just once, might behave in a normal manner. He yearned for a meaningful moment, to penetrate the dullness of the slave boy's psyche, and affix him to some semblance of reality. His thoughts were cut short by stomping; Thomas was on his back, kicking the bottom of his boots against the marble floor.

"Tom, stop it."

"Massa wants to hurt Tom."

"I don't want to hurt you," he spoke plainly. "I want you to wear the cape and mask, because that's what people wear at masquerade balls."

Thomas tilted his head from side to side in a playful manner. He heard the pleasant dark pinks his master's words carried, each forming a different sweet-shaped lily across an expansive pink field. But he was in a grey mood and simply did not feel like having odd clothes pulled, tied, and pinned to his body.

"If you could grasp that," the Colonel was saying. "Grasp the concept of normalcy and put away your obtuse behavior and act like normal human beings act, the world wouldn't be such a problematic place for you."

He didn't have time to fight. "Tom, you are the greatest musician on the planet," he said, placing his hand on the slave's shoulder. "You are poised to play your beautiful music before the greatest collection of royalty on the continent tonight."

Thomas began to clap.

"Tom is the greatest musician on the planet. Tom will wear the cape."

Later, Thomas held the Colonel's hand, dressed for the party with his black cape and mask. A footman led them to the Grand Chamberlain, who led them down a long corridor, where they were met by a royal servant. The royal servant took Thomas to another chamberlain, who led him into the majestic ballroom and to the grand piano.

Laughter and music filled the corridor while the Colonel stood in the long line of distinguished masked guests waiting for the procession into the grand ballroom. He imagined himself speaking to the Emperor privately on a balcony overlooking the gardens of Paris.

His eyes searched the rows of feathers and jesters for the lovely Belle. He spotted her green lace near the middle of the masked throng. Soon, they stepped through the golden doors, into the ballroom as long as a city block with soaring gold ceilings, magnificent gilt frescoes, and dozens of massive golden chandeliers. Life-sized marbled sculptures dominated each salon. The looming space was rich with bronze, gold, ivory, and marble with the intent to inspire awe at the splendor of the empire.

With Belle adorning his arm, he descended the stairs into the boisterous Grand Ballroom. Thomas's original piano music floated across the hall as Empress Eugenie descended from an inner salon. In purple lace, framed low over her ample breasts, she made her grand entrance as the Roman Queen Zenobia. The long train required six attendants on each side, a perfect royal spectacle. Her auburn-Colored head was bedecked with the crown jewels. Her satin gown dripped with radiant diamonds, brilliant sapphires, gleaming emeralds, and precious pearls. Next to the fashionable Empress was the beloved leader of the French, His Royal Highness, Emperor Napoleon Bonaparte the Third and their adolescent son the Prince Imperial. The confident Emperor, legendary for both his daring and his relentless womanizing, was fully clad in a black hooded cloak and black mask.

His Majesty appeared poised despite the presence of his wife and his many conquests in the same room. The Colonel watched the closely guarded Emperor with the hope that the opportunity for a political exchange would present itself.

As the Emperor and the Empress made their way to the main floor, the music began for the quadrille, but the Emperor and Empress circled the edges of the room: Napoleon did not enjoy dancing. Belle caught sight of Napoleon moving in the Colonel's direction and, shifting her fan, she touched her hand to the Colonel's shoulder. "Here comes the Emperor," she said. "Do not speak of matters of the state while we are in character," she instructed. "We must feign we do not recognize him." She winked. "He likes the game, it is important to play along."

The Colonel lowered his metal visor as Napoleon made his way through the mad crowd. With two glasses of wine in one hand and one more in the other, much wine spilled on the floor. "*Bonjour, vous semblez belle,*" he said, addressing Belle with exaggerated gallantry. He bowed low and handed her a glass of wine.

"*Je suis Makeda, la reine Sheba,*" Belle responded.

"You are enchanting, *ma chèrie,*" he said, swallowing his glass of wine in one large gulp. Though his face was partially hidden by a mask, his eyes were very clearly admiring the length of her neck and the curves of her body. He made no secret of his affections for the American lady, as she was a frequent and favorite guest of his court.

"You are strange to me," Belle said and batted her lashes. "An enticing man, I must say, the likes of which one rarely encounters." She leaned her chest toward the Emperor and offered him a generous glimpse of her cleavage.

The Colonel watched the easy way Belle flirted and managed the Emperor of France. Soon it would be his moment to speak and he was anxious. His costume was hot and his head began to pound. What would he say to a figure such as Napoleon the Third? A man who liked games, but could just as readily cut off his head. How would he know the moment to mention recognition of the Confederate States? Despite his bumbling dance and cackling laughter, the Emperor was no fool. He had a reputation for being cunning, devious, and irresolute, making him a powerful man one should only fear.

A soft voice pierced his thoughts and Belle was presenting him to Napoleon. "This is my knight in armor, Sir James of the House Bethune."

The Colonel had no time, the Emperor grabbed his hand.

"Sir Bethune. One of your ancestors was a royal advisor, *non?*" the Emperor asked.

"As well as a grandfather who was an advisor to Louis XII, and an uncle who was a confidante of Louis XIV," the Colonel smiled. He was careful not to utter Emperor in his tale, so as not to offend the ruler by acknowledging that he recognized him.

Nodding, Napoleon turned his attention to Belle and dropped two satin beanbags in her hand. "We will take supper in a few hours. Will you and your knight join a stranger?" he said, keeping the facade of a man of mystery and not the ruler of France.

"*Oui, Monsieur.* You're so very generous. We take kindly to sweet offers from strangers," Belle said with a lovely smile.

"*Merçi, madame.* Go through those doors," he said, pointing to a large set of gilded double doors on the south end of the ballroom. "You will both be admitted."

The Colonel felt a rush, for his opportunity was not far away.

The Colonel and Belle approached the sentinels and handed over the velvet beanbags His Highness had given them for admission. The shimmering private salon, with its lush Louis XIV decor, was framed by large windows facing the lighted Seine. Thomas was already in the grand room, at the grand piano, performing for Napoleon

At the long dining table set for scores of people, a servant escorted them past a feast laden with lobster, veal, doves, and pigeons, carafes like waterfalls flowing with wine--and sat them beside the Emperor and Empress. The Colonel was anxious to launch into talk with Napoleon, but Belle urged him to be mindful of etiquette and cautioned him that the mercurial ruler could banish him, if displeased.

After a while, Napoleon removed his mask and turned to the Colonel. "This music your Blind Tom's playing is inspired. The slave expresses the innermost parts of his soul with innocence and poetic spirit, *non*?"

"He pleases you?" asked the Colonel in hopes to segue toward political matters.

"His music is sweet harmony to my ears." Napoleon said. He took Belle's hand. "Madame, I had heard of the blind slave pianist from Brahms," he said. "And of course from you, *ma chère* Belle, but this slave boy is far greater than any of your superlatives described," he declared.

The Emperor watched Thomas play, his face an eruption of joy, as the slave began to play Sonata No. 2, Op. 35 from France's own beloved Chopin.

He raised his bejeweled hand in a toast. "In the words of Brahms, Blind Tom is the Eighth Wonder of the world!"

"The Eighth wonder of the World," was whispered all over the room. "*La Huitième Merveille du Monde!*"

"Bring the boy to me," he said gesticulating grandly when the Sonata was finished. "I want to see him close up, head to head, as we say."

Vivian stood beside him in a pink gown with black ribbons and a black mask. She held her hand against Thomas's back and bowed deeply, to the Emperor, then spoke in his clearest French. "*Bonjour, votre Majesté, Napoléon Bonaparte le Troisiéme. J'aime la France, sa langue est une sonate agréable à mes oreilles,*" he said.

"He speaks French! He speaks French!"

"Music's the voice that tells us the human race is greater than it knows," Thomas said, quoting Napoleon Bonaparte.

Napoleon was sincerely flattered. "Did you hear him? He quoted Bonaparte!"

The Colonel felt encouraged at the unanticipated, yet welcome moment. Thomas must have heard the quotes from one of his own children. It was an amazing stroke of luck. Thomas had unwittingly touched a soft spot in the Emperor's heart, Napoleon adored his uncle, Napoleon Bonaparte, erecting monuments and commissioning grand portraits of him all over Paris.

"He knows my uncle!" the Emperor repeated. He stood and gestured for the Colonel and Belle to withdraw with him to a more private area of the salon. "Bordeaux. We must have Bordeaux," he said, and motioned for servants to bring his favorite wine.

He chatted on about the greatness of France. The Colonel listened while taking in the great salon. It was a large, warm room with velvet walls; the entire chamber, ceiling included, seemed to be covered in marble and gold. There were gilt chairs and a large gilded self-portrait: the Supreme Ruler posing in a general's uniform between two large Corinthian columns.

"I must say, I admire your President Jefferson Davis," the Emperor said. "I am kept abreast by wire of the South's progress. This must end soon. The embargo the Americans have is not good for France."

"A good reason for you to recognize our country, Your Excellency," the Colonel ventured, relieved he did not have to broach the subject himself.

"If only for England and Russia," Napoleon averred. "Some in their realms are pro-South behind closed doors, but reluctant in public. Their unwillingness presents a delicate quandary for France." The Emperor stood before an immense window taking in the magnificence of the gas lamps lighting up his city.

"Your victory at Manassas was encouraging, very encouraging."

A rush of hope blossomed in the Colonel's breast and he was about to speak when a soft knock came at the salon door. The chamberlain entered and whispered in the Emperor's ear, then handed him a telegram. A grave expression shadowed the Emperor's face.

"I'm afraid your country has suffered a horrible defeat." Napoleon said with a sigh. "You will give my regards to your Mr. Davis. He is no longer any kind of President."

They were dismissed with one wave of his hand. And heading homeward.

VII.

1863

A falling star streaked the night sky as the steamer cut through the Atlantic. It was New Year's Eve and on the bow of the ship, the songs of slaves could be heard on the wind. Soft-melodic baritones mingled with sweet sopranos, balanced by the harmonies of honeyed alto voices. There was singing from freedmen washing the top deck. And singing from the cooks and firemen below. And the slaves loading coal in the engine room at the very bottom of the vessel were singing with the hope of freedom. Their voices floated upward, soaring past the highest decks, tickling the ethereal ears of heaven.

An eerie tension filled the air. Something was happening.

The Colonel passed a table where two English gentlemen were dining.

"It seems the Negroes are happy tonight."

"Let them sing. The Americans are finally joining the rest of the civilized world and are going to end the abomination of slavery," the cultured gent with a pencil moustache stated.

The Colonel felt as if his legs had melted. He was staggered.

"Well, it's certainly long overdue. After all, it's an antiquated practice."

"Yes, indeed. That old rusted chain of slavery has finally been broken, crumbling right inside the closed fists of those aristocratic Southern hands," he said, with an arrogant sneer.

The Colonel roiled. It took all his will to refrain from regaling them with the consequences this path would have for America and for the world. An economy decimated, a way of living unraveled. He scanned the deck, looking for Belle, and caught sight of her sitting at a table with friends from Paris. The Colonel walked toward the pink and purple-laced ladies in their corsets and fine frocks. He bowed politely and interrupted their conversation, pulling Belle by her ruffled elbow to the side.

"Is it true, about the slaves?"

"Yes, it is true," she said calmly, though she would not let her eyes meet his. "Lincoln is ready to issue an Emancipation Proclamation. Soon, they will be free and our lives will never be the same."

She said it as simply and casually as if she was saying Lincoln was announcing his wife's birthday. As if his entire life wasn't crashing down all about him.

"I must go to Tom," the Colonel's voice was a distant whisper. He took a step, but had to steady himself with the ship's rail. He was surprised to find himself shaking, his hands, and his legs. *Soon, they will all be free and our lives as we know them will never be the same.* The reality of that life changing information was rippling through his body. The hour he had always dreaded was finally upon him. He stood there still and silent.

The only hint the enigmatic Belle Graham gave that she too felt the enormity of it came when her bottom lip quivered, ever so slightly, as she lit the match for her thin cigarette. Despite her unflappable facade, she had not escaped the war unscathed. News had come around at the start of the social season that her own beloved Savannah plantation, *The Pearl*, had been burned to its foundation by Federal troops. She had inherited the land through her mother's lover. She planned to rebuild the mansion, check on the levees, reconstruct the canals, and redesign her gardens. Mistress there her entire life, she had sent word to the remaining slaves: the kitchen staff, maids, and foremen that she would see to it they were taken care of along with their families.

She did not crumble with her losses. No, the lovely Belle had made preparations, having previously transferred most of her wealth to England. She also had the good fortune, at the polo matches years ago, to catch the fancy of a well-off marquee that took pleasure in satisfying her wishes. Now, before she finished lighting her smoke, the Colonel nodded, turned and quietly disappeared.

In the cabin, the distant moon was shining brightly through the drawn curtains. The Colonel entered carrying a small lantern. Thomas was reciting a poem and continued, even though he knew his master was there. The Colonel asked Vivian to give him a moment alone with Thomas, and after she shut the door, the Colonel stood in silence while Thomas continued reciting his poem.

"Tom," the Colonel finally whispered.

"Twas mercy brought me from my Pagan land, Taught my benighted soul to understand..."

"Tom," the Colonel said again, trying to get his attention. The flame from the lantern cast a shadow over Thomas's body.

"That there's a God, that there's a Savior too: Once I redemption neither sought nor knew."

The Colonel listened curiously. He had heard Thomas recite Shakespeare, Thoreau, Plato, and the like, but never this particular poet. "Tom — Who taught you that poem?" the Colonel asked.

"Lead row slave taught Tom that poem," Thomas said. "Phillis Wheatley was a great poet. A great slave poet."

"Phillis Wheatley?"

Thomas was moving his head to the rhythm of some rhapsody only he could hear. "Yes. Phillis Wheatley. Phillis Wheatley wrote a poem for George Washington."

A scowl formed on the Colonel's face. Phillis Wheatley was a literate slave owned by an incorrigible Boston family who taught the girl how to read and write against the law.

"Phillis Wheatley was a great poet, like Tom is a great composer. Lead slave told Tom."

"Yes, Tom, you are a great composer. The greatest in the world," the Colonel said. He didn't quite know what he wanted to say and stood silent, as the steamer horn wailed. The slaves were still singing. He heard the soft whoosh of the waves lapping in thumps against the steamer's hull. What should he say to Thomas? That President Lincoln and his supporters were about to defy the Living God? The fire crackled in the lantern and somewhere on the deck a baby cried, filling up the quiet room. The Colonel could barely make out Thomas as he rocked back and forth. Suddenly, the slave started laughing.

"Do you hear that baby?"

"Tom, something very serious is happening," the Colonel said, adjusting the lantern. He tried to find the words, experiencing emotions he was never conscious of until that moment.

But Thomas did not focus his attention on the pinkish, yellow tones floating from his master's voice. He was completely distracted by the crying infant at the opposite end of the deck. "Do you hear that baby, massa?"

"Tom, there are people," the Colonel said, "...forces who want to separate us."

"That baby's crying like that baby Tom cry 'til massa get 'im," Thomas said. "Do you hear that baby, crying like Tom was crying that day massa got 'im?"

The Colonel's eyes widened. "What are you talking about, Tom?"

"Do you hear that baby, massa?" Thomas asked.

"Yes, I hear the baby Tom," the Colonel said. "What did you mean? The baby cried like you cried that day?"

"That baby's crying like Tom cry 'til massa get 'im," Thomas said. "Massa got Tom. That baby's crying like Tom cried when Tom was a baby."

"When did I get you Tom?"

"Massa Colonel picked Tom up when Tom was a baby. Tom was crying."

The Colonel expelled a stream of air. Thomas was talking about the smokehouse! How? How could he remember that day?

"That picanniny ain't worth a kernel a corn I tell ya," Thomas said, repeating mean old Wiley. "Massa Colonel picked Tom up. Massa Colonel saved Tom."

Through the wisps of flickering light, the Colonel's eyes began to mist. "Yes, Tom," he said softly. "Yes. I did pick you up when you were crying in the smokehouse."

At that moment, the Colonel vowed in his heart to carry Thomas somewhere far away. Some place so remote that Lincoln and his depraved laws would be unable to touch them. As the steamer cut across the ocean, the Colonel made his way back to the upper deck where every person seemed engaged in the raging debate between those who despised Lincoln and those who worshipped him as a hero.

"Abraham Africanus the First. A mulatto mutt is what he is! Who's his real father?"

"More of a hero than George Washington!"

"Hope he hangs from a Kentucky oak."

The Colonel padded his way to his cabin. Once inside, he kneeled next to his bed, set his lantern on the small table. Clasping his hands, he leaned over the bed. He lifted his head to the heavens, closed his eyes, and pleaded earnestly with God.

"You are the Most High God," he began. "The God of Abraham, Isaac and Jacob.

And with all his heart he prayed God would smite Abraham Lincoln, and every Northerner and every Southern traitor who defied the South's divinely ordained right to own slaves. He pleaded with God, begged, and quoted scripture.

"Servants, be obedient to them that are your masters according to the flesh, with fear and trembling, in singleness of your heart, as unto Christ. You blessed us Lord! You blessed the men of the South. We are your obedient servants. Are not the slaves our obedient servants? You ordained us. Are you not the God of Right?"

Before peeling off his clothes, he made a vow: as long as he had breath, he would never let Thomas be taken away. He would keep and protect him, as was his duty and his right.

VIII.

The docks of Atlanta came into view. It had been a grueling four-week journey from Germany, a trip slowed by stormy weather and filled with uncertainty and concern. Once, the ship was docked there was a tempest of activity. Suddenly, there was shouting. The Colonel watched his fellow Southerners, the way they moved with trepidation toward the gangway, shoulders sagged, confused and apprehensive. He walked along the top deck with Thomas and glanced over the rail: waiting below was a swarm of confusion.

A regiment of U.S. Federal Marshals on horseback and on foot, snarled orders, and pushed and shoved passengers as they disembarked. Alarmed by the massive show of federal force, the Colonel paused. At last, he took a breath and weaved through the thick throng of bodies on deck, with Thomas close by his side. But Thomas was agitated. A small, pulsating whimper came from his throat and his feet stopped moving.

"It's all right Tom. Hold onto my arm," the Colonel said, and he waited to make sure Thomas's hand was firmly fastened on his arm. He spotted the ship's Captain and swiftly made his way to him.

"What's going on, Captain?"

"God never intended it, but all the niggers on this ship are free," the Captain said in a resigned tone. His eyes flickered, as he looked pointedly at the Colonel with Thomas hanging onto his arm. "Got to turn 'em loose."

The Colonel's legs buckled beneath him.

"Good luck, Colonel," the Captain said, steadying him with his free arm.

The Colonel leaned more heavily on his cane and headed toward the gangplank. Halfway down the ramp, his eyes met with a Federal Marshal who seemed to have his eyes on Thomas, his jaw set and a determined look on his face.

"Stay close to me, Tom," the Colonel said, clutching Tom's hand with his. "Everything's going to be all right." But there was a catch in his voice, and Thomas took hold of his hand with two hands tight.

The pounding of hundreds of footsteps were like explosions of thunder, for Thomas, and he began to shake. Suddenly out of the crowd came the arm of a Federal Marshal who grabbed Thomas's arm and tried to separate him from the Colonel.

"What do you think you're doing?" There was fear in the Colonel's voice but he extended his hand to ward off the marshal. A fierce skirmish erupted and the Colonel was swarmed by a mob of federal agents who worked to separate the slave from his master.

"Take your hands off of him!" the Colonel called over the noise of the stirring crowd. "He is Thomas Bethune."

Thomas clung to him with all his strength. "Massa, please! They want to hurt Tom," he yelled.

"The blind boy is with me! Unhand him." the Colonel screamed, clutching Thomas so tight his knuckles went numb.

The Colonel struggled ferociously against what became a horde of officers, boots slamming into flesh. He chomped down on fingers with his teeth and spat in one soldier's face.

"He's a blind child, he relies on me. Leave him be."

The melee knotted the ramp, which federal troops scrambled to cordon off. Soldiers with muskets prevented other passengers from passing through. It was chaos until a musket shot rang through the air and a roaring voice declared,

"TOM WIGGINS IS A FREE MAN!"

The Lead Marshal, large as a mountain, sat atop an enormous mare at the bottom of the ramp. "He is no longer your property, Colonel! Let him go!"

"I will not!"

The Lead Marshal turned his horse around and spurred it forward. The mouth of the ramp cleared and he climbed down from his horse to address Thomas directly.

"Mr. Wiggins Bethune. We are not here to hurt you," he said, while handing over the reins of his horse. He leaned down and spoke straight to Thomas whose face was confused, his chin lifted, his half-closed eyes still searching. The Marshal's voice was clear but strong. "We are not here to cause you further harm. You are a free man, just like all other men. The Colonel is no longer your master. He is no longer your owner. Do you understand?"

"Tom wants Massa Colonel!" Tom squirmed and tugged at his captors.

"You are no longer in bondage, Mr. Wiggins. You are free to go wherever you will."

"Tom don't wanna be free! Tom wants Massa Colonel," he cried.

"He doesn't understand." The Colonel spoke with resignation. "You're scaring him." He grabbed one of Thomas's arms so the two could not be easily separated.

"This is your last warning, Colonel. Stand down!" The marshal yelled.

But the Colonel refused the command and held on even tighter. The tug-of-war continued, when from down the road John's coach rattled toward the harbor and made a grating noise as it came to a stop.

John peered out at the busy dockyard through the carriage's back window. He could see the violent disturbance. He alighted quickly into the loud clamor of voices and wove his way through the onlookers to get a closer view. When he had pushed his way to the front, he saw Thomas and his father at the heart of the disturbance. "Father!" he called out. He pushed closer, but marshals used their rifles to push him back.

"Massa Colonel!" Thomas still screamed as little by little their hands slid apart. "Massa, Tom needs you!" Thomas wailed, resisting violently. Suddenly, the slave's legs were cut from beneath him and he was lifted in the air. His hand unclasped from his master's hand.

"Unhand him!" The Colonel yelled. As the men carried Thomas away. "Release him! That is an order!" The Colonel yelled, as if commanding his troops.

"He is a free man!" The Lead Marshal shouted. "Go to your family, Mr. Wiggins. You are free. Slavery is over."

"Is he not free to stay with me?" The Colonel countered, maneuvering to keep Thomas in view.

"Free with you!"

"FREE WITH ME!"

When John finally fought his way through, the Colonel was shaking. John took his arm and helped support him as they struggled along the dock, trying to stay close to Thomas, as the marshals half carried and half dragged him along.

"Were not two-hundred-and-fifty years of free labor enough?" the Marshal asked as he maneuvered his horse back to the Colonel and smashed him in the face with the butt of his rifle.

The Colonel keeled over, blood ran from his forehead. He struggled to wipe the blood from his eyes, as Thomas was carried past the mélange of wagons, past horses, and past mounted federal marshals, carried away from the frenzy of marshals on horseback and the tangle of free bodies and the beating of drums.

John helped his father up off the ground.

"He needs me," the Colonel pleaded.

"I'm sorry, Father. We'll get him back." John held his father's bleeding head in his arms.

"He is Blind Tom. He plays the piano at two in the morning. He hates butter in his chocolate cake." The colonel muttered, inconsolably.

The Lead Marshal's mare, held on a tight rein, trotted beside the Colonel, who held his wounded head. The officer and his horse loomed over him. "Colonel Bethune," the Lead Marshal began, "we know who your boy is. You are an able bodied citizen. Now, you must seek your own fame and fortune, you must go to work with your own hands," he spat with contempt.

The Colonel's face lost its color. He made a sudden motion to try to break away, but was trapped by a wall of rifle barrels and muskets. The Colonel knew the way these men judged him, but they knew nothing of his character, of his care for the blind slave, of his sacrifices. The training he'd given him, the teachers and kindness. He gazed into the many frowning faces.

His judgers knew nothing of the operation he'd paid for in Germany, an unsuccessful attempt to give Thomas sight. The Colonel drew strength from anger. He despised these presuming and arrogant men of the North.

"He is mine!" the Colonel shouted. "He's mine!"

"Quiet, father, quiet now." said John.

Another marshal sent the butt of his weapon into the Colonel's side with a crack against his ribs. The Colonel screamed out in agony, crashed to his knees, and grabbed the flesh above his stomach in the most excruciating pain. Blood trickled from his lip.

The Lead Marshal turned back and pointed his pistol at the Colonel. He aimed it at his head.

"I am an American!" the Colonel spat.

"UNDERSTAND THIS COLONEL. TOM WIGGINS IS A FREE MAN! A FREE CITIZEN OF THE UNITED STATES OF AMERICA! You, sir, are a citizen of the Confederate States of America, a country that never legally existed! You, sir, are a traitor to the Union, a traitor to its people, a traitor to these United States. You, sir, are lucky that you are not being arrested for treason!

Now retreat. Return to your plantations where you will have to do the work yourself or pay wages for the labor you require." He pocketed his pistol and rode off.

The Colonel staggered to his feet, the Lead Marshal a blur in the growing fog off the shore. His hand clutching his side, desperately trying to keep his eyes fixed on Thomas, not wanting to lose sight of him again.

"It's all right Tom!" He shouted, struggling for a reassuring tone, so Thomas wouldn't be afraid. "I'm right here! Be careful with him! He's Blind Tom. Be careful with his hands!"

Thomas was screaming. He was carried past the parade of Ashanti, Yoruba and Basimbi singing and performing religious chants around a sacred tree. Shaking tambourines, and clapping their hands, they called Iwa spirits, and conjured ancestors to celebrate freedom with them.

"He needs his piano and his Bible," the Colonel said to John. "And he eats supper at seven. Sweet meats are his favorite. And he must have his piano. Where's his piano?" he asked, with pained desperation.

"Father, please." John wrapped his father's arm around his shoulder and helped him to walk. "He will be taken care of. We will get him back, Father."

They were clear of the dock now, following the men carrying Thomas. They set him down as a burgundy carriage appeared out of the low fog. The top of the carriage was down and there were two people, one opening the door and beginning to reach for Thomas's hand. Where are they taking him?" the Colonel asked.

John's hands closed on his father's shoulders.

"Father, please, we must go," John said softly. He pulled the Colonel back, and firmly grabbed him by the arms, but the Colonel dragged himself close enough to see it was a woman in the carriage, and then to see more clearly, it was Eliza, smiling at him. He scowled. For he knew it wasn't Eliza smirking at him, but surely the face of the devil. "Why is she here?" he asked John. Then he saw it was Charity sitting next to Eliza in the open carriage.

"He belongs to her now," came John's reply, flat and leaden.

Thomas seemed to hear his mother's voice and eagerly climb toward it. The driver cracked his narrow whip and the carriage rolled down a dark alleyway and out of sight.

The Colonel stood motionless.

They had walked away from the noisy confusion of slaves and masters at the dock. The Lead Marshal, and the men who ripped Thomas from his arms, had ridden or walked away. The street was suddenly quiet. John's carriage rolled close and, wordlessly, John helped the Colonel climb the steps and settle in against the velvet cushions. Distant and spent, the Colonel was bleeding still from a wound to his head; his mind was dull, his mood depressed, his spirit uncomprehending. *What just happened?*

He refused John's offer of whiskey. Paralyzed by fury, a diabolical sequence of events ran through his mind, flashing memories of the ball at which Eliza wormed her way into the core of his son's heart, the same ball at which he met Belle, or were those different balls, and what of the mysterious men who lurked in shadows in London and Paris. A bolt that held his life in place was missing and now a paranoid cacophony of silent screams resounded. He was shocked by the sudden turn of events, holding his hand against his forehead as if trying to figure out the incomprehensible. *Tom was gone? His soon to be ex-daughter-in-law took possession of him?* His fists shook. He would die one day, but not before he ruined Eliza!

But what of John's part in it? Bringing the snake into their midst.

He ran through how it might have come to this, where the plots lay, how he'd been so deeply betrayed.

Frances. At the thought of Frances, his heart welled with longing. Frances could never, would never betray him, he knew that. Her hand was held beneath God's hand in heaven. He would have to trust that. His mind held a singular focus: he would win Thomas home again and then not rest until Eliza was utterly destroyed, shamed, and reviled by the world.

"She's merciless," John finally whispered. "I see the pain and the rage in your eyes, in your heart, father. And you are right to feel it. I am ashamed." His flat, emotionless voice broke the silence. "She's a witch who has most certainly been planning longer than I dare to imagine."

"She teased about superstitions, enchantments, and spells, but I made light of it. She spoke of the fortune at our finger tips, in Tom, and I did nothing about it. I didn't take it seriously enough. There were warnings. She snuck long chats with Charity and taught her to write her name. It seemed a generosity, so I did nothing to curtail it from happening."

The Colonel's jaw tightened. He stared at John, his eyes vacant and cold.

"When I realized it, Charity could sign her name on the transfer of custody."

Days before the announced emancipation, Eliza had persuaded Judge Johnson with a healthy bribe and Charity signed the transfer of custody.

"She's vile, father," John whispered. "I was a fool, a credulous fool."

"I knew what kind of woman she was." The Colonel closed his eyes, his body had no heft in it any longer, and so he swayed and bounced as the carriage rolled along the path.

He made a sure promise to himself and peered over at the rectangle brass carriage clock: It read 6:47 p.m. He gawped so fixedly at it that he didn't hear John continuing to apologize. He wanted to remember the time. Have it seared into his memory so he would never forget the day. The hour. The minute. Down to the second when he had made the vow to himself for the last time - *he would die one day, but not before he destroyed her.*

He leaned back against the cushions. His eyes moist, now, as he breathed the shock subsided and he felt pain, hurt, loneliness, nostalgia. The Bible was beside him. He looked at the Holy book and slid open the trap door. He demanded the coachman to stop. The servant pulled back on the reigns. The Colonel picked up the ancient scriptures. John watched as the Colonel slid out of the vehicle, then he pulled back the curtains and watched his father walk into the brush and set the sacred tome down upon the brush.

I WILL NOT SERVE A GOD WHO DOES NOT LOVE ME, the Colonel screamed in his heart. He struck a match to set the sacred book afire!

John leapt from the carriage and ran, screaming, "Father! By God, what are you doing?"

The Colonel's heart hardened, cemented by the frigid coldness of disappointment. His son's entreaties went unheeded, and they struggled. John didn't relent, until the Colonel dropped the match and it fell atop a mound of dry wood. Black smoke arose as the flame died. "Let me go to hell," the Colonel screamed. "Let me go!"

His expression horror-struck, John pleaded, "Father, think of Mother, now. Think of where she is. Think of what matters now and how little we know, as men. Father, it's sacrilege." The Colonel's eyes blazed, his breaths were heavy, his jaw set. But John stood in front of him until the Colonel turned toward the carriage. John bent to retrieve the book.

The Colonel's face was stone. "If my God, my Lord and Savior, would abandon us here, then I will abandon Him." He turned back toward the carriage with revenge on his mind and hatred in his heart.

IX.

1866

Columbus, Georgia

Drawing out his handkerchief, the Colonel wiped his forehead and continued to recite scripture over and over in his mind, *fracture for fracture, eye for eye, tooth for tooth,* as he walked toward the courthouse. He held a leather case in his hand with papers declaring Thomas insane, and recommendations suggesting he was the right and only one to continue to care for the colorful boy. It had been nearly two years since Eliza had taken Thomas from him.

It was like a J. Purdy Brown circus on Main Street, the sidewalks teeming with people watching the Colonel wend his way to the courthouse. All the wealthy merchants and planters were out, mingling with mill workers, bakers, watchmakers, and newspapermen. The Colonel's mind was preoccupied, but as he walked past the clock shop, he nodded at Mr. Haynes, a tall man with friendly eyes who owned a rice plantation burned down by Union troops. Mr. Haynes bid the Colonel good luck.

The impending trial was the talk of the state. The *Columbus Enquirer,* still the Colonel's paper, gave the custody battle between the former master and his former daughter-in-law front page space every day. Northern journalists questioned his rights: "Why is Blind Tom compelled to support the Colonel and his able-bodied son who, fresh from the ranks of treason, are seeking custody so they can tour the country, including the North which they claim to abhor?"

The courtroom was standing room only. Friends of the Colonel crowded in the benches behind him, for the trial. Charity, her children, and the other *Solitude* slaves who had known Thomas since he was a baby turned out to watch from the balcony. The Colonel was nervous. He turned left and right hoping to see Thomas, but he wasn't in court. The Colonel searched for Charity. She was in the front row just above him, wearing a self-stitched dress, sitting with her hands clasped, her eyes puffy from crying. Any one of these now freed slaves might be called to testify, for or against the Colonel.

Across the court, Eliza sat at the defense table yawning while twisting the strings on her dress. Her new husband, Attorney A.J. Lerche, was a mousy man of modest wealth, age thirty, who seemed numbed to his wife's humiliations. He adjusted his glasses and stared without expression at legal documents before him, while she squirmed in her seat.

The trial was already one hour behind schedule, when the Colonel's lawyer started in with an opening argument delivered like a sermon. A slim, wide-shouldered man in his forties, Job Walton was a high priced lawyer from an old Atlanta family, and he knew the Southern system and how to make it work.

The courtroom was hot, humid, without fresh air, and the Colonel kept wiping his brow.

"The deceptive Mrs. Eliza Lerche, formerly Mrs. Bethune, is a cold-hearted bigamist of the worst kind," Job argued.

"No self-respecting woman could do what this woman's done. Mrs. Lerche married the young John Bethune while still married to Mr. A.J. Lerche with a plan to steal the Negro prodigy Thomas Wiggins Bethune, to most of you known as "Blind Tom". While her first husband was away on business in Persia, she married Mr. John Bethune. She then connived to steal Tom while her second husband was fighting for the Confederacy. All for a good deal of money."

Eliza's face flushed and she tried to stand, but her husband's hand on her thigh kept her seated. Mr. Walton continued.

"I dunno how they do things up north in the city of New York, but that's not what God-fearing folks do here in Georgia. Our ladies are ladies." His opening statement appealed to public opinion as much as the judge. There was a burst of claps and an echoing "Amen".

Eliza fumed while her husband whispered in her ear, convincing her to stay seated. Job continued in his thick southern drawl to accuse Eliza of fraud, of unlawfully removing Thomas from the state of Georgia, and of physically abusing the prodigy by forcibly placing the pianist, in spite of his pleas and cries, into her carriage on the day the Colonel returned from Paris.

The Colonel showed no emotion, he was ready for a lengthy fight, but Eliza seemed irritable and bored; she twitched in her seat, *tsked* and shook her head, and rolled her eyes. She was a little less impatient when her own attorney addressed the court, but still she moved excessively and moaned in agreement, often sighed.

The trial dragged on and Eliza grew increasingly bored, but one hot Thursday, the Colonel's attorney cleverly argued that she was never legally married to John and therefore had no right to gain custody of Thomas from his mother Charity. Her half-tilted head straightened at once. Her husband could not restrain her.

"Your Honor," she interrupted, out of order, "this is uncalled for." She fanned herself, enthusiastically, while rounding the table. "The Negro is no longer a slave for the Colonel to exploit at his will." Presuming to abort the proceedings, she produced letters from Boston requesting weeks of Blind Tom concerts at Horticulture Hall. The trial, she complained, was keeping her captive in Columbus, not unlike the slaves who'd just been freed. There were rumblings in the courtroom. Judge Cobb slammed his gavel and denied her request.

"Enough of all of this," he said, addressing Eliza as well as both lawyers, "It's about time I meet this Thomas Wiggins Bethune, and see for myself."

The following day, sweet flute music could be heard coming from inside the courtroom. Judge Cobb took full advantage of having Blind Tom in his courtroom, and the young man filled the chamber with the wind instrument's lovely whirr, entertaining the court for nearly half an hour.

At 18, Thomas was nearly six feet tall and rather husky in girth. Charity from the balcony made several attempts to get her son's attention, but Thomas seemed to ignore her. He seemed to ignore Eliza as well though the Judge made it clear no one should come close to the prodigy. Eliza's husband/attorney, Mr. Lerche had argued the Colonel's presence would unduly influence the boy, who'd been under his absolute authority and control for so long. He requested that the Colonel be barred from the courtroom, but his request was denied.

When the Colonel finally settled in next to his lawyer at the prosecutor's table, Thomas was on the far side of the chamber, but through all the chatter and stirring of bodies, Thomas recognized the Colonel's footsteps. He leapt to his feet and ran toward him, as if he could see.

"Massa Colonel! It's Tom."

A soft gasp came from the gallery while Thomas was restrained.

Tears came to Charity's eyes as she watched her son struggle for the Colonel his former master.

"Tom, you're free!" Eliza called out. "He no longer owns you."

Judge Cobb banged his gavel, as the Colonel called out to Thomas.

"Soon you will be back where you belong, Tom. Soon."

Eliza stood up from the defense table, outraged at the spectacle master and former slave were creating. "You see, judge. You see, how he's brainwashed him?"

"Order." Judge Cobb demanded, swinging his mallet hard against a wooden block.

Thomas was so charged with excitement, he had to be forcibly dragged away. He hadn't had contact with the Colonel since that fateful day at the docks, and everyone could see he was most undisguisedly distraught.

Judge Cobb regained order in the courtroom. "With or without reduced mental capacity, it is clear this young and talented man's response is evidence of how he clearly feels for his former master. Bearing this in mind, we shall proceed."

Mr. Lerche finally called Charity to the stand. Charity seemed to lose balance in her seat. Her children helped her stand. She was nervous, visibly shaken as she made her way from the balcony to the main floor. The Colonel tried to make eye contact, but she wouldn't look in his direction.

"Lift your right hand and repeat after me," the bailiff commanded.

Charity spoke so low the judge instructed her she'd have to speak up during her testimony so he and the rest of the court could hear. Mr. Lerche stood right in front of her, speaking to her slowly in a childish tone as if she were a toddler.

"So Mr. Bethune provided better living quarters and better food for Tom?"

"Yes, suh"

"And why do you think Colonel Bethune treated Tom so much better than he did his other slaves?"

"I's think." She twisted a rag in her hands. "'Tom filled 'is pockets."

"Tom, filled his pockets, meaning, made him a lot of money."

"Yes, suh."

All the sound went out of the courtroom.

Mr. Lerche interjected swiftly, "Are you grateful to Colonel Bethune…" He moved close enough to take her hand, but didn't. "…for saving the life of your youngest, weakest child?"

Charity nodded mutely.

"You'll have to say it out loud."

"Yessuh. I's grateful."

"Only to have him take your son away from you, had him perform, travelled with him for years at a time?"

She shook her head and tears poured from her eyes.

"That he didn't live with you and his father and siblings, have meals and…" Mr. Lerche paused and looked around the courtroom. "That he made your son, the son in most desperate need of you, a stranger." He repeated it more loudly. "That he made your son a stranger to his mother." She didn't answer, but twisted the rag into a tight corkscrew of tears and sweat.

"The Colonel had his slaves beat, did he not? He dragged Tom through the fields and tied him to the whipping post before the entire plantation."

"Objection, Your Honor." Mr. Walton cried. "Leading the witness…"

"Withdrawn," A.J. said, turning back to Charity. "So Tom was treated differently than the other slaves?"

"Objection…"

"Let me rephrase. Were you ever beat or physically punished by the Colonel?"

Charity looked down. Her lip trembled and when she looked up her eyes were filled with water.

"Not by Massa Bethune. But Mistress Frances git ta drinkin' an' git riled up 'bout somethin' not bein' done ta her likin' an' slap me. An Miss Sarah when she git ol' enough."

"Was Tom ever beaten like the other slaves? By hand or by whip?"

Charity shook her head no. "Only almos'." Tears spilled down her cheeks.

"Then Colonel Bethune did not treat you or his other slave property as well as he treated Tom? Showed some restraint with corporal punishment for only Tom?"

Charity bit her lower lip before speaking. "'Reckon massa treated him good 'cuz the boy fill' his pockets up more den all o' us other slaves put tagether," she said.

A collective murmur spilled out from the Northern crowd seated around the room.

"Order, order," the judge commanded.

For the first time in weeks, the Colonel saw Eliza's muscles relax.

In time, the judge announced he'd heard enough of the evidence to rule. He'd listened, for weeks and weeks on end, his tired head resting in his hands, to every detail. Though he was an old friend and frequent billiards companion of the Colonel, he believed he ruled impartially.

"Colonel Bethune has legitimate medical papers documenting Tom Bethune's lunacy and his ability to understand and handle the Negro's needs; this gives him a strong claim for custody. Though Charity Wiggins, Tom Bethune's mother, did confirm that the signature, transferring custody to Mrs. Eliza Lerche, is indeed her own signature, such as it is, I find Charity Wiggins was fraudulently and maliciously coerced and the State of Georgia does not honor contracts that have been signed under duress. In the judgment of this court, the young man's will is to be with Colonel Bethune and therefore..."

Cheers erupted in the court, so the rest of Judge Cobb's ruling could not be heard.

The Colonel sighed with relief and was smiling, the gavel banging. The courtroom became a circus atmosphere worthy of P.T. Barnum. Eliza stood to her feet and as Judge Cobb screamed, "Order, order in the court," that dapper Colored man, Tabbs Gross, unexpectedly appeared in front of the courtroom. As the good citizens of Georgia settled down to allow Judge Cobb his last words, the Colonel's face turned ashen, like he'd seen a ghost.

The caramel colored Tabbs strolled up to Judge Cobb followed by a stout lawyer who wore a cheaply made suit and carried legal papers held together by rubber bands. The Negro showman's lawyer announced that Blind Tom's official custodian at the time of his enslavement was Tabbs Gross and not Colonel Bethune. A gasp came from the courtroom. Tabbs Gross had purchased the rights to Blind Tom and his family in gold. Therefore, Mrs. Lerche had no rights to Thomas nor even did Colonel Bethune. Therefore, Blind Tom was a free man, before slavery had officially ended and custody should be turned over to Mr. Gross immediately, his attorney argued. Then, the lawyer unwound some rubber bands and produced a bill-of-sale.

The Colonel sprang from his chair and objected. "He is a fraud. Any signature he claims to have would be a forgery." The Colonel managed just the appropriate amount of indignation. His pulse quickened and he sat down. He never thought he'd see Tabbs Gross again.

Judge Cobb asked the Colonel, "Do you know this man?"

"I've never seen this Negro in my life. This fancy man from Cincinnati is duplicitous in all ways. That he would come to Georgia and make such accusations after all I've contributed to this community, here in Columbus, and to this state." He all but roared.

The courtroom erupted with cheers and then jeers.

A bottle sailed across the room, hitting Tabbs in the back, exploding on contact. Blood spilled out from his neck. The proceedings disintegrated into violence at once. Chairs and fists flew, pistols were pointed, and yelps went out to lynch the smooth talking "nigger." The southerners felt deeply disrespected by the uppity man of color daring to insult and besmirch a fine white man's reputation. "Tar and feather that boy!"

Judge Cobb slammed his gavel on the bench then stood from his seat and, looming over the court in his black robe with both arms outstretched, demanded order. Shielded by his attorney, Tabbs managed to safely escape the dense mob out the back of the courthouse. The smooth Colored man entered a waiting carriage and left Georgia that afternoon, deciding it was best to file his case for Blind Tom in Cincinnati where he was less likely to be hung.

Judge Cobb ruled the Colonel would allow Charity and her family to stay at *Solitude* rent-free for compensation. In addition, the Colonel would pay Charity and Mingo $750 per year to manage Blind Tom until the age of 24. Thomas would receive a stipend of $30 per month. The Colonel would retain more than 90 percent of Thomas's earnings, estimated conservatively at $35,000 per year. The Colonel agreed, Eliza protested and a swell of cheers erupted.

Extending his hand, the Colonel thanked his lawyer as the mushrooming crowd spilled into the aisles. A roar went up outside the courthouse. He was about to leave when he looked up and saw Charity, tears dripping down her cheeks. Her legs buckled and her children had to prop her up. He felt a pang seeing her face overcome with anguish. "My baby, my son!"

"He's better off with you, Colonel," Job Walton said. But the Colonel was numb. He'd been staring so hard at Charity and her heartache that he didn't feel the pats on the back, didn't register the handshakes. He tore his eyes from Charity's slumped frame, her eerie howl. He knew that Thomas was hers, but in his heart of hearts, he believed Thomas was his own son! He clutched his cane as everything blended together: the thickened celebration around him, Charity's keening howl. In his mind, Judge Cobb had done what was right and Thomas would accompany him back to *Solitude* where he belonged. Yes, it was best, Thomas would be returned to his rightful family at once and his mother could see him plenty while working in the house. He looked away from the moaning and despondent mother and smiled.

X.

The dreadful trial had taken a toll on Eliza. Now she was drinking almost constantly. She walked the hallways of her sprawling New York boardinghouse with her hair uncombed, collecting rents while the church bells rang, tipsy. Piano music trickled out from Thomas's room, and felt like both a blessing and a curse. Since returning from Columbus, he'd refused to play outside of his apartment, so she listened to him play music, day by day, which brought her not one penny.

Morning, noon, or night she could be found inside a cloud of cigarette smoke slumped over the sofa in the sparsely decorated drawing room. Her head miserably bent, she listened to Blind Tom's gorgeous chords singing heavenly tones, while not one ticket had yet to be sold. It was a miserable victory. Thomas had not been taken from her, after all. The Long Island Superior Court made a separate ruling against Judge Cobb's ruling. New York lawmakers found that Blind Tom, as a resident of the state of New York, could not be forced to move to Georgia. The Colonel, as a Georgian, had no right to Thomas whatsoever, insane or not, as long as Thomas was considered a resident of New York. Eliza had been giddy with triumph; she had every right to exhibit the blind prodigy wherever she chose, until custody was fully resolved.

But Thomas would not play for her, would not so much as put his fingers to the keys.

The sun cast a soft light through the boardinghouse windows. She drew on a cigarette and blew out a stream of smoke. Cigarette dangling between her lips, she crossed toward the liquor cabinet, adjusting a green shawl over her lavender brocade dress. Lifting a bottle of Krug out of ice, she mixed the champagne with orange juice. She felt her stomach jump.

She'd been granted an important meeting in the city with the esteemed piano manufacturer and concert purveyor, William Steinway. It was finally an opportunity. Smoothing the back of her satin dress, she sat by the crackling fire and waited for news of the carriage. Money was tight and a private carriage was no longer possible. Mr. Lerche had gone to see about letting one. Annie fussed over the brass buttons on Thomas's new frock in the hall, Eliza watched through the doorway. Already in an alcohol haze, the gaslights danced in her eyes as she tried to focus. She frowned at Annie, her stringy hair in a mess of a bun, her frumpy slip of a dress wrinkled. The servant's unsightly looks further dampened Eliza's spirits. Suddenly, she felt inspired to explain to Thomas the significance of being on his best behavior when they reached Steinway Hall. She called him in and he approached reluctantly.

"It's the best concert venue in New York, Tom," she said, speaking loudly as if blind suggested he couldn't hear. She flicked her ashes on the floor. "There are rumors Rubinstein is coming to perform a series of concerts at Steinway Hall. Rubinstein is an important man and you should be proud to be asked to play there. Tom?"

"I'm sure Mr. Tom would love to play there, wouldn't you Mr. Tom?" Annie said, while pulling the material of his vest tight so she could fasten the buttons over his rounded belly.

Eliza snorted. "Shut up, girl. You speak when spoken to you, you filthy Irish nigger," she said, eyes flashing.

Annie flinched. "Yes, mam." she finished buttoning Thomas in silence.

"As for Tom, you'll do for me what you did for that Colonel or I'll see to it you're sent away forever. And it won't be back to *Solitude,* that's for sure."

Thomas ignored her, letting the rising sun warm his face through the window.

A flicker of fantasy danced in Eliza's eyes. She was eager for the prodigy to prove profitable and replenish the money they had already spent fighting for custody in court. Blind Tom had made a fortune for the Colonel and she was fully expecting the same. The New York ruling meant the Colonel could not legally stop her from putting Blind Tom on tour, while they continued their drawn out battle over his sanity in the courtroom of his crony back in Georgia.

Eliza poured and finished off her champagne and juice before her husband walked in and offered his hand. Numb and full of liquid courage, she slipped her hand into his with a smile. She snapped for Annie to follow with Thomas and descended the front steps to the carriage.

The cab arrived at the corner of 14th Street, in front of the world-renowned Steinway Hall, at ten o'clock that morning. The horses stood still in front of the arched four-story building. Passing the elegant pilloried entrance Eliza's heart pounded. She stared ahead at the frescoed ceiling of the graceful rotunda. She ushered Mr. Lerche and Thomas toward a lovely azure grand, beneath the domed ceiling, and left them there while she hurried over to speak with William Steinway who had just entered. William was a man of stature, refined in manner with perfectly groomed beard and moustache and a tailored black suit accented by a black bow tie.

"Mrs. Lerche. William Steinway. It is my pleasure to make your acquaintance." His throaty English accent hit the consonants hard.

"Our London office speaks highly of Blind Tom's recitals for Queen Victoria. I do, however, believe the city's been abuzz regarding the difficult matter surrounding him. It's been front page news in the New York Times."

"I can assure you I have every legal right to exhibit Tom," Eliza said, trying to allay his concerns. "My husband will show you the court papers. Darling," Eliza called over to Mr. Lerche. "Show Mr. Steinway the legal papers."

Mr. Lerche opened his leather valise and handed over the letter. Mr. Steinway carefully examined the court documents.

"You have my word it will be a feast of music with an absolutely smashing performance, Mr. Steinway," Eliza said while he read.

"Well, we had Charles Dickens perform a reading here last night to standing room only. It will be hard for Blind Tom to top it," he said, traces of his German roots evident in his guttural speech.

"Why Mr. Steinway, I presume you have never heard him play. Blind Tom is beloved all around the world, even in your ancestral country. He is of equal reputation with Gottschalk and Paderewski."

As if on cue, a flurry of notes filled the hall like firecrackers, the interpretation coming from the azure grand in a virtuosic manner.

"Tom," Eliza called out, somewhat embarrassed.

"No, my lady. Let him play. It is..." William paused mid-sentence, spellbound. "Beethoven's *Appassionata?*"

Eliza gushed. She had no idea what it was, but was satisfied William Steinway recognized it. Enchanted, William walked toward the azure grand. A faint smile formed and he nodded his approval. He turned to Eliza.

"There's something stirring to the soul, isn't there?" he said. "I'm taken aback, I must confess. You are quite right, my lady, he is a true artist."

"Did not Shakespeare conceive of him when he describes Caliban being touched with the magical sounds heard in Prospero's island?" Eliza gushed.

"Mrs. Lerche, we at Steinway have found that famous concert pianists on Sunday, mean piano sales on Monday. And Blind Tom is as famous and accomplished a pianist as one gets, yes?"

"Yes, Mr. Steinway, he is," Eliza said with heartfelt confidence, though a pulse was beating hard in her chest. She was so close.

William Steinway went to his office rattling on about Thomas's "most perfect ear" and returned with paperwork and a quill. Eliza signed a contract for a four day schedule, agreeing to split fifty percent of the ticket sales with the hall. The event was scheduled for the following Sunday.

East 14th Street was bustling more than usual that Sunday afternoon Blind Tom made his debut in New York City. The Colonel walked from Union Square along a tree-line sidewalk toward the large building with the "Steinway Pianos" sign. Enjoying the warmth from the sun and a soft April breeze, he was glad he'd left his greatcoat at the hotel. There was a long line of men in top hats and women in ribboned bonnets, ahead of him, waiting to purchase tickets. Head tilted, he took in the banner advertising "Blind Tom," high above their heads.

The Colonel took his place behind a woman in a white dress and, while waiting to buy his ticket like any other patron, he thought about the times he'd shared with Thomas on tour: entertaining the *bons vivants* of Philadelphia, astounding the President in Washington, charming the crowned heads of Europe. For a moment, he forgot of his vendetta against Eliza and cherished the unexpected and exceptional times he'd had with Thomas, his former slave.

Why did he come? He did not want to be seen, was not there to cause trouble. Once he settled into his seat, discreetly tucked away in the back row of the hall, he recognized members of the most prominent New York families and felt his displacement. His ire, over Eliza and her treachery took hold of him again, and he fumed at the indecency of all she'd done – from her seduction of John to her manipulation of Charity to steal Blind Tom from the family. All the betrayals.

Lights sparkled from a Viennese crystal chandelier, and the Colonel tipped his head back to take in the ceiling painted with allegories of angels and saints. Gaslights throughout the theater fluttered an amber hue and he frowned at Eliza standing at the end of the stage, serving as master of the ceremony.

The house lights lowered and the curtains were drawn revealing the magnificent New York City Orchestra. And Thomas, who should have been seated at the piano in front of the musicians, was pacing back and forth across the stage. The corners of the Colonel's mouth lifted in a smirk of knowing, and he sank back into his chair to enjoy the spectacle. From behind the velvet curtains, Eliza looked like a clown, gesticulating frantically behind the blind musician.

The Colonel was pleased at the familiar sight.

Eliza couldn't soothe Thomas the way he could. She knew nothing about him, was too cheap even to hire Vivian, the musician's favorite teacher, who understood his peccadilloes. Now, she was out on the stage awkwardly attempting to push Thomas toward the piano. "Tom, now play boy," she coaxed. "Come on, boy, play."

"Tom can't play. His fingers is broke."

Eliza gasped. A murmur rose from the audience and soon laughter erupted.

"Tom, you were playing all morning."

"Today's Sunday. God said keep it Holy."

The Colonel savored the moment. Eliza looked like a bumbling idiot, her face damp and flushed red with strands of hair tumbling down from her once perfectly coiffed bun. She stopped to smooth her dress and tuck a hair back into place, glancing at her audience, and Thomas crossed the large stage and stood on the edge facing the guests.

"This is Eliza Lerche," he said making a sweeping gesture toward his custodian. "A big city gold-digger. She only wants Tom for the money. Tom won't play for her."

The audience gasped. Eliza covered her mouth with both hands, as if she could take back his utterance. She made an anguished shriek and scuttled behind the curtains again. The Colonel had seen all he needed to see. He straightened his smartly tailored frock and departed the hall, walking straight past the grim-faced William Steinway. He walked away, down East 14th street to a local coffee shop, filled with joy and relief. Eliza was indeed the fool he knew her to be, and fate would take care of things. He knew it'd be the disaster he'd hoped, as soon as he learned the concerts were to take place on a Sunday.

Steinway Hall was empty. William Steinway sat behind a large maple desk writing notes in his accounting book. His face was grim. For Eliza, a lifetime passed during the walk from the concert hall's rotunda to the elegant executive office, two lifetimes while he calculated.

"Twenty-five thousand dollars." His words landed hard as the punch of a heavyweight boxer. Color drained from Eliza's face. *Twenty-five thousand dollars.* She squeezed Mr. Lerche's hand so hard it turned pale. "Tonight, Mrs. Lerche, was the worst in Steinway Hall history."

"But there wasn't an empty seat in the house," Eliza sputtered.

"Yes, all the shows have been sold out, but Blind Tom will not play."

"With that in mind we could reschedule today's performances," she stammered.

As she spoke, William's face turned sour. "No. No reschedule Mrs. Lerche," he said firmly. "The onus is upon me to protect the Steinway name which my father worked so very hard to build."

"You heard him with the orchestra during rehearsals..."

"He is an extraordinary composer and a phenomenal performer, yes," Mr. Steinway interrupted. "But, you have a big problem that you refuse to accept, no?"

Eliza's restraint abandoned her. She rose to her feet.

"It's all his fault. His old master," she said, defending herself with passion, desperately hoping to turn William's opinion around. "He poisoned the idiot's mind toward me. The problem is easily fixed with two days of multiple concerts, I'll even have him perform an encore for free."

William leaned back in his chair and said slowly, "I admire your passion Mrs. Lerche. But I do not see how you will cover your expenses."

"If you reschedule the shows," she insisted. "I assure you we'll sell even more tickets."

William lowered his chin, and leaned forward, placing his folded hands on his stomach. "Ah, but you are being a bit disingenuous, no? Because your big problem is not the ticket sales is it?" His eyes firmly held hers. She stood there with her mouth open, the question lingered without an answer.

"You want to exhibit the Magnificent Blind Tom, Mrs. Lerche, but the maestro wants his old master. He will only play for him, yes? And that puts you in a quandary, does it not? Because the boy will never pay off. Such are the facts, yes?" The blood drained from Eliza's face. "We must resolve this matter. So how are you going to pay, Mrs. Lerche?"

The following morning, a crowded steamer train chugged out of the New York station headed toward Atlanta. Its whistle blew, several short hoots announcing its departure. The Colonel relaxed with a cup in one hand and a newspaper in his lap detailing the cancelled Steinway Hall shows. He snapped the paper straight, pleased, very pleased with the front-page: BLIND TOM REFUSES TO PLAY. PINES FOR FORMER MASTER.

The Colonel folded the daily with a satisfied smile. He sat the paper in his lap and took a swallow of peach sling. Since his emancipation more than twenty-four months ago, Thomas had not played one note for the public. He huffed with satisfaction. He didn't have to do anything other than keep bleeding her in court. Thomas would take care of the rest.

He looked out at the passing landscape. His former daughter-in-law didn't have the good sense to realize she was going to wind up a pauper when it was all said and done. He chugged the last of his drink and leaned back in the chair with a sigh of satisfaction. Yes, he would die, someday, but not, until he'd completely ruined her.

XI.

Hoboken, New Jersey

Eliza sat listlessly on the *fauteuil* in the boarding house living room, alone with the ugliness of her thoughts. Her hands clutched a drink not in celebration of the New Year, though all the tenants of their sprawling fifteen room boarding house were out toasting and waltzing. Though the servants had made dinner and cakes, even prepared her favorite Camembert cheese and crackers, she skipped all but the champagne. Now dressed for bed at nine or ten, she wasn't sure of the hour; she listened to the soft rain and was all but unaware of her husband who had just placed new logs on the fire.

A heavy gloom hung in the air. Her head was pounding. She drank her champagne from a wine glass and numbly watched the flames flush against the grate.

"What is the purpose of holding onto the idiot if we can't make money from him?" her husband asked. "It's senseless. Why don't you make a deal with the Colonel."

Eliza finished her champagne and scoffed. "Never."

"Then you've got to make him play somehow, Liza, that's all there is to it. You've got to get him to play."

She tucked her feet beneath her dress and a thought came into her soddened brain. After a moment of stewing the idea – there was one way of controlling men that had never failed her –she stumbled down the long corridor to Thomas's room. She did not have a clear plan when she opened the door to his room, but what she was about to do, for her, came naturally.

She peered through the shadows and saw his thick, dark figure sitting on the edge of the bed, rocking. "What goes on in your head?" she asked with slur. "What goes on in there?" she whispered and Thomas stopped rocking. She caressed the length of her bare arm under the silky sleeve of her robe. She moved closer. "I think I know what goes on inside you," she slurred. Seeing he was listening, she sat beside him on the bed.

She moved the candle to see him better. "I think what you want is me. Is that why you've been so angry? What you've wanted all this time, Tom, a white woman?"

Eliza was sure the idiot had never possessed a woman. She had convinced herself she would be giving the Negro a pure, human pleasure unlike any he'd ever imagined. If she could make a physical connection with him, make him see angels by sharing her body with him, then he would crave her. Then she would rule over him and he would finally play the piano to earn his keep, and she would have the ultimate delicious revenge against the Colonel.

She gently removed her robe and let it fall to the ground. "I think you've wanted me this entire time," she murmured, caressing his shoulder. Thomas made a low noise. She touched him softly and gently; she moved her hand stroking the inside of his thigh to arouse him.

Thomas stiffened. The low sound became like a percolating growl in his throat. But Eliza, drunk from whiskey, did not hear it, did not pick up the warning. She let her hand travel to the flesh between his legs. Thomas shifted his body at once.

"Miss Eliza's tryin' to hurt Tom," he said and shoved her hard, shoved her with such violent force she flew off the bed, crashed with a heavy thud on the hardwood floor. Her head slammed into the ground.

Stunned for a moment, she stirred and screamed. "You idiot. You fool!"

The flame from the candle she'd been holding set fire to the fabric on the bed, and Eliza struggled to her feet. "I hope you burn to death," she said.

Annie ran from her room down the hallway and saw the flames. "Oh my, Mrs. Lerche, what's happened ta ya? Mrs. Lerche, are yous okay?" Annie grabbed a pillow off the bed.

"She tried to hurt Tom," Thomas moaned, over and over, rocking back and forth, hitting his head against the wall.

"It's all right Mr. Tom, please, calm down!" Annie shouted, as she beat at the flames, pounding the blaze out.

"This idiot attacked me. I want him the hell out of here!" she spewed with hatred. A spray of saliva hit Annie's face. "He'll sleep outside with the dogs, then he'll go to the crazy house where he belongs," she said with contempt. "You crazy, retarded idiot"

Mr. Lerche appeared and tried to convince his hysterical wife to go to bed.

"She tried to hurt Tom," Thomas kept saying.

"Get him out of here!" Eliza screamed, her face disfigured with fury. There wasn't anything Mr. Lerche could say to calm her.

Annie slipped her arm around Thomas's shoulder.

"Come on Mr. Tom," Annie said, as she led him out of the bedroom. She guided him down the hallway as he cried in despair.

"Take him to the dogs!"

Hand on his shoulder, Annie kept walking. She had no intention of leading him out to sleep with the dogs. She took him out of the boardinghouse, only to slip in through a back door where she prepared a cot for him in her room, beside her bed.

XII.

1869

Solitude

A shotgun blast cracked. Then another blast, and there was flapping of wings.

"Pull!" The Colonel shouted.

He adjusted the long gun in his hands before pulling the trigger. Annie stood beside him with plugs in her ears. He aimed, pulled the trigger and the grouse exploded in the air. Satisfied with the hit, the Colonel, head fully white now, lowered his 12-gauge and adjusted his fingers in his gloves. It delighted him to be outside in the woods with nature, shooting game. He turned to Annie. "You were saying?"

Twisting her skirt with her hands, Annie took a deep breath.

"Somethin' terrible's happened. She' done it, sir." She mumbled.

"Done it?" The Colonel raised his eyebrows. He grabbed a peach from a nearby bowl and took a bite. "What do you mean, done it? Come on, you had Ensa bring you here to find me. Spit it out."

She shifted from one leg to the other. "She was always threatenin' 'bout puttin' Mr. Tom in a crazy home, sir. After she accused him of attacking her, some men come to the boardinghouse an' I ain't seen Tom in a long time."

"Attacking her? *Mon Dieu,* woman. What are you talking about? Attacked?"

"Unh huh," she whispered. "That's what she said."

"That Tom attacked her?" The Colonel clutched the rifle as Annie nodded. "Tom doesn't have a malicious bone in his body." But his shoulders sank. He knew of a few rare occasions when Thomas didn't like someone that he'd physically shove them away.

"She done something to him one night an' he pushed her an' she fell clear back an' hit her head. When I come in, a fire was burnin' in Tom's room."

"*Mon Dieu,* is he all right?"

Annie shrugged. "She made me take him out to the dogs, but I snuck him into my room. Now he's been gone an' she put me out, with no wages. Took me nearly a year jus' ta get wages ta get here to see you, sir."

The Colonel leaned his shotgun against a tree. "Gone? What do you mean, Tom's gone?"

"Just that sir," Annie said. "That's why I took all I had ta come here an' see you. Mr. Tom ain't been at Mrs. Lerche's no more for a long time."

For a moment, the Colonel lost his breath. He stood back against the shade of the tree, a malevolent gleam formed in his eyes. "He's not at the Lerche's. Where the hell is he?"

"I dunno." Annie shook her head. "But I found this in Mr. Lerche's den when they'd gone to sleep," she said, lifting her skirt. "I can't read too good, but I think this might tell where she took him." She handed him the sheaf of papers she'd stolen.

The Colonel unfolded the pages and looked them over. His brows furrowed. "This is a psychological evaluation from the Superintendent of State Lunatic Hospital in New York."

"I heard Mrs. Lerche talking about a mind doctor who would say Mr. Tom was insane. She said if she can't make money off him, she was gonna be sure you couldn't."

The Colonel continued to read, his vivid blue eyes dimming with each sentence. A smoldering rage began to disfigure his face. That callous wench had the world's greatest musician committed! The Colonel shuddered. He'd had Thomas declared insane to ensure his custodianship, but to actually commit him! He felt like his lunch was going to come up. Lunatic hospitals were notorious for inhumane treatment and filthy, unsanitary conditions. He picked up his shotgun from the tree. She was low, low, but oh he did not know she could go that low. What kind of numbed, desolate heart did that woman have? That glacial island in the center of her being that was so impenetrable, so frigid? *Despicable. Despicable!*

He stared at the document in his hand. *Despicable*, he repeated over and over. His thoughts trailed off and he stood listening to the pigeons coo.

"She will never get away with this," he finally said, "not as long as I'm alive."

Shoulders lowered, relief swept over Annie and again she sighed.

The Colonel thanked her for informing him and assured her he would reward her handsomely for her loyalty as well as restore the wages Eliza denied her. Then he shared a most shocking revelation of his own; Eliza had requested a meeting with him.

Initially, the Colonel had been inclined to ignore Eliza's request, but the troubling report he'd just received stoked a fire in him, a fire that inflamed his heart. He decided the time had come to execute the final plan for Eliza's complete and total destruction.

"Pull!" the Colonel said, blasting the bird right through its heart.

XIII.

The New England roads had finally thawed enough for Eliza to travel safely from Hoboken to the Colonel's plantation in Georgia. Eliza blew in her gloves to warm her hands before climbing out of the carriage upon reaching *Solitude*. She was relieved the Colonel had finally responded to her request to meet. She descended the coach steps. The hem of her long coat was encrusted with mud and dragged behind her as she mounted the Colonel's wide front stairs. The air was cold and unusually dry, for Georgia in April, and it took what seemed forever for the Colonel's servant to answer the front door.

"Eliza Lerche. I'm here to see the Colonel."

"Mr. Bethune is expecting you," said Ensa.

She nervously played with her gloves, rehearsing in her mind the words she might speak, adjusting her sage green evening dress, as he led her down the hallway to the drawing room. She pushed away thoughts of foreclosure and reminded herself it was important to smile as she greeted the Colonel.

"Colonel!" she effused as soon as the doors were opened and she glimpsed him in his ample chair behind his desk. He stood slowly and seemed to move with care, as he came out from behind his desk. He leaned heavily on his cane.

"It's so wonderful to see you. Absolutely wonderful," she cooed.

"Eliza," he said, his voice chilly. His vivid blue eyes so cold, his gaze sent ice through her veins. She couldn't afford to wither; her entire life depended on striking a lucrative deal: Blind Tom for cash.

The Colonel offered her a glass of fine sherry and poured it from a sparkling crystal decanter, as if to taunt her. The house was pristine and well-kept. She took in what looked like brand new crushed velvet drapes, the clean smell of lemon polish, the richness of the Persian rug she stood upon, the garden outside the window pruned and opening to its first spring blooms. She took a large sip from her glass of wine and steeled her emotions under the Colonel's hawk-like glare. Without a word, he led her out of his study and down the hall. He stopped to adjust a gilded painting, moved his arm to the right as if pointing to a freshly upholstered Louis Quinze *settee*, and as they entered the living room dropped his head back to admire the massive crystal chandelier, lit in the middle of the day and sparkling. His fortune was intact thanks to the war time efforts of Blind Tom.

He noticed she was merely a shell of her former self, beneath the carefully applied makeup and the attempt at a proud, lifted chin. Though pretty, it did not escape him that she was dressed in a green fabric from two or three seasons before. Her hair was swept into a ponytail with dangling curls, but the the pink lace of her bonnet didn't hide the many strands of gray. The stress over custody had evidently taken its toll. And it pleased him to see her thus.

Taking his time, still holding silent, he poured a single glass of fine vintage wine. He turned finally to face her, and sipped it without a word.

"Colonel Bethune, it's been far too many years," she finally spoke. She slipped off her gloves and placed them on the back of a chair. "How is the family?" she asked, feigning a casual air.

The Colonel held back a snort. The gall of that woman, he thought.

Her smile broadened and she continued. "Thomas is a joy and New York is spinning with admiration for him. His performances...well, you know how stunning his music is. Still, I concede I've been in turmoil..."

The Colonel's cold stare was unabated.

"...deciding on the right thing to do, for him. You see, the boy misses you. "

He turned toward the hearth, and watched the flames. Eliza stopped rambling. He took his wine and sat down at the game table where he was in the middle of a chess game with himself. He rested his cane on the chair. He remained silent and soon enough she rattled on.

"Tom's repertoire is over seven thousand songs now," she said, "and he still asks for cake everyday."

He moved his pawn. Just this morning, he had received confirmation that Thomas was at one of New York's wretched insane asylums. He moved his imaginary opponent's knight while his anger boiled.

She faltered. He heard her skirts as she paced.

"And,and that's why I'm here," she stammered. "It's gone on long enough, this silly feud. It pains me to even think of giving him up, but I so want what's best for him," she said with melodramatic effect. "I mean after all, he is a national treasure..."

"Enough!" he growled. He stood. He couldn't tolerate one more word. "Stop your filthy and deceitful talk." He walked toward her. He was finished.

"Yes, Colonel, we can find a way to make the most ..."

Smack! He slapped the spit out of her mouth. His palm left a print on her face. Her legs gave out, and she steadied herself with the arm of the sofa. The Colonel resisted the urge to slap her face again.

"I know exactly what you are," he hissed. "You are a third rate peasant with pretensions to wealth, a woman with a cunning display of breast and the heart of a serpent." He hissed.

Eliza's mouth dropped open. "I didn't come all the way from New York to be assaulted," she said, tears falling. "I came here —."

"You came here because he's useless to you," the Colonel snapped, "You slithered here with the apple of treachery in your fangs. As if you had anything to offer me…"

"I came to give you your wretched freak back!" she spat.

"I am not another foolish man to be beguiled by your tawdry charms."

Eliza's mouth trembled. She touched her lips, checking for blood.

"I've fought men less scheming, but more deadly," the Colonel continued.

He still had not revealed his knowledge that Thomas sat alone somewhere in a New York asylum. "It was a fine tactical move you pulled, gaining custody of him. I should have made better preparations to protect Tom. I'm still marveling at how you won him away a second time." He smirked. "New York residency, indeed. It hadn't occurred to me. Well done, Eliza."

She sat down, now, perching on the very edge of a straight backed chair.

His words were belied by his glare. A quaking shook his body. *The time, the time*, he thought. *The time lost, the time she stole, the years she destroyed. There was nothing she could say, no excuse she could give no words she could form to explain, to justify, why she had done what she had done.*

"And imagine how proud you must be that he's performing so well. The gowns you have now must be bursting the doors of your many wardrobes. I dare say." He sneered at her as she withered in her faded green satin.

"Steinway Hall was an impressive showing." He called to Ensa to open the doors. "We need air in here. The room grows fetid with the stench of this woman's treachery."

Ensa opened the French doors onto the patio and the cool breeze brought in the perfume of jasmine vines and honeysuckle. The Colonel's eyes narrowed. He pulled a pistol from his top drawer and turned it in his hand. Eliza's eyes widened and she froze. He smiled, then put the weapon back and closed the drawer and walked toward her.

"I think I should leave," Eliza said.

The Colonel spoke in a low voice, barely audible but resonant with rage. "How dare you meddle with God's Will! Look at what you've done. You've rendered mute one of the world's great wonders. Single handedly, you have ruined him. Thomas Wiggins Bethune, the eighth wonder of the world, you have ruined him."

"It's your fault that he won't play," she said. "I don't have to take this."

"Sit down!" He spat as she started to stand. The hatred and authority of his command forced her to take her seat again, but she turned her face away from him.

The Colonel dragged a chair to sit upon, drew it close to hers. "What were you thinking when you stole him away? You know nothing about music. You know nothing about his complicated needs. And now because of you, wayward and vicious woman, he hasn't performed in six years! SIX YEARS that boy has languished! A gift, robbed from the world."

"What you've done is unforgivable." The winds would not subside and a wild fire raged inside him. He brandished his cane as if he might hit her. "A snake, a black widow spider," he said bitterly. "If you had children, I have no doubt, you would eat them for your supper. You are wickedness without shame."

Eliza winced at the forcefulness of his loathing, but then he saw the muscles of her face rearrange themselves into a twisted sneer and she pushed his cane aside. She stood and straightened her skirts, her tired pink lace bonnet. Her voice was tinny.

"Since you insist on a vulgar exchange I won't tire myself with pleasantries. A half a million in cash and the idiot boy is yours."

The Colonel did not blink at the staggering sum. Instead, he laughed. *"Mon Dieu.* When did I become the fool?"

He glared at her and she lowered her head.

He walked back to the chess game, studied his pieces for a moment and moved the Queen. The game was won.

Five hundred thousand dollars? Eliza might need to be committed, he mused.

He pulled a velvet covered rope and Ensa entered the room with a black leather bag he placed on the floor. He looked at her, and then the bag.

"You will take this bag and sliver back to whatever hole..."

Her face was flushed in the firelight and her shoulders sank.

"How much?" she asked, indecorously.

"Seventy thousand dollars."

"That is an insult, Colonel? I'd never..."

"Thirty," he shrugged, cutting her off.

He did not blink, nor did he quaver, not for one instant. He knew the lawsuits, the wanton lifestyle, and the disaster at Steinway Hall had put her in financial ruin. Seventy thousand was a small fortune. He looked at her bare fingers, not even a piece of jewelry to show off. He'd made an offer low enough to offend her, but high enough it would pay off her debts and leave a portion one might live on for a decade or so. He knew she couldn't say no.

"Well, *Madame,* what is it?" His eyes coldly focused on his ex-daughter-in-law. An inferno of flames in the fireplace behind her. "You are running out of time."

Her eyes narrowed. "Seventy-five thousand, not a penny less."

The Colonel picked up the leather bag. "You will sign his guardianship over to me. You will get him from the asylum you've locked him inside."

Eliza flushed.

"…and deliver him to me within the month. Believe me, you will be watched and if you fail to deliver the boy…" His hand dismissed the threat he was making. "Most importantly, Mrs. Lerche, you will never show your face at *Solitude* or anywhere near my family again."

He slammed the quill against the table and slid its inkwell toward her. It was surreal, the simplicity of it after so many years. She took the quill with smug resolve and signed the paper.

XIV.

It was the dead of night and the rain poured down in heavy sheets, as if a dam had broken in heaven. Eliza was miserable, having traveled by train back to New York from Georgia, then to the outskirts of the state to get the Negro from the insane asylum. The doctors had to medicate the former slave with shots before he'd leave with her. Her bloodstream was full of brandy. "You know you're near the man you love, the one who kept you in chains, don't you idiot?" Eliza spat. She regarded him with a near-noxious scowl. "You deserved to be in shackles. Get out!" Eliza put Thomas out of the carriage at the bottom of the long lane that led to *Solitude*. She pushed him off the last step. He was crying, only wore a light coat, and had no umbrella to protect him from the pelting rain. The driver guided the horses into a turn and the sound of the carriage wheels disappeared into the darkness leaving Thomas on a muddy lane without direction.

But after a moment, Thomas recognized the sounds and smells of *Solitude*. He slowly began to walk toward the Big House. With each step, the heavenly choir sang and Thomas's heart beat with excitement. He knew the grooves of the trails, the scent of raccoon, the clicking of the opossums, the flutter of bats' wings, the smell of wet cotton. He knew the fragrance of jasmine flowers, wild tea, and pine. Thomas let his feet guide him, as he trudged through the sloshing mud three miles to the front porch of his old master. He stood a moment to catch his breath, before he dragged himself up the steps and knocked on the door.

"Tom's home," Thomas shouted at the closed door. "Tom's home Colonel." He was so excited he could not stop rapping his knuckles against the oak.

The Colonel emerged from his bedroom in a blue velvet robe, his cane in his hand, his head confused. He hurried down the halls and stairs and when he turned the knob and beheld Thomas standing there, he released a deep cry of relief and joy. "Tom," he said, his arms opening for a hug.

"Tom's home," Thomas said softly, sopping to the bone.

"Yes, you are Tom, yes you are home," the Colonel's eyes misted as he summoned servants to bring fresh clothes. "And blankets. He needs blankets," he said.

A few of the servants scrambled off to the servants' quarters to fetch coverlets, socks, slippers, and a fresh set of clothes for Thomas. The Colonel stared at the young prodigy, muddy, and soaking wet. He went to look out the front door and did not see a coach nor hear the hooves of horses trotting away. Good riddance to her, he thought. She was not worth another thought, not another word, for a moment, he resolved.

"Build a fire, Ensa," he commanded. "Build a good fire we can get close to and bring warmth to this poor boy's flesh."

Tom began to tell the Colonel, "Massa, Miss Eliza left Tom…"

"It's all right, Tom. It's over, Tom. She is gone and will never be back again. We must get you warm, now."

His voice was calm for Thomas's sake. The Colonel shook his head in disgust as he guided Thomas toward the fire. He took off his robe and placed it on Thomas's shoulders. The Colonel fumed at the soggy sight of Thomas. She had managed to commit one final act of depravity.

Thomas's teeth chattered. His body shook. The servants wrapped Thomas in a blanket and helped him change into dry clothes. They brought him warm soup from the kitchen.

Suddenly Thomas turned his head, recognizing footsteps. "That's Miss Vivian," Thomas whispered, as she approached.

Vivian regarded Thomas with alarm, startled by his sallow color. "Why Tom, you're shaking worse than a leaf." She slid wool socks onto his feet.

In the morning, the excitement over Thomas's return was replaced by concern. Thomas had been fragile since the day the Colonel rescued him. Now, he was very sick from the cold and weak from malnourishment. There was no knowing what horrors he had faced in the asylum. All the candles in Thomas's room were lit. The Colonel was greatly preoccupied by the need to get the young man well, but the first week stretched by with slow, swelling fear, as Thomas grew weaker and developed a fever. He was seriously ill.

A hired nurse had finished giving him a bath and put him back to bed. The Colonel was eating Butterscotch in an old leather chair by the musician's side, hoping he'd smell the sweetness and wake to ask for some. Instead Thomas began to moan and his body shook violently. The Colonel put a cool cloth on his head and whispered one of Tom's favorite scriptures. It hurt to see him suffering so; he would not allow Thomas to die. He would stay by his side. Pray over him. He would will him to live. He refreshed the cool cloth and put it back on his forehead.

"Tom's sick. He's gonna die," Thomas groaned. His old fears about death still prevalent.

"You're going to be well, old boy, but you must rest," the Colonel whispered, his voice confident. Thomas closed his eyes and fell back into a deep sleep. The Colonel poured himself a glass of wine and rang for dinner to be brought to him there. He fell asleep in the chair and was startled awake when Vivian placed a blanket over him. He shared an old memory.

"When I went into that smokehouse that day…" Vivian had heard the story in pieces over the years. "…on the day I found him, he was crying fiercely, with all his might, but it was weak and more like the mewl of a kitten, he was barely alive."

"It was an act of great kindness," Vivian said.

"Kindness?" He shook his head. "Not kindness, no, not exactly. It was human decency. I am not a kind man. But I am a man of basic decency," he held Thomas with his gaze, as Thomas slept and Vivian listened. "What I saw was a child separated from its mother. I didn't know if he would live or die. I couldn't know." He put his hand on Thomas's forehead. It was a bit cooler now. "The scope, the depth, the nature of his future, I could not have known. But I knew, a child should never be separated from its mother."

The Colonel felt someone in the doorway, and turned to see the physician there watching and listening to him, but the Colonel felt not a hint of shame for his feelings for Thomas, now a grown Negro man. With a gesture, he signaled his permission for the physician to enter.

"Tom, the physician is here, he is going to make you better." The Colonel gently shook Thomas until he stirred. The physician moved toward the bed, unpacked a few medical tools and checked the prodigy, then shook his head without saying a word. The physician cocked his head toward the hallway and the Colonel limped after him.

"What is it?"

"Colonel," the physician's voice broke. "It's difficult to say for sure," weary, he padded away from the sick room. "It could go either direction. I simply can't say for certain."

The atmosphere was gloomy that night at supper. The wind howled outside and a draft from somewhere made the candle flames quaver. The lace curtains blew as if a window were open. Thomas was on everyone's mind as they served themselves mutton, rice, and green beans.

As he prepared to say grace, the Colonel cleared his throat. His heart was heavy. The servants stopped serving and the smell of sweet, fresh cornbread rose from the baskets on the table. Fingers interlaced, heads bowed, all the Bethune children and their families were at *Solitude* to see Thomas. The Colonel cleared his throat and thanked the Lord for his family, asked Him to bless the food before them, and as he began to entreat the Lord to heal their beloved boy, he heard strains of piano music.

At first it seemed a proper backdrop to the prayer. The Colonel opened his eyes, to see if anyone was hearing what he was hearing. John's eyes also opened, peering to one side and then the other and then around the table. His blue eyes met his father's blue eyes. They knew those sweet tones. There was a flurry of chatter. The grandchildren giggled and squirmed. The Colonel commanded quiet. He pushed away his plate and slid back his chair. He clutched his cane. His heart skipped with pleasure, as he hobbled out of the dining room behind his eldest son. He shuffled down the hallway to the *grand parlor* trailed by his children and grandchildren.

That clever trickle of sixteenth notes, the melodic runs. Only Thomas could play such sweet motifs, such intricate *arpeggios* with equally inspired ease. What a charming sight it was to see Thomas in his cotton pajamas seated at the gleaming black Knabe, stroking away with memorable grace.

"This song here is for the Colonel, so he kin get his attitude right," he said. And he began to strum *Theme et Etude* Op. 45 from Thalberg. The Colonel smiled, his shoulders lifted with relief. The children shrieked and laughed and then were quietened. Everyone took a seat around the piano as Thomas played his master's favorite song.

XV.

The first years following Thomas's return passed in quiet on the rambling grounds. *Solitude* was still a cotton plantation with many of the Colonel's former slaves now working in the fertile fields as sharecroppers. On Saturdays, the Colonel took Thomas fishing at the lake near the hunting lodge, where the morning was tepid and thriving with whirring creatures. A morning mist mixed with the waking sun's rays as the Colonel and Thomas sat side by side with their lines dangling in the still water. And every evening, in the hours before supper, Thomas sang hymns before playing the black Knabe in the grand parlor, while the Colonel reclined on his favorite divan and smoked a cheroot.

When the Colonel went to town, for law work or meetings at the newspaper, Thomas wandered alone around the Big House. He mostly spent time in the fragrant gardens, picking apples in the orchard, or sitting at the piano, but never venturing off the grounds. The custody trial, the angry mobs, and the newspaper articles had faded into distant memory.

The knock on the front door came after ten o'clock. Dishes from supper had been scraped clean in the kitchen, the dining room floor swept and waxed. The Colonel was in the library sipping bourbon while pouring over bills. Ensa appeared at the door.

"The Dover family is waiting to speak with you in the *petit parlor*."

"The Dover family? From Tennessee?" Ancient floorboards and the Colonel's joints creaked when he rose from the leather chair. "Mr. Dover must have business..." he mumbled to himself, grabbing his cane.

Fatigued and in want of a warm fire, Mr. and Mrs. Dover sat close to the hearth and their four beautiful teenage daughters shared two couches. These somber, unexpected visitors made a perplexing vision. Each girl held a woven basket with comfort foods whose aroma filled the air. Ensa took all four by their handles, careful not to disturb the fresh cookies, fried chicken, steaming corn and lemon cakes. The Colonel buttoned his silk dressing gown before entering the room, then welcomed the family. Everyone stood about awkwardly for a moment, until Mr. Dover spoke. He was a tall man in a meticulous dark frock, perfectly tailored with a diamond watch chain. His voice was deep and silky.

"Our condolences, Colonel. We read about it in the paper and came as soon as we could." He offered the Colonel the clipping.

"It's terrible, just terrible," Mrs. Dover said. She was a slim woman with high cheekbones, a small waist, long neck, and fine lips with pretty brown eyes.

"We saw Blind Tom when he performed in Chattanooga before the War of Northern Aggression. It was the best show we'd ever seen, including Liszt in Versailles."

"He made the piano itself seem gifted," Mrs. Dover opined, furrowing her finely arched eyebrows.

The Colonel unfolded the paper. There'd been a flood in Jonestown, he read, and several citizens reported that the great Negro Blind Tom had been drowned in the rising waters. A couple of witnesses confirmed that the musical genius who played piano at the local saloon was swept away by the current, crashed into a tree, and was taken under. The Colonel stared at the words, captivated.

Of course Thomas's fame had given rise to imitators. Blind Negroes with piano abilities were contracted by shifty promoters to travel the countryside and pretend to be Blind Tom. Glancing from the newspaper to the Dovers, faces long and eyes filled with empathy, there was no doubt the family believed the article to be true!

The Colonel stood still. He should dispel it. Tell them it was some terrible mistake. But he stood still. There was silence in the parlor, but for the pop of the fire, the tock of the clock. While holding the newspaper clipping, his breath caught in his throat. Mr. Dover wrapped his arm around his shoulders to prop him up. They thought Blind Tom was dead!

He had a thought. A rather twisted, maniacal sort of plot. While the Dovers sipped hot chocolate and nibbled teacakes, sharing his grief, he conspired with himself to do something. He worried it was a thought from the pits of hell, but it sent a tantalizing chill through his body. The likes of which he hadn't felt in some time. He imagined a minister with the Bible, flowers on a casket covered with dirt, a tombstone, and the casket lowering six feet, the carnations covered with falling dirt. And he felt a sense of peace. A sweet, sweet rush came over his body. His face drawn into a mournful pout, he looked over at Mrs. Dover dapping her eyes with a handkerchief.

"Thank you. He was indeed a great treasure," the Colonel said.

Ensa startled and everything on his tray rattled until he steadied himself. He gave the Colonel a curious look, which the Colonel returned with a deliberate message to keep his peace.

"You're most thoughtful in coming all this way," the Colonel continued, pretending to hold back emotion. "He was, as you know, a part of our family."

The Dovers were shown to the best guest rooms, for the evening, and the Colonel told Ensa to take Thomas to the hunting lodge. In the wee hours of the morning, Thomas – with his piano, violin, flutes, and harmonicas – was taken by wagons to the remote lodge, just beyond the peach orchards, a few miles from the Big House. It was well stocked with a wood-burning furnace, stove for the maid to re-heat Thomas's meals, and warm blankets. Ensa was assigned to look after the musician, make sure he didn't wander up to the main house, and take care of his needs until it was safe for him to return.

Over the next few days, carriages, buggies, and wagons crowded in and out of *Solitude* as news of Blind Tom's death spread. A large laurel wreath with black bows greeted the bereaved admirers as they climbed the stairs to pay their respects. The Colonel came out to receive visitors, dressed in all black, his air appropriately listless, as he clutched the many gift boxes filled with gloves and gilded rings. He gestured with languid waves and shaped his face into the proper mask of sorrow while the best of society offered memories of Blind Tom.

"I saw him in Pittsburgh."

"Oh how he thrilled in New Orleans," they reminisced between kisses on the cheek and solid hand grasps intended to console him.

"To think we will never hear his beautiful music again. He will always be remembered."

The Colonel spoke to visitors between calming sips of chamomile tea and bites of mourning cakes. The details for the burial had been carefully arranged, he'd tell callers, the best mortician had already washed and prepared the body. He sighed for effect, before he lifted the porcelain cup with two fingers of one hand. A fine wood coffin with gold mountings had been chosen and the Negro would be laid to rest within the Bethune family cemetery.

On that gray morning of the funeral, bells rang out above Columbus, signaling the beginning of the ritual for an important citizen. The Bethune mansion was staged with drawn curtains. Dark clad servants passed out funeral biscuits, and there was the eeriness of motionless clocks, their hands set at the estimated time of the Thomas's death. The Bethune children wore dark mourning clothes and chatted together in hushed tones. The grandchildren sniffled, their faces wet with tears over the death of the Negro musician they'd come to love. John stood biting his lip next to Sarah beneath her veil, and Mary in her cape munched on scones. The siblings kept their heads low, fully aware of their father's sin. Nevertheless, their gloved hands covered dry eyes as they dutifully awaited the procession from the house to the cemetery.

Columbus shops closed, flags were lowered to half-staff. A military band's horns played the funeral march Thomas had composed. Hundreds of Columbus residents: planters, merchants, butchers, and bakers, assembled along Main Street, light coats tight around their bodies. The gentry were gathered in front of the Boll estate while Judge Cobb stood and watched from the top of the courthouse steps. Mrs. Alit the seamstress was dressed in a proper black dress. She stretched her neck to catch a glimpse of the golden casket adorning the bed of a wagon, slowly inching behind the 10-piece band. There was pushing and squeezing to the front, as the vehicle passed by with the body of the world famous Blind Tom. The Colonel's barouche, followed by the trail of Bethune carriages, completed the lengthy procession to the cemetery.

It was a bittersweet sense of finality when the gilded casket was lowered into the ground. The Colonel tossed a white carnation onto the casket. He felt a twinge of guilt when he glimpsed Charity, Mingo, and her children weeping at the edge of the hole. Nevertheless, the matter was finished. Back at Solitude, that evening, he retired to his den, took a seat behind his mahogany desk, and began to sift through the invoices that had piled up during the time he'd spent entertaining mourners. "It had to be done, *mon Père,*" John whispered from the door.

The Colonel nodded, hands on the leg of his cotton pants. He felt alive again. He went out by moonlight, met with the smell of wood and smoke, and the perfume of flowers in the garden. He mounted his mare and rode to visit Thomas. But he did not send for him to return from the hunting lodge right away. He discouraged his children to speak of the prodigy and the Colored staff was sworn to secrecy. No one would ever again take Thomas away from him again.

XVI.

Richmond, 1905

It was gloomy in the makeshift cell. "You did it." Matthew's face was one of horror.

"Matthew, are you all right?" John asked, noting the pallor of the young attorney's skin.

"You bought Thomas, after he was free?"

"I paid for her to go away."

"You kept him from his family, and then faked his death?" Matthew cringed. "You did it," he whispered, turning to John. "You knew of all this?" Now he looked at the Colonel. "What kind of people are you?" His arms were limp, his eyes glazed with incredulity. He took a few steps back, as if the Colonel were contaminated.

"The truth is rarely simple, is it?" the Colonel set his chair rocking and sipped his cup of hot tea with brandy. John closed the Bethune annals and tied the ribbon. "Matthew, you heard the story."

The young attorney turned to face the old man. "Any jury would find you guilty, Sir. You bought him like he was property, just like you purchased his family. You paid—"

"I paid for that hideous woman to go away!" the Colonel snapped.

"No man is good enough to govern another man without that other's consent. Is that not what Lincoln said?"

"As a matter of fact, I saved him!" the Colonel said. "I gave him life."

Matthew said nothing, having no appetite at all for the conversation.

The Colonel accepted the young lawyer's malevolent glare; he understood that the gulf between them was as wide as the gulf between the North and the South.

"A human being God created," Matthew muttered, "…with a mother, a father, siblings who loved him," he drew himself straight and looked the Colonel in the eye. "They had no say when you took him away."

"I am not afraid, nor will I apologize for what I've done," the Colonel said softly.

For a moment, neither man spoke. "You fabricated the entire thing."

"Yes, to protect him." The Colonel stabbed the floor with his cane. "Sometimes the end justifies the means, Young Shaw."

Matthew peered at him, still, with distaste. "Thomas reportedly earned more than one hundred thousand dollars a year. How much money does he have in the bank?"

John jumped to his father's defense. "Tom doesn't understand the concept of money!"

"Did his family understand the concept of money?" Matthew spat each consonant.

"I've always treated Tom as my family," the Colonel offered with a soft murmur.

"His family lives in squalor while you sip *Veuve Clicquot* and race horses his labor purchased, and recline beneath the roof he helped keep over your head."

The Colonel gestured for him to go away.

"Did you ever know that his family, never called him Tom?"

"You don't know anything about me or about Tom," the Colonel stared at him with scorn.

"They only called him Thomas," Matthew argued with resigned bitterness. "According to his mother, Tom, is what the white man called him. She despised the moniker Blind Tom."

At that, neither the Colonel nor John responded.

"Love is unconditional," Matthew whispered. "Love is generous and kind. Love is protecting, not exploitative. Not buying and selling, and making a profit off of another human without compensation."

Matthew watched as the Colonel withdrew, watched him turn the chair so that he sat facing the window.

"Tom's greatest love was playing music," the Colonel whispered. "There wouldn't be a Blind Tom if it wasn't for me. He wouldn't be the famous idiot genius, there'd be no money to fight over, or any Eighth Wonder of the world. I will never apologize for abetting him in that endeavor."

"You should have seen to his financial well-being!" Matthew retorted. "The social fabric of entitlement that bred you has blinded you to inexorable depths."

The Colonel avoided his gaze. The young man wouldn't understand how it had begun again, one quiet afternoon. One long rainy day, years after the false funeral, Thomas had been strumming one of his own rhapsodies on the piano in the *petit parlor*, the Colonel was playing solitaire, at the card table in the bay, when Thomas began shouting out grand introductions, as he started to play.

"Now Tom will play his own *March Timpani.*"

The Colonel had smiled to himself, that first night. But each night that followed, before Thomas played, he announced himself more theatrically.

"And now, for you fine ladies and noblemen Thomas will play a bit of Chopin…"

The Colonel thought not much of it until one afternoon, walking deep inside one of the gardens at *Solitude*, he found Thomas sitting on a tree stump playing Mozart on Sarah's old violin. Birds seemed to sing along with his music, and the Colonel noticed Thomas's sightless eyes resting peacefully in the cavern of his rounded face.

"Paris, the lovely Paris, Colonel," Thomas said, lowering the violin.

"What of Paris, Tom?" he asked.

"Tom will go to Paris and play for Emperor Napoleon the Third."

Throughout the following weeks, Thomas brought up Paris again-and-again. "Tom will play for Emperor Napoleon III," he'd say while strumming Chopin. "Now, Tom boy play," he mimicked the Colonel's tone and tenor.

One of these nights, the Colonel set down his playing cards. He leaned back in his chair and puffed on his cigar. He gazed at Thomas.

"Now, Tom will play for Queen Victoria," Tom began to play *The Battle of Manassas.*

"Tom," the Colonel said, and Thomas stopped playing. "Would you like to play on grand stages again?"

"Yes, Tom would like to play his beautiful music on grand stages."

The Colonel studied Thomas. He was now a full grown man and knew his own wants.

Through dinner, the Colonel contemplated the possibilities; the risks and complications kept him up at night. Thomas was calmer with age, less prone to tantrums and difficulties. His music was as inspired as ever. As calm as life was at *Solitude*, in isolation from a world that considered Blind Tom dead, it was intriguing, for both of them, the prospect of concerts again.

Weeks later, in the back of a portrait studio in Atlanta, the Colonel met with a heavy-set Canadian concert manager, an old friend of Judge Cobb. There, a deal was signed for Blind Tom to perform for five days in *La belle province* of Quebec. Traveling in Europe or the United States would be tricky, though the Blind Tom imposters had muddied the waters and the world had moved on, still Canada was pristine ground to start. With its sprawling chateaux and winding waterfalls, it was the perfect place to reignite Blind Tom's concert tours.

At the Thespian Theater in Quebec, each of ten performances was sold out. The Canadians were duly beguiled by Thomas's odd antics and wit, and they were enchanted by his rich and complex melodies.

After Quebec, Blind Tom delighted audiences in St. Pierre before the Colonel took him by steamer to perform in Denmark. Renewed news of Blind Tom's brilliance spread. The local funeral hadn't made international papers. By the time Thomas and the Colonel reached Havana, swarming crowds greeted them at the port, the docks filled with the beat of *bata drums* and the sweet high plucking tones of *marimbulas*. The Afro-Latin purrs thrilled Thomas, who performed with native musicians at the *Plaza de las Armas* and *Gran Teatro Tacon*. He rocked his large body and stomped his feet with the audience in the great opera theaters. The Havanese, dazzled by Thomas's original compositions, fell in love with *Imitation of a Sewing Machine* and shouted *"La Increible"* whenever he performed.

So yes, it was true that Thomas had toured in Europe after the funeral. After the funeral, Blind Tom entertained high society for decades, all over the world. The last years of the Colonel and Thomas had been spent traveling without the complications of ownership and war. They would come back to *Solitude* and sit at the long dining table, sometimes with family, eating grits and baked ham or chicken with gravy and biscuits. They'd rise in the morning, at first light, the air moist with dew and the fragrance of the damp earth. They'd ride in the early morning light in a simple carriage to a boat and transfer to a steamer leaving from Atlanta and heading to Glasgow or Melbourne, where Blind Tom would perform for months at a time. There were no conflicts, no torn allegiances. It was simple, in Thomas's last years.

"If I'm wrong for giving him his dignity," the Colonel muttered from his rocker, "and setting him free through the music he loves. Then, by all means, let them hang me. Only our God of mercy can judge me."

Matthew stood and stared at him in silence. He turned away from him and no more words were spoken, until that familiar jingling sound came of keys clashing against copper and a dull rubbing sound as the chosen key slid into its lock. A large guard entered with a bottle of wine. "Colonel? Sir, you're free to go. Judge Cobb sends his regards," he handed the congratulatory bottle to John.

"Free to go?" Matthew asked, a look of confusion on his face.

"All charges have been dropped."

The Colonel's blue eyes lit with a twinkle as he grabbed his cane. Ah, yes, the deep tapestry of tradition, of an intricate, impenetrable latticework of complex morals and class privilege that haunted the South. And in the South, in Virginia, a white man, a white gentleman of the Colonel's standing would always have the benefit of the doubt.

John clapped his hands together and walked over to his father's rocker to help him up. "Good will always prevail over evil, father," he said in triumph.

"Any word on Tom?" the Colonel anxiously asked the guard.

"Same, sir. He's breathing, but unconscious."

"I must go to his side," the Colonel said, pressing his body up on his cane.

"See to it my belongings are properly returned to my plantation."

The Colonel turned to address Matthew. He took in the dread on his face, the shaking of his head. "I've repented for my sins," he said. "Think of me as you will Young Shaw, but when I die, when Tom dies, the Bethune name will be immortalized."

The Colonel hobbled out of the cell. Outside, he placed a top hat on his head and padded his way through a crushing mix of protestors and supporters, his chin ever high.

"Scoundrel!"

"You should rot in hell, Colonel!"

He took small, slow steps toward the carriage, before he stopped and gazed at the faces in the animated throng. They would never know him. They would never know the pungent smell of Thomas's blanket that sweltering afternoon when he picked up a screaming nigger baby and saved its life. They'd never know how he felt in the dim light of the servant's quarters cradling Thomas's bony frame against his chest, or the delight he felt when Thomas ran to wrap his arms tightly around the belly of the grandfather clock, or the warmth in his heart the first time he'd heard Thomas's music like angels singing in the dead of night.

He stepped onto the first step of his carriage and spoke as loudly as he could. "The earth is a better place because of Blind Tom Bethune," he said, as the sun drenched the pillared portico. "Richmond, Columbus, Seattle. New York, London, Paris, and Montreal. Australia, Havana, and the golden thrones of Germany. The pyramids of Egypt. All have been enriched by the brilliant music of Tom Bethune."

"He's not your slave anymore!"

The words no longer penetrated. John touched him gently on his elbow to usher him forward.

"Honor his greatness by remembering him," he said, not turning away. *"Blind Tom* Bethune. *The Black Mozart. The Black Swan. The Eighth Wonder of the world.* Poets have exalted him, folk songs have been written about his genius. Never forget him, for the angels sang through him."

A caramel Colored servant helped the Colonel into the black carriage.

Men and women cursed his name, waving their fists.

But he smiled, satisfied that his promise to his dying father had been fulfilled. History would prove him correct and the Bethune name would be carried forward, with honor and reverence, through the legend of Thomas Wiggins Bethune.

The Colonel settled against the back seat and clutched his cane. He was happy knowing that he and Thomas still had a final phrase of the grand symphony they shared together. For however long or short the heavenly conductor willed they would remain together, playing *pianissimo*. He prayed the Almighty might extend Thomas's days, like a maestro might the final notes of a wondrous song: sweet and slow, with his foot gently pressed upon the damper pedal.

The Colonel's Colored servant with clear blue eyes shut the carriage door, and the sun began to set behind the Colonel in his old fashioned carriage. The wheels bumped and rocked along the untended road, and the Colonel smiled out at the changing landscape. As his splendid carriage disappeared into the expanse where the earth meets the horizon, he felt the universe had been set right and he had to see about important matters, to see about *Thomas Wiggins Bethune.*

HISTORICAL NOTES

This novel is based on actual events in the life of Thomas Bethune. Thomas was indeed rescued by Colonel Bethune from a sweltering smokehouse where his former master Wiley left him to die. He was given to Colonel Bethune for free. He began playing Mozart at the age of three or four, composing his first rhapsody shortly after taking to the piano. He played the flute, violin, harmonica, and sang baritone. He spoke more than six languages fluently and could recite poetry. Famed pianists lauded his feats and his concerts are well documented. We know he performed at the White House for President Buchanan and performed in the Blue Room for the Japanese Samurai. We also know Thomas held many concerts for the crowned heads of Europe. Olé Bull was a fan and Thomas trained with Ignaz Moscheles. All kinds of rumors surrounded Blind Tom, who was a major celebrity, including an obscure plot to kidnap him and set him free for the abolitionist cause that allegedly involved Abraham Lincoln, as well as rumors he'd died in the Jonestown flood. Fascinated by Blind Tom, Mark Twain trailed his concert tour around the states and wrote about him. Blind Tom is also noted in William Steinway's diary and was written about by poets. Perry Oliver is reported to have paid the Colonel between $15,000 and $50,000 per year to tour Blind Tom, the equivalent of $270,000-$900,000 in modern currency. It is true that Tabbs Gross paid a large sum for Thomas and his family's freedom that the Colonel reneged on. The Colonel, sometimes referred to as General Bethune, died of natural causes and John Bethune was killed in a train accident. Thomas was never out of the Colonel's power after slavery, as he declared Thomas insane and toured him in Europe. Newspapers accused the Colonel of keeping the musician enslaved. The years of court battles in the U.S. over Thomas were real. In his published will, John wrote that his wife Eliza was an opportunist and bigamist. He left her nothing. However, Eliza did get custody of Thomas as the only living Bethune heir, but the pianist, who was in his twenties, refused to play in public due to missing John, thus Blind Tom and his music fell into obscurity. During a custody trial, Charity told the court the family never called him Tom. It's also true that Thomas died of a stroke while at the piano. He could not lift his arm to play, he collapsed, and his last words were, "the angels have stopped singing. Isn't that terrible? Tom is done." He died in 1908.

AUTHORS BIO

A.M. Cal is an award-winning t.v. writer/producer who lives in Los Angeles, while her heart lives in Seattle. She is a double doctoral student at Pepperdine University. She earned her B.A. from the University of Washington, an M.A. from Cal State University, Northridge, and is a member of Zeta Phi Beta Sorority, Inc. *Eighth Wonder* is her first novel. She is currently working on a second historical book.